The Strange Appeal of Dougie Neil

Keith A Pearson

Inchgate Publishing

For more information about the author and to receive updates on his new releases, visit...

www.keithapearson.co.uk

Chapter 1

Another bead of sweat rolls down my back.

It's warm in the bar, but I daren't remove my jacket because of the dark sweat patches around my armpits. They developed in the taxi on the way here, and I nipped to the toilet the moment I arrived to check for odour. A little musty perhaps, but not potent enough to overpower almost half a pint of aftershave.

I always sweat when I'm nervous, but I don't remember it ever being this bad.

A gulp of cold lager helps.

I toyed with the idea of ordering something sophisticated like a cocktail or a fancy gin, but I don't want to pretend to be someone I'm not. Dougie Neil only drinks lager, or white wine if he's desperate.

There's a clock on the exposed brick wall opposite my spot at the bar. We agreed to meet at eight o'clock, but I arrived forty minutes early so I could mentally prepare.

In hindsight, a mistake.

Being a Tuesday evening, the bar is quiet. I feel self-conscious, sitting here alone. Why didn't I suggest Friday when I could hide in the crowd? Saying that, I don't remember suggesting any day—it all happened so fast it's now a bit of a blur.

I still can't believe she responded to my profile in the first place.

It will be three years next month since I first published my profile on the Somebody2Love.com dating website. Put another way, thirty-six monthly payments totalling £1,080.

I can't say it's been money well spent, but back then I still harboured the teeniest hope I might avoid spending the rest of my life alone. It coincided with my thirty-eighth birthday, so perhaps the decision to try online dating was a midlife crisis; a final desperate roll of the dice.

Having spent hours and hours carefully honing the text for my profile, I then had to choose a photograph. In a way, it was akin to baking the perfect cake and then decorating it with the contents of a cat-litter tray. Still, I eventually settled on the least-worst photo I could find and added it to my profile. With one final click, I officially joined the dating market.

Then, nothing.

Days turned into weeks, and my inbox remained empty. Those weeks became months and despite changing my profile photograph sixteen times, it didn't make one jot of difference. As any angler will confirm, you won't catch anything with sub-standard bait.

One year later, I removed every single photograph and updated the text on my profile. In short, I said I wanted to meet someone who cared more about a partner's character than their looks.

Still, nothing. Month after month of nothing.

If it wasn't for the regular debits leaving my bank account, I might have forgotten I even had an account with Somebody2Love.com. Then, three days ago, I received an email saying someone had posted a message on my profile. That someone was Carol, and any minute now she'll walk through the door and see me for the first time.

The anxiety is almost overbearing. I summon the barman.

"Same again, please."

I've already sunk two pints but I'll go easy with the third. If ever there was a situation demanding Dutch courage, this is undoubtedly it.

I glance at my watch—7:52 pm.

"Can I get you anything else?" the barman asks.

"I don't suppose you've got a spare shirt?"

"I'm afraid not."

"Never mind."

He heads off to deal with another customer. I sip from the full pint glass and then surreptitiously sniff my right armpit. The aftershave is still winning the battle.

7:55 pm.

There's piped music playing in the background and, up until now, I've not given it much attention—probably because it's what today's kids listen to, and I'm no kid, unfortunately. What they're playing now, though, is worthy of my attention because it was in the charts the last time I went on a date ... eleven years ago. *Bad Romance* by Lady Gaga couldn't have been more apt at the time. The date was such a cataclysmic disaster I vowed never to try again. And yet, here I am, with Lady Gaga still taunting me.

Perhaps this was a mistake.

My stomach growls, but it's not because I'm hungry. It's the same gnawing sensation I experienced as a teenager, back when I didn't have the first clue what the dating gods had in store for me; the evil bastards.

I attempt to wash away the doubts with another glug of lager.

Rather than dwell on the rising negativity, I let my thoughts drift back to those teenage years and the moment it all began.

I distinctly recall my first rejection in the hall during our school's annual Christmas disco—I was fourteen. The DJ played Roxette's *It Must Have Been Love*, and I finally plucked up the courage to cross the dance floor to where Annalisa Andrews loitered amongst a small group of girls. Annalisa was my first crush, and despite her rabid acne and braces I thought she was the most beautiful girl in school.

"Would you like to dance?" I squeaked.

"With you?"

"Err, yes."

Two of her friends sniggered.

"Eww, no way!" she squealed. "You're a right minger."

The rest of her group burst out laughing. Annalisa turned her back on me and joined in with the merriment.

I think there was still twenty or so minutes before the disco was due to end, but I couldn't get out of that hall quick enough. I grabbed my jacket and trudged home in the rain, my tail between my legs.

Stupidly, I told my parents about what happened, and they laughed it off. My experience was all part of growing up, apparently. They said I shouldn't worry, and based upon the law of averages, the next girl I asked to dance was more likely to say yes. So, at the monthly Youth Club disco, I approached Dawn Beech. She didn't say no to a dance, probably because she couldn't stop laughing. A month later, I asked Gemma Cole. She didn't laugh—she burst into tears.

My luck didn't improve at college. I tried befriending girls before asking them out, and although they weren't as cruel in their rejection, the net result was the same: no date. Naomi Walker did say yes to a date, but the day before we were due to go out, I discovered she stood to win a fifty quid bet if she could tolerate two hours with me. The date never happened.

I turned eighteen and left college, my strike rate still at zero and my virginity intact. I hadn't even managed a snog. I would have settled for that.

However, I felt sure the pickings would be richer in the adult world of pubs, bars, and nightclubs where the lighting was dim and the women worldly. Over a period of five months, I struck out nineteen times. I know it was nineteen because I recorded every rejection in my diary, hoping to identify a common mistake I might avoid at my next attempt.

It's funny, I don't remember making a conscious decision to stop, but I did. I think it was around the first anniversary of leaving college when I realised how soul-destroying my strategy had become. Naively, I believed my parents when they said it was only a matter of time before I found Miss Right. Mum kept telling me that she kissed a lot of frogs before her Prince Charming came along, but I was nineteen and hadn't kissed anyone, amphibious or otherwise.

I still harboured the faintest hope I might meet someone, but I stopped going out because hope can only take so much rejection. I had to retain it; keep a candle flickering at the end of the tunnel.

It wasn't long afterwards I met Denise Gresty. I later discovered it wasn't a candle at the end of my tunnel but the spark of a fuse wire.

8:00 pm.

The main door swings open, and an attractive, middle-aged woman enters the bar, alone. My heart stops beating momentarily.

The woman scans the room but looks straight through me like I'm invisible. I think it's safe to say she's looking for someone who isn't me. A split second later, her face lights up, and she waves. To my right, a guy strides over and the couple embrace.

A pang of envy cuts right through me, but it's tinged with relief. Life has taught me to be realistic and to keep my expectations low. They say opposites attract, and that might be true when it comes to personality, but rarely is it true when it comes to aesthetics. There are exceptions but life is not a fairy-tale, and the chances of a beauty dating this beast are remote. I have no problem with that because I'd hate to be in a relationship where I wake up every day feeling unworthy of the woman lying next to me.

8:02 pm.

Carol is now officially late. Either that, or she's come to her senses and decided not to turn up at all. In a twisted way, I think I'd rather suffer disappointment over flat-out rejection. I've suffered so much of both that neither sting as much as they used to, but rejection is always more personal. I suppose it's like applying for a job. If your application fails, you can always tell yourself it was because they found a better-qualified candidate. However, being told you're simply not good enough is flat-out rejection.

8:04 pm.

I'm about to empty my glass when the main door swings open again. A short, stocky woman enters, looking flustered. She checks her watch and then heads straight to a spot near the bar fifteen feet away. The barman approaches her.

"Rum and Coke, please," she says.

The barman nods and readies her order. As she waits, the woman slowly casts an eye across the tables until I appear in her line of sight. Her mouth bobs open.

I can't be certain but there's a passing resemblance to the picture on Carol's dating profile. It's hard to say as that photo featured a woman a good decade younger than the one at the bar.

"Carol?" I enquire.

She replies with a crooked smile and then turns to the barman.

"Better make that a double."

Chapter 2

Some people will tell you that looks aren't important, but in my experience, those people are kidding themselves. Looks *are* important. The desire to mate with a suitably attractive partner is hard-baked into our genetic code, as it is with almost every species on the planet. I mean, who wants ugly offspring?

"Yeah, I'm Carol."

Her voice is much deeper than I remember from our brief telephone conversation, and it carries the rasp of a seasoned smoker.

"I'm Douglas," I declare. "Lovely to meet you."

I step forward and shake her hand. A peck on the cheek doesn't feel right.

"Let me get that for you."

I hand a ten-pound note to the barman as Carol receives her drink.

"Ta."

Drink and change acquired, I try to take control of the situation. There's nothing I can do about the physical first impression but I can demonstrate I'm more than just an ugly face.

"Shall we grab a table?"

"Okay."

"Before they all run off," I chuckle.

"What?"

"Err, sorry. Just a silly joke."

Carol rolls her eyes. Undeterred, I lead her to the darkest corner of the bar and pull out a chair. She sits down without saying a word and takes a long sip from her glass. I need to fill the silence.

"So, um, are you new to the dating scene, Carol?"

"Not really."

"How long have you been single, if you don't mind me asking?"

"About a year. You?"

"Let's just say my search for Miss Right has taken much longer than I anticipated."

"That ain't an answer."

"If you need me to be precise, twenty-odd years."

"Christ on a bike! Why?"

"Um, because I'm not everyone's cup of tea in the looks department."

"That why you don't have a photo on your profile?"

"Exactly that."

"Don't matter to me," she responds, shrugging her unusually broad shoulders. "I've dated some right ugly bastards over the years."

"Well, I'm glad that you're not the type who judges a man on looks alone."

"Nah, but that doesn't mean I'll go out with just anyone, you know. I have standards."

"What is it you're looking for in a man, then?"

Carol reaches for her glass and duly empties it.

"Fetch me another rum and Coke, and I'll tell you."

"Okay."

"And make it a double."

Barely five minutes after arriving, my date is on her second drink. Perhaps it's just to ease her nerves. I hurry back to the bar and order her rum and Coke and half a pint of lager. While I wait for our drinks, I assess my first impressions of Carol. Having been judged my whole life, I don't like to judge others without getting to know them, but there's no ignoring her coarse demeanour. Still, I'm sure she has many redeeming qualities that'll shine through once I get to know her.

I return to the table, and Carol is still there—never a given in my experience.

"One rum and Coke."

Retaking my seat, I hold my glass aloft.

"Cheers."

Half-heartedly, Carol clinks her glass against mine. It's the first time I've noticed the chunky sovereign rings and tattoo of a swallow on her hand.

"I like your tattoo," I lie.

"Got it done years ago."

"Do you have an interest in birds?"

"Nah. I had it done 'cos of my nickname back in the day—Swallows. I was pissed out of my box when I had it done."

"Why were you called Swallows?"

"Why do you think?" she snorts.

"Err ..."

"Let's just say I got myself a bit of a reputation. I ain't like that now, though."

"Right. Good to know."

It feels appropriate to take a moment, and a large gulp of lager, before pressing on.

"You were going to tell me what you're looking for in a man."

"Oh yeah. Firstly, he's gotta have a steady job. My ex-husband was a right lazy tosser, and I ain't gettin' myself tied to another layabout."

"How long were you married?"

"Four years the first time. Six years the second."

I can't imagine why, but Carol failed to mention her double divorce on her profile. Maybe it'll be third time lucky.

"Well, I have a steady job," I reply confidently. "So steady, in fact, I've been there for twenty years."

"What do you do?"

"Have you heard of The Wombles?"

"Those furry little feckers from kids' TV?"

"Yes, although I don't think that's how most people remember them. They lived on Wimbledon Common and spent their days cleaning up after humans."

"You tellin' me you're a Womble?" she coughs.

"I suppose I am, in a way. I work for Ashbridge Borough Council in their street cleaning and grounds maintenance team."

"A street sweeper?"

"It's a bit more varied than that, but yes, I use a broom now and then."

"You don't seem the sort. I'd have put money on you working in an office or somethin'."

"That's how I started out after I left college—working in an office for an auditing company. I did that for a couple of years but ... but I had to leave that position. I took the job with the council thinking it'd only be temporary, but I enjoyed it. The rest is history."

My choice of employment remains a puzzle to many, not least of all my parents. I left college with A-levels in English and Maths, but I couldn't face university. Carol appears nonplussed.

"What do you do for a living?" I ask.

"I don't work on account of my asthma. Ain't had a job in years."

"I'm sorry to hear that."

"Ain't a problem, but it's why I need a decent bloke in my life. Someone who doesn't mind spoiling his woman."

I've no clue what Carol's idea of being spoilt is, so I just nod.

"And the other thing," she continues. "I want a bloke who likes the same things I do, and he's also gotta have a decent girth."

"Okay. What hobbies ... sorry? Girth?"

"Yeah, you know."

I don't know. Carol then winks at me.

"I ain't dating a bloke with a pencil dick."

She cackles loudly, to the point a couple across the room shoot a disapproving look our way. Out of pure embarrassment, I manage a feeble chuckle in reply. I need to move the conversation on from Carol's carnal needs.

"Um, shall we talk about your hobbies?"

"If you like."

"What do you like doing in your spare time?"

"I go to the bingo twice a week and karaoke on Friday nights."

"That sounds fun."

"You ain't heard me sing, darlin'."

Another round of cackling ensues. I wonder if Carol's merriment is down to her glass being empty again.

"What about you?" she eventually asks. "You got any hobbies?"

"I have. I'm a passionate twitcher."

"A what?"

"Birdwatching."

"You mean you're one of those blokes who hang around Tinkerton Meadow all hours?"

I'm surprised she's aware of our local nature reserve.

"Yep, I'm one of them. How do you know about Tinkerton Meadow? Did you read about our conservation work in the local newspaper?"

"Me and my ex used to go there sometimes. That's another of my hobbies."

"Oh, really?" I respond excitedly. "You're into birdwatching too?"

"No, you silly sod. It was one of our favourite dogging spots before they put gates on the car park."

I choke on a mouthful of lager. The couple across the room get up and leave.

"Dogging?" I splutter. "As in ... not taking a dog for a walk?"

"You've never tried it?"

"Noooo."

"Why? You shouldn't knock it till you've tried it, darlin'."

My knowledge of dogging is limited, but I do know the Tinkerton Meadow Management Committee had gates installed because of the sheer number of used condoms left in the car park overnight.

"I, err ... I don't think it's my cup of tea if I'm being honest."

"That's a shame. I would have thought a bloke like you would be up for anything."

"A bloke like me?"

"Yeah, I mean beggars can't be choosers, and you can't have many opportunities for an easy shag, right?"

"I ... I'm not looking for an easy shag."

"What are you looking for then?"

"A loving, long-term relationship. Maybe children."

"I ain't havin' more kids for no one."

"I did say maybe. It's not a deal-breaker."

"That's alright, then. So, you and me are on the same page, eh? We both want some lovin'?"

"Err, I guess so."

"Good, 'cos I'm warming up nicely. Go fetch me another drink, and if I'm buzzin' enough, maybe we can go back to your place."

"My place?"

"Don't tell me you still live with your mum and dad?"

"No, I have a little end-terrace house across town, but ..."

"That's settled then. Get me another drink, and then we'll head back to yours."

"I, um … I'm not entirely comfortable with that, Carol. We barely know one another."

"What's the matter? Don't you fancy me?"

It's an interesting question. I've reached the point that I'm so desperate to meet someone I don't much care who that someone is or if there's any initial attraction.

"It's not that," I respond. "I'm just a bit old-fashioned in that I'd like to get to know someone before … you know."

"There ain't no better way to get to know someone than what I've got in mind, darlin'."

I inwardly shudder.

"Listen, Carol. You seem lovely, and I'm sure we've got a lot in common, but can't we take it slowly?"

"I'm fifty-two, darlin'. I ain't got time to take it slow."

"You're fifty-two? You said forty on your profile."

"Whatever," she says with a shrug. "Everyone lies on dating profiles."

"Not everyone. I didn't."

"What do you want? A medal?"

At this very moment, a valid excuse to leave would be preferable. As much as I desperately wanted this date to be a success, I suspect we're probably not compatible.

"So, we gonna get it on or what?" Carol asks. "I've only got a babysitter for three hours."

"Err, I'm really sorry, but I can't sleep with someone I've only just met."

This revelation agitates my date. She scowls back at me.

"Are you sayin' I shaved my fanny for nothin'?"

I have no answer and just stare back, dumbstruck. Carol stands up and snatches her handbag from the table.

"You're pathetic," she spits. "No wonder you're on your own, you limp-dicked loser."

And there endeth our date.

I watch Carol storm towards the exit and out the door without a second glance in my direction. If there's any consolation, it's that I still have a few mouthfuls of lager left. At least I don't have to sit here and conduct a post-mortem with an empty glass.

That post-mortem begins with a damning conclusion. Sad as it is, my brief date with Carol was nowhere near the worst I've endured. If I overlook the insults, the lie about her age, and the fact we were incompatible on every level, she did at least seem keen to have sex with me.

Saying that, she cited sex with strangers in a car park as a hobby. That might imply she's not the fussy type.

What am I saying? She's *definitely* not the fussy type. Why else would she want to sleep with me, of all people?

I don't wish to dwell on the negatives, but it's hard not to when the result is always the same. I'll head home to an empty house and watch a bit of TV on my own. Then, I'll slip into an empty bed where I'll be kept awake by the same thought that won't let me sleep most nights—I'm alone, and I always will be.

Perhaps another date might miraculously materialise months from now, but why should the outcome be any different? It's not as though Mother Nature is likely to undo her curse, and I'll suddenly blossom into an attractive, middle-aged man. No, that's not going to happen because Mother Nature hates me.

My parents are both in their early seventies and they're still a good-looking couple. Roger and Fay Neil are the kind of model couple you might see posing in a brochure for luxury cruise holidays. And my younger sister, Kathryn, is what most folks would describe as conventionally attractive. Me, though, I don't know what went wrong. It's almost as if Mother Nature scraped together all the shitty leftover parts when putting me together.

I've got this egg-shaped head left in the reject bin. You can have that, Douglas. And, I've got a pair of unusually small, beady eyes. You can have those, and I'll position them too close together. Then, I've been trying to get rid of this nose with a ridiculously

bulbous end. That's yours. Now, what about a chin? Tell you what,
why don't we forget about a chin altogether? And to top it off,
why don't I throw in male pattern baldness and a permanently
pock-marked complexion?

I finish my beer and nip to the toilets. As I wash my hands, I
make eye contact with my reflection in the mirror behind the
sink.

"You're a loser, Dougie", I mutter. "Just accept it."

Chapter 3

Ten years ago, my parents surprised me with forty thousand pounds as a birthday present, although Dad said it was more an advance on my inheritance than a gift. As such, it was strongly suggested I invest the money as a deposit on a home of my own. Anyone who doesn't know my parents would consider such a gift extremely generous, but I knew they had an ulterior motive—two, in fact.

Firstly, they wanted the house to themselves, and I understood why they didn't want their thirty-something son cramping their retirement years. Fair enough.

Secondly, I think they thought I'd be more likely to attract a girlfriend if I had a home of my own. Again, there was no arguing with their logic.

More excited than nervous, I failed to anticipate the reality of living on my own for the first time in my life.

With some guidance from Dad, I spent months searching for a suitable house and finally settled on a solid, end-of-terrace house in a relatively quiet street. The previous owners were a married couple with a young son, and when I first viewed the house, it had a warm homely feel. I remember daydreaming that perhaps the little house might host another family one day—mine.

On the day I moved in, the daydreaming abruptly ended. Without any furniture or personal possessions, the rooms were just soulless boxes.

Despite making numerous trips to IKEA, and my sister's help with redecorating, I couldn't recapture the feeling I had when I first viewed the house. Consequently, those first six months were tainted with a sense of loneliness as the realisation slowly dawned—a home isn't a home if there's no one there to love.

I did toy with getting a dog, but I hated the idea of leaving the poor thing at home on his own all day. My mum suggested a cat, but I wasn't keen. I've always considered cats a bit shifty.

Ten years after moving in, No.9 Cargate Road still doesn't feel much like a home, but at least it's a place I can call my own. And, if I were searching for a silver lining, there's no one to disturb when I get up at ungodly o'clock to get ready for work.

A horn blasts outside. I glance out of the lounge window and frown.

I've told my workmate, Ady, to text me when he arrives but every now and then he forgets his phone. It wouldn't be such a problem if our working day began at a civilised hour, but it doesn't. It begins at 7.00 am.

I grab my keys and hurry downstairs.

"Sorry, mate," he says, as I open the car door. "I keep forgetting."

"It's not me you need to apologise to—I was already awake. It's my neighbours who want to kill you."

"They'll have to catch me first."

Grinning, he revs the engine and lifts the clutch. I sometimes wonder why I agreed to this arrangement, besides the fact that Ady lives a few streets away and our depot is in the middle of nowhere. Is the fifty per cent reduction in travel costs worth it?

"Reckon the weather should be good today," Ady remarks, as we leave Cargate Road and my irate neighbours behind.

"Define good?"

"Gonna be warmer than usual for September, like twenty-four degrees. That's what Leanne said, anyway."

Leanne is Ady's long-suffering girlfriend. They live together with his mum and two Staffordshire Bull Terriers named Ron and Reg. He's got a good heart but by his own admission, Ady isn't the brightest star in the sky. Fortunately for him, we're not employed for our intelligence.

The ten-minute drive passes quickly and, as we trundle past the depot gates, I glance up at the sign that's greeted my arrival at work every day for so many years: *Ashbridge Borough Council — Street Cleaning and Grounds Maintenance Depot.*

Ady parks up, and we make our way to the office. Our day begins with a briefing from Jonny Strang, the cheerless depot manager. This briefing is usually short because very little changes from day to day in our job. There are seven two-man crews, and each crew is responsible for a designated section of the borough. Our schedule is almost always the same. We spend the first few hours emptying the scores of public bins dotted around our patch, and then we're on fly-tipping duty, which involves clearing up waste abandoned in public spaces. If there's still time in the day, we'll spend our afternoons litter picking on roadside verges.

Considering the early hour, it's no surprise there's not a lot of revelry in the office. Most of my colleagues are silently sipping coffee from paper cups or staring bleary-eyed into space. Grunted greetings are exchanged before Jonny confirms there's nothing to confirm besides another health and safety course looming at the end of the month. Briefing over, we can begin our working day.

The first task of the day is to sign out a vehicle. We all typically use the same van every day, but someone somewhere in the council's management team decided to make it as convoluted a process as possible. Every set of van keys now has to be issued by the depot administrator, Keira.

"I'm just gonna have a quick smoke before we set off," Ady says, as we file out of the meeting room.

"Okay."

I venture into Keira's office.

Besides those I'm related to, I don't regularly interact with many women, Keira being one of the few exceptions. The council have tried to address our depot's apparent lack of gender diversity but to no avail. For reasons unclear to management, the women of Ashbridge don't seem keen on clearing crap from the streets. Saying that, neither do the menfolk, which is why we're perpetually understaffed.

"Good morning, Dougie," Keira says in her usual perfunctory tone.

"Morning."

Keira, like Ady, is in her early thirties. Unlike Ady, Keira is the model of reserved professionalism.

After a glance at the computer screen and a few clicks of a mouse, Keira rolls her chair across the tiled floor to a cabinet. She then tosses a key in my direction.

"Thanks."

"Where's Ady?" she asks.

"Having a smoke."

"I thought he'd given up."

"He has ... kind of."

"Does Leanne know?"

"Um, probably not."

Keira's eyes narrow. I think I've just dropped Ady in the shit.

"I best be going," I mumble.

After my quick getaway, I head out to the lot where all the vehicles are parked. I find Ady loitering.

"Does Leanne know you're still smoking?" I ask.

"What she doesn't know won't hurt her."

"Yeah, I think that might be about to change."

"Eh?"

"I inadvertently told Keira you were having a fag."

His shoulders slump.

"Ahh, crap."

This is a problem for Ady because Keira is friends with his better half on Facebook. Actually, Keira is Facebook friends with every one of her colleagues' partners, and for a good reason.

Three years ago, our then office administrator, Joan, retired. Keira was hired as Joan's replacement, and a number of my colleagues revelled in having a new, young, and admittedly pretty face in the office. Some of their antics were wholly inappropriate, but Keira seemed to take it all in her stride.

Then, after she'd been with us for a month, Keira announced during a morning briefing that she'd been secretly recording the conversations in her office. Using her mobile phone, she then played back some of those recordings. It didn't make for pleasant listening and went way beyond what could be labelled harmless banter; more smut, innuendo, and casual sexism. The public shaming had the desired effect, and there were plenty of red faces and apologies, but her strategy for dealing with unruly male colleagues didn't end there.

Having tracked down everyone's wife, fiancée, or girlfriend on Facebook, Keira made it clear that if anyone stepped out of line again, their partner would also get to hear the recordings. To date, no one has dared test that threat.

"Do you think Keira will grass on me?" Ady asks, as we pull out of the depot.

"No idea, mate, but I'd be on my best behaviour for the next few days if I were you."

We set off on our route and the morning unfolds in the same way it unfolds every single day. From street to street, bin to bin, we remove the full sack of rubbish from each and replace it with a new one, ready to be refilled within twenty-four hours. Although we visit the same bins five days a week, every week, no one seems to notice us. For me, that's a perk of the job, but if we ever miss a bin, someone will soon notice and complain to the council.

Lunchtime looms.

Depending on how busy we are, we'll usually grab a sandwich and eat it in the van, but if we're ahead of schedule, we sometimes pop in to a little cafe on our route. Today feels like a beans on toast for lunch kind of day.

"Fancy lunch at The Vale?" I ask Ady, as he hurls the last sack of rubbish on the van.

"I'm skint."

"Already? There's still ten days till we get paid."

"It's been one of those months."

"I'll buy, and you can pay next time."

"Nice one."

It's only a two-minute drive to The Vale Cafe, and the car park is near empty when we arrive. So, too, is the cafe itself, besides an elderly couple sipping tea near the window and a guy in oily overalls tucking into a full English.

"Alright, lads," Colin beams from behind the counter. "How's tricks?"

"Not bad, ta. Can we get beans on toast twice and two mugs of tea, please?"

Colin scribbles our order on a small notepad, rips the page out, and then slaps it on the ledge of a serving hatch behind him.

"Grab a seat. I'll bring your teas over."

"Cheers, Colin."

We sit down at the nearest table.

Since the first week I started working for the council, The Vale Cafe has been a comforting feature of my life. Some might call it old-fashioned, but I prefer to call it traditional. I love the vinyl tablecloths, the fluted glass salt and pepper pots, and the black and white photos of vintage aircraft dotted around the walls. Yes, there's sometimes a faint whiff of damp in the air, and

Colin's daughter, Heather, is somewhat lacking in the charm department, but I wouldn't change a thing about the place.

Our teas arrive and, soon after, Colin brings our lunch over. We're only supposed to have thirty minutes, so there's no time for conversation as we wolf down a thick doorstep of toasted bread and a generous serving of baked beans.

All too soon, it's time to get back to work. Ady heads outside for a smoke while I settle the bill at the counter.

"Everything alright?" Colin asks, as I hand over a note.

"Lovely, as always."

"Glad you enjoyed it," he replies with a half-smile. "I'm afraid you'll have to fend for yourself from next week, for a while at least."

"Eh? Why?"

"The hospital had a last-minute cancellation, so they've moved my hip replacement op forward to Monday. I'll be out of commission for at least four weeks."

"You're closing the cafe?"

"It looks like I've no choice. A mate had agreed to step in and help, but he's done his back in, the stupid bugger. Heather can't run the place on her own, and I'm struggling to find anyone willing to help out at such short notice."

I wonder if it's because he can't find anyone willing to work with his daughter. Heather has barely spoken a dozen words to me in the five or six years she's worked in The Vale's kitchen. At first, I thought it was just me, but she's just as standoffish with Ady.

"If I think of anyone, I'll let you know."

"I'd appreciate it, Dougie."

As Colin plucks coins from the till, I catch sight of Heather on the other side of the serving hatch. Her attention appears fixed on a cheese grater, which is just as well. On the odd occasion I've caught Heather's eye and smiled, she's inevitably looked away—in disgust, probably. Ady says she's no right being so prickly with me because, in my esteemed colleague's words, she isn't exactly beating away men with a stick. There's definitely no ring on her finger, or likely to be with such a standoffish attitude.

I thank Colin and head out to the van where Ady is waiting.

"We might have to find somewhere else for lunch next month."

"Why?"

"Colin is getting his hip fixed, so he won't be able to work for a while."

"Does that mean we can have McDonald's for a change?"

"No, it doesn't."

"Killjoy."

"We'll see if you're still so keen on McDonald's once you've picked half-a-ton of their packaging from the next roadside verge we're tasked to clear."

"Yeah, fair enough."

Point made, it's time to see what delights the fly-tippers of Ashbridge have in store for us today.

Chapter 4

The rest of our afternoon proved uneventful, not that there's ever much excitement in clearing sofas and fridges from remote lay-bys. We completed our last pick up and drove to the municipal tip, where we unloaded the spoils of our day's endeavours. The only good thing about starting work so early is that we're usually finished by three.

After Ady drops me home, it takes twenty minutes to shower and change, and then I hop in the car for the short drive across town to the place I spend most of my free time.

Once a quarry, Tinkerton Meadow is now a two-hundred-acre nature reserve and the only place I feel truly happy. It's been three decades since the quarry closed, and within weeks of the last excavator departing the site, Mother Nature began reclaiming the land. There's no denying she did a much better job with Tinkerton Meadow than she did with Dougie Neil. Now, it's a mosaic of glistening ponds, gravel islands, reed beds and brush, surrounded by wild hedgerows and thicket.

As tranquil as Tinkerton Meadow is, the peace is not the main reason I love being here.

I pull into the car park and enter the reserve through a wooden gate. From there, it's a short walk along a path shadowed by young trees to what we all affectionately refer to as Falbert's Mount, named after the man who campaigned for Tinkerton

Meadow to become a nature reserve, Martin Falbert. In reality, it's just a broad hillock roughly thirty feet high.

I've clambered up the grass slope to Falbert's Mount well over a thousand times, but I'm still mesmerised every time I reach the top and drink in the view. Today, the sky is cloudless and the air still, so the pond is like glass.

I'm not the only one here to enjoy the scenery.

Kenny Seddon spends more time on this Mount than almost anyone. Apart from being the most avid of twitchers, he's probably the closest thing I have to a best friend.

I cross the grass to where Kenny is standing. I'm sure he's aware of my presence, but he doesn't remove the binoculars trained on the pond.

"Alright, Kenny."

"Not so bad," he mumbles.

"Anything interesting today?"

"Four juvenile Greenshank, a pair of Garganey, and a Great White Egret."

"Nice."

"You see much after I left yesterday?" he asks.

Kenny was born and bred in Glasgow but left the city twenty-five years ago. Even so, there's still more than a hint of his Glaswegian accent. In my head, it sometimes makes even the most innocuous of questions sound like a veiled threat.

"Nope. Not a thing."

Kenny lowers his binoculars and turns to face me. In his mid-fifties, he's a semi-retired landscape gardener, and I reckon most people could guess Kenny's profession just by looking at him. His weathered face has an almost bark-like quality, and his mane of grey-blond hair is as wild and untamed as any Highland strath.

"There's rumour of a Marsh Harrier in the area."

"I'm surprised you're the only one here, then."

There's about a dozen of us who visit the reserve daily, but three times as many will turn up whenever there's a rare sighting. I like to come up here for a few hours after work and almost every weekend, just before dawn.

"Give it a while, and all the usual suspects will turn up," Kenny smiles. "But until then, you've got the sole pleasure of my company."

"Lucky me, eh."

"Aye, you're a lucky man indeed, young Dougie."

"I think we both know I'm neither young nor lucky."

Kenny frowns, or at least I think he's frowning. Frankly, it's hard to tell. If he did, it's because he's one of life's perpetual optimists. Ironic as he hails from a city not renowned for the sunny disposition of its residents.

"How many times must I tell you not to be so negative? It's not a trait that'll help you find a lassie."

"I know, but I had a disastrous date last night, so I'm not feeling particularly positive today."

"What went wrong?"

"It'd be quicker to tell you what went right."

"That bad, eh?"

"Truth be told, I've had worse dates," I concede, trying to match Kenny's positivity. "And she did offer to sleep with me."

"Did she now?" he responds with a knowing smile. "And did you accept her offer?"

"No."

"Why on earth not?"

"Several reasons, but primarily because we'd only just met."

"So what? Sometimes in life, you've just got to jump in feet first and to hell with the consequences."

"I'm not sure you'd stand by that advice if you'd met Carol."

"Any port in a storm, my friend," he chuckles. "And, what's the worst that could have happened?"

"Take your pick: chlamydia, syphilis, gonorrhoea."

"Ah," he winces.

"Exactly."

Kenny steps over and puts his arm around my shoulder.

"Listen," he says. "Do you remember my mentioning Sara's best pal, Lucy?"

A decade his junior, Sara is Kenny's wife.

"Can't say I do, no."

"Nae matter. It's Lucy's fortieth this weekend, and she's throwing a big party on Saturday evening. I'm sure I could swing you an invite if you're up for it?"

"It's kind of you, Kenny, but ..."

"Before you say no, it's in a nightclub in town, and there'll be plenty of single lassies there, for sure."

I try to remember the last time I went to a nightclub. It was so long ago it might have been in the previous millennia.

"But, I won't know anyone."

"You'll know me, and you'll be doing me a favour if you come along."

"Err, how?"

"I guarantee Sara will be on the dancefloor with her buddies most of the evening, and you can keep this old fart company."

"But, I ..."

"You'll enjoy it, I promise."

"Honestly, Kenny, I don't think I will."

"Yes, you bloody well will."

Despite his broad smile, I'm almost certain my friend will stab me to death if I decline his offer.

"I suppose an hour or two won't hurt."

"Good man," he replies, squeezing my shoulder. "I'll clear it with Sara and message you the details."

My only hope is that Kenny's other half is as unenthusiastic about the idea as I am. It's unlikely, though. Some years back, during a barbecue at Kenny's place, Sara declared that she intended to help me find a girlfriend. Despite her initial enthusiasm for the mission, all attempts to find a suitable date within her circle of friends proved futile. Being the slightly scatty type she is, Sara soon forgot about *Project Dougie*, but I fear she won't pass up this opportunity to resurrect it.

"Thanks, mate."

I find a thin smile, and Kenny removes his arm from my shoulder.

Conversation over, we both train our binoculars on the pond's nearest shore. It's always nice chatting to Kenny, but we're both here for one reason, and one reason only.

It's a depressing fact that few people understand bird watchers. To most, we're somewhere on the anorak scale between train spotters and those who enjoy battle re-enactments—sad little men who have nothing else in their lives but their pathetic hobby. It's fair to say we are obsessive because we don't have packed social calendars, but there's nothing pathetic in what we do.

From my perspective, I find birds aren't judgemental, and neither are those who hold an interest in spotting them.

Within a few minutes of putting the binoculars to my face, I spot a lone Garganey searching for insects in the reeds. The Garganey is a type of small, migratory duck, and this is only the third year they've graced us with their presence. An exhilarating start to today's session.

Time then passes by in the same way it always does when I'm here—unnoticed. If I'm ever on the Mount alone, I like to pretend I'm the last remaining human on the planet. On the one hand, I'd have zero chance of ever going on a successful date, but at least there would be no more disappointment. I think I'd prefer the certainty of knowing I'll forever be alone over the cruelty of hope. Inevitably, an aeroplane will pass by overhead or a dog walker will hail their canine companion, breaking the illusion.

Today, though, it's a mobile phone that cuts the daydreaming short, vibrating away in my pocket. After a glance at the screen, I accept the call in a hushed voice.

"Hi, Mum."

"Hello, darling. Have I caught you at a good time?"

"Not really. I'm at Tinkerton."

"I'll keep it brief, then. Are you around later?"

"Possibly. Why?"

"Your father, in his infinite wisdom, ordered a new television, but it's so damned big he can't get it out of the box on his own. Would you mind popping over and giving him a hand?"

"Sure. Seven'ish suit?"

"Could you make it half-seven?"

"Is there some reason why that half-hour is important?"

"No, not at all, but seven-thirty would be better for us."

"Alright. I'll see you then."

"Thank you. Bye, darling."

I end the call and tuck the phone back in my pocket. My plans this evening involved a modern-history documentary and a long soak in the bath. It's not as though either requires much in the way of rescheduling, and there might be cake on offer.

It says a lot about my life that the likely highlights of the week will include watching a small duck paddling in the reeds and a slice of lemon drizzle cake.

Still, beggars and all that.

Chapter 5

Roger and Fay Neil married forty-seven years ago, and that fact still blows my mind. I just can't imagine being with someone for so long. To experience what my parents have, I'd need to marry someone tomorrow, and we'd both need to live to ninety. Considering my track record with women over the last two decades and my fondness for cake and beer, that seems unlikely.

I pull up on the driveway of their bungalow, next to Dad's almost-new Tesla.

My parents sold our family home shortly after I moved out. They decided moving to a spacious bungalow might make life easier should their mobility deteriorate. Ironically, they're more active now than they've ever been. Their typical week involves a schedule of tennis, ballroom dancing, yoga, rambling, golf, and other physical pursuits that Dad boasts about far too frequently for my liking. No one wants to know their parents are rutting away like rabbits on a near-daily basis, especially me.

I ring the doorbell and, after a moment's wait, hear Dad whistling his way down the hall.

"Evening, Son," he beams. "Good to see you."

I step over the threshold, and Dad slaps me on the back.

"You well?" he asks.

"I'm alright, ta."

He closes the front door and briefly checks his reflection in the hallway mirror. I wouldn't say he's a vain man, but if I hear his anecdote again about the time his thirty-something hairdresser called him a silver fox, I won't be responsible for my actions. No, he's not vain, but Dad is definitely image-conscious. Saying that, so is his wife. Alas, I inherited my looks from my late grandfather, Donald, who possessed a passing resemblance to Frankenstein's monster. He's been dead a long time but I do remember he was a happy-go-lucky character. Fuck-ugly, but always smiley.

"We're in the conservatory," Dad remarks, as he heads back up the hallway.

"We're? Do you have company?"

He doesn't reply.

I follow him through the kitchen and out to the conservatory, where I get my answer.

"Evening, Douglas," Mum gushes, getting to her feet. "Thanks for dropping by."

We share a peck, and my attention then turns to the middle-aged woman perched on the rattan sofa, cup of tea in hand.

"Douglas," Mum says, "this is Veronica. Her mother moved into number six last week."

"It's err, nice to meet you, Veronica."

"You too," she replies, getting to her feet. "But, I really must be going."

"Nonsense," Mum responds. "Surely you can stay for another cuppa?"

"As I said, I have to pick my son up at eight."

"Oh, that's right. It must be so hard being a single mother."

Mum's strange intonation on the term *single mother* coincides with a sly wink in my direction. Now I know why she wanted me here at such a specific time.

"I never said I was a single mother," Veronica objects. "What gave you that idea?"

"When we were chatting at your mother's house this morning, you said you didn't have a husband."

"I don't, but I do have a partner, and we're very happy together, thank you."

"Oh. My mistake."

Veronica hands her cup to Mum, mutters a curt goodbye, and leaves. Later this evening, I'm sure she'll discuss with her partner how Mrs Neil tried setting her up with her aesthetically-challenged son.

"What was that about?" I ask.

"What was what about?"

"The formal introduction to Veronica. Is that why you suggested I drop by at such a specific time?"

"Not at all."

"Don't fib, Mum. You're at it again, aren't you?"

She puffs a long sigh.

"Yes, guilty as charged," she says, hands raised. "But you know my heart's in the right place."

I love my mum, but her attempts at playing Cupid wore thin years ago. I wouldn't mind so much if just one of those attempts had proven remotely successful, but they've all ended in varying degrees of disaster.

"Please, Mum," I plead. "Promise me this'll be your last attempt at matchmaking."

"Fat chance," Dad snorts from his chair. "You know your mother won't be happy until you're walking down the aisle."

"Did you know about this latest attempt to palm me off on some poor unsuspecting female?"

"Possibly."

"Thanks for warning me."

"She's a nice-looking woman that Veronica. You could have done a lot worse."

"Jesus wept," I groan. "She wasn't even single."

"But she wasn't married, was she? You could have still made an effort."

I slap my palm against my forehead.

"Dad, I know you're only trying to help, but it's degrading. Stop it, please."

Mum steps forward and puts her hand on my arm.

"Your father and I have been talking, and ... you know, you can be honest with us, Douglas."

"Yes, I know."

"If there's something you need to share with us, we'll support you."

"Mum, you've lost me."

Dad perches on the edge of his chair, hands clasped together.

"You know, Son, your mother and I might be getting on a bit, but we're not complete fuddy-duddies. We accept the world has changed a lot since we were young."

"Right."

"What I'm saying is that we love you, irrespective of your ... orientation."

"My what?"

"It's okay," he says softly. "I think we've been kidding ourselves, but tonight's little episode with Veronica confirmed our suspicions."

"What suspicions?"

"That you're not interested in women, and I want you to know we're fine with it."

"Wait ... you think I'm gay?"

Too late, I realise my tone sounded a bit too close to incredulous.

"It's nothing to be ashamed of, Douglas," Mum chides. "It's not our cup of tea, but if you like a bit of cock now and then, good on you. As long as you wear a rubber, it's fine. Really, it is."

"Oh, God," I groan.

In their strange little way, my parents are trying to be supportive, but they just don't understand. How could they?

They've never found themselves short of attention from members of the opposite sex.

"I'm not gay."

"You're sure?" Dad asks.

"Yes."

He appears puzzled.

"You can't blame me for thinking you might be. You're forty-one and still single."

"Not through choice."

"Are you being too picky?"

"No."

"What is it then? You haven't dated anyone since Denise, and …"

"Enough," I snap. "How many times have I told you I don't ever want to hear that woman's name again?"

"Son, that was a long, long time ago. You really need to get over it."

A throwaway statement, but it strikes a nerve.

"Are you fucking serious?"

"Douglas!" Mum barks. "Language, please."

No matter what age we reach, the parent-child dynamic rarely changes.

"Sorry," I mumble like a scorned teenager.

"Your father is simply making the point that you can't let one bad experience put you off for life. I know you had your troubles with Denise, but it was a lifetime ago."

"Mum, I've asked you countless times never to mention … her."

"Fine, but whatever is holding you back from meeting someone, you need to fix it."

I'm in no mood to continue the conversation.

"Dad, do you need help with the TV, or not?"

"I might have sorted it before you arrived," he replies sheepishly.

"In that case, I'm going home."

"Do you have to leave so soon?" Mum asks.

"Yes."

She sees me to the door, where I lean forward and plant a peck on Mum's cheek.

"Are you okay, Douglas?"

"I'm fine."

"I feel a bit silly now, trying to orchestrate that meeting with Veronica. I'm sorry."

"It's not me you should be apologising to. Did you see Veronica's face when the penny dropped?"

"We meant no harm."

"I'm sure you didn't, but enough is enough, Mum. I'm coming to terms with the fact I'll probably be alone for the rest of my life, and I can live with it."

"Don't be so defeatist. You'll find someone; I know it."

"Goodbye, Mum."

"But, Douglas ..."

I stride away.

On the journey home, I chew over the doorstep conversation with my mother. There's one word she used that rankles a bit, not that I let on: defeatist.

I remember reading an article about the author, JK Rowling, and that her manuscript for the first Harry Potter novel was rejected by twelve different publishers before she found one willing to sign her. Ms Rowling is now considered a model of persistence, like being rejected twelve times is reason enough to admit defeat. If she'd experienced my levels of rejection, she'd have tossed her wizardly manuscript in the bin long before she found a willing publisher.

Compared to what I've been through, JK Rowling doesn't know the meaning of the word rejection.

There's little comfort waiting for me when I arrive home; the emptiness weighing heavier than usual. Although it was unseasonably warm earlier, the temperature dipped dramatically as soon as the sun set. The house is now too close to cold for my liking. I turn the thermostat dial a couple of notches.

I make myself a hot chocolate, flop down on the sofa, and switch the television on.

The documentary doesn't prove to be the distraction I hoped it might. My parents have inadvertently unleashed memories I've spent most of my adult life trying to suppress. As for getting over what happened, little do they know I still relive those months with Denise almost every day.

I really should stop reading those bloody diaries.

22nd January 2001

What's the point of Tuesdays? I don't like Mondays much but at least they serve a purpose—a signal that the week has begun. Tuesdays are shit, though, because nothing of interest ever happens.

This Tuesday started on a bad footing. My alarm didn't go off, and I'd have still been in bed if Mum hadn't banged on my bedroom door at eight o'clock. I didn't have time for breakfast.

I got to the office on time and then wondered why I bothered. I don't think anyone would have noticed.

I've just checked my 1999 diary to be sure, and I've now been working at Temple-Dane Auditing Services for almost eighteen months. I don't know where the time has gone, but I thought I'd be dating someone by now—fat chance of that.

The morning was a drudge, up until the primary server crashed just after eleven. There wasn't much to do but stare out of the window until the IT guys got it running again. One of the bosses then suggested we work through our lunch breaks to make up for the lost productivity. That didn't go down well.

After lunch, we were introduced to Julia's replacement while she's away on maternity leave. Denise is a bit older than me, I think, and a million miles out of my league, so I didn't pay much attention until I bumped into her in the break room, mid-afternoon.

She asked if I wanted a biscuit. I can't stand digestives, but I took one anyway so I didn't appear rude.

Talking to a really attractive woman isn't easy. I could feel my cheeks burning when Denise asked me where the teabags were kept. Then I stupidly asked if she knew what the word tepidophobia meant. No one ever knows it's the fear of badly made tea.

She laughed and it felt kinda good.

That was the highlight of my day. I suppose it'll probably be the highlight of my week unless I bump into Denise in the break room again. She seems nice, and unlike all the other women in the office, not so judgy.

Mum made toad in the hole for dinner, and Dad nipped into Blockbuster on the way home from work. He hired Wall Street with Michael Douglas and Charlie Sheen. I thought it was okay, but the main guy, Gordon Gekko was an absolute arsehole.

It's my turn to choose a film next week. I wonder what kind of films Denise likes.

Chapter 6

Ady is in a subdued mood this morning. I ask him what's up, but whatever it is, he seems reluctant to discuss it.

"Just a few money worries," is all he's prepared to say before suggesting I change the subject.

Ady always has money worries, so I'm not overly concerned. I stupidly tell him I'm going out on Saturday evening.

"Where?"

"A nightclub."

"I didn't think that was your scene."

"It isn't, but my mate, Kenny, insisted I go along to some random woman's fortieth birthday. I really don't fancy it."

"Why are you going then?"

"If you'd met Kenny, you'd know why. He can be very persuasive."

"Do you know what you're gonna wear?"

"No idea."

The prospect of shopping for clothes fills me with dread; trawling shops staffed by attractive youngsters and mirrors everywhere. There must be something suitable in my wardrobe.

I spend the rest of our journey conducting a mental inventory. The pickings are slim.

The start of our working day is no different to any other day, with Jonny conducting the briefing like he's just left his wife in bed with another man and Keira going through her perfunctory motions.

Once the bin emptying routine is over, we consult the list of fly-tips we need to clear today. It's long, and the locations are spread right across our patch.

"No time for lunch at The Vale," I sigh, as I work out a route from our current position.

"Busy one, then?"

"Fourteen collections."

"Great," he groans. "I was hoping for an early finish."

"Sorry, mate. Not today."

After quickly demolishing a sandwich and a bag of crisps from a corner shop, we set off.

"Where are we heading first?" Ady asks.

"Lawton Close on the Kempshot Estate. A sofa."

It's a short drive and, thankfully, the streets on the estate are relatively quiet when we arrive. Last year, we dropped by to collect an oven that some idiot had lobbed from the third-floor balcony of one of the tower blocks. The nearest place we could park the van was a good hundred yards away and, when we returned with the battered oven, the van was full of crap that wasn't there five minutes prior.

I turn into Lawton Close. Our prize is sitting in the middle of a flowerbed.

"Fuck's sake," Ady groans. "Why dump it there?"

"Why dump it anywhere?"

I pull up, and we make our way across an area of scrubby grass to the flowerbed. At first sight, the leather sofa looks in pretty good condition, and it's not apparent why someone saw fit to abandon it. Then, as we get closer, the reason becomes clear.

"I think we'll need gloves for this one, mate."

We both don our protective gloves, but they don't help with the stench of stale piss emanating from the sofa.

"On three, lift. One, two, three."

The piss-sodden sofa drips all the way back to the van. We shove it on and stand back before daring to breathe again.

"One down, thirteen to go."

Our next stop is a semi-rural spot about half a mile from Tinkerton Meadow. Despite the warning sign fixed to a post, the lay-by is notorious for fly-tipping. Today, it looks like a tipper truck has deposited its entire load.

"A cowboy clearance job, I reckon," Ady remarks as we survey the scene.

There's a fridge-freezer, an old television, a dismantled wardrobe, a load of toys, a desk, and eight bin liners full of god-knows-what.

"Yep, I think you're right."

You could argue that the previous owner of the waste did the right thing in hiring a clearance company to take away their unwanted junk. Unfortunately, they didn't check if they were hiring a legitimate clearance company.

I step over to the nearest bin liner and untie the neck. Strangely, this is one part of the job I quite enjoy.

Besides collecting fly-tipped waste, we're also tasked with finding clues to who it once belonged to so the council can levy a punishment. Most people are unaware that they risk a hefty fine if the fly-tipped crap can be traced back to them. I like the investigative angle, and occasionally we'll unearth a discarded letter or Amazon package with an address. If we do, a brown envelope from the council will eventually land on some unsuspecting soul's doormat.

It doesn't take much rummaging to establish who this waste once belonged to.

"A-ha," I declare, withdrawing a piece of unopened junk mail. "Sorry, Mr Robert Worrall of 19 Orchard Gardens, but you're in for a nasty surprise in the post."

I photograph the scene from a dozen angles and bag the evidence before we set about loading it all onto the van.

Our next stop is a residential street about a mile away, where some moron has dumped a washing machine on the pavement outside a row of upmarket townhouses.

On arrival, we're able to park right next to the offending item. We hop out of the cab, and just as we're about to lift the washing machine from the pavement, a woman emerges from the nearest townhouse.

"Excuse me," she says. "Are you from the council?"

Tall, slim, and blessed with the kind of beauty you rarely see beyond a fashion catwalk, the woman has far more than her fair share of good looks.

She saunters over and stands in front of me. My cheeks redden.

"Yes, err ... we're from the council," I mumble, avoiding eye contact.

"Have you come to collect our old fridge-freezer?" she asks. "I booked a collection on the council website yesterday."

"I'm afraid not. We're just here to pick this up," I reply, nodding towards the washing machine.

The woman looks at the washing machine. Then at the half-laden van.

"Well, you might as well take the fridge-freezer while you're here."

"I'm sorry, but we can't."

"Why not?"

"Because we're only authorised to collect fly-tipped waste. Another crew will collect your fridge-freezer."

"That's not good enough," she snaps. "I want it gone, and you're here, so just take it."

"As I said, we can't."

The woman's brow develops a deep furrow.

"Don't be such a damn jobsworth. Take it, or I'll ring your boss and tell him you're being deliberately obstructive."

I can't stand confrontation and decide it'd be better if I just ignore the woman and get on with loading the washing machine. I signal to Ady.

"Ready?"

"Yep."

We're supposed to use a trolley to shift heavy items, but it's more hassle than it's worth. It's much quicker and easier just to lift the machine and slide it onto the back of the van. We both squat down and grab hold of the abandoned appliance.

"How dare you ignore me!" the woman yells. "My taxes pay your wages, you know."

"On three, mate."

It takes less than ten seconds to transport the washing machine from the pavement to the back of the van. Task complete, we shut and bolt the tailgate. Rather than accepting defeat gracefully, the woman's anger boils over. She stands directly in my path, blocking the route back to the cab.

"You're pathetic," she seethes, jabbing a manicured finger inches from my face.

"Madam," I respond in a conciliatory tone. "I have explained the situation, and if you're unhappy with it, feel free to complain to Ashbridge Council. We're just doing what we're told to do."

Only minutes ago, the woman's face was beautiful. Now, that same face is red with fury. It's the opposite of beautiful.

"I bet you've got a tiny cock, and ... and haven't touched a woman since you fell out of your mother's snatch."

Insults rarely hurt because I've heard them all a thousand times. What I haven't experienced in a long, long time is this kind of spiteful rage. Shocked, the woman's outburst renders my legs and mouth inert.

"I ... I ..."

Ady comes to my rescue.

"Stand back," he says to the woman, forcibly but with restraint. "If you think verbally assaulting council staff is okay, you'll be waiting a long time to get that fridge-freezer shifted, darlin'."

"I beg your pardon?"

"You heard. We ain't paid nowhere near enough to put up with people yelling abuse at us."

"It's your word against mine, and you're the ones being obstinate."

"Fair enough," Ady shrugs. "We'll see what our gaffer has to say when we show him the video."

"What video?"

"All council vehicles are fitted with CCTV, just for situations like this ... you know, when an entitled member of the public thinks they can lay into us for no good reason."

Ady's statement—bullshit as it is—has the desired effect. The woman curses under her breath and storms back to her front door. A second later, that door slams shut.

"You alright, mate?" Ady asks.

"Err, yeah. Thanks."

I shake off the residual shock and join my colleague in the van.

"Bleedin' cheek," he says, putting his seatbelt on. "Shame she had such a narky attitude 'cos she was a looker."

"You know what they say about beauty being skin deep, right?"

"Yeah, you're not wrong there. Can you imagine having to live with someone so bloody stroppy?"

I don't reply and turn my attention to the clipboard.

"We're behind schedule now," I mutter. "We'd better get a move on."

Ady grabs his phone and taps silently away at the screen as I manoeuvre the van through the back streets of Ashbridge to our next collection, trying to make up for lost time.

We reach a junction with a main road just as the traffic lights turn red. With Ady still preoccupied with his phone, I stare out of the window towards a car park on my right. A red hatchback pulls into a space some thirty yards away, and the four occupants gather by the side: a man, a woman, and two boys who I'd guess are three or four years of age. The parents are both smiling, and the boys look excited about something. Maybe they're heading into town for a pizza before an afternoon trip to the cinema. It's just a guess, but whatever their plans, they look so happy. Perhaps they're just happy to be together. I breathe a heavy sigh and pull away as the lights turn green.

The mournful thoughts soon catch up.

Wanting a partner isn't just about sharing my life with someone. It'd be lovely, but it's so much more than that. I don't think anyone relishes growing old, but most are lucky enough to be surrounded by family as they enter their twilight years. My parents won't be around forever, and while I love my sister and my nieces, I don't want to become sad Uncle Dougie, the lonely bachelor who only gets invited over for the occasional barbecue or Christmas lunch just because he's nowhere else to go. I want my own family.

At forty-one years of age, that dream is as good as over, and it hurts far more than the constant insults thrown my way.

"Earth to Dougie," Ady quips. "Anyone at home?"

"Eh?"

"You've just driven straight past the next pick-up."

"Have I? Shit."

I turn around at the next junction. My colleague puts his phone in the glove box.

"She got under your skin, that woman?"

"A bit."

"That's Joe Public for you. Ain't you glad we don't have to deal with them that often?"

"It's a definite perk of the job."

"The only perk," he huffs. "It certainly ain't the pay."

"Can't disagree with you there."

"So why do you do it?"

"The job?"

"Yeah. I ain't no Einstein, so this is as good as it gets for me, but you're a clever bastard. I don't understand why you've stuck at it so long."

"As you say, we don't have to deal with people ... well, most of the time. And, I don't ever want to work in an office again."

"Even on days when it's pissing down, or you're freezing your nuts off?"

"Yep, even then."

"You're such a weirdo, mate," he says with a grin. "I'd give anything to be smart like you and sit on my arse in a nice warm office all day."

Ady wouldn't be so confident if he knew what happened to me the last time I worked in an office. Fortunately, he doesn't—very few do, and for that, I'm grateful.

Chapter 7

My day did not start well.

Ten minutes before we were due at work, Ady sent a text saying he'd just woken up. I had to hurry down to my car and hit the road like Lewis Hamilton. I made it on time, just. Then I had to wait fifteen minutes for Ady to arrive and another five whilst Jonny administered a bollocking.

Despite oversleeping and being given a verbal warning for poor timekeeping, Ady is in surprisingly good spirits.

"Shall we have lunch at The Vale?" he asks, as we empty the last bin of the morning. "My treat."

"I thought you were skint."

"I was, but I ... I got a refund on a pair of trainers. I bought them on a whim."

"Fair enough. Seeing as it's Friday, I think egg and chips are in order."

We hop into the van and head to The Vale Cafe to find it no busier than the last time we visited. Ady nips to the loo while I head to the counter.

"Afternoon, Dougie," Colin smiles as I approach. "What can I get you?"

"Egg and chips twice, and two teas."

"No worries."

"How's the search for an extra pair of hands going?" I ask. "Any luck?"

"Nope."

"That's a bugger. Four weeks is a long time to go without a decent cuppa."

"Don't go finding another cafe just yet. Heather is going to manage the place on her own."

"Oh. She'll be serving customers, will she?"

Colin chuckles to himself and then leans across the counter as if he's about to share a secret.

"I know what you're thinking," he says in a hushed voice. "But Heather insists she can cope."

"We'll be on our best behaviour, and if there's anything I can do to help, just let me know."

"Is that a genuine offer, or are you just being polite?"

"It's genuine, Colin, but obviously, my motives aren't entirely selfless. If this place isn't open, Ady might drag me to McDonald's. Have you ever tried their tea?"

He pulls a face that suggests he has.

"I don't finish till three'ish most days, but if Heather needs a hand after that, I'll be glad to help."

"You're a good man, Dougie. Leave me your number, and I'll tell her she can call on you if she's desperate … not when you're at work, obviously."

I scribble my number on a pad, and Colin tucks the slip of paper in his apron pocket.

"Sit yourself down. I'll fetch those teas."

Ady joins me at the table and spends the entire twenty minutes staring at his phone while we eat. All too soon, it's time to get back to work. Ady heads to the counter to settle the bill, and I wave Colin goodbye. As I do, I catch sight of Heather standing on the other side of the serving hatch. It's hard to interpret her expression, but she immediately turns her head away when she notices me looking. I think it's more likely hell will freeze over before she asks for help. At least I made the offer.

The rest of the afternoon passes in a haze of fly-tipped wardrobes and a spot of roadside litter picking. The weather is about as perfect as it ever gets in our job—mild and dry, and just enough breeze so we can't smell each other.

Back at the depot, I sign the van back in while Ady loiters outside for a smoke. In her office, Keira is on the phone.

"I'm just on hold with accounts," she remarks. "Bear with me a minute."

"Sure."

With the two of us waiting in silence, the situation soon becomes uncomfortable. I feel compelled to say something.

"Any plans this weekend, Keira?"

Looking up at me over the rim of her glasses, she answers my question with a stern glare.

"Sorry," I respond sheepishly. "None of my business."

I guess Keira has to take a hard line with small talk because a handful of my colleagues don't know where to draw the line. In hindsight, asking Keira about her plans could easily be misconstrued as a clumsy opening line to a date request.

I get my phone out and randomly prod the screen, just to avoid another conversational pothole. Long seconds pass.

"Can I see you on Tuesday?" Keira suddenly asks.

I look up from my phone.

"Tuesday? Err ..."

"About 10:00 am?"

I realise her question is aimed at whoever is on the other end of the phone. As my cheeks burn red, Keira concludes her conversation and hangs up.

"Key, please."

I hand over the van key and then try to rattle through the return procedure as quickly as possible. Once complete, I hurry away.

"You took your time," Ady complains, as I exit the office building.

"Sorry. Keira was on the phone. Why are you waiting, anyway? You do remember I had to drive in myself this morning?"

"Roy and some of the lads are heading to the Golden Lion for a few beers. You up for it?"

"I'll pass, thanks."

"I dunno why I asked. You're never up for beers on a Friday."

"That's not true. It's just … I've got plans this afternoon."

"What plans?"

Much like Keira, I prefer to keep my private life private. If any of my colleagues found out about my birdwatching hobby, I'll likely suffer a stream of unoriginal and unfunny jibes about *great tits* and *common shags*. Our profession isn't renowned for its sophisticated humour.

"I, um … need to buy something to wear to this bloody party tomorrow."

"Suit yourself. I'll see you Monday."

We both depart, and within thirty minutes, I'm back in my car heading towards Tinkerton Meadow.

When I arrive, there's only one other vehicle in the car park: Kenny's beaten-up old Volvo estate. Despite the shabby bodywork, my friend refuses to trade it in for a newer model on the basis it's solid and reliable. If I were a psychologist, I might question if Kenny sees the same qualities in me as he does his car—not much to look at but always dependable. I, however, do not regularly deposit fluids when I'm stationary, like the old Volvo. Not yet, anyway.

I make my way to Falbert's Mount and climb up the grassy bank. Upon reaching the top, I regret not bringing my sunglasses. The autumn sun is exceptionally bright, floating just above the tree line directly ahead. A low sun isn't ideal as it makes it difficult to view birds flying in a westerly direction.

Kenny is standing with his binoculars trained on a patch of thicket west of the main pond. Almost as if he has a sixth sense, he lowers them and turns to face me.

"Have you got eyes in the back of your head?" I ask, using my right hand as a sun shade.

"That'd be handy, but no. No one needs a second pair of eyes to know you're here. We can smell you coming, my friend."

His observation is valid and a consequence of coming straight from the shower to Tinkerton Meadow.

"Have I overdone the deodorant?"

"Maybe just a wee bit," he chuckles. "But I suspect it's preferable to your odour at the end of the working day."

"You know how it is. It's not a proper day's work if you don't break sweat."

"Aye, you're not wrong."

I remove the lens caps from my binoculars and take up a position next to Kenny.

"Anything interesting to report?"

"Not a bad day so far: half-a-dozen Snipe, too many Lapwing to count, and I was just watching a couple of Meadow Pipit as you arrived."

Shoulder to shoulder, we raise our binoculars. In any other situation, the silence would become awkward within seconds. In the birdwatching fraternity, it's the accepted norm. Many a time, I've loitered on the Mount alongside a small gaggle of twitchers, and we've barely said a word to one another. I understand why: Tinkerton Meadow is as much a sanctuary for us as it is for the birds we spot.

I'm happily studying a wading Green Sandpiper when Kenny breaks the silence.

"Are you looking forward to tomorrow night?"

"Honestly?" I reply, lowering my binoculars. "I'm close to crapping my pants already. It's been a long time since I stepped foot in a nightclub, and I never felt comfortable the first time around."

"The party is in a private area with its own bar, so it won't be too crowded. And, as it's a fortieth birthday, so you'll be amongst people your age ... apart from a few dinosaurs like me."

I reply with an unconvincing smile.

"You know," Kenny continues. "If you really don't fancy it, stay at home, but you'll not find a lassie sat on your arse watching the Discovery Channel."

"That much I do know, and please don't think I'm being ungrateful. I'm just ... ah, forget it."

"You've lost your mojo. Is that what it is?"

"I never had it."

"So, maybe you'll find it tomorrow. And, what's the worst that could happen? We have a few drinks, a few laughs, and end the evening putting the world to rights over a bag of chips."

Kenny's reassurance adds a bit of conviction to my smile.

"Yeah, you're right. Sod it ... I'll be there."

"Eight o'clock sharp," he replies warmly. "And remember: fortune favours the brave."

"Let's hope so."

"And on that note, I need a piss. Keep an eye on my bag for me?"

"Sure."

Kenny squats down to put his binoculars in his rucksack. Facing the sun, I no longer have his six-foot frame acting as a shade, and once again I'm forced to shield my eyes. With most of the sun's rays blocked, I notice we're not alone on the Mount. There's a figure standing right at the far end, which puts them at a distance roughly half the length of a football pitch away from us.

"Who's that?" I ask Kenny, nodding in the direction of the figure.

"Not a clue. I didn't even notice them arrive."

Us twitchers might not be the chattiest of creatures, but it's common practice to say hello when you arrive and to ask about the day's bird activity.

"Maybe it's a newbie," I suggest. "Do you think we should go introduce ourselves?"

Kenny turns towards the figure, shielding his eyes.

"Is he wearing a cloak?" he asks.

"A bloke in a cloak? Perhaps it's Dr Seuss."

My attempt at humour misses the mark, so I squint hard in an effort to answer Kenny's question. The sun is almost directly above the figure, and all I can make out is a vague silhouette, edged with a striking white halo. Whoever it is, they appear to be staring out towards the lake.

"It looks like he or she is wearing a dress?" I suggest.

"Who wears a full-length dress to go bird spotting?"

As we continue to squint into the distance, a sudden but distinctive sound splits the silence: *kak, kak, kak.* Our heads snap in the direction of the sound, just in time to catch a young Peregrine gliding towards the safety of a beech tree at the far edge of the meadow.

"Whoever startled him," Kenny says. "They did us a favour."

Peregrines are one of the rarer birds to visit Tinkerton Meadow, and although I've spotted hundreds over the years, I still get a thrill seeing one in flight.

"You'd better take that piss before he heads off."

"Typical," Kenny snorts. "Some birds have lousy timing."

Just as he turns to walk away, the sun dips below the tree line. The view beyond my friend's shoulder has changed.

"Where'd they go?"

"Who?"

"Our mystery visitor."

Kenny spins around and double-checks my claim. More than a passing glance, he scans the vista for a good few seconds.

"Must have been a flying visit," he says casually. "I just hope they're not in the Portaloo, for their sake."

Kenny hurries off to empty his bladder.

With the sun's warming rays no longer reaching the Mount, a slight shiver crosses my shoulders. Only then do I notice the silence. Even after dark, our avian friends continue to squawk and chirp and trill. The complete lack of sound is so disconcerting, I cough just to confirm my ears are still working. In an instant, the reserve's soundtrack resumes.

All seems normal again, apart from a peculiar sense of ... I don't even know how to describe it. It's like I'm standing in a queue at the Post Office and whoever is behind me is too close. I turn around. Unsurprisingly, there's no one there.

In need of distraction, I raise my binoculars and aim them towards the beech tree.

The Peregrine is nowhere to be seen, but then I catch movement near the base of the trunk. Fleeting, I couldn't even say what caused it.

It was probably just a deer. Yes, it must have been.

Chapter 8

There are two types of weather no twitcher wants to see in the forecast. The first is fog because birdwatching in low visibility is pointless. The second is thunderstorms. Mid-evening yesterday, the weather forecasting app on my phone suddenly displayed a lightning bolt icon against this morning's timeline. That is why I'm lying in bed at eight o'clock on a Saturday morning, rather than standing on Falbert's Mount.

I can tolerate most weather conditions: biting winds, torrential rain, and even heavy snow. However, as much as I love birdwatching, I'm not crazy enough to stand on top of an exposed hillock during a thunderstorm.

Instead of my usual Saturday morning routine, I'd planned a long, lazy lie-in, but as my eyes flickered open just after dawn, my brain immediately reminded me about tonight. The resulting jolt of anxiety put paid to further sleep. I've now been lying under the duvet for almost an hour, desperate for the loo but lacking the motivation to get out of bed.

I finally relent.

Twenty minutes and one mug of steaming hot tea later, I'm at a bit of a loss. There is one chore I've been putting off, and I still don't want to do it, but time is running short.

With much reluctance, I trek back up the stairs and open the doors to my wardrobe.

Because I don't have a social life to speak of, I only purchase clothes with function in mind. Consequently, there's not much on the rails suitable for a nightclub. I spot a pair of black corduroy trousers, which are probably okay, so I pull them off the hanger and try them on. They still fit and, in a dark nightclub, I reckon they'll look a bit like jeans.

Trousers sorted, I kneel down and inspect my modest collection of footwear. It doesn't take long to dismiss all but a pair of black leather Oxford brogues I purchased for a wedding years ago.

As I feared, it's what to wear on top that proves problematic. What goes with black cords?

The first contender on the rail is a white dress-shirt.

"No, you'll look like a waiter."

I continue the search and stop on a mid-grey pullover.

"An adult in school uniform," I mutter. "Definitely not."

The third possibility is a maroon cardigan. It's a bit baggy around the arms, but it'll look acceptable over the white shirt.

I slip on the shirt and the cardigan and steel myself. I've no choice now but to look in the mirror.

Such is my aversion to my reflection, there's only one full-length mirror in the house, and it's strategically hidden behind the door of the bedroom I use as a home office. A deep breath and I cross the landing.

As I enter the spare bedroom, an ominous rumble of thunder marks the end of the brief journey.

Another deep breath and I swing the door towards me.

The horror of seeing my own reflection never seems to dampen. In many ways, what I'm wearing is almost inconsequential because I look like a cartoonish depiction of a human whatever I wear. My odd body shape is the reason I've never owned an off-the-peg suit—my torso is too short and my legs too long, and I've no arse to speak of. It's a ridiculous body, or freakish as I once overheard a supposed friend in college describe it.

I turn away in disgust and scuttle back to my bedroom. Try as I might, I can't displace the mirror's image as I change out of tonight's attire. Even recounting Kenny's words doesn't help to stem the negativity. I've heard all the platitudes and sentiments there are, and they've all proven baseless. There isn't someone for everyone, and no matter how many fish there are in the sea, the number is inconsequential when you consider how much cold, empty water there is.

"Enough," I snap.

If I allow myself to wallow in negativity every time I consider my situation, my mental health will quickly spiral out of control. Things could always be worse—much worse—and I certainly don't want to go back to the dark days of therapy again.

I look out of the window at my sodden back garden and the puddles of murky water dotted across the lawn. Relentless, the rain continues to pelt down from a slate-grey sky. If I'm looking for cheer, there's not a lot of it outside.

To keep myself occupied all day, I need a plan. A late breakfast at The Vale will kill an hour, and then a few hours at the cinema, perhaps. I've no idea what's on, but it doesn't matter as I'm willing to watch almost anything except romcoms. I've seen too many where the quirky oddball protagonist ends up with the beautiful girl, and I can't stomach another plot that bears no resemblance to reality. My reality, anyway.

By mid-afternoon, the plan is underway, and four hours of the day are taken care of. It began with a full English, served with a smile from Colin and a cold glare from Heather, and then the joy of an almost empty cinema.

I discovered years ago that if you wait to see a film as late as possible after its release, you can avoid being crammed into a full auditorium. This strategy became a necessity once our local cinema started serving nachos and chilli dogs at the refreshments counter. It's bad enough listening to someone behind you slurping a drink through a straw or munching on popcorn, but at this rate, people will soon be watching a film whilst tucking into a three-course meal, including a soup starter. It's unacceptable.

I arrive home just after three and spend the rest of the afternoon watching a couple of avian documentaries. The first is about the remarkable 40,000-mile annual migration of Arctic Terns, and the second, narrated by Stephen Fry, documents the exotic mating rituals of certain bird species. If only I could improve my mating record with a show of brightly coloured plumage and a few dance moves. I'd even consider a journey of 40,000 miles if it meant finding a partner, truth be told.

Dinner time arrives, and I select my microwave meal carefully, avoiding anything with garlic or too much spice. If, by some miracle, I should find myself chatting to a lady this evening, the last thing I want is to risk putting her off with my offensive breath. I settle on shepherd's pie, served with a side order of delusional optimism.

At six o'clock, I shave, followed by a long soak in the bath. It's gone seven by the time I get dressed and apply a liberal amount of Polo cologne. The expensive scent was a birthday present from my sister, maybe nine or ten years ago, and it's testament to how infrequently I have cause to wear it that the bottle is still two-thirds full.

I've just got enough time to down two large vodka tonics before the pre-booked taxi arrives. The swarm of agitated butterflies in my stomach need subduing.

A friend once told me that taxi drivers prefer single passengers to sit in the back of the car rather than the front passenger's seat. When my taxi arrives, I duly oblige that preference. The driver confirms the destination and turns up the stereo volume before pulling away. To my surprise, his choice of music is a slow bluesy-jazz number, probably best suited to the end of an evening rather than the beginning. Still, combined with the warming glow of the vodka, it helps to ease the nerves.

As we travel through the dark streets of Ashbridge, I think back to the last time I left the house on a Saturday evening, destined for a nightclub. I couldn't say when it was or if anything unexpected happened, but I do remember the sense of anticipation. In my late teens, I still harboured some semblance of hope, maybe even excitement about what fate had in store for me. I felt like a gold prospector, panning for the rarest nugget in an over-mined backwater. The odds were stacked against success, but I never believed they were insurmountable. I later learned that naivety is both a blessing and a curse for the young.

We arrive at our destination.

"£8.60, please."

I hand the driver a tenner and tell him to keep the change. Even the tiniest grain of goodwill is worth harvesting. Then, I stand on the pavement and watch the taxi pull away.

No turning back.

I glance up at the sky and offer a silent prayer that, at the very least, my evening doesn't end in disaster. The rain-heavy clouds have finally moved on, and a few pin-prick stars are just about visible beyond the street lights. In hindsight, my decision to wear a waterproof kagool might have been a tad pessimistic.

A deep breath and I turn around.

The nightclub we're heading to is called Zinc, although in my day it was Ragamuffins. What doesn't appear to have changed are the opening hours, as the doors to the dimly lit foyer are currently closed. Kenny confirmed that he and the rest of the party-goers are meeting in the bar next door to Zinc. That bar isn't named after a chemical element.

I cover four paving slabs, but my legs stop of their own accord before I reach the door. Although the large panes of glass are tinted, I can still see what's going on inside the bar. It's crowded, and from what I can see, most of the clientele are young and attractive.

Is it really too late to turn back?

I'm still assessing my options when the clack of heeled shoes catches my attention. I turn to my left, to the source.

"How's that for timing?" Kenny says with a broad smile. "Have you just got here?"

The clacking continues courtesy of Sara's high-heeled shoes as the couple approach.

"Um, yes. Just."

I can't help but look Kenny and Sara up and down. They both look effortlessly cool: Kenny in jeans and a black leather coat, and Sara in a short dress, knee-length boots, and denim jacket.

Sara steps forward and plants a kiss on my cheek.

"It's really good to see you, Dougie. I'm so glad you decided to come along."

"Thank you for inviting me."

"No need to thank her," Kenny interjects. "You just buy the first round, and we'll call it quits."

"Fair enough," I chuckle.

My legs re-engage, and I step towards the door, pulling it open so Kenny and Sara can enter first.

"Cheers," Sara chirps.

My gesture has nothing to do with chivalry and a lot to do with cowardice. It's easier to hide behind my friends if I let them lead the way.

They enter. I count to three and follow.

The change in atmosphere is stark. Inside the bar, it's overly warm, and the thrum of a hundred simultaneous conversations fight with the baseline of the background music. It's like walking into a wall of white noise.

With Kenny leading, we push a trail through to the far side of the bar. A woman wearing a plastic tiara and a 'Birthday Girl' sash spots Sara and charges towards us. Sara dashes forward, and the two women embrace. They excitedly chatter words I can't hear.

"I'm probably stating the obvious," Kenny says, leaning into me. "But that's Lucy, and it's her fortieth."

"I gathered."

Lucy is as pretty as she is happily married, so Kenny tells me. I really hope I'm not the only singleton here tonight. Just as I'm about to make a break for the bar, Sara drags her friend in my direction.

"Dougie, this is Lucy."

"Um, hi," I splutter, offering a handshake. "Many happy returns, and, err ... thanks for letting me gatecrash your party."

"You're very welcome," Lucy replies, shaking my hand. "Any friend of Kenny and Sara's is a friend of mine, and the more the merrier, I say."

"That's very nice of you. I was about to get a round in if you'd like a drink?"

"I've already got three on the go, thanks, but I might take you up on that offer later."

Lucy then drags Sara away.

"She seems very nice," I remark.

"Aye, she is," Kenny replies, nodding towards the group of twenty-odd revellers Sara and Lucy are now part of. "And, I'm sure all her friends are too."

There certainly appear to be far more females than males amongst Lucy's guests.

"You never know, Dougie-boy, tonight might be your lucky night."

"Hmm, if I can get through the evening with my dignity intact, I'll consider that lucky."

Kenny shakes his head.

"Give it a rest, Captain Pessimistic, and get the drinks in. Sara will have a large Prosecco."

"Alright. Pint?"

"Please."

I edge my way to the bar and, after a two-minute wait, grab the attention of a guy who doesn't look old enough to consume alcohol, let alone serve it. I shout my order at him and, while I wait, reflect on Kenny's words. Perhaps I am being too pessimistic. Sara has always been kind to me, and on first impressions, Lucy seems very pleasant. It stands to reason their mutual friends are probably lovely people too.

Would it hurt to rekindle some of that naive optimism from my youth?

"That'll be £16.20, mate," the young barman says.

"Thanks," I reply, handing him a twenty-pound note. "Have one yourself."

"Nice one. Cheers."

He keeps three quid and returns eighty pence.

"Thanks for the drink," he says. "You have a good evening."

As I drop the coins in my pocket, I respond to the barman's suggestion.

"You know, I think I just might."

Chapter 9

We stayed in the bar for a little over an hour. Kenny and I nursed our pints for the duration, but Lucy, Sara, and their friends were keen to make the most of the half-price cocktails on offer. By the time we left, the group had grown in number, noise, and levels of intoxication. Still, they all seemed in good spirits.

Being a private party, we didn't have to join the queue outside Zinc. Lucy's husband, Ryan, spoke to the door staff, and they swiftly guided us through the foyer and up the stairs.

Kenny suggests we deposit our coats in the cloakroom.

"I'm already sweating like a pig on heat," he says.

We stray from the rest of the group to the end of the corridor, where a young woman stands idle behind the cloakroom counter. We pay a fiver for the privilege of leaving our coats on a hanger for a few hours.

We then head back along the corridor towards the set of double doors leading through to the main nightclub. As we walk, I have to admit I'm curious how much the club has changed since my last visit, so many years ago.

It turns out that nightclubs don't change very much because there's not much to change. The dancefloor is still the dancefloor, and the two bar areas are still bar areas. There's a lot less neon lighting, but everything else is as I remember it. What I don't remember is ever seeing it so empty. As the doors have only just opened, there's barely a handful of people milling around by the bars.

"I think we're over there," I say to Kenny, pointing to a set of open doors on the far side of the room.

"Lead on."

As we get nearer, another doorman appears and checks we're on the guest list for the private party. Satisfied we're not a couple of over-aged gatecrashers, he ushers us in.

Considering I wasn't the coolest of youths, the private party room is one part of the club I never got to see. It's smaller than I imagined, with a bar at one end and a square dancefloor at the other. There are tables and chairs arranged down one side, but only two of the tables are currently occupied. Most of Lucy's guests are assembled at the bar. The DJ has selected to play *Free* by Ultra Naté, which I think was released in the late nineties. I guess Lucy has requested the music from her youth. It's a great choice as it's also the music of my youth, although I think my experience of that period was very different to Lucy's.

Kenny tells me to grab a table while he gets the drinks in. I don't argue and make for a table in the corner.

When he returns, we do what all middle-aged men do once they're left alone with a few pints—we enthusiastically debate everything that's wrong with society and whose fault it is. The conversation proves thirsty work, and we get through two pints in a little over an hour.

On the whole, we're left alone. Sara makes a half-hearted attempt to drag Kenny to the dance floor, but he's nothing if not resolute. I'm grateful she doesn't ask me.

With Sara back amongst the throng, Kenny and I continue where we left off, and then I fetch another round. If I were stone-cold sober, I'd probably feel more self-conscious as I amble from our table to the bar, but no one gives me a second glance. I'm confident it would be a different story if I stepped through the doors to the main nightclub, where the crowd are likely half my age.

As the barman pours our pints, I concede that maybe coming along tonight wasn't such a bad idea after all. Granted, the chances of meeting anyone now seem slimmer than they were at the beginning of the evening, but that's just par for the course.

I return to the table.

As I pass by the edge of the dancefloor, it becomes apparent Kenny is no longer sitting alone. Sara is seated next to her husband, and a woman with blue hair is in my seat. With some trepidation, I approach and put the drinks on the table.

"Dougie," Sara says. "This is my mate, Gail."

She looks up at me and smiles.

"Gail felt a bit faint on the dancefloor," Sara adds. "So, we're just having a brief sit down if that's okay with you?"

"No problem."

I flop down in the last remaining chair, with Kenny to my right and Gail to my left. I've barely had chance to sip from my glass when Sara suddenly gets to her feet.

"Can I get you a glass of water, Gail?"

"Please."

Sara then grabs Kenny's hand.

"And you, Mr Seddon," she says, "can buy your wife a drink while we're at the bar."

Kenny stands, and before I can say anything, they're away. Left alone with Gail, I realise too late that I've been set up. Now, I can either sit here in the most awkward of silences or make small talk. I choose the lesser evil.

"Are you having a good evening?" I ask.

"I was," Gail replies with a long sigh.

"Right. Would you rather I leave you alone?"

Her eyebrows suddenly arch.

"Oh, my God," she gasps. "I didn't mean it's suddenly bad because I'm talking to you. I meant ... I think I've had one too many Mojitos."

"Ahh, right. Is that why you were feeling faint?"

"Probably. I'm not a big drinker, so it always goes to my head."

I glance across to the bar to see where Sara is, and more importantly, the promised glass of water. There's no sign of either.

"Would you like me to fetch that water? I don't know where Sara has got to."

"No, you're alright," she replies, stifling a burp. "I think I need some fresh air."

Slowly, Gail clambers to her feet, keeping one hand on the back of the chair to steady herself. Wherever she's heading for fresh air, I have grave doubts she'll make it unaided. Is that my problem, though?

"Would you, um, like me to come with you ... just to make sure you're okay?"

She ponders my offer for a few seconds.

"That's nice of you. Ta."

I stand up and offer her my arm. She releases her hand on the chair and grabs on to me. Not being judgemental, but Gail is no slip of a girl, and I do well to maintain my own balance.

Now I'm committed, I've no idea where we're heading for air. The thought of slowly edging our way through the main nightclub and down the stairs fills me with dread. Fortunately, Gail confirms there's an outside smoking area along the same corridor as the toilets.

Destination confirmed, we slowly make our way across the room, along the corridor, and out through the fire door. Having never smoked, I had no preconceived idea what a smoking area might look like. In this instance, it's a square of flat roof with a rusting guard rail along the edge, offering a view of a dark alleyway below.

A bloke leaning up against the guard rail turns to us, flicks his cigarette away, and departs with a nod in my direction. Now we're alone, I don't know what to do.

"Do you want to sit down for a minute, Gail?"

"Sit where?"

A quick glance confirms there's nowhere to sit, apart from the damp floor.

"To be honest, I hadn't thought that far ahead."

"Thanks, anyway," she chuckles. "I'm fine here."

She then leans up against the guard rail, closes her eyes and sucks in a lungful of the cold night air. My good deed complete, I wonder if my presence is still required.

"Would you like me to leave you alone?" I ask.

Gail opens her eyes and looks down towards the alleyway.

"It's up to you," she replies. "I feel a bit icky, but I'm not suicidal."

I glance over the guard rail.

"That's just as well. I don't think a ten-foot fall would do the trick."

"No," she snorts. "Probably not."

"If you don't mind me asking, why the suicide reference?"

Gail turns to face me.

"Sara didn't tell you?"

"Err, Sara didn't tell me anything about you."

"I split with my boyfriend a few weeks ago."

"Oh, I'm sorry to hear that."

"Yeah, everyone is. I thought I'd try drowning my sorrows, but it hasn't worked."

"Too much sorrow, never enough alcohol, eh?"

"Something like that," she replies wistfully.

I don't know this woman from Adam, so besides the usual platitudes, there's nothing I can say to ease Gail's suffering.

"Would you like me to call you a taxi?"

"Not really. It's still early, and if I go home now, I'll just sit and wallow in self-pity."

"Been there, done that."

"You've been dumped before, have you?"

"In a manner of speaking."

"You got any tips for getting over it?"

I wouldn't want to underestimate whatever Gail is going through, but it's highly unlikely the circumstances of her break-up are even remotely close to what I endured.

"I'm afraid not."

Gail pushes herself away from the guard rail and then, quickly realising her balance is still impaired, grabs hold of it again.

"There's only one sol-solution, then," she says, slightly slurring her words. "Buy me a drink?"

A few hours ago, I could only have dreamed about a woman asking me to buy her a drink. However, that dream didn't involve a semi-paralytic woman in the throes of a post break-up meltdown.

"Is that a good idea?"

"You got a better one, Dave?"

"Not really, and it's Dougie."

"What is?"

"My name."

"Is it?"

She screws her face up as if I've just asked her to solve a quadratic equation.

"Yes, my name is Dougie or Douglas. I don't mind which."

Gail once again leaves the security of the guard rail, resting her hand on my shoulder.

"Well, Dougie, do you fancy getting shitfaced with me?"

"Err, possibly, but wouldn't you rather go back to the party and get drunk with your friends?"

"No, 'cos I fancy getting drunk with someone who isn't a friend."

"Why's that?"

"Because I can say whatever I want and not have to worry about it. No sympathy, no judgement."

It's a fair point, and as if to enforce it she looks me straight in the eye. Hers are possibly the greenest eyes I've ever seen. I might even go as far as to call them enticing.

"Okay. I'm game."

"Nice one."

If there's any moral question to be asked about encouraging an already drunk woman to drink more, I decide not to ask it. As Kenny advised, sometimes you've just got to jump in feet first and to hell with the consequences.

We wander back to the bar, and I help Gail onto a stool. I'm not sure it's the best place for someone with compromised balance, but it's better than standing.

"What can I get you, Gail? A Mojito?"

"Christ, no," she replies, stifling another burp. "I'll have a glass of Merlot, please."

I order her wine and half a pint of lager for myself. While I wait, I scan the room for Kenny and Sara. They're seated at the same table and seemingly content in their own company. I don't think they're missing mine.

Drinks served, I throw a random question at Gail.

"How long have you known Sara?"

"Ten years or so. We both used to work with Lucy."

"Ah, right."

"It was Sara who introduced me to Tom."

"Sorry. Who's Tom?"

"My cheating bastard ex."

"Oh."

I can't think of anything meaningful to say in response, but it doesn't matter. Gail takes my silence as a cue to relay the highlights of her relationship with Tom and the fateful final days.

For fifteen long minutes, Gail vents. She only pauses to swig wine and seek the odd nod of affirmation. Yes, it's easy to miss the obvious signs of an affair. Yes, all couples have their difficulties. And yes, all men are cowardly wankers. There's a brief respite while she orders another large glass of Merlot, but then the venting continues.

Finally, Gail runs out of steam, ending with a slurred conclusion: she is very drunk indeed.

"Are you sure you don't want me to order you a taxi?" I ask.

"No, I wanna ... will you dance with me?"

"Is that a good idea?"

"Wassamatta?" she replies with wobbling indignation. "Don't you wanna dance with me?"

"Um, no, it's just that ..."

"Come on," she pleads. "I wanna dance."

Her voice is shrill enough to attract the attention of the barman. He looks across and rolls his eyes as I weigh up my options. Now would probably be a good time to go home.

Before I can make my excuses, Gail manages to clamber off the stool. She keeps one hand on the edge of the bar and holds the other in my direction.

"Dance with me, Dave. Sorry ... Darren."

Despite Gail's inability to remember my name, a battle ensues between common sense and ego. She is not an unattractive woman, and she wants to dance with me. Notwithstanding her level of intoxication, she's happy to be seen on a dancefloor with me, in full view of her friends. It's been a very long time since I've had such an opportunity and who's to say if or when I'll ever get another one.

I hop off my stool and take Gail's hand.

Somehow, we make it to the dancefloor. I probably should have warned Gail that I can't dance, but she'll find out soon enough.

"I love this tune," she yells, finally letting go of my hand. "It's a banger!"

Seemingly oblivious to anyone else on the dancefloor, Gail loses herself in the music. Her movements are wild and uncoordinated whilst mine are stiff and mechanical. We must look like a ridiculous couple, but I don't much care because my dance partner clearly doesn't.

The track comes to an end, and the DJ mixes in a more down-tempo tune. Gail stumbles towards me, and before I know it, our bodies are pressed tightly together. She then puts one hand around my waist and leans towards my left shoulder.

"You're alright, you know," she says, a little too loudly, considering her mouth is only inches from my ear.

"You too," I reply.

Her hand slips from my waist to the top of my buttock. I swallow hard.

"I feel ... I feel ..." Gail then says breathlessly, without finishing the sentence.

What does she feel? Is she attracted to me? What is it?

I lean closer.

"What is it? What do you feel?"

"I feel ..."

All of a sudden, her shoulders judder, and her body stiffens. This strange spasm coincides with the most troubling sensation like someone has just poured a jug of warm custard down my back. It's followed by the arrival of a sickly-sweet odour and one or two shrieks from those nearby.

My lager-addled brain finally puts the pieces together, and realisation dawns—Gail has just emptied the contents of her stomach straight down the back of my neck.

I can't move, but Gail wobbles back a few feet and then draws a hand across her mouth. The crowd have parted around us and are now standing open-mouthed, horrified. Gail looks just as horrified, right up until she turns and staggers towards the toilets. I'm left alone, standing in the middle of a dancefloor, the back of my shirt and cardigan sodden with warm sick.

The horror amongst the onlookers then turns to ridicule. Most are laughing, but a few have their mobile phones in hand, capturing my humiliation so they can relive it and share it later.

I drop my head and storm away, the sound of raucous laughter ringing in my ears.

Yes, this was a mistake. I should have known better.

Chapter 10

It's no surprise I'm alone. The sun has only just crept above the horizon, and there's a distinct chill in the air. It's also a Sunday—a day for long lie-ins and browsing the newspapers over a cooked breakfast.

Most people would think I'm insane, getting up whilst it's still dark and standing on top of a hillock with just birdsong and the whispers of a pre-dawn wind for company. Given the events of last night, perhaps I am insane. I'm undoubtedly stupid for thinking I might be able to go out and enjoy an uneventful evening or that some sane, rational woman might be interested in me.

I spent much of the long walk home kicking myself, metaphorically. Sobriety returned within the first mile and with it, a conclusion: never again. A tiny fragment of hope led to my disastrous evening, and if I'd listened to that little voice in my head, the one warning me not to indulge hope, I wouldn't be feeling so wretched this morning.

No, that will be the last time I allow hope to lead me astray. From now on, I'll stick to my lane. It's far better to be alone than risk making a fool of myself again. If some mystical force has been at work over the last week, it's proven beyond all doubt where my future lies. I'm not willing to risk upsetting that force again.

Douglas Neil: bachelor. That's how it has to be, and if I just accept it, there won't be any more Carols, any more Gails, or God-forbid, *her*.

I stare out across the lake, towards the smudge of muddy-yellow sunlight trying to break through the clouds. That smudge is mirrored on the lake's surface as a family of Little Grebe paddle around the edges of the reed bed. The sight is reward enough for the early morning, and it helps to temper my gloomy mood.

Time passes, although I've no idea how long because here it's an irrelevance. I could loiter around till dusk if I wanted to because I'm not expected anywhere, and it's unlikely anyone will care where I am. My parents play tennis on a Sunday morning and then typically indulge in a long, boozy lunch with friends at their favourite gastropub. Kathryn will be enjoying a family day with her husband and daughters: a trip to the zoo, or a drive to the beach, perhaps. They have their lives, and I'm happy for them. I have mine, and it's here.

As the sun continues to climb, so too does the temperature. It's close to eight o'clock, and I'm surprised no one else has joined me on the Mount. I don't mind because I'm not in the mood for company. Besides, a number of Cetti's Warblers are skulking in the nearby nettle bed, and I'd much rather listen to their chatter. They're a difficult bird to spot, but their almost constant song is distinctive enough that any twitcher worth their salt would recognise it.

With the tepid sun on my face and the warblers providing a calming melody, I close my eyes and breathe deeply. A sense of contentment rises, and I embrace it. Not everyone can find contentment in their life, not even those who are married or in long-term relationships. That's why people stray, isn't it? Maybe my contentment is better because it'll never leave me.

I'm still wallowing in the moment when the Cetti's Warblers abruptly fall silent. I open my eyes to a darker scene, prompted by a cloud passing in front of the sun. It would explain the sudden chill that rolls across my shoulders and down my spine. Then, I sense movement off to my right.

I turn my head, expecting to see a fellow twitcher approaching, but there's no one to be seen. So convinced my senses aren't playing tricks, I spin around one-eighty degrees.

"What the hell?"

There's not a soul around.

The warblers then pick up where they left off, and the cloud breaks past the sun. All is as it was, except for the inescapable and perhaps irrational feeling someone is watching me. I turn around again and scan the tracks and pathways crisscrossing the reserve, but the only life I spot is avian.

I puff a long sigh. This is what happens when I don't get enough sleep, and as I barely scraped four hours last night, it's no surprise my brain isn't firing on all cylinders. Skipping breakfast probably didn't help.

I'm far from feeling alright.

I don't want to leave, but I can't ignore what my body is telling me. If I stay here much longer, I'll probably start hallucinating and report a flock of Emus wading in the shallows. As if I haven't suffered enough humiliation for one weekend.

Reluctantly, I take one last look out to the lake and shuffle carefully back down the bank. No matter how hard I try to ignore it, the sense of being watched follows me all the way back to the car park.

I'm keen to get back into my car when a white Volvo passes through the gates and pulls up beside me.

"There you are," Kenny remarks, clambering out of his Swedish tank. "Why haven't you answered my text messages?"

"Sorry. I haven't switched my phone on this morning."

"And last night? I tried calling four times."

"I think my battery died."

Kenny steps towards me, blocking the path to my car door.

"Are you okay, pal?"

"Okay?"

"We saw what happened with Gail. I don't know what to say."

"There's nothing to say," I reply with a half-shrug. "Crap happens ... well, to me, it does."

"Sara was mortified."

"Did she speak to Gail?"

"Aye, eventually. Sara found her crying in the loo, and it seems the poor lassie has some problems she's not coping with."

"Clearly."

"I'm sorry. We didn't realise."

"Forget it," I sigh. "It wasn't anyone's fault."

"Maybe not, but you know what Sara is like? She thought you two would be good together."

"We were ... until she vomited into my collar. I'll never get the smell of Mojito out of that cardigan, you know."

Kenny tries hard not to smile.

"Was Gail okay in the end?" I ask.

"Kind of. She told Sara she was going to go stay with her mum for a few months, to sort her head out."

"Let me guess where her mum lives—Peru?"

"Not quite. Spain."

"That figures, not that she'd want to see me again, anyway."

"It's not you, mate. She's ..."

"Stop," I groan, holding my hands up. "I don't want to hear another word about last night or Gail. Okay?"

"Fair enough."

"And, please, can you tell Sara that I appreciate her efforts, but I'm no longer in the market for a girlfriend."

"Come on, you can't give up just because of one bad experience."

"I'd agree, Kenny, if it were just one bad experience, but my love life has been a succession of bad experiences. I've come to realise that some people just aren't meant to be in a relationship, and up until last night, I was ninety-nine per cent sure I was one of them. This morning, I'm one-hundred per cent certain."

Kenny knows me well enough not to push the point. He puts his hand on my shoulder and nods.

"You're my friend, and that much will never change."

We share a too-close-to-awkward smile until Kenny removes his hand.

"So, are you coming or going?" he asks breezily.

"Going. I've been here since daybreak."

"Much out there?"

"There's … listen, do you mind if I shoot off? I'm not feeling too clever, and I desperately need to eat."

"Sure. Will you be back later?"

"Hopefully."

"I'll be here till lunchtime if you're feeling any better by then."

I nod my acknowledgement and fall into the driver's seat of my car. Kenny stands by the boot of his tank and sees me off with a single wave.

At home, I half-heartedly eat a couple of slices of toast, washed down with a strong cup of tea. I fancy a nap, but I know I'll pay for it tonight if I sleep now. Instead, I sit in front of the television and flick through the channels, finally stopping on a documentary about the Great War. I struggle to maintain interest, right up until the narrator mentions a term I've never heard before: *the war to end all wars.*

He goes on to explain the meaning behind the term. Coined by the author HG Wells, it implied a hope that the sheer destructiveness of the Great War would persuade mankind to abandon warfare as a means of solving conflict.

Sadly for mankind, Wells' hopes were dashed only twenty-one years later when the Second World War kicked off. The Great War was not the war to end all wars.

I wonder, though, if my only relationship was the relationship to end all relationships? Deep down, was it so destructive that I've subconsciously sabotaged every subsequent attempt to start another one? I don't think so, but I am willing to accept the psychological damage has left its mark. Why can I only remember the bad, though? It wasn't all bad, was it?

16th February 2001

It's nearly one in the morning, but I'm too wired for sleep. I'm probably too drunk to write, but I don't want to forget what an amazing evening I've just had ... the best evening of my life!

To think, it nearly never happened.

I don't even recall who first mentioned drinks after work—maybe it was Steve—but I wasn't really in the mood. Then, ten minutes before the end of the day, Denise wandered past my desk and mentioned that a few of the team were meeting up at The Plough after work. I don't know why she wanted me to come along, but maybe it's because we've got chatty on lunch breaks and being she's still relatively new, she just feels more comfortable with my familiar face at the pub.

I never got around to asking her.

There were nine of us there in the end. Steve got the first round because he's now certain he'll get the promotion he's been chasing for months. I can't remember who bought the next round, but two drinks were enough for those who'd driven to work, and I think five of them left after an hour.

Steve then made his excuses, then Paul and Claire left together. I reckon they're secretly shagging, but Claire has a boyfriend so they're trying to keep it quiet.

That left just Denise and me. We talked shit for ten minutes until she finished her drink, and when she got up I thought she was leaving too.

But she didn't leave.

Even though there were only two of us there, Denise offered to buy me a drink. We finished another round and then I offered to buy her one, but I was positive she'd say she had to go. No, she said she was having a really good time and would love another drink.

We stayed until closing time, and we laughed and played pool, and even sang along together to a few tunes on the jukebox, including that new single they're playing on the radio all the time at the moment: Teenage Dirtbag, by a band called Wheatus, I think. If the evening had ended there, I couldn't have been any happier, but then Denise asked me to walk her to the taxi rank.

We stopped on the way at Toni's for a bag of chips—her idea, not mine—and then ate them in the bus shelter opposite the Co-Op. It was bloody freezing, but Denise squeezed right up to me to keep warm. I can still smell her sweet perfume like the scent is trapped in my head. I remember thinking I wish I had some so I could squirt a bit on this page, so that I'd never forget it.

We finished our chips, and that was that. I walked her to the taxi rank.

Just before she got into her cab, she told me what a great evening she'd had, and that we should do it again. I thought she was just being polite, or too pissed to know what she was saying. I said yes, obviously, and she stepped right up to me.

I thought I might get a peck on the cheek, but no ... SHE KISSED ME!!! A proper kiss, my first proper kiss, and even if Denise wakes up tomorrow and says it was a mistake, I don't care. It was AMAZING!!!

That's not true. Now I've thought about it, I do care. It's stupid to think we could be anything more than colleagues but, up until tonight, I thought it was stupid that a stunner like Denise would even want to be seen in public with someone like me—I might have told her that. I can't remember.

I walked home on a cloud, and even now, an hour later, I can't stop smiling. If there is a God, I hope he's listened to my prayers because I've never wanted anything in my life so badly as Denise. I would give literally anything to go out with her. ANYTHING!

I'm getting tired so I'll finish for now. Stupidly, I didn't ask Denise for her number so I won't see her now till Monday. Maybe tomorrow I'll wake up and realise this was all a dream, but for now I'm going to assume I've just had the best night of my life.

I never thought I'd ever write this, but Monday morning can't come soon enough.

Chapter 11

A fresh week, or to put it another way, the first week of acceptance. I had hoped the change in perspective might bring a sense of relief, but it's yet to materialise. I've carried hope for so long it's bound to take some getting used to.

"This is it now, Dougie," I mumble, as I lace up my boots. "You're going to be single for the rest of your life. Accept it, live with it, embrace it."

I can just about accept it now, but living with it will take time, and embracing it even longer. I gave the matter a lot of thought last night and concluded my situation is akin to that of a professional footballer who's never fulfilled their ambitions. At some point, they must accept their career is over, and they'll never experience the fame, fortune or glories enjoyed by some in the game. They could look back with regret and resentment, but surely it's better to look back and say at least you played football professionally, even if you've little to show for it?

Understanding that mentality is one thing, but living with it is quite another. This is going to be a process.

My thoughts are interrupted by the trilling of a mobile phone. Plucking it from my pocket, I don't recognise the number but answer anyway.

"Hello," I huff.

"Is that you, Dougie?" the female voice responds.

"Leanne?"

"Yeah."

My heart beats a little faster. There must be a compelling reason why Ady's girlfriend is calling me at this hour, and I can't think of a benign one.

"What's the matter?" I splutter. "Is everything okay?"

"Have you heard from Ady?" she asks.

"No, but seeing as you're calling me at this time of the morning, I'm guessing you don't know where he is?"

"He didn't come home last night. I last saw him just after seven yesterday evening—he said he was nipping to a mate's house to play poker for an hour or two."

"I don't know what to say, Leanne, but I'd wager he had one beer too many and fell asleep on someone's sofa."

"Do you think?"

I glance up at the clock.

"Probably, yes," I sigh. "But to be frank, I'm more concerned with getting to work on time."

"I'm worried, Dougie. He's been acting odd of late, and every time I ask him what's wrong—"

"Leanne," I interject, a little too forcibly. "I'm sure he'll turn up at work later, and I'll get him to call you. I've got to go. Bye."

I end the call and scrabble around for my car keys. Bloody Ady.

Once I'm on the road my annoyance eases a touch, but it doesn't dissipate entirely. Yes, I'm annoyed at Ady because if Leanne hadn't called, I'd almost certainly be late myself, but I'm also miffed about a couple dragging me into their relationship problems. I don't get to have a relationship myself, so why should I help those more fortunate than me? They get to enjoy all the smooth, so bollocks to it—they can deal with the rough, too.

Almost a minute earlier than usual, I pull into the depot and park up. I'm still annoyed and decide I won't be covering for Ady.

I head inside for the morning meeting and wait for Jonny to realise that Ady isn't there. Five minutes later, our agitated manager marks Ady as absent and informs me I'll have to go out solo today. With my mood still some way from sunny, that suits me just fine. Everyone is entitled to the odd day of self-pity, I reckon.

It's no great surprise to find that Keira is equally unsunny this morning and she barely says more than a few words as I sign out a van. Task complete, I hit the road.

When I first started this job, my then boss paired me with a fifty-something bloke called Mike. He was a real council stalwart, joining our department straight from school. I liked Mike, but he was a lazy bugger who knew how to play the system.

Mike imparted some advice early on and stressed the rules about working solo. Apparently, a month after he started working for the council, Mike was sent out on his own after his workmate called in sick. Keen to make a good impression, he finished his bin round in less time than it usually took two men. One man on his own doesn't tend to waste time chatting about the weather or generally dicking around. When Mike returned to the depot early, he got hammered when his workmates found out. His efficiency could have given management an excuse to halve the workforce without reducing productivity.

To this day, that unwritten rule remains in force. If you go out on your own, you're expected to take at least one hour more to complete your bin round than it would with two men. That hour is usually wasted away in a cafe or spent hiding in a quiet layby somewhere.

I won't be breaking the rule any time soon. I'll complete my bin round and enjoy a longer than usual lunch break at The Vale Cafe. After lunch, I'm on litter picking duty because the one job we can't do on our own is load fly-tipped waste. However, I don't mind litter picking because there's a quiet lane on our patch which skirts the furthest boundary of Tinkerton

Meadow. If I park up there, I can while away the rest of my working day by clearing litter from the verges and hedgerows whilst birdwatching at the same time.

Come to think of it, perhaps working on our own wouldn't be such a bad thing, unless you're one of the poor sods made redundant.

With my day planned, I feel a bit better. It also helps when the early morning fog departs, and a hazy sun breaks through.

Without Ady's inane chatter to distract me, I manage to empty every bin on the round by late morning. I can't say I even hurried, but I have worked up an appetite. I hop back into the van and make my way towards The Vale. Only then do I remember that Colin is due to receive his new hip today, and Heather will be running the cafe on her own. That prospect tempers my mood somewhat. For a moment, I consider having lunch elsewhere.

The lure of a full English proves too enticing.

I arrive just before noon, and I'm pleased to find the car park empty. Dealing with the standoffish Heather will be effort enough, but it'll be a nightmare if she's stressed by too many customers at once.

With a degree of trepidation, I venture inside.

Besides Ron—a curmudgeonly pensioner who regularly nurses a single cup of tea for an hour—the place is deserted. I approach the un-staffed counter.

"Hello?"

Through the serving hatch comes the sound of pans clattering. It's followed by the foreboding figure of Heather, her expression unreadable but not exactly welcoming.

"Morning, Heather," I chirp. "Any news on your dad yet?"

"No," she mumbles, avoiding eye contact. "He's not due in surgery till later this afternoon."

"Well, give him my regards when you see him."

She nods.

"Can I get a full English and a mug of tea, please?"

"Yes ... um, sit down."

I overlook Heather's curtness and respond with a smile. She doesn't notice because she's writing my order on a notepad, ever so slowly.

"Is everything okay?" I ask.

"Yes."

"Did Colin mention that I'm happy to help if you're desperate?"

"He did."

Still no eye contact.

"Okay, great. I'll, err, grab a table."

Heather nods and then hustles over to the other end of the counter, and a hot water urn. I sit down at the nearest table.

If someone asked me to describe Heather, I think I'd struggle because she has no discernible features. She's not particularly tall or short, fat or thin. Everything about her is either average or nondescript, from her plain choice of clothes to her mid-brown hair, which is permanently tied into a ponytail. Ady once joked that Heather is a Rich Tea biscuit in human form. I frowned at his unkind remark, but I must admit it is accurate.

My tea arrives.

"I'll fix your order now," Heather says, still staring at the mug. "It'll be ten minutes."

"No problem. Thank you."

The service is a far cry from when Colin is at the counter, but at least Heather appears to be making an effort. I guess some people are better at dealing with customers than others. Sadly for Heather, she hasn't inherited her dad's affable manner.

As promised, my lunch arrives within ten minutes. There's no small talk to accompany it, but I don't mind as I'm keen to tuck in. As soon as I've unwrapped the cutlery from a napkin, I delve in.

With time on my side, I'm able to savour every mouthful. Heather isn't blessed with a sparkling personality, but by God, she knows how to cook a breakfast. The bacon is crisp, the sausage plump, and the egg perfectly runny.

Once my plate is empty, I sit back in my chair and wallow in a contented glow for a few minutes. Heather then returns and picks up the plate.

"That was probably the best full English I've ever had," I remark.

She pauses.

"Was it?"

"Err, yes."

"Oh."

"But, that's why we come here—the food is always top-notch."

"Thank you," she mumbles.

"You're welcome."

Heather then hurries back to the kitchen. She didn't say much, but that's as close to a conversation as we've ever had. She even managed a pleasantry, which is most unlike her.

With my stomach full, I snatch a discarded newspaper from an adjacent table and flick through it while I finish my tea. All too soon, it's time to get back to work.

I approach the counter and spot Heather on the other side of the serving hatch. She bustles out to the till and rings in my order.

"£6.00, please."

I hand over a ten-pound note, and Heather scrapes four coins from the till.

"Your change," she says, slapping the coins on the counter.

I take two and leave two as a tip.

"Thanks, Heather. I'll see you again soon."

She doesn't reply, and her eyes remain fixed on the pound coins. No thank you is forthcoming, so I leave.

Back in the van, I check my phone just in case Ady has surfaced. There are no missed calls and no messages. Nonplussed, I drop it into the door pocket, glance at the dashboard clock, and start the engine. It's only a five-minute drive to Garwood Lane, which means I have just under three hours of litter picking ahead of me.

I set off.

My destination sits on the very edge of the patch we're responsible for. Garwood Lane itself is a single-track road, roughly half a mile long, bordered by a grass verge on one side and wild hedgerow on the other. It's often used as a cut-through if traffic is bad on the main route out of Ashbridge. And, because there are no houses, no cameras, and it's typically quiet, it's an ideal place for any inconsiderate arsehole to lob rubbish from their vehicle. Sadly, they do it so often that litter picking in Garwood Lane is a regular feature in our work schedule.

I turn into the lane and proceed slowly forward until I reach one of two short laybys. The last time we left this spot, there wasn't a single piece of rubbish anywhere. Not so today.

Once I've donned a pair of protective gloves, I lock the van and pull a small wheelie bin off the back. We find it's so much easier to haul a plastic bin along the road than using plastic bags, which tend to snag and split on the thorny bushes.

I plan to move down the left side of the lane first and then return on the other side. That means I get to spend the first half of the afternoon on the interesting side of the lane. Beyond the hedgerow, there's a steep bank leading down to a copse. That copse stretches along the lane, and my elevated position affords a view straight into the branches of the trees. It's ideal for spotting, but there isn't the same diversity of birds as around the lake in Tinkerton Meadow. Still, it's a damn sight more interesting than staring at a graffiti-splattered brick wall.

I set to work.

I'm constantly surprised by what people throw from their vehicles. There's always a ton of fast food packaging and drinks cans, but occasionally we'll find something that beggars belief. Ady once found some Levi jeans entwined with a heavily soiled pair of underpants. We spent a good half-hour speculating why someone would pull over, remove the bottom half of their clothing, and then hide the shit-smeared garments in a hedgerow. Presumably, the culprit also had to drive home half-naked.

The mind boggles.

There's nothing out of the ordinary in the first hundred yards of verge, but there's an unusual amount of rubbish. Why people can't take their crap home with them is beyond me. Then, I stumble upon something buried deep in the hedgerow.

"No way."

It really falls under the banner of fly-tipping rather than littering, but some twat saw fit to dispose of an old car battery by throwing it into the hedge. Why not take the bloody thing to a recycling centre? How can it be any more troublesome than driving out here?

The battery is far enough into the hedge I could just leave it, and no one would be any the wiser, but the problem with car batteries is they contain lead and a not-insignificant amount of sulphuric acid. If those elements leak out, they pose a real threat to wildlife, not to mention the hedgerow itself.

I can't leave it there.

Resigned to the task, I look for a spot where the foliage is sparse enough for me to clamber through to the other side. I notice a potential spot six feet to my right. On closer inspection, there's a gap just large enough I should be able to force my way through the thick hedgerow without damaging it, or me.

I put my hood up to protect my head against the thorny branches and push my right leg into the gap, carefully shimmying the rest of my body into the hedge.

Then, ducking below a thick branch, I thrust my left leg forward until my boot touches solid ground. All that remains is to push past the thinner branches, and I'm out. I shift my weight forward and stand up straight, simultaneously swinging my right leg forward.

Without warning, the supposed solid ground under my left boot gives way.

"SHIIIT!"

Suddenly, the sky is where the ground should be, and gravity has gone the same way as Ady—absent without notice. With my hands grabbing at nothing but thin air, I can't arrest my forward motion. Before I know it, I'm tumbling down the steep bank on the other side of the hedge.

In the middle of a forward roll, I spot a worrying sight directly in my path. The silver birch is a good age, with a thick trunk. It won't give way if I crash into it.

Helpless, I close my eyes and brace for impact, praying I make contact with a shoulder or buttock rather than my head.

Chapter 12

The pain is so acute I can't even draw breath to scream.

During my final somersault, I ended up falling forwards with the silver birch trunk directly ahead and only a few feet away. A collision seemed inevitable, and all I could do to avoid hitting the trunk headfirst was to twist my upper body in the split-second available.

I achieved my aim, but my right shoulder paid the price. It struck the trunk hard, and if the pain is any barometer of injury, something is definitely broken. To make matters worse, I must have turned my ankle when the ground gave way, and the constant throbbing does not bode well.

Lying motionless, I focus on my breathing. A minute or so passes, and the pain eases a fraction, straying just within the cusp of tolerance. It's a state I'm willing to endure for now.

The only part of my body I dare move is my eyeballs. I assess my surroundings. I'm on my back, looking up at the branches of the same silver birch that put me here. All I can smell is damp soil and decaying vegetation. I love being close to nature, but this is too much.

I pull a few shallow breaths and attempt to formulate a plan. It's a simple one—I need help.

Gingerly, I move my left hand towards my coat pocket, searching for a mobile phone. It does not go well. For reasons beyond my understanding, just moving my hand is enough to enrage the pain in my right shoulder.

I suck air through gritted teeth.

The searing pain, unwelcome as it is, brings clarity of thought. I can search every one of my six pockets, and I won't find a mobile phone because I dropped it in another pocket an hour ago—the door pocket in the van. That realisation attracts more thoughts and a fair dose of panic. What if I can't get back up to the road and summon help? How long will it be before anyone notices I'm missing? I could be stuck here for days, and what if my injuries are more severe than a broken bone or two? I could be dead long before anyone discovers me.

The fear induces a welcome shot of adrenalin. No matter how unbearable the pain, I must get back up the bank and scramble to the lane. If I can make it that far, I shouldn't have to wait too long for a passing vehicle and rescue.

I need to move before the pain-easing effects of the adrenaline subside.

"Come on, Dougie," I pant. "You've got this."

Summoning every ounce of resolve, I roll onto my left side. It hurts so much I could cry, but there's no alternative—face the pain or risk a fate I'd rather not contemplate.

From my side, I manage to get onto my knees through a series of slow, eye-watering movements. If I can stand and shuffle the short distance to the silver birch, I can take a moment to regroup and regain my resolve. That's my next goal.

I've suffered some atrocious hangover headaches in my time, but they pale into insignificance compared to the agony of simply standing up. Once upright, I learn how little weight my ankle can bear—next to nothing. My only hope is to hop towards the trunk,

I steel myself and take the first hop.

"Fuuck!"

Considering my situation, I had no reason to recall a buried memory about kids playing hopscotch in the school playground. If I had, I might have remembered those kids hopping on one leg and using their arms to maintain balance. I might also have considered how instinctive that action is.

Unable to move my right arm at all, I've no hope of maintaining balance. That is why I am now face down on the floor, staring at the base of a silver birch tree, and in abject agony.

This isn't good.

Utilising the last remnants of adrenalin, I manage to twist myself around and sit with my back up against the tree trunk. That final effort takes everything I have, both physically and mentally. I need to face facts: even without injuries, it'd be tricky climbing up the steep bank. Doing it on one leg without using my disabled right arm for balance is near-on impossible.

I'm screwed.

What can I do? What does anyone do when they're in desperate need of rescue?

"Help!"

Even shouting hurts. I wait for a response, but all I can hear is the wind rustling through the leaves above me and the chirping of chaffinches from the hedgerow. So close, but a distance I have no hope of covering.

I yell a few more times, but the pain is compounded every time I suck in air. It feels like being filleted from my shoulder to my breast bone.

My chances of being found are now down to Jonny and Keira. At some point, they'll realise there's a van missing, and they'll wonder where I am. A call will be made, but it will go unanswered. Surely, they'll then inform the police or at least come and search for their missing van. When they find it abandoned, they'll look up the lane and see the blue wheelie bin near the verge. It won't take much imagination to work out where I am from there.

The thought of just sitting here waiting for rescue fills me with dread, but what choice do I have? God-willing, it'll only be a few hours

The only consolation is that doing nothing is far less painful.

Resigned to my fate, I try to relax and cast the worst-case scenarios from my mind. I need to think happy thoughts.

I close my eyes and picture the view from the Mount. It's a beautiful spring morning, just after daybreak, and the meadow and lake are teeming with bird activity. I can feel the warmth of the sun on my skin as I watch the silvery ripples lapping at the shoreline.

My breathing slows, and peace descends. Much better. I can live with this till help arrives.

I slip towards a state somewhere between sleep and semi-consciousness.

Time passes, although I've no idea how long. The world continues to slip in and out of focus as I drift between reality and the land of nod.

Crack.

Was that sound in my head, or did I just hear someone step on a twig? My eyes slowly peel open, squinting in the half-light of the glade.

"Hello?" I croak. "Is someone there?"

As I listen intently for a response, I catch movement in the corner of my eye. I carefully turn my head just in time to see a figure emerging from beyond an oak tree, some forty feet away.

"Can you help me?" I call out.

If the roles were reversed and I stumbled upon some poor sod lying against a tree, begging for help, I'd move with a bit more urgency than this individual.

Forty feet becomes twenty, and I'm able to ascertain further details about my rescuer. It's a woman dressed in what looks like a monk's habit. My assumption about gender is based solely upon the mane of straw-coloured hair flowing from beneath her hood. With their head bowed forward, I can't see a face.

She, or he, comes to a stop no more than six feet away. The fact they haven't verbally responded to my cry for help, or made eye contact, summons a sense of unease.

"Do you have a phone?" I ask, my voice surprisingly high-pitched.

The figure takes another two steps forward before lifting their head. It is a woman, but there's something off about her expression. There's no outward sign of concern like you'd expect in someone who'd found a stranger injured in the woods. By contrast, her lips are too red to be natural, and her glacier-blue eyes are more Siamese cat than human.

I have no idea if she's willing to help or if she's here to kill me—there's nothing in her face to indicate what's going through her mind.

The panic returns.

I don't understand the woman's lack of urgency or concern.

"I ... I'm Douglas," I splutter.

Her lips curl at the edges. It's not quite a smile but enough to soften the starkness of her face.

"I know," she replies, taking another step forward. "Are you in pain, Douglas?"

My need to answer her second question trumps my need to ask how she knows my name.

"Yes," I whimper. "A lot."

In one fluid movement, the woman steps over and kneels by my side.

"Where does it hurt?" she asks, tilting her head a fraction.

"My shoulder ... and my ankle."

"I understand."

Her voice is so soothing I'm slightly less concerned the stranger has shown no sign of summoning help.

"Can I ask your—"

A bolt of pain streaks across my shoulder, cutting off my question and invoking a gasp.

"Shush now," the woman says gently. "Don't talk."

I want to ask her why, but my attention is drawn to her hand as it slips into a pouch-like pocket at the front of her habit. She withdraws a small glass bottle, full to the brim with a brownish liquid.

"You must take this," she says, removing a cork stopper from the neck.

"What is it?"

"It will make you feel better. I promise."

She moves the bottle towards my mouth, but I turn my head like a sulky toddler unwilling to take their medicine.

"Douglas," the woman says calmly. "You need this. You really do."

"For God's sake," I snap. "I've broken something. I don't need medicine ... I need a doctor."

If her blank stare is anything to go by, the woman is unmoved by my outburst.

"You're in pain, Douglas. I know that."

"Then please, call an ambulance."

"You misunderstand," she replies. "Your pain lies much deeper than a broken bone. No doctor can fix you."

"And your medicine will?" I scoff.

"It's not a medicine. Let's just call it a herbal remedy."

"With respect, you're crazy."

"That's disappointing to hear," she responds, her eyes wide and bright. "I thought you had faith in Mother Nature."

"Eh?"

"You appreciate the beauty of the natural world, do you not?"

"Of course."

She raises the bottle until it's directly in my line of sight.

"Then have faith in nature's remedy. I promise you won't regret it."

I shake my head as she moves the bottle closer to my lips.

"You only need a mouthful, Douglas," she says. "That is all it will take for your pain to go away."

This woman is clearly nuts, but I can't afford to offend her.

"Listen, I'll try your potion on one condition: if I'm still in pain five minutes after I've taken it, swear you'll call an ambulance."

If a face can smile without the lips curling upwards, the woman achieves the feat.

"I accept that condition."

She moves the bottle towards my mouth, close enough I can smell the liquid within. The scent is organic, almost floral. Is it likely to do me any harm?

"Are you sure this is safe to drink?" I ask.

The woman pauses and looks me straight in the eye.

"It will give you what you need, Douglas."

I'm still trying to decipher her response when the lip of the bottle touches mine.

"Now, drink."

I don't know who's crazier: me, or this random homoeopath. Still, I open my mouth, and she gently tips the bottle forward.

To my surprise, the liquid has barely any taste, and it's warmer than I imagined. It's like sipping an exceptionally weak cup of lukewarm tea. I swallow it down, and the woman returns the cork bung.

"There," she says. "That was not so bad, was it?"

"I guess not."

She returns the bottle to her pocket.

"You will soon feel sleepy. Do not fight it."

"What? Why would I feel sleepy?"

"Don't worry. Just allow yourself to drift away, and when you awake, you will feel like a new man."

This was not the deal I had in mind.

"You said you'd call for help."

"If you were still in pain. You will not be."

She stands up. The sense of panic returns with a vengeance.

"Are you going?"

"I must. Goodbye, Douglas."

"Please, you can't just leave me here."

The woman gently places her hand on the top of my head. Immediately, I'm engulfed by a calm so deep and so serene, it's like lying back in a hot bath on a winter's evening. My eyelids flutter and then close.

I slip away.

Chapter 13

I awake with a start—confusion reigns.

Where am I?

Piece by piece, the memories fall into place: the abandoned car battery, the hedgerow, the tumble down the bank, and ... was the peculiar woman part of a dream or did that actually happen?

Whilst I'm trying to separate reality from make-believe, a fly buzzes past and lands on my forehead. Without thinking, I brush it away.

Wait.

"What the ..."

I slowly roll my right shoulder, fully expecting a jolt of pain. Nothing. How can that be? I move it the other way, with a bit more vigour. Everything functions as it should. Did I pop my shoulder out of its socket, and it's now worked its way back in? It's the only explanation I can think of.

Unfortunately, the damaged shoulder wasn't my only injury.

I wriggle my toes, then turn my feet left and right. Again, there's no pain. Relief melds with confusion. The only test still to perform is getting up off my arse and getting out of here.

Half-expecting a relapse, I carefully stand up. I then bounce on the balls of my feet to test the ankle that couldn't bear my weight the last time I tried. There's no evidence of the injury whatsoever, no tinge or latent stiffness.

What the fuck was in that woman's herbal remedy?

It's not a question I can answer, and for now, I'm more concerned about getting back to the van. I've no idea how many hours have passed since I tumbled down the bank, but now I don't want anyone finding out about it—I'll never live it down.

Still cautious, I proceed towards the lower part of the bank. With every part of my body functioning at least as well as it did this morning, I clamber to the top. I then locate the gap in the hedgerow and burst through it like a marathon runner breaking through the finish-line tape.

I made it. I'm safe.

Then I remember the bloody car battery. I'd rather not leave it where it is, but I'm not willing to risk another tumble. I'll come back tomorrow with Ady, and he can retrieve it—penance for skiving off today.

I don't wear a watch at work, so the only way of knowing the time is to return to the van. With the wheelie bin in tow, I hurry back along the lane and unlock the cab.

A quick check of my phone confirms two hours have elapsed since I parked up. It's a relief because it's almost time to call it quits for the day. My mind is ablaze with questions and one or two concerns, so I'd rather be at home on the sofa where I can process this afternoon's events.

I put on my seat belt and start the engine.

After a quick visit to the recycling centre where I dump my modest load, I return to the depot. Four vans are already back, so my timing won't raise any suspicions. There's no way I'm willing to disclose any part of what happened to me this afternoon.

After noting the van's mileage, I ensure all the doors are locked and make my way to Keira's office. As I arrive, one of my colleagues, Big Fal, is just leaving.

"Alright, Dougie," he booms.

"Not bad. You?"

"Mustn't grumble."

Big Fal lumbers away, and I'm left alone with Keira. She continues staring at her computer screen, seemingly oblivious to my presence.

I place the van key on her desk. Keira glances up and her mask of indifference suddenly slips away. Strangely, she's staring at me like I'm Father Christmas and she's a six-year-old child.

"Sorry, Dougie," she beams. "I didn't realise it was you."

"Err, no problem."

"You had a good day?"

Keira never engages in small talk. Is she drunk?

"It was … uneventful, thanks."

She plucks the van key off the desk, but rather than get on with the check-in procedure, she sits back in her chair and continues to stare up at me.

"Everything okay?" I ask.

"Yep, everything's fine," she replies, twirling a length of hair around her finger.

I'm not convinced. She doesn't sound drunk, but this is not the punctilious version of Keira we're all used to.

"I need to get going," I remark. "Can you finish signing the van in, please?"

Her mouth bobs open like she's just remembered an urgent appointment.

"I'm so sorry, Dougie," she replies, clearly flustered. "What must you think of me?"

I don't think anything I'd willingly share with Keira. I've already suffered too much odd this afternoon, and her behaviour isn't helping.

"It's fine."

She quickly completes the check-in procedure, and I sign the form to confirm I've done what I need to do. At this point, Keira usually ends our interaction with a curt goodbye. Not today.

"Any plans for the evening?" she asks.

I'm about to reply when Big Fal returns. Keira's change in demeanour is as instant as it is obvious.

"What is it?" she snaps, glaring up at Big Fal.

"Err, I left my phone in the van. Can I borrow the key for a minute, please?"

Keira spins around in her seat, snatches a key from the cabinet, and tosses it at Big Fal.

"I want that back in under five minutes. Clear?"

"Yes, Keira," the big man mumbles before hurrying away.

The moment he's gone, Keira adopts her strange demeanour again, gazing up at me with an almost dreamy smile.

"Where were we?" she asks.

"I was just about to go home," I reply, edging towards the door. "Bye, Keira."

I've never been so glad to finish work for the day. Even the tedious act of driving home is a welcome relief from the weirdest of workdays.

Once I've showered and changed, I decide against a visit to Tinkerton Meadow. I've had enough fresh air today, and I want to work through what happened with the strange woman earlier.

I turn the television on as background noise and make myself comfortable on the sofa. There, I switch between moving my shoulder and my foot, assessing what I already know—there's no indication either were injured only hours ago. There's no way injuries so painful can heal in just a few hours. No way at all. What's more, a thorough check before my shower confirmed a total absence of bruising across my back and shoulders. Doing a manual job, I'm used to collecting bruises for the odd innocuous bang or bump, so why aren't there any bruises after I smacked into a tree trunk?

It appears I have defied medical science simply by taking one mouthful of an unknown herbal tonic.

Or have I?

I vividly remember tumbling down the bank, and I'll never forget the pain of hitting the tree for as long as I live. What about the rest of it, though? Did I knock myself out and merely dream about a mysterious woman and her potion?

No, I didn't. She was as real as the pain I endured. So, who is she?

It doesn't take long to determine there's no way of answering that question. Stupidly, I didn't even have the wherewithal to ask her name, let alone why she was wandering around a glade in the middle of the day, dressed like a Benedictine monk. Something about her seemed familiar, though.

Could it be a coincidence that Kenny and I saw a figure in a cloak on the Mount on Friday? Was it the same woman? Unable to answer either question, I turn my thoughts to the herbal remedy. I am living, breathing proof that the woman's potion is close to a miracle cure. That doesn't correspond with my previous experience of herbal medicines.

My mum was into homoeopathy for a brief spell. Whenever I complained of any ailment, she'd insist I try one of her herbal concoctions rather than any over-the-counter medicine. I took feverfew for a headache and ended up with a migraine. I tried St. John's wort to help sleep and subsequently suffered horrific nightmares. And, I took Gentian root to help with trapped wind. Less said about its side-effects, the better.

Even if I were a staunch advocate for herbal medicine, I'd struggle to believe that a single mouthful of muddy-brown liquid is capable of fixing broken bones and damaged ligaments in less time than it takes to see a doctor in A&E.

What the hell did I take?

With answers still elusive, I grab the TV remote and flick through the channels. Maybe, rather than stressing about questions I can't answer, I should just be grateful I'm not still lying in the glade in agony.

My phone rings: Ady.

"Oh, there you are. Nice day off?"

"I'm sorry, mate. I had a nightmare evening yesterday and ... let's just say I'm in as much trouble at home as I am at work."

"I gathered. Did Leanne tell you she called me?"

"What?"

Ady sounds surprised.

"She called me this morning, asking if I'd seen you."

"Right. I'll have a word with her. In the meantime, I need to ask a favour."

"If you're hoping I'll cover your arse while you skive off again, forget it."

"Nah, it's not that. I need to borrow some money ... just twenty quid."

"Fine," I sigh. "We'll stop at the cash machine on the way in tomorrow."

"I really need it now. The electricity is about to go off unless I put some money on the key."

"Hasn't Leanne got any money?"

"She asked me to do it, and I'm a bit skint at the moment."

"So, you'd rather ask me than risk your girlfriend's wrath?"

"That's about the strength of it."

I'm comfortable on the sofa, and I really don't fancy a walk to the cash machine, but a friend in need is ... well, a pain in the arse.

"Okay," I sigh. "Give me half an hour."

"You're a lifesaver."

"And just like a lifesaver, I hope you don't expect me to come to your rescue every five minutes."

"Yeah, I know."

I hang up.

Five minutes later, I'm wandering the dark streets towards the petrol station a few streets away, and the nearest cash machine. My right ankle is performing just as well as my left, as if the injury never happened, but that's not the only peculiarity. It's cold enough I'll likely wake up to a frost tomorrow morning, and yet my skin feels warm to the touch. The only explanation is that I'm coming down with something, but I don't have any other symptoms: no aching limbs, no runny nose, no sore throat.

I put it out of my mind. Since turning forty, I've come to accept that the human body works in mysterious ways. Only last week, I woke up with an aching left bollock, and for the life of me, I couldn't understand why. I checked it thoroughly, but with no signs of damage or inflammation, all I could do was swallow a couple of painkillers and hope for the best. Mysteriously, it was fine the next day.

When I arrive at the petrol station, there's a woman already using the cash machine. I stand back a respectable distance and wait for her to complete her transaction. The machine then makes the familiar churning sound, and a few seconds later, the woman turns around.

I wait for her to walk away so I can take my turn, but she remains standing directly in front of the cash machine, staring at me.

"Um, excuse me," the woman says. "Do I know you?"

In her early thirties, I'd guess, she's too pretty to be my acquaintance because she's the kind of woman I typically avoid.

"I don't think so," I reply, staring at her designer trainers.

"Are you sure," she persists. "Didn't we date a few times?"

I look up, gobsmacked.

"You ... err, you think we used to date?" I splutter.

"Ten years ago, perhaps. I'm terrible with names and faces, but you look so familiar."

"I don't think we dated, no."

"Oh, okay," she chirps. "I feel better now."

"Err, why?"

She steps towards me, invading my personal space to such an extent I can smell the mint on her breath and the scent of her overly sweet perfume.

"If we had dated," she purrs. "I'd now be kicking myself for letting you get away."

With that, she sashays across the forecourt and hops into the passenger's seat of a BMW.

"Weirdo," I mumble under my breath.

Why anyone would put on such an overtly sarcastic performance without a crowd is beyond me. When the girls taunted me in secondary school, at least I understood their motives.

Once I've acquired Ady's cash, I hurry home to find him waiting on my doorstep.

Favour sorted, I head inside in search of a mug of hot chocolate and a good documentary to watch before I take an early night.

Today has been too much. Way too much.

Chapter 14

It isn't quite cold enough for a frost, but Ady has the car's heater to maximum.

"Are you coming down with something?" I ask, as we head towards the depot.

"No. Why?"

"It's baking in here."

"Mate, it's not. I'm only just warming up."

Much like my walk to the cash machine last night, I'm positively radiating heat. Perhaps I'm the one coming down with something, but I still feel okay. In fact, I woke up this morning feeling unusually chipper.

"Did you get your electricity sorted?"

"I did. Cheers, I owe you one."

"You owe me twenty."

"I'll sort you out on payday. Scout's honour."

Ady is always borrowing money, but I rarely ever need to remind him to pay it back, so I'm not concerned.

We arrive at the depot and head for the meeting room. We're the last to arrive, and Jonny is just about to start running through his list of announcements no one wants to hear. It's so dull I tune out and almost miss him mention my name.

I glance at Ady, but his mind is elsewhere.

"Sorry?" I call out. "I didn't quite catch that, Jonny."

"I said you need to do a household collection this afternoon. Mrs Parker-Roan on Huntingdon Terrace."

"Why us?"

Household collections are usually handled by Big Fal and Eddy, and they're both in the room.

"Because Fal and Eddy are going to be tied up all day, and we've got an irate resident demanding we collect her fridge-freezer yesterday."

Ady wakes up.

"Ahh, shit," he mumbles under his breath. "I bet it's that narky cow with the attitude problem."

I calculate the odds as Jonny wraps up the briefing.

Minutes later, Ady's assumption is proven correct as we inspect a job docket, confirming the collection address.

"I wish you'd taken the bet," Ady huffs. "I knew it had to be the same woman."

"Betting is a mug's game."

"You wouldn't say that if you'd won."

"We'll never know, and seeing as you owe me a favour, can you sign the van out today."

"I guess so. Have you upset Keira?"

"Um, no. I'm just a bit warm, that's all. I'll meet you out in the yard."

Ady shrugs and wanders off to Keira's office. I don't know what happened yesterday, but experience tells me I'm being set up for a prank. I assumed Keira was above all that, but her behaviour suggests otherwise. Whatever her game, I'm not playing.

Van keys secured, we set off on our route.

The morning passes like any other, apart from a couple of bizarre moments involving members of the public. On Bransome Road, I stupidly opened the van door without checking my mirror properly, and a female cyclist screeched to a halt only inches from my door. She'd have been perfectly within her rights to yell at me for putting her life at risk, but halfway through my bumbling apology, she said she'd forgive me if I took her out for a drink.

I suspected foul play and gave her a false phone number. Ady thought I was mad, but I said it was likely a set-up. There's no way such an attractive woman would ask me out for a drink, but I could imagine turning up at a pub to find her muscle-bound boyfriend waiting for me. He'd then beat the shit out of me for almost killing his girlfriend—a far more likely scenario.

Then, as I waited in the van while Ady used the public toilets, I noticed a middle-aged woman sitting on a bench next to a bin we'd just emptied. I inadvertently caught her eye, and she smiled back at me. I presumed it was no more than a coincidence, so I looked away. However, over the ensuing minutes, I caught her smiling in my direction at least four times. This led me to conclude the poor woman was in the throes of a psychotic episode. Not wanting to encourage her delusions, I refused to look in her direction again.

Our final task before lunch involves a return visit to a street in an affluent part of town. It's not a visit I'm relishing.

We arrive and park up outside the house.

"Can you go and knock?" I ask Ady. "I'm not keen on speaking to her after last time."

"Yeah, no worries."

Ady makes his way to the front door whilst I head around the back of the van and undo the tailgate. I then stand and watch until Mrs Potty-Mouth eventually answers the door. Dressed in gym gear, she says something to Ady that can't be positive if her scowl is anything to go by. He then turns around and summons me with a wave.

"It's in the back garden."

"Right."

We're only supposed to collect items from the front of a property but having already endured Mrs Parker-Roan's rage once, it's probably best we make a concession.

She disappears back inside and slams the door. We traipse around the back and through a gate to her garden, where the fridge-freezer awaits us. Not wanting to hang around any longer than is necessary, we manhandle the unwanted appliance out of the garden as quickly as we can. Once it's on the back of the van, Ady begins tying it down to ensure it doesn't escape before we reach the recycling centre. That job in hand, I make my way back to the cab. I don't quite get there.

"Excuse me."

I turn to the source of the voice. It's Mrs Parker-Roan, standing in the doorway of her expensive house.

"Yes?"

"You forgot these," she shouts, pointing to the hallway floor.

I've no idea what we've forgotten, and I'm half-minded to say tough, but it'll guarantee a complaint on my personnel file. With reluctance, I amble up the pathway.

As I approach the doorstep, I attempt a smile to show willingness. To my surprise, Mrs Parker-Roan smiles back.

"You're an angel. Thank you."

Her kind words and soft tone are a million miles from the angry harridan who screamed at me during our last encounter.

"It's just these," Mrs Parker-Roan adds, pointing to three plastic trays which look like they came from the fridge-freezer.

"No problem."

"I wish they'd sent you last week. The guy I dealt with was horrible."

"Pardon?"

"There were two men here last week, collecting an abandoned washing machine. Your colleague was one of them, but there was this other guy ... he was just vile."

"Err, I was that other guy."

"Don't be silly," she smirks. "I'd remember such a super-hot guy."

I stare back at Mrs Parker-Roan, a model of bodily perfection in her figure-hugging Lycra.

"Sorry? A what?"

"Don't pretend I've embarrassed you. I bet you get propositioned all the time."

"Err, I can't say ... forget it. I really should be going."

I bend over and grab the trays from the hallway floor.

"While you're down there," Mrs Parker-Roan then chuckles as my head reaches the level of her crotch.

"Pardon?" I reply, standing upright.

"I'm kidding, but if I wasn't happily married, I'd be tempted to drag you upstairs."

The last time I saw this woman's face, it was red and puckered. Now, she's smiling at me like I'm the object of some messed-up fantasy. I'm not sure if it's any improvement.

"That's ... nice. Thanks."

"My pleasure, handsome," she replies with a wink before closing the door.

Confused, I throw the trays in the back of the van and return to the cab.

"What was she bending your ear about?" Ady asks.

"Honestly, mate, I don't have the first clue."

"Was she giving you a hard time?"

"No, but she wanted to apparently."

"I'm not with you."

"Did I never tell you about Steve Saunders?"

"No."

"He transferred to our department from the bin lorries after he got involved with some married woman on his round."

"Lucky bugger."

"You say, but Steve was a dirty bastard."

"Dirty, as in ..."

"Dirty, as in unclean. Steve was seeing that woman for months until her husband found a pair of skid-marked underpants under the marital bed. It turns out the wife had a fetish for men with dirty jobs, and Steve wasn't the first."

Ady grimaces.

"Some people are into weird shit."

"Indeed, and I think our Mrs Parker-Roan is one of them."

"Takes all sorts, I guess."

"It does, mate."

I start the engine and then turn up the air conditioning.

"What's wrong with you?" Ady complains. "It's brass monkeys in here."

"I don't know, but I've been feeling odd since yesterday. Think I might be coming down with something."

"Whatever it is, I'll have some—I could do with a few days off."

"And what if I've got Ebola?"

"Dunno what that is, mate."

"It's a … never mind."

Before we grab lunch and collect the first fly-tipped waste of the day, I decide to make a quick detour.

"I just want to nip to Garwood Lane."

"What for?"

"I spotted a car battery in the hedge yesterday."

"So, why didn't you pick it up yesterday?"

"Because … because I didn't have time, alright."

As Ady was skiving yesterday, he's not in any position to question my work ethic. He doesn't.

We arrive in the lane, and I park in the same layby. Prior to yesterday's events, I wouldn't have thought twice about salvaging the car battery on my own, but there's only so much weird one man can handle in a week.

"Give me a hand, Ady."

He reluctantly joins me on the verge, and we walk in silence towards the fated spot. It's not too hard to find as I trampled the grass on my previous visit.

"Where is it then?" Ady asks.

I slowly move back along the hedge, trying to spot what was evident yesterday. After two passes, I stand and scratch my head.

"That's odd. It was definitely here."

"Well, it ain't now."

Ady isn't right about much, but he is right about this. To demonstrate how right he is, he shrugs his shoulders and begins a slow walk back to the van. I feel compelled to check the hedge one final time.

My theory about being ill receives credence as a sudden chill rips right through me. I'm so cold I physically shiver. Then, as quickly as it arrived, the chill retreats and I'm warm again.

If this keeps up, maybe I should see a doctor.

With Ady skint and our time limited, we grab a quick sandwich for lunch. The rest of the afternoon is as gruelling as it is long, with seventeen loads of fly-tipped waste to collect. By the end of it, the van is fit to bursting, and it's a relief to offload it at the recycling centre.

After sending Ady to check-in the van, I decide I'm in the mood for an hour or so at Tinkerton Meadow. It might be chilly, but clear, bright days like today won't be around much longer. When the clocks go back in October and dusk arrives an hour earlier, my post-work spotting opportunities will be over until the spring.

Ady drops me home, and after a quick shower I hop into my car and scoot over to Tinkerton Meadow. There's already a white Volvo in the car park, so unsurprisingly, I arrive on Falbert's Mount to find Kenny in his favoured spot.

"Alright, Kenny."

"Ahh, there you are," he replies, removing his binoculars. "What happened to you yesterday?"

"Don't ask. I had a nightmare at work."

"That's good."

"Not for me, it wasn't."

"Sorry, pal," he responds. "I didn't mean it like that. I meant, it's good that you're not pissed off with me."

"Why would I be pissed off with you?"

"You know, Saturday night?"

"It's forgotten."

"No hard feelings?"

"Of course not."

"I'm pleased," he says, slapping me on the back. "Because if you were still pissed with me, I'd have to buy you dinner in the Fox & Hounds by way of an apology."

"Well, maybe I am still a bit annoyed. Certainly enough to warrant a pie and a pint."

"I can do that," Kenny smiles. "Any plans once you've finished here?"

"Nope."

"How about we loiter here till dusk and then head over to the Fox & Hounds? Deal?"

"Don't you need to consult with Sara?"

"It was her suggestion, actually. I told her you'd be okay, but it's her way of making amends."

"And she thinks my forgiveness can be bought so easily?"

"She said we can have a pudding."

I hold out my hand.

"Deal."

Chapter 15

We spent almost two hours on the Mount until dusk stopped play. It proved a good session with sightings of seven Green Sandpiper, nine Snipe, five Skylark, a pair of Peregrine, and an entire flock of Redwing.

Now though, I just want to spot a menu. The fresh air and paltry lunch have left me with a ravenous appetite.

I follow Kenny's Volvo into the car park at the Fox & Hounds and we park up. This is my friend's favourite pub because he can stagger home in ten minutes whilst it's a good few miles for me. Still, as I'm not buying tonight, I'll take the concession.

We then enter a bar with thick oak beams, exposed brick walls, and an inglenook fireplace larger than the average flat in central London.

"Kenny, Dougie," the landlord, Greg, greets us. "How are you two fine gentlemen doing this evening?"

"Pretty good," Kenny replies. "We'll be even better with some food inside us."

Greg hands over the menus before pulling us a pint each. Conscious of my fried food intake, I gravitate towards beef casserole with herby dumplings. Kenny chooses the same and confirms our order. We're about to grab a table when a blonde-haired woman appears through a door behind the bar.

"Have you got a sec, Greg?" she says.

"Be right with you," the landlord replies.

The woman then lets her gaze linger in our direction before disappearing back through the door.

"That's our newest member of staff, Zoe," Greg confirms.

"Are your staff getting younger, or are we getting older?" Kenny asks jokingly.

"Sadly, my friend, the latter."

Kenny's interest in the new recruit ends there, and we take our drinks to a table.

"So, what happened yesterday at work?" he asks.

"Eh?"

"You said you had a bad day."

"Oh, right. I'd tell you, but you'll think I'm losing my mind."

"Try me."

There aren't many people in my life I'm comfortable confiding in, but Kenny is one of them. I explain what occurred yesterday, including my meeting with the peculiar woman. He doesn't scoff at my tale, but his eyebrows bob up and down throughout.

"I take your point," he says. "If it were anyone but you, I'd dismiss it as bullshit."

"You believe me?"

"I believe you fell down a bank and injured yourself, for sure, but the rest of it is … would you believe me if the roles were reversed?"

"I'm not sure I would, no, but something happened in that glade. However, the more I try to get my head around it, the more unreal it feels. I'm now doubting myself."

"And you were stone-cold sober?"

"I was at work, Kenny. Of course I was sober."

"Do you think maybe someone slipped something in your tea at the cafe?"

"Is that a serious question? What reason would Heather have for spiking my tea with a hallucinogenic drug?"

"I don't know, but she is an odd one."

"It's a ridiculous theory," I huff. "But now you've mentioned odd, I've had a few strange run-ins with women since yesterday."

"In what way strange?"

"First, there was Keira in the office. She was acting goofy towards me, and that's not like her at all. Then, I was at a cash machine last night, and this random woman asked if we'd ever dated as she thought I looked familiar."

"And had you?"

"God, no. She was at least a decade younger than me, and on her appearance alone, I'd say she was the kind of woman who only dates professional footballers."

Kenny appears confused.

"You're a good pal, Dougie, which is why I can't lie to you—you're no professional footballer in talent or looks."

"Exactly. Then today, I think an attractive housewife propositioned me."

"Seriously?"

"She said if she weren't happily married, she'd have dragged me upstairs and ripped my clothes off."

"Bloody hell," my friend sighs, shaking his head. "Are you positive you haven't taken anything?"

"I'm not losing my mind, but something strange is happening to me, and ... Christ, it's baking in here."

Having already removed my coat, I unbutton my cardigan and slip it off.

"What was I saying?"

Before Kenny can answer, our food arrives courtesy of the newest staff member.

"Two beef casseroles," Zoe confirms, placing our bowls on the table. "Can I get you anything else?"

"I'm good, thanks," I reply.

"Actually," Kenny responds. "Would you mind settling a wee problem we're having?"

"I can try."

"See my friend here? Is there anything about him that appears odd to you?"

I throw a severe glare across the table towards Kenny.

"I'm not sure how to answer that," Zoe replies, her cheeks flushing pink.

"My apologies, lass. I didn't mean to embarrass you."

"Oh, I'm not embarrassed. I'm just really awkward around good-looking guys."

"That's nice of you to say," Kenny replies, trying hard to stifle a smug grin. "If only I were twenty years younger."

"I meant your friend."

Zoe looks down at me, flashes a sultry smile, and then hurries back to the kitchen.

I turn to Kenny.

"What just happened there?" he asks, seemingly dumbstruck.

"I told you, didn't I? Ever since I sipped that herbal tonic yesterday, women have been acting weird around me. And, I'm constantly warm, like I'm close to getting a fever."

My friend snaps out of his stupor.

"Ahh, this is a wind-up, right?" he snorts. "You're getting your own back for what happened on Saturday."

"And how would I have arranged such a pointless prank? Besides, it was your idea to come here for dinner tonight. I didn't even know Zoe existed until fifteen minutes ago."

"You're telling me that what just occurred wasn't your doing?"

"On my mother's life. Now, do you believe what I told you about those other women?"

"But, there's got to be a rational explanation."

"I don't even know what's wrong with me, let alone how to explain it."

Kenny ponders my reply for a moment.

"You first noticed something odd after you took that herbal tonic, correct?"

"That's right."

"There must have been something in it."

"Like what?"

Hungry as we are, Kenny's focus isn't on his dinner.

"Wander around your average woodland, and you'll find a range of plants with remarkable properties. For example, elder has antiseptic and anti-inflammatory properties, and nettles are a natural anti-histamine. Then, at the other end of the scale, a handful of deadly nightshade berries will kill you within hours if you don't seek treatment."

"I understand that, but have you ever heard of a herbal treatment that affects … I can't believe I'm about to say this … that affects attraction?"

"Attraction?"

"Yes, like what just happened with Zoe."

As I wait for a reply, Kenny unfurls his cutlery from a napkin and digs the fork into his bowl.

"Maybe that tonic affected your pheromone levels—supercharged them," he then declares.

I'm partial to the odd wildlife documentary, so I understand how pheromones work in nature. Essentially, some creatures secrete a potent chemical that helps to attract a mating partner.

"It's a good theory, Kenny, but I know for sure it's not pheromone-related."

"How so?"

"Do you promise you won't laugh or tell another living soul?"

"You can trust me; you know that."

I bolster my resolve with a large chunk of dumpling.

"Do you remember those magazines for men in the nineties: Loaded, Maxim, and the like?"

"Aye. They were like porn mags without the porn."

"Exactly. I used to buy Loaded now and then, and in one edition, I noticed an advert in the classified section at the back. It was for a cologne called MegaMan, and the advert claimed it contained androsterone—the most potent of pheromones, apparently. It was scientifically proven to make the wearer more attractive to women."

"Ah, shite," Kenny groans, rolling his eyes. "Don't tell me ..."

"Yep, I paid eighty quid for a bottle."

"I think I know the answer but indulge me: did it work?"

"In a way, yes. I wore it to the pub one evening, but on the way, a swarm of wasps caught my scent and attacked. The stripey little bastards stung me eleven times."

Kenny's face turns crimson; such is the effort not to laugh.

"Go on," I sigh. "Let it out."

He duly does.

"You silly bugger," he cries. "I'm sorry, but that's the funniest thing I've heard in ages."

"I can laugh about it now, but I didn't think it was so funny at the time. Have you ever been stung on the nipple? There's no pain like it, I can tell you."

"I'd beg to differ, pal. I once grazed my bollocks, skinny-dipping in a swimming pool in Lanzarote."

Just the thought is wince-inducing.

"Ouch."

"I couldn't wear pants for a fortnight."

"Tragic, but your shredded scrotum aside, my experience with pheromone-laced cologne undermines your theory, don't you think?"

"Maybe, maybe not. All I'm saying is that you shouldn't underestimate the potency of native plants. Thinking about it, you were a bit stupid drinking that tonic without asking what was in it."

"I didn't have much choice."

"Course you didn't," my friend replies with a hint of scepticism in his tone.

"I didn't. I was in agony."

"Yet, you seem perfectly fine now."

Something in Kenny's eyes suggests he's still not convinced about my tale. I'm so short of facts it's unlikely I'll be able to change his mind.

"Just forget I said anything," I mumble. "I don't want to talk about it anymore."

Happy to oblige, Kenny changes the subject and chats mindlessly until both our bowls are empty.

"That was fantastic," my friend proclaims, sitting back in his chair.

"It was and, fortunately for you, I'm stuffed."

"I was hoping you'd say that—saves me a few quid. Do you fancy one for the road?"

"No, I'm okay, thanks."

"Fair enough. I'll just need to visit the loo, and I'll settle up."

"Sure."

Kenny disappears, and a minute later, Zoe arrives to clear away our empty bowls.

"Was everything okay?" she asks.

"Lovely, thanks."

"Can I get you anything else?"

"No, we're just leaving."

"That's a pity."

"Is it?"

She glances towards the bar and then slides onto the chair next to mine.

"I was hoping you might let me buy you a drink when my shift ends. I'm Zoe, by the way."

"Um, I'm Dougie. You want a drink ... with me?"

"Oh, you're not married, are you?"

"No, no. I'm very much single."

"Cool. So, how about it?"

"Err, can I ask how old are you?"

"Twenty-nine. Is my age a problem then?"

"I'm forty-one, which means I'm biologically old enough to be your dad."

"How many twelve-year-old lads father a child?"

"Fair point," I concede. "Perhaps your much older brother."

"So?" she shrugs.

"That doesn't bother you?"

"No."

"Right, err, I mean ... it's not just your age."

"What is it then? If you don't fancy me, that's cool. Just be honest, please, before I make a complete fool of myself."

Zoe's question drags me back to the day I purchased my car. With only a five-grand budget, my options didn't extend beyond a run-of-the-mill hatchback, which was fine. I found a Ford Focus online and went to see it at a local car dealership the next day.

When I arrived, the salesman pointed out the Focus and suggested I take a closer look at it while he fetched the documents. I wandered over and after I prodded a few buttons on the dashboard, checked the engine bay and kicked the tyres, I decided to buy it. As I shut the bonnet, I couldn't help but notice the forty-grand Mercedes Coupé parked opposite. I was still admiring it when the salesman wandered over, and he asked if I fancied taking it for a test drive. In many respects, his assumption that a street cleaning operative could afford a high-end sports car is less ludicrous than Zoe's assumption I don't fancy her.

"I ... sorry, is this a joke?"

"Why would I joke about buying you a drink?"

It's not a question I can answer. All I can do is pose one of my own.

"Do you think we're, um, compatible?"

"You seem like a nice enough guy, and it's not like I'm asking you to marry me. So, what's the big deal?"

"You'll have to forgive me, Zoe. I'm just trying to understand why you want to have a drink with me."

"That's kind of where you start when two single people meet. We have a few drinks and see where that takes us. I'm not looking for anything heavy—just a bit of fun if you're up for it?"

There's a good chance I'm being an idiot here, but I can't fathom which brand of idiot. It would be idiotic to ignore the fact there might be a sting in the tail somewhere, but would it be more idiotic to say no just because I'm scared of being stung? Again.

"I'm flattered, Zoe, but my head isn't in the right place at the moment. Would you mind if I slept on it?"

Zoe then leans in and rests her hand on my thigh.

"Is that a phone in your pocket?" she asks in a suggestive tone.

"Yes," I gulp.

"Do you want to take my number, then?"

I pull out my phone and almost drop it. Once I've stopped my hand from shaking, I thumb Zoe's number into the contact app.

"Message me when you've decided," she says, getting to her feet. "I'd better crack on before Greg fires me for skiving."

Zoe then sashays away. I watch on as she disappears back into the kitchen. Long seconds pass, and I have to physically pinch myself to confirm that what just happened, happened.

"You fit?"

Kenny is standing at the edge of the table.

"Err, sure."

"Everything alright, Dougie. You look a bit flustered."

"No, no. I'm just warm."

Like a kid telling his best mate what he got for Christmas, I so badly want to share my news with Kenny. However, a significant part of me still believes the news might be fake. Did a stunningly attractive girl just ask me on a date? Did I really tell her I'd have to think about it?

I must be crazy, one way or another.

Chapter 16

It's every parent's job to impart good advice to their off-spring. However, if a parent has to reinforce that advice on a near-monthly basis, it becomes dogma. My dad is an inherently sceptical man, and throughout my childhood, he constantly warned me that if something seems too good to be true, it almost always is.

Sitting here with my mug of breakfast tea and staring at Zoe's number on my phone screen, I can't blot out Dad's warning.

I didn't sleep well last night as my mind wanted to unpick the day's events. Consequently, I got up half an hour early and, after my shower, I did something I've never done before—I spent ten whole minutes examining my face in the bathroom mirror.

Such is the aversion to my own face, the only time I look at it is when I shave on a Sunday evening, and even then, I keep my eyes firmly trained on my puny jawline.

What I hoped to see was a metamorphosis. I've heard it said that some men become more handsome as they age. In my case, there were more lines than I remember, and years of working outside has added a grainy quality to my skin, but the overall effect wasn't what I'd call distinguished. Unattractive, certainly.

And yet, despite the mirror's damning evidence, I seem to be catnip to members of the opposite sex. There's even a name and eleven digits stored in my phone's memory belonging to an attractive woman as proof.

I finish my tea and put the mug in the dishwasher. Ady isn't due for another fifteen minutes, and I've plenty to ponder.

My mind begins dissecting the conversation with Kenny in the Fox & Hounds. Although he might not have believed me, he did help pinpoint the catalyst for my alleged condition—the herbal tonic. It only took a few hours for me to conclude that I couldn't possibly have been as badly injured as I thought I was, and maybe the tonic had some anaesthetic properties. But, there's no explaining how it has affected my interactions with the fairer sex.

Come to think of it, every medicine I've ever taken, herbal or otherwise, has lost all potency after six or seven hours, maximum. My encounter with Zoe occurred some thirty-odd hours after I sipped that herbal tonic, so that can't be the reason. If not that, what in God's name is happening to me? Is anything happening to me, or am I in the midst of a mental breakdown?

More questions arrive.

I could be losing my mind, but if for some miraculous reason I'm suddenly able to attract women like Zoe, what does that mean for Dougie Neil in the short, medium, and long term?

As I put my boots on, another snippet of Dad's advice floats into my mind: women admire confidence in a man. I don't know why that particular pearl of wisdom stuck. Over the years, Dad has offered an entire encyclopaedia of advice relating to my inability to find a partner. So far, none of it has helped, but maybe today, the odds are stacked a little differently.

If whatever is happening to me continues today, I should find the confidence to utilise it. Frankly, I've nothing to lose. For all I know, this gift is temporary, and it could be taken away at any moment—if it hasn't already gone.

"Gift," I mumble under my breath. "Maybe that's just what it is."

I'm not willing to discount the mental breakdown theory, but if you're heading towards insanity, you might as well enjoy the journey.

That thought sets off a jittery sensation in the pit of my stomach. I can only equate it to the times I've received a text about a rare bird sighting at Tinkerton Meadow, and I've rushed over only to find it was a false alarm.

Ady pulls up outside—a welcome distraction. I hurry out and hop in the passenger's seat.

"Morning,"

"Ain't it just," he spits.

"Someone got out of the wrong side of the bed."

"Fat chance. The wrong side of the sofa."

"Ah. Trouble at home?"

"Yeah, but can we talk about something else, or not at all?"

He revs the engine hard, and I'm pressed back in my seat as the tyres find grip. I've enough on my mind without worrying about Ady's woes, so I don't attempt conversation until we're walking across the car park to the briefing room.

"Are you going to be in a shitty mood all day?" I ask.

"I'll be alright once I've had a coffee."

"Let's hope so."

The morning meeting is brief, and before I can ask Ady to sign out the van, he's already making his way outside for a smoke. On one level, that's not such a bad thing as it means I have to confront Keira. The first test is to see if normality has returned.

As I make my way to her office, it dawns on me that whatever happens when I arrive, I can't lose. Either she'll treat me in the same business-like manner she treats all of us, or her odd behaviour will continue from our last encounter.

I pass through the doorway. Keira's eyes are fixed on her monitor for a good ten seconds before they flick in my direction. Her face lights up.

"Hey, Dougie," she chirps. "How are you?"

I've never given it much thought before now, but it's incredible what a difference a smile makes to a face. In Keira's case, it's almost as if I'm looking at an entirely different person.

"Pretty good, thanks."

"That's good to hear."

Pleasantries over, the situation becomes awkward in a heartbeat. It's not helped that Keira is grinning up at me like a teenage girl staring at a poster of her favourite boy band.

"Err, can I get a van, please?"

"Sure, Dougie. Not a problem."

Her almost seductive tone has the opposite effect and, as she spins around in her chair, I inwardly shudder. Under normal circumstances, I'd be elated if Keira threw the odd half-smile my way, but this is too much. Whatever is the cause, this overly flirtatious character is so far removed from the real Keira it's disturbing.

"Here you go," she says, dangling a key out in front of me.

I reach forward to grab it, but Keira pulls it away at the last second.

"What's the magic word?" she asks.

"Err, *please,* may I have the key?"

"No, the magic word is *dinner.*"

"Sorry?"

"Yes, dinner. You, me, Friday night. What do you say?"

Ohh, shit!

"Um ..."

I can think of many good reasons why going out with Keira would be a bad idea. What I can't think of is a single plausible excuse for declining her invite—not one.

"Dinner?" I parrot. "You and me?"

A series of heavy footsteps suddenly stomp up behind me. I've never been so pleased to see Big Fal.

"Morning, Keira," he says.

"Can't you see I'm dealing with Dougie?" she says flatly. "Come back in five minutes, and close the door on your way out."

Big Fal shrugs and duly obliges.

"Where were we?" Keira asks, her soft tone restored. "Oh yes—dinner."

"Well, err ... that's really, um ..."

"Oh, no," Keira then suddenly blusters, her eyes wide. "I didn't think to ask if you're actually seeing someone at the moment."

I feel like a prisoner, granted a last-gasp pardon by my own executioner.

"I'm afraid I am," I reply with a sigh of faux disappointment. "I'm genuinely flattered, Keira, but I wouldn't want to ... you know, err, mess anyone around."

"No, I understand," she sighs. "She's a lucky woman."

"Thanks."

"But if anything changes or it doesn't work out, my offer stands, okay?"

"I'll definitely bear that in mind."

Not only have I never seen Keira smile so much, but I've also never seen her look so disappointed. She slides the van key across the desk and mutters a few words I don't quite catch.

"I'd better be going. See you later, Keira."

Waiting for a reply doesn't strike me as a sound idea. I scuttle out of the office, passing a disgruntled Big Fal waiting outside, and don't stop until I'm in the Keira-free confines of the yard. Ady is loitering in an empty parking bay, mobile phone in one hand and cigarette in the other.

"Let's get going," I call over, making my way to our allocated van three bays along.

Ady flicks the cigarette away but keeps his eyes on the phone screen. His interest doesn't wane once he's sitting next to me in the van. It seems my colleague still isn't in the mood for conversation. I'm not fussed as I can use the silence to consider what just happened with Keira, and there's a lot to unpack.

Driving on autopilot, I replay the scene in my mind's eye. Even thinking about it makes my skin prickle, but I need to think of the implication beyond a few minutes of crippling awkwardness. For reasons unknown, women are attracted to me. No, that's not the right word because attraction wouldn't compel a woman like Keira to cast aside her principles and act like a giddy teenager.

Whatever this is, it's far more potent than attraction; it's almost spell-like.

The only time I've heard about such a radical change in a person's behaviour came courtesy of the man sitting next to me.

"Can I ask you a question, Ady?"

"What's up?" he replies, without looking up from his phone screen.

"Do you recall telling me about that stage hypnotist."

"The one at Dave's stag do?"

"How many stage hypnotists have you seen?"

"One."

"Well, then, yes," I groan. "The one at Dave's stag do."

"What about him?"

"Remind me. Didn't he convince one of Dave's mates his shoe was a phone?"

"Oh yeah, Jimmy," Ady snorts as the memory returns. "He was convinced he was on the phone to Beyoncé, and she asked him to talk dirty. The bloke made a right mug of himself."

"Do you reckon it was real?"

"Why are you interested?"

"Err, a mate of mine is having a fiftieth birthday party next year, and he mentioned hiring a stage hypnotist. I was curious if it was just bullshit."

"Jimmy swore blind he didn't know what he was doing, and he ain't the sort of bloke who'd do something like that for a giggle. He got the piss ripped out of him for months afterwards."

"Right, thanks."

Ady returns to his phone, and I return to my thoughts.

What my colleague just described isn't too far removed from the way Keira behaved—so far out of character that it defies a logical explanation. In itself, that might explain Keira's behaviour, but it doesn't come close to explaining why or how or who put her in that trance. Nor does it explain why Zoe from the Fox & Hounds asked me out or why the previously obnoxious Mrs Parker-Roan suggested she'd like to bounce up and down on my gentleman's sausage.

With no obvious answer, I turn to Kenny's theory about pheromones. What are the chances that one sip of a herbal tonic could invoke such potent pheromones that women lose their minds when I talk to them? Absolutely none. And yet, that's as close to a viable explanation as I can think of. It's a long way from plausible but theoretically viable.

Any further thought on the subject will have to wait as we arrive at the first bin collection.

As we move from pick up to pick up, I catch several women glancing in my direction, and more than a few throw a smile my way. If I wasn't at work, I might have been tempted to chat with one or two.

We empty the last bin of the day, and Ady says he needs a favour.

"I need to go see someone on the Kempshot Estate. It'll only take five minutes."

"Can't you do it after work?"

"It's urgent, mate. Please?"

I check the list of fly-tip sites we need to visit, and Ady's luck is in; there's one just on the edge of the estate.

"Five minutes."

"Nice one. It's a flat above the shops, so we could grab a sandwich while we're there."

"I was hoping to visit The Vale today."

"If you can wait till tomorrow, I'll treat you."

A compromise reached, we make our way across town to the Kempshot Estate.

"Pull in here," Ady orders as we approach a row of three shops: a Chinese takeaway, a convenience store, and an off licence.

I park in a layby.

"Cheers," Ady says, his hand on the door. "I'll be five minutes. Fifteen tops."

"Wait, you said ..."

He hops out of the van before I've time to argue. Having been conned, I watch my duplicitous colleague hurry to a set of stairs at the side of the takeaway, presumably leading up to the flats above. After furtively checking his surroundings, Ady darts up the stairs, out of view.

That man is running out of favours, and goodwill.

As the Chinese takeaway is closed, my options for lunch are limited. I lock the van and wander into the convenience store in search of a sandwich. There's a paltry range on offer, so I settle on a ham salad sandwich, plus a bag of crisps and a bottle of Coke.

I join the queue behind a woman wearing pyjama bottoms, a fluffy dressing gown, and slippers. I'm not one to judge, but how can anyone be so lazy they can't be arsed to change out of their nightwear before popping to the shop?

The woman turns her head and notices me.

"Wotcha," she says and then spins around. "Ain't seen you in here before."

"I'm not local."

"Didn't think so. I'd have noticed a good-looking bloke like you. I'm Julie."

What am I supposed to say to that? Fortunately, the man at the counter moves off, and the assistant requests the next customer.

Julie shuffles over and asks for a packet of cigarettes. I breathe a sigh of relief when she pops them in her pocket and steps towards the door. I'm halfway to the counter when she stops and calls over to me.

"I'm at number nineteen Amber Court if you fancy ... a cup of tea."

Her invite is accompanied by an exaggerated wink.

"Um, thanks. I'll bear that in mind."

Julie shuffles out the door.

"Just these, please," I say to the young assistant, placing my lunch items on the counter.

While he's scanning, I happen to notice the headline on the front page of the local newspaper, piled high in a stand just to my left. It warns of impending job cuts at Ashbridge Borough Council.

"I'll take one of these, too," I say to the assistant, snatching a paper from the pile.

I return to the van, but there's no sign of Ady. I might be annoyed if I wasn't so preoccupied with my own issues. As it is, I sit and read the paper whilst eating my lunch. It transpires that the job cuts at the council are in departments other than mine, which is good news for me but not such good news for those in the affected departments.

I'm only partially paying attention when I flip the page to the 'What's On' guide. I'm not that interested but give the page a cursory scan. An advert then grabs my attention.

The advert in question is for an over-forties speed dating event. I've tried speed dating once before and, despite sitting down and chatting with eleven women, I came away without a single match. I vowed never to put myself through that humiliation again.

I'm about to turn the page, but my mind wants to linger on the advert. It then poses a question: what would happen if I attended a speed dating event, blessed with my supposed superpower?

Without thinking too deeply about the answer, I re-read the advert. The event is tonight at seven o'clock, at a pub in town.

I can imagine three different scenarios if I show up. The first, and least welcome, would be a repeat of my first attempt at speed dating. The second would be a complete reversal of my prior fortunes whereby I match with every woman there. The third scenario, and perhaps a stretch of the imagination, is one where I go on a second date with a woman who might turn out to be Miss Right.

I close the paper and weigh up the pros and cons. A few minutes spent listing each, but I keep returning to the same question: what is the point of this—whatever *this* is—if I don't take advantage of it?

By the time Ady returns to the van, I've reached a decision.

Chapter 17

I consider myself a good person. Not perfect, but good. If not, I wouldn't currently be lying in the bath, wrestling with my conscience.

Growing up, my parents were huge fans of board games, and once a month, we'd enjoy a family games night. This involved the four of us battling it out to see who would be the house champion that month. One of my favourite games was called Scruples. When it was your turn, you'd pick a card containing a random moral dilemma, and the rest of the players had to guess how you'd answer.

Some of the dilemmas were fairly innocuous, like whether you'd leave your details if you scraped someone else's vehicle in a car park and there were no witnesses. Others were more contentious like if you could travel back in time and kill Adolf Hitler as a child, would you?

We must have played Scruples scores of times, to the point where we'd all answered every question. Thirty years on, and I still remember most of them, which is why I'm positive there was never a question relating to the dilemma I now face. It's one thing knowing I miraculously appeal to members of the opposite sex, but quite another acting on that appeal.

Zoe is a prime example of the problem. A few days ago, she wouldn't have looked at me twice, but now she's keen we go on a date. Whatever chicanery is at play here, is it wrong to take advantage? It's such a ridiculous notion, but what if we did go on a date, and she ended up back at my place? What if we had a few drinks and things became a little heated on the sofa? What if we ended up in my bed, naked?

As the bathwater reaches tepid, my moral compass continues to whirl around like a weather vane in a gale. Would I be conning women if I responded to their advances? What if this gift is exactly that, and I'm supposed to use it? In the Bible, did a crowd of five-thousand refuse bread and fish because it arrived on their plate courtesy of a miracle?

Somewhere in the maelstrom, the compass needle slows down and points towards a man I once knew: Jeremy Dane of Temple-Dane Auditing Services.

I was only eighteen when I first started working for Jeremy's company; a tiny, insignificant cog in the multi-million-pound machine he'd built. In all the time I worked there, I only spoke to him twice, primarily because his plush office was on the top floor of the building whilst I shared an open-plan office on the third floor with forty other minions. Jeremy was also more than twice my age, so we had nothing in common except one thing—we both fancied Cécile Warren like crazy.

Alas, Jeremy was engaged to the young model while I could only admire her from afar whenever she dropped in to see her fiancé.

I couldn't understand how a short, plump, ruddy-faced man like Jeremy could attract such a stunning woman, years his junior. As I got older, I noticed many more couples like Jeremy and Cécile: physically mismatched individuals masquerading as couples. Every time I opened a newspaper or turned on the television, I'd see reports of some pension-age actor or politician or business icon dating a woman half his age. It slowly dawned on me that what those men lacked in good looks, they more than made up for with their money, power, and influence.

The last I heard, Jeremy and Cécile were married with two children, although he'd lost most of his fortune in the financial crisis. Perhaps money bridged the gap between them, but they're still together. His fortune offered Jeremy a chance to find a wife beyond his physical appeal. Why shouldn't I use my gift for the same purpose?

And, come to think of it, why is my gift any different to someone blessed with good genes? Exceptionally good-looking men attract women all the time, and no one questions their morality, even though they're using their gift. I wasn't blessed with a handsome face, money or power or influence, so I've been left on the sidelines my entire life. Now, I have this miraculous opportunity, so why shouldn't I use it? It's not as though I'm an arsehole who's only interested in bedding as many women as possible. I want a wife and a family.

The compass needle stops spinning. It might waver in the coming hours, days, and weeks ahead, but it's definitely pointing in the right direction now.

I hop out of the bath, splash on a little cologne, and get dressed.

Forty minutes later, my taxi pulls up outside The Cherry Blossom—a pub I used to frequent back in the day before they refurbished the interior and upped the price of a pint by a quid. With mixed feelings, I push open the door.

I had already planned my tactics in the taxi, so I put my head down and stride straight for the bar. Ideally, I'd like to find a quiet corner in which to hide until the speed dating begins. What I hadn't factored in was the woman standing in my way, clipboard in hand.

"Are you here for the speed dating?" she asks.

"Yes."

"Fantastic," she purrs. "I'm Shelley, the organiser."

She holds out a hand, and I shake it. "I'm Dougie."

"It's lovely to meet you, Dougie," Shelley replies, still gripping my hand. "I'm sure you'll have more than your fair share of matches tonight."

Shelley reminds me of the mothers I see congregated outside the private school on Hemingway Avenue, the kind who invest an inordinate amount of time and money on beauty treatments: hair, nails, eyebrows, fake tan, the lot. That's not to say Shelley isn't an attractive woman, though.

Our host guides me to the bar, where she confirms my personal details on a form and then presents me with a scorecard and name badge. She has a habit of talking with her hands, and I can't help but notice the lack of a wedding ring.

I pay the ten quid fee, and Shelley is about to ask a question when two women breeze in through the main door.

"Sorry," she says. "More singletons to deal with. Hopefully, I'll catch up with you later."

Her eyes linger on mine for a fraction longer than is necessary. Is she being friendly or flirtatious? Before I'm able to gather further intel, Shelley flounces away to welcome the newcomers.

I order a pint and seek refuge at the far end of the bar. A psychologist would probably cite past dating trauma as the cause for my racing heart and sweaty palms, but such a diagnosis would be wrong. If Shelley's warm welcome is anything to go by, the gift is working just as well as it did last night in the Fox & Hounds. No, I'm nervous because I don't know what the fuck I'm doing. These waters are uncharted, and I'm now bobbing around in the middle with female sharks circling. It never crossed my mind to have swimming lessons before I rocked up.

I gulp back a mouthful of lager and try to reassure myself everything will be fine. It is, however, mildly annoying that I'm not more excited. What single man wouldn't want to walk into a pub knowing that every woman will want to talk to him? I'm living every man's dream, so why am I on the verge of crapping my pants?

Pre-game nerves, I conclude. Even after hundreds of games, the world's best footballers say they still can't escape the jitters. By comparison, I'm a non-league journeyman, about to step out onto the hallowed Wembley turf in a cup final.

Ironically, the blast of a whistle breaks my thoughts. Shelley steps into the centre of the room.

"Thank you," she says, as the buzz of conversation peters out. "We're just about to get started, but I thought I'd remind you how our speed dating events work."

I listen carefully as Shelley confirms what I remember from my previous experience. There are seven men and seven women, and therefore seven tables set up in the middle of the room. The women stay put, and the men move from table to table, participating in a five-minute 'date' with each woman. At the end of that date, we note on our scorecard if we think it was a hit or a miss. If both parties say it's a hit, we have the option of chatting afterwards, and those with multiple matches can decide who they want to hook up with, either this evening or at a later date.

What Shelley fails to mention is what happens if you have zero matches. I'm sure she has a list of platitudes ready to deploy, but in my experience, all you want is the ground to immediately swallow you up.

The women take their seats, and I line up with the six other men. The whistle blows, and the first man sits down at the first table, the second at the second, and so on. Finally, I get to sit down in front of Miranda: a woman with a massive mane of red hair and more cleavage than your average *Carry On* film.

We politely shake hands, but before I can get a word in, Miranda suggests I tell her all about myself.

"I'm, um, forty-one, and I own my own house. I've worked for Ashbridge Council for twenty years, and ... err, I enjoy bird-watching."

"Birdwatching?"

"Yes."

"Please, tell me all about it."

"What would you like to know?"

"Everything, darling. Everything."

"I'd love to, but I don't think we've enough time. Don't you want to tell me a bit about yourself?"

Miranda leans forward.

"I'm going to say this now, Dougie—I already know we're a great match."

"Oh, already?"

"You have a real aura about you, And, your eyes; there's something so enticing about them."

"Thank you."

"I could sit and look into them all evening."

To prove her sincerity, she stares straight at me. I don't know where to look, so I gamble on down.

"Like what you see?" Miranda asks.

"No ... no, I wasn't looking at your tit ... your breasts. I was just ... um ..."

"I don't mind, darling. I'm flattered."

My cheeks burning, I attempt to get our date back on track.

"What do you do for a living, Miranda?"

"I'm a primary school teacher."

"That sounds like a lovely job."

"No, it absolutely isn't."

"Oh."

"Most of my colleagues are whiny windbags, and the kids are insufferable little shits."

"You don't like children?"

"Not particularly. What about you?"

The whistle blows before I can answer, bringing an end to our 'date'. Miranda then reinforces how keen she is to continue our conversation on a proper date. I'm not sure, but I don't want to rule her out. I reply with a reassuring smile.

Next, I meet Tracey, who clearly does like children because she has five of them already. She doesn't rule out a sixth if she meets the right man, and if her outrageous flirting is any barometer, I might be that right man.

From Tracey, I move on to Naila, and she virtually proposes to me within the first two minutes. I'm almost tempted to accept until she lists her menagerie of pets: two dogs, four cats, five rabbits, a cockatiel, and seventeen guinea pigs. I've always fancied owning a dog, but not a zoo.

My five-minute date with Gemma starts well enough. She's undoubtedly attractive, but her wide range of tattoos and body piercings are a distraction.

Claire insists I might be her soul mate, and during my conversation with Ruth, I mention I'd like children. She cheekily suggests we could make a start in the car park once our date is over.

Last up is Camilla, who steadfastly, almost aggressively, refuses to accept I've only ever had one relationship. I'm not keen on her attitude, and there's something in her features that reminds me of someone I don't wish to be reminded of.

With the final blast of her whistle, Shelley brings the dating part of the evening to an end. I make my excuses to Camilla and dash off to the toilets. My bladder doesn't require emptying, but I need to get my head together.

I seek refuge in a cubicle, putting the seat down so I can sit and reflect.

I've just met seven women and based upon their behaviour, I wouldn't be surprised if all seven put a giant tick next to my name. I'm confident I've never met seven keen women throughout my entire adult life. There can be no doubt that what began with Keira on Monday is still in force this evening. Seven women: seven opportunities to find love, to settle down, and to live happily ever after.

However, now I face a new dilemma.

Up until this point, I've had so few opportunities to forge a relationship I never stopped to consider what kind of woman I'd like to enter that relationship with. The old adage about beggars not being choosers always guided my thinking, and your average beggar doesn't request a menu when asked if they'd like something to eat.

Now, though, I have options.

One option I don't have is to hide away in a toilet cubicle for the rest of the evening. At some point, I need to head back to the room and confirm which of the seven women I matched with and if I want to take things any further. The issue is I've had precisely fourteen seconds to consider what I'm looking for in a partner. Going on gut instinct alone, I'm not sure any of the seven are right for me. A few days ago, I'd have crawled over broken glass for a date with any one of them, but now I need to be pragmatic.

If I want children, which I'm sure I do, that discounts at least five of the seven women I've just 'dated', and I'm not convinced the other two are ideal candidates.

I realise I'm an idiot.

If I'd had the forethought to consider this before leaving the house, I would have realised an over-forties dating event probably isn't the ideal hunting ground for women who want to start a family.

This leads me to a troubling conclusion. If I head back to the bar, I'll likely be accosted by at least one of the women, possibly more. It's not their fault I didn't think this through, and I'd rather avoid flatly rejecting them. I'm sure they'd all be understanding, except Camilla. That's a shame as physically, she's my type, and despite her combative communication skills, she did say she hadn't given up on having kids.

The thought of dating Camilla lingers for a moment.

"No, Dougie," I whisper. "Don't even go there. Not again."

22nd March 2001

I need to write this stuff down because a part of me doesn't believe it's happening.

It's almost two months to the day that we were introduced to a new member of staff, and now she's my girlfriend: official as of two weeks ago.

As it happens, we became official on the same night I lost my virginity to Denise. I've never been so nervous or wanted anything so badly, and I wish I could do it again. Maybe I should have had a wank a few hours before, so it would have lasted longer. I wasn't keeping time, but I don't think I lasted more than two minutes. Denise was cool about it, though, and we had another go after an hour. That was better, but I still felt a bit conscious that I was in bed with a proper woman, with experience, and I was an absolute newbie. Denise did promise to teach me everything she knows, so that's something to look forward to.

I suppose it's still early days, but I haven't met any of Denise's friends or family yet. She came over and met Mum and Dad last week, and they liked her, I think. I get the feeling my new girlfriend isn't so keen on Dad as she said he was a bit sexist in some of the things he said. I don't know if he was, but Denise is a strong-willed woman and doesn't put up with anyone's shit. Some might call her bossy, but I like the fact she's willing to take control and knows her own mind. I want a relationship with a woman, not a silly girl.

I'm making Denise sound like a stroppy mare, and she isn't really. She's going to look at a new flat to rent on Saturday, and she asked me to come along for a second opinion. If she didn't respect me, why ask if I'd join her? She's only hinted at it, but I think she's been badly hurt in the past, and it'll take some time to build up trust. I try to do what I can and show her that I'm different. Whenever we go out, I always pay and as much as I'd love to have sex with her every minute of every day, I wait till she's in the mood. I'm sure she'll want it more as I get better at it.

That's it for now. So far, 2001 is proving to be the best year of my life, and I hope one day I can look back at this year's diary and share it with our kids ... well, most of it. After so much disappointment, it makes a nice change writing positive stuff in my diary—long may it continue!

Chapter 18

Within a few seconds of waking up, memories of my speed dating adventure filter in. I chuckle to myself.

It's nothing to be proud of, but to spare the feelings of the seven women, I fled through the fire exit.

I can't lie—as I jogged away, the feeling was electric. It crossed my mind that only rock stars get to flee adoring women. The rock star feeling soon passed, though, and by the time I got home, guilt had taken over. Today, I'll email Shelley and ask her to pass on my apologies—I'll just say I didn't feel well and had to leave.

I'll also use the opportunity to confirm I won't be pursuing any second dates. Now I'm blessed with this incredible gift, it would be mad to settle for a less-than-ideal partner. That's why I spent an hour on the sofa last night, writing a list of the attributes my perfect girlfriend will ideally possess. I also drew up a few ground rules, so I don't find myself in another Keira-like situation. Whoever I date, it cannot be someone I knew prior to my ... transformation. It would feel like I'm conning them in some way.

Once I'd finished the list, I realised that I'd already met someone who ticked almost every box: Zoe from The Fox & Hounds. Her age was the only issue as I'd set a maximum age gap of ten years, and Zoe is twelve years younger than me. She seemed nice, though, and her pleasing aesthetic proved too tempting a proposition—I sent her a text message asking if she'd like to meet up for a drink. A reply arrived within two minutes: *Definitely!*

I clamber out of bed, shower, and get dressed. I've got two days of work before my date, but I cannot remember the last time I felt so positive.

It doesn't last—Ady is late again.

I try calling him, but it goes straight to voicemail. Unwilling to wait, I grab my car keys and leave the house.

The traffic is kind, and I waltz into the meeting room a minute before Jonny bustles in. He scans the room and spots the space next to me where Ady usually stands.

"Where's Ady?" he asks gruffly.

"I don't know, boss. He didn't pick me up at the usual time, and he isn't answering his phone."

"I'll give him two minutes, and then he's on his second strike."

I don't know why Jonny feels the need to warn me. I'm not Ady's keeper.

Those two minutes come and go, and my errant colleague fails to show. That means I'll be working on my own again today. Hopefully, it'll be less eventful than Monday.

To avoid any awkwardness, I wait until Big Fal enters Keira's office before I venture in. We swap pleasantries, but Keira is closer to her usual self, only breaking cover once Big Fal departs.

"I'm sorry if I embarrassed you yesterday," she says in a hushed voice.

"It's forgotten."

"I wish it was. I feel terrible."

"Seriously, Keira. Just forget it."

"That's easy for you to say. I kicked up such a fuss when the lads overstepped the mark, and then I went and asked you out on a date. I shouldn't have done that."

"I won't tell anyone if you don't. Please, let's just pretend it never happened."

Keira nods but avoids looking up at me while handing over the keys to a van. Not wanting to prolong the awkwardness, I depart in a hurry.

There's still no sign of Ady's car when I wander out to the yard. I loiter for a few minutes just in case he's running late, but to no avail. I hop in the van and set off.

Working alone, I'm too busy to notice any female attention as I empty bin after bin. I finish just before noon, and much like Monday, I decide I'm deserving of a decent lunch. It's an easy decision without my perpetually-skint colleague in tow.

As I make my way towards The Vale Cafe, a thought occurs. "Ah, crap."

I may have sorted the situation with Keira, but I now have to face Heather and her reaction to my newfound attraction. Is double egg and chips worth the potential trouble? It probably isn't, but it could be months before Colin is back behind the counter, and I know my favourite cafe has been struggling of late. I don't want to add to their financial woes by boycotting the place, so I've no choice but to face Heather. If it comes to it, I'll use the same excuse I used with Keira—I'm already dating.

Ten minutes later, I push open the door to The Vale Cafe. It's relatively quiet again, with no queue at the counter. It's just as well there's no queue as there's no one present to serve. I brace myself for the inevitable and call Heather's name.

A moment passes, and a clearly-flustered Heather appears, wiping her hands on her apron.

"Sorry, Dougie," she mumbles.

"No problem. Everything okay?"

"Just a glitch with the toaster," she replies dismissively. "What can I get you?"

Heather stands silent, pen at the ready. True to form, she's avoiding eye contact.

"Double egg and chips, please, and a tea."

"Okay," she replies, scribbling my order on a pad. "Anything else?"

Our eyes meet for a fraction of a second, but Heather quickly looks back down at the pad. Her reaction is confusing because it's unlike every woman I've encountered over the last four days. Heather's uncomfortable indifference is the same today as it was on Monday.

"Err, no. Thanks."

"Take a seat. I'll bring your tea over."

With that, she shuffles over to the hot water urn.

Something isn't right.

I take a seat at a table and surreptitiously study Heather as she prepares the tea. There's not so much as a furtive glance in my direction.

Panic arrives.

Lying awake the other night, I theorised about the gift losing potency over time, like ibuprofen or English mustard. Keira was certainly more constrained this morning, but I put that down to our conversation about my relationship status. Heather, though, is just being ... Heather.

The woman in question arrives at my table.

"One tea," she says impassively. "Your food won't be long."

I smile up at her, hoping to ignite the flames of attraction. I'm rewarded with a slight upturn of Heather's lips; a flicker of a semi-smile. It's so fleeting she's already on her way back to the kitchen before I can respond.

I'm left with a mug of tea and a growing sense of unease. Either Heather is immune to the gift, or its powers are already on the wane. I'm not fussed about Heather's indifference, but there is the small matter of a date with Zoe to consider. I can think of no greater humiliation than meeting her tomorrow and seeing the look of horror on her face when she realises her mistake.

I sit and stew for five minutes until my lunch arrives. It's delivered with the minimum of conversation, which only stokes my concerns. Appetite ruined, I clear half the plate and head to the counter. Rather than waste time, I put a ten-pound note next to the till and call through the serving hatch to let Heather know. I need to confirm if the gift is still giving.

Outside the cafe, I appraise my options, and a Shell petrol station just across the road seems a reasonable bet. I hurry over and enter the small shop. As luck would have it, a bored-looking woman is behind the counter, picking her nails. I approach.

"Hi."

She looks up. The badge on her jumper confirms a name: Debs.

"Oh, um … hi," she stumbles when our eyes meet. "Sorry, I was miles away."

"That's okay. I was wondering if you sell air fresheners?"

"Sure. Let me show you."

The dread I felt back in the cafe eases as Debs scuttles from behind the counter. Her bright smile and willingness to assist are positive signs, but for all I know, Debs' cheeriness might be her default manner.

I follow her to the back wall of the shop and a small stand displaying motoring accessories.

"What's your favourite," she asks. "Vanilla, cherry, or forest pine?"

"I'll take a vanilla one, please."

She plucks a tree-shaped air freshener from the display and turns to face me.

"I love the smell of vanilla. It's so moreish, don't you think?"

"Yep, it's a nice smell."

She moves closer and then tilts her head to the side.

"My perfume has a vanilla-bean base note. Have a sniff if you like."

In one sense, this situation is welcome because the gift is clearly dictating this woman's behaviour. In another sense, it's not welcome. Should I encourage her? I take a tentative sniff.

"It's very nice," I remark before glancing up at a clock behind the counter. "Oh, is that the time? I'm running late."

"Oh, right. I don't suppose ..."

"I'm meeting my girlfriend for lunch."

Her smile fades, and I immediately feel awful. I've experienced the cold sting of disappointment too many times, and I loathe the thought of inflicting it on someone else, especially as Debs has the sparkliest blue eyes and the cutest dimples. Alas, I'd wager she's also in her late forties and therefore unlikely to want kids.

I apologise and hurry out of the shop.

With no fly-tipping duties to perform, I drive slowly towards one of the town's parks, as per Jonny's instructions. Litter picking on a damp afternoon isn't my idea of a good time, but a local councillor has received complaints about it, so needs must.

As I pull up outside the park, I'm still no closer to understanding what happened with Heather. The problem trying to understand the incomprehensible is that there's no room for logic. I have no idea why women suddenly find me so appealing, so how in God's name am I supposed to unpick why one particular woman doesn't?

With a headache brewing, I switch my focus to an equally unfathomable subject: littering. Manor Park isn't particularly large at just over three acres, and there are nine bins dotted along the pathways. By my reckoning, the furthest anyone would have to walk to dispose of their rubbish would be a hundred yards. And yet, even that short distance is too far for some, judging by the food wrappers strewn across the lawns, the cans and bottles shoved in bushes, and a dirty nappy dumped under a bench. Some days, I despair at people. I really do.

Fortunately, a steady drizzle ensures the park is near-deserted, so I'm able to get on with my job undisturbed. The hours drift by, and the working day finally comes to an end. Back at the depot, I check the van back in with minimal fuss and head home.

A good omen, perhaps, and, by the time I unlock the front door, the rain has stopped. The change in weather is reason enough to spend the rest of the afternoon at Tinkerton Meadow.

I hop into the shower and get dressed. I'm just about to leave when the doorbell rings. I rarely have visitors, so it's likely a delivery driver with a parcel, although I can't remember what or when I last ordered online.

I hurry down the hall and open the front door. It's not a delivery driver, but one of the last people I expected to see on my doorstep.

"Oh, Leanne. Hi."

Ady's girlfriend tries hard to find a smile. Her coffee-coloured hair is unusually windswept, and there's not a trace of makeup on her face. She looks washed out.

"Hey, Dougie. I'm sorry to drop by unannounced, but I was wondering if you've seen Ady?"

"Err, no. I haven't seen him since yesterday afternoon."

"He wasn't at work today?"

"No. I tried calling him this morning, but it went straight through to voicemail."

Leanne reacts to my news by bowing her head and pinching the bridge of her nose.

"Is there something going on, Leanne? He's been acting out of sorts for a while now."

She looks up, straight at me, as if she's about to answer my question. No words follow, but her wide eyes say an awful lot.

"Can I come in, Dougie?"

Shit. This could become very awkward very quickly.

"Err, I was just on my way out. Can it wait?"

"I'm worried sick, and I've no one else to turn to."

"What about his mum?"

"She's not well, and I don't want to put her in a panic unless I really have to."

My conscience makes the decision.

"Come in."

I wave my unannounced guest into the hallway and invite her to go through to the lounge. As she removes her coat, I question how a girl like Leanne ended up with Ady. He's a good-looking lad but unquestionably shallow and prone to bouts of naivety. Leanne, on the other hand, is strait-laced and sensible. On more than one occasion, Ady has joked that his girlfriend acts more like his mum than his actual mum, but she gives better blowjobs. I never asked, but I assumed he meant Leanne.

"Do you want to sit down?"

"Thanks."

She perches on the edge of the sofa. I consider offering a cup of tea, but I don't want to make her too comfortable. Instead, I sit down in the armchair. Before I can open my mouth to say anything, Leanne's mobile chirps a notification. She hurriedly checks the screen and then puffs a prolonged breath.

"It's Ady," she says, shaking her head. "He's at home and wants to know what's for dinner."

"Panic over, then."

"For now."

Rather than get up and leave, Leanne stares silently at the carpet.

"Are you okay?" I ask. "Is there something going on with that boyfriend of yours?"

"If I tell you, will you promise not to say anything to him?"

"I guess so."

She takes a moment to compose herself, and then looks straight at me.

"I think Ady is cheating on me."

"Oh. I didn't think he was ... wait, what evidence do you have?"

"This isn't the first time he's done a disappearing act. The last time, he said he was playing cards at a mate's house and ended up crashing on his sofa."

"That sounds plausible."

"Yes, but then he's really guarded about his phone—he takes it with him everywhere, even to the bathroom."

I can't deny I've noticed Ady's obsession with his phone of late.

"Is there anything else?" I ask.

"He's always skint. He's never been great with money which is why we have separate bank accounts, but when he used to waste money, at least I knew what he was wasting it on because he'd order all sorts of pointless crap from Amazon. Now, I've no idea where Ady is spending his money."

"Okay, I guess you've grounds for suspicion, but why not just ask him?"

"I have, and he swears blind he's not being unfaithful."

"And you don't believe him?"

"I don't know," she replies meekly. "Maybe I'm just being paranoid, but if you'd ever been cheated on, you'd understand how hard it is to trust again."

"Ady's cheated on you before?"

"No, not Ady—a previous boyfriend. This feels like history repeating itself, and I'm starting to wonder if it's me."

"You?"

"If two blokes cheat on me in succession, maybe I'm doing something wrong."

"No, you mustn't think like that."

"Why not?" she gulps. "Stands to reason, doesn't it?"

"Firstly, you don't know that Ady is cheating on you, and secondly, if someone is willing to cheat on you, they're the one with the problem. You shouldn't ever blame yourself."

"Easier said than done. You've no idea how hard it is."

I open my mouth to launch a defence but stop before the words reach my lips. This isn't about me, and I don't want to get too embroiled in my colleague's domestic affairs.

"Listen, Leanne. I wish I could help, but Ady has never said anything to me about another woman."

"He might if you asked him."

"I doubt it."

"He looks up to you, like a big brother. You're one of the few people he'd listen to."

"So, you want me to discuss your concerns with him?"

"God, no. He can't know I've been talking to you … airing our dirty laundry."

"What am I supposed to do then?"

"I know you can't ask him outright, but if you casually dropped the odd question into the conversation, he might eventually open up. You could ask where he was last night and why he didn't make it into work."

"I've tried that before, but he just closes up."

"Please, Dougie," she pleads. "I don't know how else to deal with this."

"As I said, can't you just ask him?"

"If he is seeing someone else, he'll just lie. If he's not, he'll think I don't trust him. It's a lose-lose situation. I just want to know for my own peace of mind. Please, Dougie."

She fixes me with the saddest pair of eyes, like the last puppy in the pet shop. Then, to smash any final resistance, she starts crying.

"Okay, okay. I'll do what I can."

"Thank you," Leanne sniffs. "I do appreciate it."

I stand up and glance up at the clock on the wall. There's barely an hour of daylight remaining. Taking the hint, Leanne stands up.

"I'm so sorry. I didn't mean to hold you up."

"It's okay."

"I'll give you my number, and then I'll get out of your hair."

"Err, your number?"

"So you can call me if Ady says anything."

"Oh, right."

We swap phone numbers, and I see a still-weepy Leanne to the front door. I'm about to open it when she places a hand on my shoulder.

"You're a good man, Dougie."

Without warning, Leanne then throws her arms around me. I'd be lying if I said I don't like a nice hug, and it's definitely one of the things I miss the most as a bachelor. However, Leanne's hug is so tight it verges on inappropriate. It continues too long, and I sense an unwelcome stirring in the trouser department.

I clear my throat. Leanne finally unlocks her arms, and I'm able to take a step back, but not before I receive a peck on the cheek.

"Thank you," she says, less tearful than she was a moment ago.

"No problem."

Her reluctance to leave is matched only by my motivation to see her gone. Eventually, I manage to usher her out the door. Within seconds, I vow that any future communications with Leanne will be by phone and phone alone. I would never mess around with a mate's other half and, based upon the half-a-dozen times I've met Leanne in the past, she wouldn't ordinarily look twice at me in that way. However, we're no longer in ordinary times.

Being attractive is an amazing feeling, but attracting the wrong women is a side-effect I can do without.

Lesson learned, I hope.

Chapter 19

I woke up in the middle of the night, courtesy of a vivid dream. It was more of a nightmare, really; a wholly improper scene involving Leanne and Keira, a king-size bed, and six litres of Ben & Jerry's cookie dough ice cream.

Still perturbed as I munch on a slice of toast, I think I understand why my imagination is conjuring up such taboo imagery—sex.

Years ago, I watched the film *Cast Away*, starring Tom Hanks. It was about a FedEx executive who ends up stranded on an uninhabited island after his plane crashes into the ocean. As I watched it, I pondered how I might fare in such a situation, and I concluded that I'd have no choice but to live on plants because I couldn't catch, kill, or butcher my own dinner.

If I had to spend four years on that island, as Hanks' character did, I'd try to forget all about eating meat because it'd be like a punishment for a man who loves a bacon sandwich. I'd likely return to civilisation a fully-fledged vegan, but it wouldn't take more than the aroma of fried chicken to reactivate my inner-carnivore.

I reckon there are parallels between that enforced veganism scenario and my sex life.

Having lived a life of enforced celibacy for so long, I've trained my mind not to dwell on sex. Now and then, I might indulge in a spot of self-relief if the mood takes me, but it's like eating vegetarian sausages—a pale imitation of the real thing.

Now, though, sex is no longer just something other people do. It's a realistic possibility in my not-too-distant future. Perhaps I didn't realise how much I missed it, and that hug with Leanne was enough to remind me. Thank Christ I'm not so desperate I'd ever act on those inappropriate urges, but for the first time in my life, I have a faint inkling of why people cheat. Impulse, plus attraction, plus opportunity equals ... I don't want to think about it.

I'm never buying Ben & Jerry's ice cream again.

Two minutes early, Ady pulls up outside whilst I'm still buttoning up my coat. He's already in for the mother of all bollockings, so I guess he can't afford to be a second late today. I lock up and hurry down the path to his car.

"You made it today, then?" I joke, as I fall into the passenger's seat.

"Just," he grunts.

We set off, but there's little in the way of conversation. I find myself questioning what I should say, comparing it to what Ady might expect me to say and what I need to say to get the answers Leanne wants. Between those three positions, I'm just confused. Why did I agree to this? I'm a terrible liar, and I'm not much better at subtlety.

"What happened yesterday?" I ask.

"Nothing."

"Why didn't you show up for work?"

"I wasn't feeling too clever."

"That's twice this week. Shouldn't you see a doctor?"

"Nah, I'm fine."

"But what if you're not fine tomorrow?"

"Just drop it, eh."

"Suit yourself, but don't come crying to me when Jonny fires you."

"He can't fire me. I've got rights."

"Alright," I shrug. "You know best."

I fold my arms and look out of the side window. A minute or so passes before Ady speaks again.

"Can he fire me?" he asks.

"He said something about yesterday being your second strike. By that, he probably means you're a hair's breadth away from being fired ... unless there's a good reason you've been off this week?"

I wait for an answer that doesn't come.

"Listen, mate," I say in a conciliatory tone. "I don't want to pry into your personal life, but I'd be gutted if you got the sack."

"You would?"

"Yes, because they'd set me up with a new partner, and he might turn out to be an even bigger bellend than the partner I've got."

My attempt at ice-breaking works as Ady snorts a laugh.

"Seriously, though," I continue. "You said the other day you had a few money worries—losing your job won't help with those worries, will it?"

"No."

"So, if you've got a problem you're struggling with, you only need to ask, and I'll do what I can to help. You know what they say about a problem shared, eh?"

"I know," Ady replies. "I appreciate it."

The silence returns. I've said enough, and if I keep pressing him, he'll wonder what I'm up to. Ady might be a bit slow on the uptake but he's not a complete moron.

We arrive at the depot, and as soon as the morning meeting is over, Jonny summons Ady into his office, leaving me to visit Keira and sign out a van. The last time I saw her, in my dream, she was provocatively licking a dessert spoon. With that image still fresh in my mind, it's a brief but uncomfortable conversation.

I wander out to the yard where Ady is waiting by the last remaining van. He's puffing on a cigarette like it's his last.

"You've still got a job, I assume?" I ask, unlocking the van.

Ady doesn't reply until we're both seated in the cab.

"Yeah, you were right. Jonny gave me a final warning about my attendance."

"Didn't you tell him you weren't well?"

"That wasn't the issue. If we're sick, we're supposed to call in before our shift starts, but I didn't call in till late morning."

"Oh, I see. Why didn't you call when you knew you wouldn't be coming in?"

"I was up half the night and didn't get up on time."

"Didn't Leanne wake you?"

This is the moment. Will Ady lie, or will he tell me where he really was?

"I wasn't at home."

"Where were you, then?"

"I crashed at a mate's house."

That's exactly what he told Leanne. He's either telling the truth or he's a consistent liar.

"Twice in one week?"

"Yeah. So?"

"So, nothing. What you do with your evenings isn't any of my business."

"No, it ain't."

"Alright, stroppy arse. If you want to fuck up your job and your relationship, go ahead—it's no skin off my nose."

My point made, I start the van and pull out of the yard without another word. I should have known not to get involved, and now I have to suffer Ady's sulky attitude all day.

I turn my thoughts to this evening and my date with Zoe. The residual angst with Ady is immediately diluted by a frothing cocktail of excitement and trepidation.

As the day progresses, my moody colleague lightens up a bit. Not wanting to provoke another strop, I steer our conversations well away from his home life. Leanne is probably right to be suspicious, but I'm far from convinced Ady is seeing someone else. If he's having his cake and eating it, surely he'd be in a better mood.

We finish for the day, and on the drive back to my place, Ady asks what I'm up to over the weekend. I'm just about to brag about my date with a beautiful young woman but stop just in the nick of time. Ady couldn't keep a secret if his life depended upon it, and if I tell him, it'll be all around the depot by lunchtime Monday. As Keira thinks I'm already in a relationship, it'll make an already awkward situation ten times worse if she discovers I lied, no matter how white that lie might be.

"Nothing exciting," I reply.

Seeing as I never do anything exciting with my weekends, Ady isn't surprised.

"Right. I'll see you Monday," he mumbles before speeding away.

As soon as I get in, I check the time and then my phone: the former to confirm how long I've got before I leave at 6:45 pm, and the latter to confirm Zoe hasn't sent a message to cancel. I've got a few minutes shy of three hours to get ready, and if Zoe is inclined to cancel, she's leaving it late.

An hour later, I do receive a message from Zoe, but it's only to say how much she's looking forward to tonight. I reply, saying I'm also looking forward to it. In truth, I'm petrified.

Just after five o'clock, I sit down in front of the television with a microwaved lasagne. I pick at the starchy pasta, but my earlier excitement is now laced with anxiety, and I've no appetite. If someone could bottle the side effects of anxiety, they could sell it as the world's most effective diet aid. Admittedly, the heart palpitations, sweaty palms, and the threat of explosive diarrhoea are a slight downside.

The only antidote to my jitters is a relaxing bath. I throw the remains of my dinner in the bin and head upstairs.

If nothing else, lying in a tub of hot water does wonders for my aching muscles. With no distractions, though, it also allows my mind to wander.

Ten days ago, I was lying in this very bath preparing for a date with Carol. Although I was a little nervous, my expectations were so low they stifled the worst of the anxiety. Now, the game has changed. With the gift in play, I don't have to worry about being rejected because of my looks, but there's plenty to be worried about. What if she thinks I'm dull or the sound of my voice grates? What if she can't stand the way I laugh, or I say something she vehemently disagrees with? What if she hates the scent of my cologne or my choice of clothes? What if she …

"Jesus, Dougie! Give it a rest."

I hold a breath and slip beneath the water. Hopefully, the prospect of drowning will serve as a distraction.

As it transpires, I don't drown, but I can't wholly banish my qualms either. I keep telling myself it'll be fine, and I shouldn't be so nervy. I have an advantage most men would give their right arm for, and I need to focus on that advantage. Hell, it's the only reason this date is happening.

By the time I've finished getting dressed, I feel fractionally better, but I could do with some extra insurance, so my anxiety doesn't ruin the date before it starts. I raid the kitchen cupboard for a bottle of vodka and pour a generous shot into a glass together with a splash of orange juice.

Once that's dispatched, I refill the glass twice more, just to be on the safe side.

Out on the street, a horn blares—my taxi awaits. I glance up at the kitchen clock.

Show time.

Chapter 20

What is it with taxi drivers? When you're not in the mood for a chat, you get one who won't shut up. When you want a spot of light conversion to help ease pre-date nerves, you end up being driven by a mute.

He drops me off outside the bar Zoe suggested and takes payment with an insincere thank you.

I'm five minutes early—time enough for another drink.

I head inside and immediately regret not researching this establishment. It's just the kind of uber-cool bar I'd go out of my way to avoid. Too late now.

On the upside, it's busy but not rammed. Judging by their attire, I'd guess the majority of the customers are enjoying post-work drinks. I navigate past a group of suits milling around by the bar area. No one pays me any attention.

I order a lager and stare at rows of coloured bottles lined up on the back wall whilst the barman pulls my pint.

"That'll be £6.50, please, mate."

"Sorry, did you say £6.50 ... for a pint?"

"I'm afraid so."

There's no sense complaining to the messenger. It must be galling that the price of one pint probably isn't much less than he earns in an hour. I hand him a tenner.

"Keep the change."

"That's good of you. Thanks."

I had hoped my generous tip might encourage the barman to chat, but he drifts off to serve another customer. I guess this isn't the kind of place where the bar staff have the time or inclination to chew the cud with regulars.

I perch on one of the high stools lined up alongside the bar and wait.

It doesn't take long to establish I haven't chosen the best vantage point. My view of the door is blocked by a couple of wide brick pillars, a growing gaggle of office workers, and a steady stream of customers ordering drinks.

There's not much I can do but hope that Zoe spots me.

The minutes tick by, and I happen to check the time at precisely seven o'clock. As I look up, I catch sight of a woman with blonde hair hurrying in my direction, maybe fifteen feet away. She doesn't look much like the woman waiting tables in the Fox & Hounds until her head turns in my direction.

"Dougie!" she almost shrieks. "You're here."

I am here, but I now wish I wasn't. If Zoe's looks were intimidating before, she's now off-the-scale stunning. She steps forward and offers a hug, which isn't easy to reciprocate while perched on a stool.

"Hi," I squawk. "Can I get you a drink?"

"Ooh, please. I'll have a gin and tonic."

I catch the barman's eye, and my earlier tip ensures prompt service.

Zoe takes a quick sip of her drink and then removes her coat, revealing a beautifully tailored mini-dress with a pair of heeled shoes that look impossible to walk on. On looks alone, I have no right even breathing the same air as my date.

"You look amazing," I remark, as she drags a stool right up to mine and hops on to it.

"Thank you, but I bet you say that to all the girls."

"Ha-ha ... yeah."

She takes another slow sip from her glass whilst my urge to flee intensifies. I am so far out of my comfort zone I might as well be sitting here debating world politics with Barack Obama or astrophysics with Professor Brian Cox. Admittedly, neither would look as good in a mini-dress.

"Are you okay?" Zoe asks. "You look a bit ... uncomfortable."

"I, err ..."

This is ridiculous. What was I thinking?

"I'm sorry, Zoe. It's not you, it's me."

Christ. Did I just say that?

"Eh? Are you bailing on me?"

"No, it's not like that. If I'm being honest, I feel a bit of a fraud sitting here with you."

"I don't understand. I asked you out, didn't I?"

"Yes, but let's be frank: you're gorgeous, and I'm ... I'm not."

"That's bullshit and you know it. Every woman in this place is giving you the eye."

I slowly turn my head and catch at least three sets of female eyes looking in my direction. I also catch one or two blokes throwing a puzzled frown our way. I've got a good idea what they're thinking.

"If I ask you a question, Dougie, will you give me a straight answer?"

"Of course."

"Do you regret saying yes to this date?"

I pride myself on being open and honest, so I have to tell Zoe the truth ... or a version of the truth she'll understand.

"I don't regret saying yes to the date, but I do feel a bit un-comfortable."

"Is it this place?"

It's a good question. The venue certainly isn't helping ease my imposter syndrome.

"Honestly, this isn't my scene at all."

Her smile returns.

"Why didn't you say so, silly? It is a bit pretentious, but I wanted to impress you."

"You did?"

"I'm just a waitress in a pub. That's not exactly glamorous, is it?"

I can't help but chuckle.

"What's so funny?" Zoe asks.

"Trust me—I couldn't care less what you do for a living."

"Oh."

"And you don't have to impress me. I'm a simple man with simple tastes."

Her lips curl into a mischievous smile.

"In which case," she says, her hands resting on my knees. "I have a proposition for you."

"I'm listening."

"There's an off-licence up the road. Why don't we go there, grab some drinks and head back to my place ... if you're looking for somewhere a bit more down to earth."

I've never had an out-of-body experience before, but all of a sudden, I'm no longer perched on a stool but floating up near the ceiling, looking down on a stunningly beautiful woman trying to entice a flabby, middle-aged loser back to her flat. The scene is so surreal, so unbelievably fanciful; I don't even flinch when the flabby, middle-aged loser nods his head.

"We have a plan," Zoe says excitedly. "Shall we finish our drinks and split?"

"Sure."

I'm back in my body, but the sense of detachment remains. I gulp back my overpriced lager and stand up.

"Oh, before we go, can I get a selfie with you?"

Zoe fishes her phone from the pocket of her coat and stands up.

"You want a picture of me?"

"No, I want a picture of us together."

"Dare I ask why?"

"It's our first date, and I want to post an Instagram story tomorrow."

I have a Facebook account I haven't used in years, and that's about as far as my social media usage goes. It's a stark reminder of the difference in our ages.

"Um, okay."

Zoe moves to my side and rests her chin on my shoulder, the feel of her hair brushing my cheek and the scent of her perfume adding to the surrealism. She then raises her phone, so both our faces are in the middle of the screen and then taps the camera icon. If my gift ever wears off, I hope Zoe's photo-editing skills are up to scratch.

"Perfect," she coos before tapping the screen a few times.

Being the gentleman I am, I help my date into her coat and politely nod a goodbye to the barman. Much like the other men in the room, his face is a picture of mild bewilderment, or perhaps envy. He is precisely the kind of handsome young man who *should* be leaving with a girl like Zoe. I don't think either of us can quite believe I am.

Once we're out on the pavement, Zoe takes my hand. It might be dark, but the street is well lit, and despite that, the raised chin and permanent smile suggest Zoe isn't in the slightest bit embarrassed to be seen with me.

We reach the off-licence and pick up eight cans of lager and two bottles of Prosecco.

"It's only a five-minute walk to my place," Zoe says. "But we could always get a cab if you can't wait."

"I'm fine walking," I reply confidently. "I can wait five minutes for another beer."

She responds with a look I can't quite decipher. We continue up the road, hand in hand.

On the way, I do my best to stoke conversation. Zoe likes to talk, I discover, which is fine by me as I prefer to listen. She tells how she moved back to Ashbridge a few months ago after living in Birmingham for six years. The job at The Fox & Hounds is only temporary whilst she tries to work out what she wants to do with the rest of her life.

"My parents keep telling me I should settle down," she says.

"Is that what you want to do?"

"I like to be impulsive, whereas my older sister is the sensible one. She's always on my back about my irresponsible ways."

"Would I be right in saying she wouldn't invite a man back to her flat on a first date?"

"Absolutely not. In fairness, though, she had a bad experience with a guy at uni, and that put her off men for ages."

We arrive at a small block of flats, and Zoe opens the door to the communal hallway.

"I'll apologise in advance about my flat," she says. "It's a bit of a dump, but it's all I can afford at the moment."

"I'm sure it's fine."

I'm not, but I don't know how else to respond.

We climb the stairs to the first floor, and I follow my date to flat three. She removes her coat and suggests I hang mine next to hers in the cramped hallway. I then follow her through to the lounge with a kitchenette area at one end and just enough room for a sofa, coffee table, and a bookcase.

"I did warn you," she chuckles.

"It's cosy."

"It'll get cosier," she purrs, taking the carrier bag from my hand. "Sit down, and I'll fetch some glasses."

On the way to the kitchen area, she presses the button on a stereo, and a slow track begins.

"Do you like Celeste?" Zoe asks as she opens the fridge.

"Err, I can't say I've ever heard of her."

"She's so cool. I love this album."

All modern music sounds the same to me, but Celeste's voice has a distinctly vintage edge, like she's singing from a stage in a smoky jazz club.

Zoe returns with one of the Prosecco bottles, two glasses, and a can of lager. She pours us both a drink and sits down next to me.

"Cheers, and here's to a fun-filled evening."

I clink my glass against hers.

"Cheers."

I drink more when I'm nervous, which is probably why I down three cans within the first hour—Zoe matches me drink for drink, demolishing the first bottle of Prosecco. Despite a few flirty touches and a lot of innuendoes we haven't reached first base yet, but we are becoming increasingly tipsy.

And then, that changes in an instant.

I put my glass on the table and sit back. Zoe then suddenly leaps from her seat and sits astride me. Before I can react, her mouth is on mine, her tongue thrashing around like a grounded salmon. I'm so taken aback by the dramatic change in speed, I remain a passive participant for a moment or two. It then crosses my mind that Zoe may have made an incorrect assumption. Kenny once told me that some younger women prefer a mature man because they're more experienced in matters carnal.

As it is, I'm responding to Zoe's affections like a virgin teenager. I need to up my game.

I lose all track of time as we kiss and fondle and groan and gasp. Every now and then, I open my eyes just to be sure I'm not asleep. Never in my wildest dreams could I ever have imagined making out with a woman like Zoe. Not only is she stunningly beautiful, but her enthusiasm appears boundless.

Unsurprisingly, she notices the prominent bulge in my trousers.

"Someone's come out to play, I see," she whispers in my ear whilst stroking my erection through two layers of polyester.

"He has," I whimper.

"Wait here."

She leaps off my lap and disappears through the door to the hallway. I use the break in play to down a few mouthfuls of lager. I've barely got my breath back when Zoe appears in the doorway.

"Ohh ..."

She strides towards me, wearing nothing but the skimpiest thong and her high-heeled shoes.

"Stand up," she orders.

I do as I'm told. If my erection wasn't obvious before, it sure as hell is now.

Zoe moves in for another bout of heavy kissing, but this time, she has other plans for her hands. As she slowly unbuckles my belt, I grasp the opportunity to run my hands across her peach-smooth backside. It's been so long since I last touched a woman. I can't remember if it always felt so amazing.

Having removed my belt, Zoe unbuttons my trousers. Three rapid beats of my heart pass, and I know what's about to happen. Then, it does.

"Ohhhh ... sweet Jesus!"

Rather than grab hold of my erect penis, Zoe delicately strokes her hand up and down the shaft. It is the most divine sensation.

"Do you like that?" she asks, her voice low and husky.

"Very much ... indeeeeed!"

My response only encourages Zoe, and the stroking intensifies. A tiny voice in my brain suggests I should ask her to ease off, but a much louder, more enthusiastic voice tells me to shut the fuck up and just enjoy it. This time last week, I was watching *Who Wants to be a Millionaire* on TV and working my way through a tub of Twiglets. I like a quiz as much as the next man, but ...

Oh, no.

Ohh, noooo!

Much like the operators at Chernobyl, I realise too late I-
'm facing a critical pressure issue, albeit testicular rather than
nuclear. It is now apparent I'm only seconds away from an
unplanned and catastrophic explosion.

"I ... I ..."

I seem to have lost the ability to talk. I've no option but
to interject physically. I withdraw my hand from Zoe's pert
buttock, intent on grabbing her wrist before she administers
the fatal stroke, but the timing is lousy. Without warning, she
increases both her grip and intensity in one cataclysmic stroke.

"Hummmphhh!"

My knees buckle, and it's all I can do to keep myself upright
as the orgasm arrives. I don't think I've ever experienced such
exhilaration *and* humiliation in the same intense moment. As
the final orgasmic waves ebb away, I dare to open my eyes.

Zoe is standing a foot or so away, her right hand dangling in
the air like she's just plunged a blocked toilet without a plunger.

"Oops," is all I can say.

"You could have warned me," she says flatly.

"I'm so sorry. It's been a while, and I couldn't help myself."

Her expression softens a touch.

"It's okay. Let's just call that an appetiser, shall we?"

"Yes, let's."

"Come with me."

She takes my hand and leads me back to the hallway.

"Right, I need to visit the bathroom to clean up. Why don't
you make yourself comfortable in here," she says, opening the
door to the bedroom, "And when I'm done in the bathroom,
you can return the favour, eh?"

"Return the ... oh, yes. Of course."

She flashes a grin, then nudges me into her lair and closes the
door. A few seconds later, I hear the shower pump whine into

action. Jesus, did my Chernobyl moment generate that much fallout?

I turn and assess my surroundings. The room is barely large enough to contain a double bed and a few items of furniture. A lamp on the bedside table offers just enough light to illuminate the clothes strewn across the floor and clutter on every flat surface.

I remind myself I'm not here to critique Zoe's domestic skills. She'll finish showering in less than a minute, and I have a crisis on my hands.

When my date returns, she'll be bringing certain expectations with her—expectations I'm not convinced I can meet. She has essentially requested an orgasm, and I can see two immediate problems with that. Firstly, it's been twenty-odd years since I last attempted to bring a woman to orgasm. Secondly, that attempt failed miserably, much like the previous attempts.

I begin pacing up and down the narrow strip of laundry-free carpet. My nerves jangling and penis limp, I stop and close my eyes.

"Breathe, Dougie. Breathe," I whisper.

When I open my eyes again, I'm looking directly at a chest of drawers up against the back wall. On top, there's a stuffed teddy bear next to a framed photograph of four adults huddled together. Even in the dim light, I can see one of those adults is Zoe, together with another woman of a similar age and two who look closer to my age. My best guess is it's a family photo featuring Zoe, her sister, and their parents.

Strangely, it's her dad's features that catch my attention: balding, tall, and slightly overweight. To the left of the photograph, there's a make-up mirror, and I can't help but glance at my reflection. I then look back at the family photo and then the mirror again.

"Oh, shitting hell."

At a guess, Zoe's dad must be at least ten to fifteen years older than me, but most people wouldn't know it due to my already-bald head and weathered complexion. What would that man think if he knew what his daughter was up to this evening? More to the point, what would he think of me?

I know what I'd think.

In an instant, my situation loses all semblance of eroticism. A measure of sobriety soon follows. This is no longer two consenting adults about to engage in passionate love-making. It's one sad, middle-aged man about to defile someone's daughter. Worse still, that daughter has no idea her lover's appeal is merely an illusion—a trick at best, a con at worst.

The shower pump ceases its whine.

In the time it takes for Zoe to dry herself, I button up my trousers, grab my coat from the lounge, and silently exit the flat.

The shame of running out on my date is hard to bear, but not as hard as the guilt I'd have suffered if I'd stayed. It's a cold consolation on a cold walk home.

Chapter 21

Half-six in the morning. I turn the shower on, and my hand stings the moment water comes into contact with it—the angry skin a result of a tic I thought I'd conquered. As a child, I'd chew my nails whenever I felt anxious. By my early twenties, I'd moved on to chewing my knuckles—I had plenty to be anxious about back then.

When I returned from Zoe's last night, I flopped on the sofa and remained there for an hour, replaying every awful moment of the evening. It took most of that hour to get past the humiliation, and then shame rocked up. I tried applying a coping mechanism taught to me by a therapist many years ago. Yes, I made a complete fool of myself, but it could have been worse, couldn't it?

After lengthy thought, I concluded it could.

Yes, I did prematurely shoot my load over a woman way too young to be fondling my manhood, but at least I left with just my dignity in shreds. My sense of morality, although bruised, remained intact. In the end, I did the right thing—kind of.

Within those few first minutes of departing Zoe's flat, I experienced something of an epiphany. I realised where I'd gone wrong. It was a question of inexperience and stunning naivety.

Flicking through a newspaper some weeks ago, I came across a photo of a badly damaged Ferrari 448 being loaded onto a recovery truck. My interest piqued, I read the accompanying story. A kid in his early twenties had purchased the high-performance supercar after winning ten-million quid on the lottery. On his first drive, he got a bit too cocky and lost control of his expensive new toy, landing it upside down in a ditch. He walked away unscathed, but the car itself wasn't so fortunate, nor were the insurance company who faced a £250,000 claim. I had little sympathy for the driver or his insurers.

However, the relevance of that story wasn't lost on me.

For the same reason young men should not be driving high-powered supercars, I should not be dating women like Zoe. Both are fine to look at, but both need to be handled by those with the relevant experience.

I reached a conclusion and coined it the Goldilocks Principle. I don't want a partner so young and pretty we'll attract bewildered gasps whenever we walk down the street together. Nor do I want a partner like Carol—too old and battle-scarred, with motherhood firmly in her rear-view mirror. I want a partner who is somewhere in the middle. Someone just right.

That someone is definitely not Zoe, so on the walk back home last night, I sent her a text message. I said I was genuinely sorry for running out on her, but it was for the best because she deserved better than me. I begged for forgiveness, but her expletive-ridden reply didn't suggest she was in a forgiving mood. I figured I'd only stoke her rage if I engaged, so I blocked her number. Sometimes you need to be cruel to be kind.

It was a night that will live long in the memory, but for all the wrong reasons.

I get dressed and hurry out to the car. My mind is still ablaze, and the best antidote is the tranquillity of Tinkerton Meadow.

When I turn into the car park, I pull up alongside Kenny's Volvo. I'm not sure if his being here is a good thing or not. Last night's events are still raw, and I don't know if I'm ready to talk about what happened, but I need to unburden the residue guilt.

I'm halfway up Falbert's Mount when I reach a decision.

At the top, the scene is spectacular; the horizon streaked with purple and amber clouds reflected on the still waters of the lake like a Constable watercolour. If I don't see a bird of note all morning, the journey would have been worthwhile for the view alone. It helps to ease my anxieties.

"Morning," my friend calls out as I approach the edge of the Mount.

"Morning. Been here long?"

"Ten minutes."

I come to a halt beside Kenny.

"Have you spotted anything?"

"I haven't even got my binoculars out yet. I was just soaking up the view."

"It's a fine one."

We stand and silently drink in the view. Lovely as it is, I need to offload.

"I had a date last night."

"You did? With who?"

"Zoe from the Fox & Hounds."

"Wait ... I thought that was a wind-up."

"No, we went out last night."

Kenny turns to face me, the deep lines on his face accentuated by the easterly light.

"She must be a good fifteen years younger than you."

"Twelve years, to be precise."

"No disrespect intended, pal, but you're punching a bit above your weight with Zoe, are you not?"

"She asked me out, remember."

"Yeah, so you said," he replies, rubbing his chin. "Maybe she's got a thing for older blokes."

"She must have."

"Anyway, how'd the date go?"

"Not great. I'll spare you the details but suffice to say there won't be a second one."

"Back to the drawing board, eh?"

"Seems that way."

Kenny turns back to the lake before speaking again.

"I happened to mention your situation to Sara."

"My situation?"

"Women coming on to you."

"A small number of women I've met over the last week, and by no means all of them. Why did you tell Sara?"

"She's my wife—we discuss everything."

"And what did she have to say on the subject."

"She thinks you're suffering from ... what did she call it? That's it ... erotomania."

Sara has always been something of an amateur psychologist, so it's no surprise she holds a theory. I probably should have stressed to Kenny that I didn't want him discussing my situation with anyone, including Sara.

"Thanks, mate," I groan, "Now your wife thinks I'm losing the plot. And, what the hell is erotomania when it's at home?"

"Do you want to know?"

"No, not really, but go on."

"It's a delusional belief where the sufferer believes a member of the opposite sex is fixated with them romantically."

"You think I'm delusional now?"

"I didn't say that. Sara googled your symptoms, and that's what she came up with."

"If this were just a delusion, how do you explain what happened with Zoe? Did I just delude myself into her flat?"

"You ended up back at her place?" he coughs, unable to mask his shock.

"Yes."

"Are you shitting me, Dougie?"

"If I had a bible in my pocket, I'd swear on it."

Seemingly lost for words, Kenny shakes his head whilst chuckling to himself.

"What's so funny?"

"I'm just trying to picture the two of you together."

"Bit pervy."

"No, not in bed—just together. You're an odd couple; you have to admit."

"We're not a couple in any sense. We had a date and decided we weren't compatible, and that's all there is to it."

"Shame. She's a cracking lassie, but I wouldn't have put the two of you together in a month of Sundays."

"Yes, and that's the primary reason we decided not to take things any further. When I said we're not compatible, I meant we're poles apart in looks, age, and ... err, experience."

"You're better off fishing in less challenging waters, eh?"

"How'd you mean?"

"When I first started dating Sara, there were times I thought we had too little in common to make a go of it. Being with a younger woman has its advantages, but there's nae denying there are challenges too."

"And yet, you're still together."

"Aye, because as we got to know each other, we realised we do have quite a lot in common, but let me tell you: there's a big difference between the perfect woman and the woman who's perfect for you."

"What you're saying, in a roundabout way, is that I should set my sights a little lower?"

"Not lower—just set them in a different direction."

Although it'll take a while to get past last night's car crash, I file Kenny's advice away for future use. There's merit in my friend's guidance, and it tallies with my own conclusions.

With our conversation reaching a natural end, we both turn our attention to the reason we're here. Over the ensuing hour, another five twitchers join us. Pleasantries are exchanged along with a smattering of small talk but, on a morning as stunning as this one, silence is the order of the day. That is, until my mobile phone buzzes in my pocket just after half-eight. I pull it out, and as I don't recognise the number, I'm in two minds about answering. Deciding it's unlikely to be a cold caller at this hour on a Saturday, I move to the far side of the Mount and accept the call.

"Hello."

"Um, hello," a mouse-like voice replies. "Is that Douglas?"

"Yes, but you'll have to speak up. I can barely hear you."

"Sorry. It's Heather … from The Vale Cafe."

"Oh, hi, Heather. What can I do for you?"

The line falls silent.

"Heather? Are you there?"

"Yes … I, err, I've got a problem and … are you busy?"

"Not especially."

"Would you come to the cafe, please?"

"Now?"

"Yes."

I don't want to leave just yet, but I promised Colin I'd help Heather if called upon.

"I'll be there in ten minutes."

"Thank you."

She ends the call before I can say another word. With some reluctance, I bid farewell to Kenny and trudge back to the car park.

True to my word, I push open the door to The Vale Cafe within the ten estimated minutes. The place is empty.

"Be with you in a moment," comes the call from the kitchen.

As I approach the counter, I catch sight of Heather bustling past the serving hatch. I call her name, and a face appears.

"Douglas. You're here."

"I'm the only one here, it seems. What's the problem?"

"Come through, and I'll show you."

She nods toward a door on the left, marked Staff Only. I push it open and enter.

I'm immediately struck by how small the kitchen is. It appears clean enough, but the equipment looks decades old.

"Thank you for coming," Heather says, clearly exasperated.

Dressed in a shapeless green polo shirt and black slacks, Heather's utilitarian outfit also features a pair of dark-grey Crocs. They're a far cry from the killer heels Zoe wore last night. Then again, Zoe probably wears equally sensible footwear when she's rushing around at work.

"No problem. How can I help?"

Heather turns and glares at an oversized, stainless-steel toaster.

"It's this ruddy thing," she huffs. "It keeps activating the trip switch in the fuse box."

I step over and take a closer look. It's a brief look because my knowledge of electrics is almost as negligible as my knowledge of the female species.

"How old is it?" I ask.

"I don't know, but it was here when I started."

"So, at least five or six years?"

"More likely double that, but it's always worked okay."

"Until today."

Heather nods.

I might not know much about toasters, but I do know they're rarely worth repairing, particularly one as old as this.

"I suspect one of the filaments has failed," I suggest. "And that's why it keeps setting off the trip switch."

"Can you fix it?"

"In a word, no, but I can pop into town and pick up a new one if that helps?"

This news, along with my offer, does nothing to lighten Heather's mood. The toaster receives another stern glare.

"I can be back within half-hour," I add.

"No, it's okay."

"How are you going to make toast without a toaster?"

Not a complicated question, but the answer seems to evade Heather. Her attention remains fixed on the knackered appliance as if she's willing it to start working again.

After a few awkward seconds of silence, she finally puffs a long sigh.

"We can't afford a new toaster."

I'm not sure if she's talking to me or the old toaster, but only one of us is capable of answering.

"They're not expensive. You can get a half-decent one for thirty quid."

"As I said," she replies, her voice not much more than a whisper. "We can't afford a new toaster."

I'm taken aback by Heather's admission. I already had an inkling money was tight, but I didn't realise The Vale's finances were quite so stretched.

"Don't worry about it, Heather. I'll cover the cost."

My offer receives barely a flicker of acknowledgement—just a slight nod of the head.

"I'll be back shortly."

I return to my car and head to the Tesco superstore just over a mile away. They seem to sell just about everything these days, so I'm sure they'll have a modest selection of toasters.

My hunch proved correct, and I return to The Vale with a new four-slice toaster under my arm and a few quid change from the estimated thirty quid. When I enter, Heather is at the counter, and one lone customer is sitting at a table.

"Here we are," I announce, holding up the toaster. "Would you like me to set it up?"

"Please," Heather replies, focussing on the cup of tea she's preparing. "Go on through to the kitchen, and I'll be there in a tick."

I push through the door and set about unpacking the new toaster. I'm just about to plug it in when Heather bustles in.

"Have you got a couple of slices of bread handy?" I ask. "We'll give it a test run."

She opens a cupboard and hands me two slices of thick white bread. I slide them in and wait a couple of seconds to check everything is working as it should be. Satisfied all is well, I turn to Heather and catch her staring at the bulge in my jacket pocket.

Over the years, I've discovered that people tend to think negatively about middle-aged men who wear rain macs, especially when there's a pair of high-powered binoculars poking out of the pocket. I did consider buying a tabard with the words 'Off-duty Bird Watcher' printed on the front and back, just to avoid such negative thoughts.

I lock eyes with Heather for a fraction of a second, and I feel compelled to explain myself.

"They're for birdwatching ... the binoculars."

In my haste to explain, I wonder if I sound even more suspicious. Heather's expression suggests I might.

"I was birdwatching when you called, you see."

After a brief pause, she poses a question.

"You like birdwatching?"

I thought I'd already established that fact, but Heather still seems perplexed.

"It started as a hobby, but it's become something of an obsession. So much so, I spend an inordinate amount of time up at Tinkerton Meadow."

Sad as it is, most people have no interest in birdwatching. The moment I mention my favourite pastime, they tend to feign interest and then promptly change the subject.

"I ... I like birds," Heather suddenly splutters.

"Really?"

"Yes. We've ... we've got feeding stations in the garden at home, and I spend hours watching them from my bedroom window."

If I didn't know better, I'd say I detected a nervous excitement in Heather's voice. By her usual standards, it's quite the outpouring of emotion.

"That's great. Do you have any favourites?"

"Well, there's a pair of goldfinches who seem to like the seed mix, and they pop by every morning just after sunrise, but they only stay until the rabble arrive."

"The rabble?"

"A gang of house sparrows. They're lovely, but such greedy creatures, and noisy."

"Ahh, yes," I chuckle. "They live in colonies, and when one finds a food source, it's not long before the rest descend in numbers. My friend, Kenny, calls them feathered locusts."

"I can see why, but I do have a soft spot for them."

Just as quickly as our conversation began, it comes to an end when the lone customer calls out from the counter.

"I'd, um, better go see to them," Heather says, defaulting to her usual self.

"Sure. I need to be going anyway."

"I'll pay you back for the toaster as soon as we can afford it."

"There's no need. Consider it a very early Christmas present."

Her cheeks redden, and she mumbles a few words I don't catch.

"Sorry, Heather. I didn't quite hear you."

"You're very kind," she repeats softly.

She then hurries out to the counter, leaving me with a pair of toasters and a nagging thought: Heather has never been in the slightest bit chatty with me before. Could that be down to the gift?

Once again, my thoughts turn to Zoe, and her wild, unbridled behaviour last night. Heather, on the other hand, struggled to maintain eye contact. I can't decide if she's immune to the gift or not, but on balance, I think she might be. I don't know how or why, but it's probably no bad thing. Encouraging her would break several of my rules, and I don't think Colin would be too pleased if I messed with his daughter in any way, shape, or form.

I say goodbye to Heather and leave her to deal with The Vale's one and only customer. Her unenthusiastic reply is reason to believe I might be right about her immunity to the gift.

Blessed as I might be, I'm still no closer to understanding the inner workings of the female mind.

That, I suspect, may never change.

30th April 2001

No one likes Mondays, but this Monday has been one of the best days of my life.

It's been five weeks since I tagged along with Denise when she went flat hunting. We looked at five different flats, but she hated all of them. Three were too small, one had a damp problem, and the last had too many stairs. After we'd finished, we went to the pub for lunch, and I tried to put a positive spin on the morning. I said two of them weren't so bad but that just pissed Denise off. She said I was lucky that I'd had the luxury of living in a lovely detached house and never had to cope with living in a poky box.

That's when I had my idea.

Even now, I can't believe Denise agreed to it. Granted, we've not been dating that long, and it's still early days, but it just seemed like the right thing to do.

I don't care what anyone thinks—if they don't like it, fuck them. Today, I'm officially living with my girlfriend, and that's all that matters.

I keep thinking back to the houses we viewed the following weekend, and I really liked the two-bed semi in Weston Road. It was within walking distance of the town centre, and although it was a bit basic inside, it was a decent size. I reckon it would have been Denise's choice before we viewed 8 Norton Rise.

I'm still not sure why we needed a three-bedroom house, but Denise loved the en-suite shower room and the big kitchen-din-

er. We had a takeaway pizza in that kitchen tonight, and then Denise popped out for a few hours to see an old school friend while I finished unpacking. She's now in the en-suite, having a shower while I write this. She's singing to herself so she must be happy, and so am I. In fact, I don't think I've ever been happier.

The only slight concern I have relates to our finances. This house was right at the very top of our rent budget, and we'll have to tighten our belts until I get a promotion, but I don't care. As long as I've got my Denise and a TV, that's all I need. It's a shame Mum and Dad aren't on board with us moving in together but they'll come around in time. I know this has all happened so fast but that doesn't mean it's wrong.

I'm trying not to think too far ahead, but I'm already planning how I can ask Denise to marry me. She's not the most romantic woman in the world but I'd like my proposal to be special. That's probably a year or two away, so I've got plenty of time to plan.

Anyway, the shower has stopped and Denise will be joining me in a minute—our first night in our new home, together. We're still not quite there with the whole sex thing, but fingers crossed my luck will be in tonight.

I can't wait to christen the bedroom … and all the other rooms!

Chapter 22

I could happily live on takeaways and convenience food, but the older I get, the more my body wants to cling to every gram of fat I consume. So, when I turned forty, I promised myself I'd try to cook a healthy meal three or four times a week.

That promise is the reason I'm currently trawling the aisles in Tesco on a Sunday morning, along with half the residents of Ashbridge, it seems. Still, every time I pass a family with a couple of screaming kids in tow, I count my blessings. It's not that I wouldn't give anything to have kids of my own, but dragging them around a supermarket doesn't seem much like fun for anyone, particularly the kids.

I also have to admit there's a novelty factor involved in today's shopping expedition. I read somewhere that supermarkets are one of the most popular places for single folk to find a partner. That might be true, just not in my case. I've shopped alone for years, and the only reason a woman has ever approached me is to ask for something off a top shelf. That, or they mistake me for a member of staff. That's why I no longer wear my navy-blue fleece.

Today, though, I've been smiled at, winked at, and a woman in the freezer aisle asked for my number. She seemed lovely, but I've already learned a valuable lesson when it comes to the age of a prospective partner—too young is not ideal, and I can imagine that too old is likely no better. Last weekend I might have been tempted to date a pension-age woman. Today, not so much.

I finish the shopping and head home. It doesn't take long to unpack, and within twenty minutes, I'm back on the road again. I agreed to pop in and see my parents today as they've generously found a visitation slot between Sunday morning tennis and their late lunch with friends Howard and Jenny.

As I pull up on the driveway outside their house, Mum opens the front door. I wave at her, and suddenly, a cold shiver runs down my spine. It hadn't crossed my mind until now, but what if my own mother ... no, that doesn't bear thinking about. I get out of the car and approach Mum on the doorstep.

"Lovely to see you," she says, opening her arms for our customary hug.

"You too."

Mercifully, the hug is as brief and perfunctory as it always is.

"Come on through to the kitchen. Your father is just waxing his balls."

"Oh, okay ... sorry? Dad's doing what?"

"His golf balls, darling. It helps eke out a few extra yards on the driving range."

I breathe a sigh of relief and follow Mum through to the kitchen. Dad is indeed waxing balls at the table.

"Morning, Son," he chirps. "How are we this fine Sunday morning?"

"Pretty good, ta," I reply, flashing a smile.

"Good. You seem remarkably chipper."

His observation isn't too wide of the mark. After I did my good deed at The Vale Cafe yesterday, I returned to Tinkerton Meadow with a sandwich and a flask of hot soup. I spent most of the day there, in quiet reflection, and I eventually managed to put the events with Zoe into perspective. Yes, I messed up, but there's still ample opportunity to try again, and I can learn from my mistakes. At least I have that in my favour, whereas before, opportunities were so scarce that wasting one would have knocked my confidence for months.

"I had a good day at Tinkerton yesterday," I reply by way of an explanation. "How was tennis this morning?"

"We didn't play this morning," Mum interjects.

"Why not?"

She looks at Dad as if seeking his permission to answer my question. He nods his approval, and Mum clasps her hands together—a sure sign there's a titbit of news she's desperate to reveal. It almost always relates to Kate.

"Your father had a meeting up at the golf club this morning." She pauses for effect.

"And, you are now looking at the president-elect of Ashbridge Golf Club."

I've never understood Dad's obsession with whacking a small ball around a field all day, but then he's never understood my obsession with standing on a hillock and staring at birds all day. At least I don't have to pay two grand a year for the privilege or tolerate the snobby politics of Ashbridge Golf Club.

"Wow, Dad. Congratulations."

"Thank you, kindly," he replies, his chin raised high. "And I don't mind saying I'm pretty chuffed. It's been a hard-won battle."

"A battle? I thought you'd be the obvious candidate, seeing as you've been a member since the Romans invaded."

Dad chortles at my comment. Mum doesn't.

"The committee is obsessed with the club's good reputation, so they won't just elect any old Tom, Dick, or Harry. There's a vetting process, and that involved a thorough check to ensure I'm of good moral standing."

"That sounds a bit over the top. It's a golf club—not MI5."

"Yes, but they're still smarting over the appointment of Donald Parsons."

"Who?"

"Donald was forced to resign as president four years ago. He and his wife were a little too fond of hosting dinner parties."

"Eh? What's so scandalous about hosting dinner parties?"

"Nothing, if the guests don't head upstairs after coffee and indulge in a spot of wife-swapping."

"Ohh."

"Anyway, as there are no skeletons in my closet, or my family's, the vetting procedure—long and tedious as it was—went without a hitch."

I think back a few weeks to my awful date with Carol and her offer to try dogging. I might have considered it for a nanosecond, and now I'm even more relieved I saw sense. Being caught having sex in the back of a Vauxhall Astra with a dozen blokes watching is probably not becoming of a golf club president's son.

"Well, I'm very pleased for you, Dad."

"Thank you, and I trust you'll be coming along to the inauguration ceremony next weekend?"

"Yeah, I guess so."

"Kathryn and Alec will be there, obviously."

"Great."

Of course, my sister and her perfect husband will be there.

"Is there anyone you'd like to bring?" Mum asks, more out of politeness than expectation.

"Err, I'll get back to you on that."

"Let your father know soon. They need to confirm numbers, don't they, darling?"

Dad nods, but I can tell from the look in his eye that he's already confirmed how many of his family will be in attendance, and his son won't be bringing a plus-one.

I sit and listen as my parents talk about themselves for an hour and then make my excuses. Mum did suggest I might like to join them for lunch, but it was a hollow invite, judging by her subtlest sigh of relief when I declined.

On the way home, I concede my mood isn't as upbeat as it was on the way to my parents' house. Nothing has really changed, but that's the problem—Mum and Dad still treat me differently from Kathryn because I'm single. I can't blame them because I'm that awkward square peg who doesn't easily fit in social events.

It's not just my parents. It's society in general.

I don't get invited to many weddings, but when I do, I'm always stuck on a table with the widowers, the moody youths, and that oddball cousin every family has but secretly wishes they didn't. It isn't just weddings, though. Every party and social gathering I've ever attended has been dominated by couples. Even at funerals, there's nothing worse than being that lone mourner who stands in the corner at the wake sipping tea whilst trying to avoid eye contact with the deceased's nearest and dearest.

I wish I could say it's different with my friends. I don't have many, but those I do are all in relationships, and couples much prefer entertaining other couples. If you're single, you are, by default, odd: two guests, four guests, six guests, and then the loner. We upset the seating plan and the after-dinner games.

Is it any wonder I've become something of a social recluse?

My mood shifts again as I unlock the front door. Not so long ago, I'd carry my negative thoughts with me for days, but now I have hope, courtesy of the gift. I know it'll take time to join the couple's cliques—certainly long after Dad's do at the golf club—but one day soon, I can look forward to being an even number.

However, I suppose there are certain benefits to being alone. I can do what I want without the need to please anyone else. The world is my oyster, but it's a bastard cold oyster this afternoon, and I fancy spending it slumped on the sofa watching a film.

I treat myself to a hot chocolate and retire to the lounge. There, I spend ten minutes deciding what to watch. In the spirit of positive thinking, I thank my lucky stars that I don't have to please anyone else's taste in films but my own. I settle on an action film with guns and car chases and shouty Americans.

An hour into it, I'm interrupted by the doorbell. Reluctantly, I get up and shuffle down the hallway to see who's interrupted my peaceful afternoon. I open the door and, for a second, struggle to recall the name of the woman standing on my doorstep.

"Hi, Dougie," she beams. "I hope I'm not disturbing you."

"Oh, hi ..."

"Shelley."

"Yes. Shelley ... hi."

"Sorry for dropping by unannounced, but I was in the area and thought I'd see if you had any feedback on the speed dating event. You disappeared before I got the chance to follow-up."

Shit. I never got around to writing the email I intended to send. Even so, I'm surprised Shelley is here, gauging my feedback in person.

"Sorry, Shelley. How did you know my address?"

"From your profile form—the one you filled out before the event, remember?"

"Oh, yes. To be honest, I'm not sure any of my dates were quite what I'm looking for."

"Oh, really? There were some lovely ladies there on Wednesday."

"Yes, they were all lovely, but I was looking for someone ..."

Too late, I realise I've painted myself into an ageist corner. Fortunately, Shelley pre-empts the answer I don't have.

"You're looking for someone, but you're not quite sure what kind of woman?" she suggests. "Would that be a fair assessment?"

"Pretty fair."

"Maybe I can help? I've been in the dating game a long time."

She looks at me with an expectant smile and then stamps her feet a couple of times as a gust of wind whips along the street. The penny drops after a second or two.

"Pardon my manners. Would you like to come in?"

"If you're sure?"

"Of course."

Shelley steps into the hallway, the delicate scent of a floral perfume joining her.

"Can I take your coat?"

"What a gentleman. Thank you."

As she unbuttons her coat, I can't help but compare this woman with the one I met on Wednesday evening. I remember thinking that she was attractive, but my mind was already racing ahead to the dates I was about to embark upon.

"Come through to the lounge."

She follows me in, and I turn off the television.

"This is cosy," she remarks. "But, lacking a woman's touch ... if you don't mind me saying so."

"No, I couldn't agree more," I reply with a smile. "Please, have a seat."

Kathryn has told me countless times I need to accessorise my lounge with vases and pictures and other interior design trinkets, but I struggle with style, as my wardrobe would testify.

Shelley makes herself comfortable, crossing one leg over the other and then slowly flicking a strand of hair from her forehead.

"So, tell me, Dougie: if you could list the ideal attributes you're seeking in a partner, what would be the top three?"

"Um, that's a good question, but I don't think I have an answer. I don't like to pigeonhole anyone."

"Okay, but clearly none of the women you met on Wednesday ticked the right boxes, so what was it specifically they lacked?"

"I don't think they lacked anything per se ... as I said, they were all nice."

"But?"

I squirm in my chair, unable to say the words that sound awful in my head.

"Speak freely, Dougie. I understand a man like you can have any woman he wants, but you do need to know in your own mind what you're ideally looking for, right?"

"I guess so."

"So, you met a bunch of very different women the other night—did they all share one trait you didn't like?"

"It's not a trait as such, but I realised afterwards that, in an ideal world, I'd like to meet someone a shade younger."

"Now we're getting somewhere. There's no shame in admitting you like a younger woman."

My mind flashes back to Friday night and my experience with a much younger woman.

"When I say younger, I mean someone ideally looking for a family."

"Aha," Shelley responds like she's just unearthed the key to my desires. "You want children?"

"I think I do, yes. And, in hindsight, I should probably have chosen a dating event where I'd meet women who wanted that too."

"Now you're making sense. Do you know how young this ideal partner might be?"

This feels like a trap of some sort. Am I about to be exposed as a deviant?

"I'm open-minded."

"Hmm ... how about thirty-seven?"

"That's oddly specific."

"You haven't answered my question. Does thirty-seven sound about right?"

Not that I'm about to tell Shelley, but that age fits nicely in my prefect partner profile, recently updated with a higher minimum age so I can avoid meeting another Zoe.

"Yeah, thirty-seven would work."

"That's good to hear," Shelley purrs. "Guess how old I am?"

I was right to be wary of a trap, but the lure isn't quite what or who I expected.

"A stab in the dark—thirty-seven?"

"You're good," she says with a wicked grin. "So ..."

She sits forward and puffs out her cheeks as if steeling herself.

"So, how would you feel if I asked you out on a date?"

In all my fantasies about random women asking me out, I never considered how disarming a question it might be in reality. I've only met Shelley once, and although there's no denying she's an attractive woman, I don't know anything about her.

"Your silence isn't filling me with positive vibes," she says.

"Um, sorry. I'm just a bit taken aback, that's all."

"Why? I thought you could tell I was keen when we met."

"Not really, but I'm terrible at picking up signals."

"Just as well I grasped the nettle, then. But if the attraction isn't mutual, I totally understand."

"No, I ... err, I think you're attractive, definitely."

"That's a relief. Is there another reason you don't seem keen on a date with yours truly? I'm only thinking of a few drinks in town—nothing heavy."

Is there any reason? Shelley is eight years older than Zoe, and they seem to be very different women. I can't put my finger on what Shelley has that Zoe doesn't, or vice versa, but I'm far more comfortable knowing there's only a four-year age gap between us.

"A few drinks would be great, but do you mind if I ask you a question?"

"Shoot."

"You asked me about children. Are you looking to start a family?"

"Would you like to know my back story?"

"Only if you're comfortable sharing it with me."

"It's not a long one, but a familiar one. I was married in my late twenties, but by the time I hit thirty-five, it became clear there were three of us in the marriage: me, my husband, and his business. I knew he was a workaholic, but I didn't realise it was his obsession and nothing else mattered. After he said we'd have to wait another year before starting a family, I gave him an ultimatum, thinking he'd choose me. He didn't."

"I'm sorry to hear that."

"I was sorry too, for a while. We divorced, and I met someone new at a Christmas party last year, and I thought we might have a future, but he turned out to be the complete opposite of my ex-husband ... just not in a good way. I left one man who prioritised everything over me, to another man who prioritised me to the point of suffocation."

"Oh, dear."

"We split up a few weeks ago, so I'm effectively looking for love again. Like you, I want a family."

As she looks across at me, I realise that Shelley has what Zoe sadly lacked: empathy. She isn't a woman just looking for a bit of fun, but a solid, dependable commitment. She wants what I want.

"Where and when shall we meet?" I ask.

"I take it you're not put off by my history?"

"Not at all."

"Well, seeing as we met at the Cherry Blossom, why don't we stick to the same venue on Tuesday?"

"Shall we say half-seven?"

"Perfect. You've made my day, Dougie."

She then glances at her watch.

"I'd love to stay and chat, but I promised my mum I'd pick up some groceries from Tesco before they close, so I'd better dash."

Shelley stands up, and I see her to the door, where she plants a peck on my cheek.

"See you Tuesday. I'm already looking forward to it."

"Me too."

I'm still smiling as I return to the sofa, and slightly dazed too. Have I jumped in too soon after the debacle with Zoe?

I quickly conclude it's never too soon to go on another date as long as I learn from my prior mistakes and take it slow. As Shelley herself said, it's just a few drinks. No going back to her place and definitely no sexual shenanigans.

If I stick to those rules, this could be the start of something good.

Chapter 23

Not only did Ady turn up this morning, but he also turned up two minutes early. Perhaps, being it's a Monday, he's decided to start the working week as he means to go on. We shall see.

We finish our bin round just before midday, and the subject of lunch comes up.

"Do you fancy The Vale?" Ady asks.

"I'm not paying again."

"I didn't ask you to. I've got a few quid in my pocket, so I'll treat you."

"Really?"

"Yeah, and here's the score I owe you."

He pulls out his wallet and extracts a twenty-pound note. I notice it's one of at least a dozen.

"Someone's flush today," I remark.

"Eh?"

"The wedge of notes in your wallet."

"Oh, yeah ... I won a hundred quid on a scratch card."

"Congratulations. Perhaps you should treat that girlfriend of yours to a night out."

"Why do you say that?"

"No reason. I just thought ... never mind."

Ady instantly shrugs off my suggestion and hops back in the van. Would someone cheating have reacted any differently? I don't know, and frankly, the prospect of a free lunch at The Vale is a greater priority.

We arrive to find the car park is empty. Mondays are usually one of the busier days, so I'm surprised we're the only customers. When we reach the front door, the reason becomes apparent.

I turn the door handle, but it's locked, and the scene beyond the glass hidden in darkness.

"I reckon it's shut," Ady groans.

"Well deduced, Sherlock."

"No need to be sarky."

"Sorry, I'm just hungry, and it's bloody typical it's shut on a day when you're buying."

As we traipse back to the van, I think back to Saturday, and I can't help but wonder if I misdiagnosed the toaster as the cause for the electrical problems. Heather never called or messaged me to say otherwise, but then again, I think she probably realised no help is better than the wrong kind of help.

We drive a few hundred yards up the road, and I pull over outside a convenience store.

"Sandwiches will have to suffice today."

"Suppose so."

We waste five minutes selecting our respective sandwiches and then convene back in the van. I turn the radio on, and we settle back for a brief lunch break; Ady staring at his phone while I read a newspaper. A minute in, and my colleague swears under his breath.

"What's up?"

"Tomato bloody sauce. That's what's up."

"Eh?"

He shakes a bag of crisps in front of my face.

"I thought these were ready salted, but they're tomato sauce flavour."

"Well, go and swap them."

"I'll be two minutes. Do you want anything else while I'm in there?"

"No, ta."

He tosses his phone on the dashboard and nips back to the shop. I'm about to return to my newspaper when a buzzing sound vibrates near the windscreen. Only three feet away, I can see the message bubble on Ady's phone screen.

I glance out of the side window towards the shop. There's no sign of my workmate.

I wouldn't usually snoop, but if there's any substance to Leanne's paranoia, I won't get a better chance to check who's messaging Ady.

I check the coast is clear and lean forward. The message is short, and from someone in his contact list labelled SCK: *That was some evening!! Hope we can do it again soon ;o)*

It's not exactly damning evidence, but we've been chatting for over five hours, and Ady has yet to mention going out last night. The words of the message certainly aren't proof he was up to no good, but the winking emoji at the end might imply otherwise. What exactly is it that SCK wants to do again soon, and why does it require a wink?

I'm still contemplating that question when Ady returns.

"All sorted?" I ask, returning my attention to the newspaper.

"Yep," he huffs, snatching his phone from the dashboard.

I sneak a look at his face as he reads the message, but his expression remains neutral. Seconds pass, and then he taps away at the screen, presumably replying to SCK. There's nothing I can do now without raising suspicion, but maybe later, I'll casually ask how he spent his Sunday evening.

We finish lunch and head off for our first fly-tip collection of the afternoon. With that first collection being one of eighteen, we barely have a chance to draw breath most of the afternoon. My only opportunity to quiz Ady finally arrives on the way to the recycling centre.

"What a day, eh?" I sigh. "I'm knackered."

"You and me both, mate."

I pause a moment.

"Did you get much chance to rest over the weekend?"

"A bit."

"What did you get up to? Anything interesting?"

"Not really. Went to the pub with the missus on Saturday evening ... stayed in last night."

"Right," I nod.

I wait for Ady to ask about my weekend, but he's focussed on his phone again. In fact, he barely says another word until he drops me off at home. I stand on the pavement and watch as he speeds away. Then, I ping a text message to Leanne, simply saying we need to talk whenever she's available.

With a date in the diary for tomorrow, it's unlikely I'll have a chance to visit Tinkerton Meadow so, despite the cold, I snatch a quick shower and head straight out. The car park is empty when I get there, as is Falbert's Mount.

I manage just over an hour before the light is too feeble to see anything of interest. Still, the dusky setting did tempt a barn owl out, and I managed to catch a few glimpses as she hunted over the meadow just before I left. Of all our native birds, I don't think there are many as endearing as owls. Spotting one is always a treat.

I return home cold but contented, and in the mood for a warming bowl of mulligatawny soup with doorsteps of crusty bread. I'm just about to turn on the hob when the doorbell rings.

Mildly irritated, I hurry to the front door and open it.

"Oh. Hi, Leanne."

"I got your message and came straight from work."

"Right. I kind of assumed you'd phone."

"Ady uses my phone now and again, and I didn't want him seeing I'd called you. He might get the wrong idea."

"Yeah, fair point. Um, you'd better come in."

Besides Mum and Kathryn, I've had very few female callers in all the years I've lived in Cargate Road. Now, I've had two in a few days, with Leanne visiting twice. If I keep this up, busybody Joan from across the street will start a gossip campaign, and I dread to think what conclusions she'll draw.

I invite Leanne to sit in the lounge, keeping my fingers crossed I can impart what little I know and get rid of her within ten minutes.

"Have you found anything out?" she asks, as I perch on the edge of the armchair.

"Yes, and no. Do the initials SCK mean anything to you?"

She pauses a moment to think but returns a shrug.

"I don't think so. Why?"

"It's probably nothing but a message popped up on Ady's phone earlier. It said something about last night being a top evening, and whoever SCK is, they hoped to do it again soon."

"Last night?"

"Yes. I asked Ady, and he said he was at home last night, which I'm guessing he wasn't?"

"No, he went out around seven o'clock. He said a few mates had organised a game of five-a-side football, but they were a player short."

I breathe a little easier.

"There you are then. That explains the text ... sort of."

"Sort of?"

"Whoever sent it posted a winky-face emoji at the end."

Leanne doesn't say a word in response, but she does grab her mobile phone and begins tapping away at the screen.

"What are you doing?" I ask.

"Why would one of Ady's mates add a wink to a message about football? Something sounds off about it, so I'm scrolling through his friends on Facebook to see if anyone has the initials SCK."

She continues her screen tapping. Part of me wishes I hadn't mentioned the wink emoji. It's the same part of me that is now irritated by Leanne conducting her research in my lounge.

"Bitch," she suddenly spits under her breath. "I knew it."

"Err, everything okay?"

"No, it's not. Ady used to date some slapper called Shannon King, and I thought he'd unfriended her. Apparently, he hasn't."

To prove her point, Leanne holds up her phone to reveal a photo of a female face. Typical of so many Facebook photos, it's filtered to such an extent that the subject looks like a cartoon character.

"Do you happen to know her middle name?" I ask.

"No, but pound to a penny it begins with the letter C. I bloody knew that bastard was cheating on me."

She tosses the phone on the sofa and puts her head in her hands.

"Are you okay, Leanne?"

Her shoulders begin to judder slightly, and her reply comes in the form of a low sobbing sound. Now, I *really* wish I hadn't mentioned the wink emoji.

It occurs to me that I have two options. I could nip back to the kitchen and prepare my dinner whilst Leanne works through her emotional breakdown, or I could attempt to comfort her. As hungry as I am, I can't leave the poor girl sobbing on my sofa while I slice bread and simmer soup.

I get up and slowly edge towards the sofa. With no reaction, I have little choice but to sit down and offer a few words of comfort.

Ensuring we're a reasonable distance apart, I lower myself down and prepare a suitable opening line.

"You don't know for certain Ady is cheating," I submit. "Or even if that Shannon woman sent the message."

"Who else could it be?" she sniffs.

"I don't know, but neither do you ... not for certain. If it was her, why didn't she put a kiss or two at the end of the message? Wouldn't that be the done thing between two people enjoying a fling?"

I'm clutching at straws, but if it helps stabilise Leanne's emotional state, perhaps she'll leave me in peace.

"Have you got a tissue?" she asks.

"Sure. One sec."

I hurry through to the kitchen and pluck a packet of tissues from a drawer. When I return to the lounge, Leanne is sitting up, her forehead furrowed with scowl lines.

"Here you go," I say, handing her a tissue.

"Thanks."

"Are you okay?"

"I'm angry."

"Shouldn't you get the facts before you invest too heavily in any emotion?"

"I know my boyfriend lied to you about last night, and why would he do that if he was only playing football?"

"I don't know."

"Exactly."

She takes a moment to wipe her eyes.

"I wish Ady were more like you," she then declares.

"Like me?"

"Yeah, kind and considerate. I bet you wouldn't cheat on a partner, would you?"

"Well, no, but we don't know that Ady has."

"I'm past caring," she sighs. "I only put up with Ady's immaturity because I didn't think I could do any better."

"Oh."

"I mean," she continues, "I'm not exactly a catwalk model, am I?"

She turns and looks at me, her expression beckoning an answer.

"I, err ... you're a very attractive woman, Leanne, and I'm sure Ady thinks the same."

"Are you sure? Does he talk about me when he's at work? Does he say how much he fancies me?"

"That's not really the kind of thing either of us would discuss at work, to be honest."

She stares into her lap for a few seconds and then poses another question.

"Do you really think I'm attractive?"

Ohh, shit. This is the very definition of a lose-lose question.

"Um, Ady is lucky to have you."

"Thank you, Dougie. You're very sweet."

"You're welcome."

"I don't understand how you're still single. I really don't."

It's funny how she's never shared that thought with me before.

"Well, maybe fate will intervene soon. All I can do is hope."

She finds a weak smile and then blows her nose. I throw a less-than-subtle glance at the clock on the wall.

"Sorry. I didn't mean to keep you," Leanne says.

"It's okay."

We both stand up, and after a moment of awkward silence, I see Leanne to the front door. I try to keep my distance but yet again, she pulls me into another embrace.

"What do you think I should do?" she asks, her arms still wrapped around my waist. "About Ady?"

"I wouldn't do anything. Just see how things pan out."

"You think?"

"Yeah, I do."

"And you'll let me know if you unearth anything else I should know."

"Sure."

With that, she finally releases me.

"Thanks again, Dougie. You've been a real help."

I don't think I have, but I'm not about to argue.

"Any time."

Ady's girlfriend leaves for the second, and hopefully final, time. I've got my own relationship issues to contend with, and I don't even have a relationship yet.

Still, maybe that'll change tomorrow.

Chapter 24

I've never been so nervous waiting for Ady to pick me up. After Leanne left the house yesterday, I spent much of the evening fretting about my involvement in their domestic affairs. Fortunately, when he finally arrived, he seemed to be his usual self. I subsequently spent all day keeping the conversation off-topic and vowed never to interfere again. If Ady is seeing someone else, that's on him, and I no longer want to play piggy in the middle.

With my third date in two weeks only hours away, it seems I've settled into a routine: dinner, a long bath, and a period of introspection and self-doubt. My date with Carol occurred before I discovered the gift, but the date with Zoe was no less unsuccessful, albeit for different reasons. Third time lucky, I hope.

Once I've dressed, I head down to the kitchen and open the cupboard where I store my booze. I grab a bottle of vodka but pause before removing it. Whilst alcohol helps take the edge off my anxiety, it also undermines common sense. If I'd been sober, I don't think I'd have ventured back to Zoe's flat, and I wouldn't have let events get so out of hand.

I shut the cupboard door, the bottle of vodka still on the shelf inside. Tonight, I need to be sensible, and I definitely need to keep my pants on.

Decision made, I snatch my car keys from the hook and double-check my breath is fresh. I'm a bit early, but as I'm driving, I can take a slow pootle into town and kill time. Besides, without the calming effect of alcohol, I need to keep my mind distracted.

Driving like an octogenarian, I arrive at the car park five minutes before I'm due to meet Shelley. I guess most people would take a peek in the rear-view mirror for one final check before a date, but I'm not most people. Now I'm blessed with the gift, how I look seems to be wholly inconsequential. Checking my reflection would only undermine what little confidence I have.

Two minutes later, I push open the door to The Cherry Tree. I'm struck by how quiet it is compared to last week. It's a Tuesday evening, I suppose, and there's no speed dating event tonight.

To my surprise, Shelley is already waiting. She glances over, and her face lights up.

"Dougie!"

I flash a smile and stride over.

"Hi, Shelley."

She greets me with a delicate peck on both cheeks.

"I was a bit worried you wouldn't show," she says, as we lean up against the bar, facing one another.

"As a man who's been stood up more than once, I'd never do that."

"Yeah, right," she replies, playfully slapping my arm. "As if you've ever been stood up."

There's no sense in arguing the truth so I let it slide.

"Can I get you a drink, Dougie ... or do you prefer Douglas?"

"I'll just have an orange juice, please, and Dougie is fine with me."

"You're not drinking tonight?"

"I start work at stupid o'clock in the morning, and it's hard enough getting up on time as it is. Weekday hangovers are best avoided."

"Very sensible. I got a cab, so do you mind if I have a few glasses of wine?"

"No, not at all."

Once we're both furnished with drinks, Shelley suggests we get comfortable on one of the large leather sofas either side of the fireplace. It's early days, but already I feel more comfortable on this date than at any moment during my date with Zoe.

I soon learn that Shelley is easy to talk to. Maybe it's because she's closer to my age, but we connect on most subjects. It also helps that we're not quite at the polar opposite ends of the looks spectrum. Shelley is far too beautiful to date a man like me, for sure, but that beauty is restrained, conservative. It's clear she's keen on making the most of her looks, but her cosmetic enhancements are understated. Unlike the date with Zoe, I don't feel intimidated in Shelley's company, and I'm not so concerned everyone is looking at us and wondering if I'm paying my date for her company.

The first hour flies by as we cover the usual range of subjects two strangers would typically discuss on a first date: jobs, home life, and family. I discover that besides running her weekly speed dating events, Shelley also has a part-time job as a receptionist at a law firm. To her credit, she seemed genuinely interested when I told her about my job.

The conversation then turns to relationships—the topic I've been dreading.

"So, Dougie, how does a man like you end up at a speed dating event?"

"Same reason as anyone, I guess."

"Between you and me, most of the people who attend my events are desperate. You can't possibly be desperate."

"Can't I? Why not?"

"Because of your aura. I've never met a man who's made me feel so … I can't even describe it, but it's intoxicating."

"Um, thank you."

"You must have women throwing themselves at you, I bet."

Not that I intend to tell Shelley, but up until recently, most women would rather throw themselves under a bus than date me.

"Shall we just say I haven't dated in a long time because I've not met anyone suitable?"

"And what about now? Do you think I could ever make it into the suitable category?"

Shelley's question is one I've been pondering myself over the last hour. I've already concluded that she seems perfect in every way. She's funny, smart, engaging, and although I'm not obsessed with looks, there's no denying Shelley would turn heads if she entered any room occupied by men my age.

"You're definitely in the suitable category," I admit. "One hundred per cent."

She leans closer and rests her hand on my knee.

"Do you think tonight might lead to another date, then?"

"I'd reckon so."

"Great," she beams. "And fingers crossed, many more after that."

There's a slight break in conversation as Shelley looks across at me. She pauses for a heartbeat and then tilts her head slightly. Feeling intensely self-conscious, I reach for my drink.

"I'm just going to pop to the ladies," she says with a sudden flurry.

"Yeah, err, right. Can I get you another drink?"

"That'd be lovely," comes the reply. "Thank you."

I watch her scoot away towards the toilets and get to my feet. If it were physically possible, I'd kick my own arse because I'm almost certain I just missed the perfect opportunity to enjoy our first kiss. Worse still, I suspect I leant forward to grab a glass of tepid orange juice just as Shelley tried to instigate that kiss.

Idiot.

"Pull yourself together," I mutter under my breath.

I've no doubt that a lack of dating experience is behind my inability to read the signals. I'm sure moments like the one I just blew are supposed to come naturally, but you've got to have a certain level of confidence, and I just don't have it yet.

Still, unlike my date with Zoe, there's plenty of time to make amends for my ham-fisted reaction. I just need to relax and grasp the next opportunity—be more James Bond, less Mr Bean.

I approach the bar and order another round of drinks, asking the barman to add a shot of vodka to my orange juice. It's not enough to put me over the limit for driving, but it might just be enough to bolster my confidence.

As soon as the glass hits the bar, I empty it in one swift gulp.

"Same again, please, minus the vodka."

I can already feel the warm glow of alcohol in my chest when Shelley returns. Still smiling, she sashays over.

"I noticed a jukebox on my way to the ladies," she says. "You can tell a lot about someone by the music they like."

"Can you now?"

"I hope so. Shall we go take a look together?"

"Definitely. Do you have any guilty pleasures you'd like to confess beforehand?"

"Possibly," she grins.

After paying for the drinks, I walk alongside Shelley to the far side of the bar and a digital jukebox fixed to the wall.

"Forgive me, Father," she giggles, slipping a pound coin into the slot, "For I am about to sin."

She then presses the screen with her finger to shuffle through a selection of albums. She settles on the Spice Girls' greatest hits.

"I did warn you, Dougie. I always wanted to be Baby Spice when I was younger."

I've no strong opinion on the Spice Girls, but the slow track Shelley selects isn't one that I'm keen on: *2 Become 1*. As the song begins, she turns to me.

"I adore this song. It was the Christmas number one when I was a teenager, and I must have played it a thousand times while dreaming about falling in love."

I have very different memories of the song, most of which I've tried to forget. However, I don't want to be that naive, self-doubting young man anymore.

Our faces are only a few feet apart, and as one of the Spice Girls—I'm not sure which—suggests I should free my mind of doubt and danger, I do what I should have done five minutes ago. I lean in towards Shelley and close my eyes. Before I can question the decision, her lips touch mine. The sensation is exquisite, and as our kiss slowly evolves, there's none of the animalistic frenzy that tainted my first kiss with Zoe. I don't want it ever to end.

"Bitch!" a voice growls somewhere behind us.

Shelley suddenly pulls away. I open my eyes to a very different face. Her mouth is agape, features taut with panic. I spin around to see what she's staring at.

"I knew you were up to something," the owner of the voice snaps. "You cheating bitch!"

That owner is a bloke with square shoulders and a thick neck ... and an unnaturally crimson-red face.

"Paul," Shelley splutters. "What ... how ... I'm sorry."

"Sorry?" the man named Paul responds. "Sorry for cheating on me, or just sorry you got caught?"

"It's not what you think," Shelley pleads. "It was just a kiss."

Still reeling from the sudden change in mood, my mind finally catches up with events. I turn to Shelley.

"What does he mean, cheating? You said you were single."

"I ... I don't know why I said that. I just ... I got carried away."

I turn to Paul with my hands raised.

"I'm so sorry. If I thought for one moment Shelley was seeing someone; I'd never have agreed to this date."

"Date?" Paul spits. "This ain't a date, you moron. She just wants my attention, ain't that right, Shell?"

I glance across at Shelley. She slowly nods.

"Brilliant," I huff. "Thanks for the lies, Shelley."

"What did you expect?" Paul says to me. "You're a fucking horror show, mate. You didn't seriously think she was interested in you, did you? This is all for my benefit."

Shelley is now close to tears. She briefly looks in my direction, mutters an apology, and then lowers her chin.

"Don't apologise to him," Paul snorts. "He's had his tongue down your throat—he'll be wanking over that for months. It's me who deserves an apology."

I've had enough.

"I'll leave you two to it. Frankly, you deserve each other."

I take two steps forward, but my progress quickly ends as Paul puts his hand flat on my chest.

"What's that supposed to mean?"

"It means nothing. Now, if you don't mind ..."

"You ain't getting away with it that easy. No bloke messes with my woman."

"I didn't know she was *your woman*, as you so eloquently put it, and I've already apologised. What more do you want?"

"Are you taking the piss?"

With panic setting in, I hop a couple of steps to the side in an attempt to evade his outstretched arm, but Paul brings his other arm into the mix and jabs a punch towards my ribcage. When it lands, it's potent enough to inflict a searing pain and severely undermine my balance.

"Paul! No!" Shelley screams.

Gravity grabs hold of my shoulders. My arms flailing, I turn my head to assess where I might land. To my horror, the edge of a solid wooden table zooms into focus. If that connects with any part of my head, it'll likely hurt a lot more than Paul's punch.

I stretch out my left arm at the last second, hoping it'll hit the floor before my head hits the table.

Then ...

Chapter 25

I think I'm dead or dying, or somewhere between those two states. I've heard it said that when your time is up, you'll journey towards a bright light, much like the one filling my vision. They also say that you might see your life flashing before your eyes, but all I recall is a brief, spectacular firework display.

"Hello? Can you hear me?"

Is that the voice of St Peter or Lucifer? I don't know, but I didn't expect either to have a Brummie accent.

"Jesus," I mumble.

"No, I'm Greg."

The bright light dims away to reveal the face of a middle-aged man with a goatee beard.

"What's your name, mate?" Greg asks.

"Dougie."

My voice sounds nothing like my voice.

"How are you feeling, Dougie?"

"Like ... shit," I wince. "My head is pounding."

"I'm not surprised. You took a helluva whack when you fell over."

I'm about to argue that I didn't fall over, but I've already established that talking hurts. So too does thinking.

"I don't think you've suffered any serious injury, but we'll run you down to A&E, okay? You can never be too careful when it comes to head injuries."

"Okay," I just about murmur.

It feels like a troop of monkeys are running riot in my head, and someone has given each one a toffee hammer to play with.

"Can you stand up?"

I send a message to my legs, and they both respond with a slight movement.

"Think so."

"Here, I'll give you a hand."

As my eyes adjust to the light, my surroundings come into focus. I'm on the floor in The Cherry Tree and, judging by his green uniform, Greg is a paramedic. There's no sign of Shelley or Paul, and the Spice Girls have also fled the scene, to be replaced by a slight humming sound.

I realise the humming is inside my head.

"That's it," Greg says, as he helps me to stand upright. "Do you think you can walk thirty yards to the ambulance, or would you like me to fetch a wheelchair?"

"No, I'll walk ... thank you."

Greg keeps hold of my arm as I slowly shuffle towards the exit, every step agitating the monkeys.

Eventually, I reach the ambulance, and it's a relief to sit down. Greg closes the rear doors and then ensures I'm strapped in.

"Five minutes, and we'll be there," he says.

"Okay, ta."

"Can I ask, have you had much to drink this evening?"

"No, nothing ... wait. I had one shot of vodka, but that's all."

"You're sure?"

"Positive."

Satisfied my fall wasn't the result of nine pints of Stella, Greg sits back in his seat and scribbles on a pad.

I close my eyes and try to will away the pain. With every passing minute, it becomes fractionally more bearable. What isn't so bearable is my indignation. Why the hell did Shelley lie to me?

The journey to the hospital isn't long enough for me to answer that question.

The ambulance comes to a stop and Greg eventually hands me off to a male nurse. I'm told to take a seat and, within a minute of the nurse leaving, I spot a sign on the wall stating that waiting times are currently three hours. Who knows if that'll be long enough to fathom out what was going through Shelley's mind, but I don't suppose it matters because the net result is the same as my last two dates—failure.

Fortunately, I don't have to wait three hours. A nurse calls my name and then leads me to a triage area where my injury is assessed by a doctor. He performs a series of tests, and judging by his lack of concern, I presume I passed.

"You've got a nasty bump and a mild concussion," he confirms. "Take two paracetamol every four hours, and I'd recommend you rest up for the next twenty-four hours. You should be fine by then, but if you're feeling nauseous or suffering from blurred vision, call your doctor or come straight back here. Understood?"

"Yes. Thank you."

Just knowing I haven't sustained a serious injury is enough to calm my anxiety. It looks like I'll have to call in sick tomorrow but it's better to be safe than sorry. It might do Ady some good, working on his own.

The nurse guides me back to the reception area.

"Is there someone who can pick you up? A wife or girlfriend?"

"I'd rather not bother anyone at this time of the evening. I'll just hop in a taxi."

She places her hand on my upper arm.

"Are you sure?" she asks, fluttering her eyelashes. "I finish in an hour if you'd like a lift?"

"Thanks. I'm fine."

I spot a sign for the main exit and make a beeline for it.

Somewhere along the way, I take a wrong turn and lose my bearings. A porter points me in the right direction, and I follow another featureless corridor, passing signs for various departments I pray I'll never need to visit in the future, except for the maternity wing. Alas, the prospect of fatherhood is no closer now than it was two weeks ago. I'm attracting women, which is great, but I certainly haven't attracted the right woman.

That thought rekindles my indignation with Shelley. I'm still angry, but I'm also bitterly disappointed because I liked her, and I thought we were getting on well. Christ knows what she planned to do about her thuggish boyfriend if our relationship evolved, but if I have to put a positive spin on tonight's events, at least I found out before I got too involved.

Back to the drawing board.

I reach the main reception area and call a taxi. I'm told it'll be with me in twenty minutes. I hang up and glance at the row of plastic seats lined up on the wall near the exit. Three of the six seats are occupied by individuals who appear to be carrying the weight of the world on their shoulders if their sombre expressions are anything to go by. I decide not to join them.

There's an altogether different kind of gloom waiting for me outside the main hospital entrance, courtesy of a dark sky and drizzly rain. The taxi pick-up bay is opposite the entrance, but there's no cover, so I'll loiter where I am until I see the taxi approaching.

There's not much of a view, but I do spot a couple of benches some twenty yards away, both under the canopy that covers the building's various entrances and exit points. There's a lone figure sitting on the furthest bench, but the nearest is empty. I slowly make my way over, and with every passing step, the figure on the far bench eases into focus. When I get close enough to realise who it is, I stop dead in my tracks.

"Heather?"

She looks up from the paving slabs and turns towards me. Her surprise at seeing me is evident but brief.

"Hello, Douglas."

In the seconds it takes to cover the final few steps to the bench, the reason Heather is here tumbles to the front of my mind.

"How's Colin?" I ask. "I've been meaning to pop in and see him, but ..."

Halfway through my excuse, I realise there's no good way to end it. I've been so engrossed with my love life I've given precious little thought to Colin's recovery after his hip operation.

"Can I sit down?"

Heather nods, so I gingerly ease myself down onto the cold, hard, metal bench.

"I should have popped in to see your dad by now. No excuses, but I promise I'll visit him tomorrow."

"No point," she replies, her voice not much more than a croak.

My heart drops to my stomach.

"What do you mean, no point?"

"He's ... he's in the intensive care unit, and ... they put him in an induced coma Saturday afternoon."

"But he was fine, wasn't he? I thought the operation went well."

Heather swallows hard and finally turns to face me. Her eyes are puffy and red as if she's in the grip of acute hay fever.

"Dad has pneumonia."

"Oh, no. That's ... will he be okay?"

She shrugs once and then shivers.

"Why are you sitting out here?"

"I just needed a break to clear my head. I've been here since Saturday evening when they called me in."

That explains why The Vale was shut yesterday.

"You've been here since Saturday?" I parrot.

She nods her head.

"Bloody hell, Heather. Have you slept at all?"

There's no reaction at all to my question, which I take as an answer. It begs another question. I slide across the bench until I'm as close I suspect Heather is comfortable with.

"Has no one else been here to relieve you?" I ask as gently as I can.

"There is no one else. It's just Dad and me."

"No one?"

Another shake of the head. I don't know what to do, what to say. All I do know is I can't leave her here like this, alone.

"Listen, Heather, can I make a suggestion?"

She doesn't say no, so I continue.

"Why don't you go home and get some sleep. Your dad wouldn't want you making yourself ill, would he?"

"I can't leave him all on his own. I just can't."

"He won't be on his own, and I'm sure the staff will call you if there's any change in his condition."

"And what if he wakes up? He'll be confused, and he'll want to see a familiar face."

"Well, um ... I'll wait here till the morning if you like?"

I can only put my spontaneous show of kindness down to a mild concussion. It's not that I don't care, but I desperately want to go home and lie down in a dark room.

"No, I can't ask you to do that," she says.

Her tone lacks the fortitude of someone unwilling to change their mind. If she is even half as tired as she looks, she must be exhausted. As crap as I feel, I don't think it's anywhere near as bad as the woman seated next to me feels.

"It's fine, Heather. I've got a taxi arriving in fifteen minutes, and you're going to get in it, understood? I don't want you coming back before morning."

"What if he wakes up, or ..."

"If there's any change in his condition, I'll call you straight away. I promise."

Heather nibbles her bottom lip.

"Why are you here?" she then asks. "At the hospital."

"Long story, but I suffered a mild bump on the head earlier. I'm fine, though."

"I can't expect you to sit here all night if you're not well yourself."

"Heather, it's okay," I reply with a reassuring smile. "Can you think of anywhere better to be if you've had a bump on the head than a hospital?"

My attempt at levity misses the mark.

"There is one condition, though," I continue. "I don't suppose you've got any paracetamol on you?"

"In my handbag," she replies.

"Which is where?"

"In the ICU relatives' room."

"Okay. Let's get your handbag, eh? The taxi will be here soon."

Heather stares down at her lap, and I can almost hear the cogs whirring in her head. If I were in her shoes, would I be so keen to leave my sick dad in the company of a man I barely know? Maybe if I'd made more effort with Heather over the years I've been visiting The Vale Cafe, perhaps she wouldn't now be so hesitant.

"You need some rest, Heather. You look exhausted."

With the faintest nod and a tired sigh, she gets to her feet.

With neither of us in the mood for small talk, the walk to the intensive care unit passes in silence. At the door, Heather presses a buzzer, and the lock disengages within a few seconds. On the other side of the door, a male nurse greets us in a suitably subdued manner. Heather then explains who I am.

"Douglas is a family friend, Andy. Is it okay if he waits in the family room while I pop home for a few hours?"

"Of course," Andy replies. "You're long overdue a break, Heather."

The nurse turns to me and offers a wan smile.

"Nice to meet you, Douglas."

The next few minutes pass by in a blur. After leading the way to the family room, Heather hands me a pack of paracetamol and then tries to talk herself out of leaving. I coax her towards the door and swear on my own life I'll call her if anything happens. She finally leaves, and I'm left alone, wondering if any man has set out on a date only to end the evening sitting in an intensive care unit.

How in God's name did I let this happen?

My metaphorical bed made there's nothing I can do but make the best of the situation. I source a bottle of water from the vending machine and dispatch two of Heather's tablets. I'm so thirsty I empty the bottle within seconds.

Feeling a touch better, in a physical sense, I flop down on the sofa and assess my surroundings. If I try hard enough, I could convince myself I'm in the reception area of a three-star hotel. The décor is pleasant enough, not that I'd imagine anyone unfortunate enough to spend time here would care much about the pastel-blue wallpaper or framed landscape portraits on the wall.

Then, I notice the curtains.

"Bloody hell," I murmur.

I know nothing about interior design, but I do know that the grey and teal patterned curtains hanging in front of me were sold in Argos for much of the early noughties. I know this because an identical pair used to hang in the lounge of a house where I lived briefly. I also know how many times the pattern repeats, how thick the material is, the colour of the lining, and the depth of the hem. I know all of this because I spent a very long time standing next to a window.

16th June 2001

Life has a funny way of kicking you in the balls when you're least expecting it.

Three weeks after signing the lease on our lovely new home, the fuckers at Temple-Dane sacked Denise. They said it was because of her poor work ethic, but on the odd occasions I passed by her desk, she always looked busy. I was tempted to resign in protest but Denise said that'd be stupid because, until she gets another job, we have to pay for everything with my wages.

She was pissed off, obviously, but more than anything, she was worried about paying her own bills. That day, I went to the bank and arranged for Denise to be added to my bank account. Now we're living together, it makes sense we have a joint bank account. I do feel bad that I didn't come up with the idea first, and my girlfriend had to suggest it.

It's just as well I've always saved a chunk of my wages and built up a decent amount of savings. I reckon Denise will get a job soon, and it'll be better paid than the one she lost, so this is just a blip.

Probably the worst thing about being sacked is what it does for your confidence, and Denise's mood has been up and down since it happened. Some days she locks herself away in the bedroom for hours and won't talk to me. Other days, she wants to go out and party with her best friend. I don't begrudge her going out on a Saturday evening, but I'm writing this entry at 2.30 am, and she's still not back. Last week, she didn't come home till 10.00 am on the Sunday, and I was worried sick. I stood at the lounge window until it got light but that was all I could manage before exhaustion took hold.

She promised she'd be home at a reasonable hour this week, or she'd call me if she was going to stay at her mate's flat again. Soon as I finish writing, I know I'll be back at the window again 'cos I can't sleep. I worry about her, and I know it's good that she can go out and blow off some steam, but I wish she'd let me go with her. In Denise's defence, she said we can't really afford for both of us to go out, and I kinda understand where she's coming from. She spent almost eighty quid last Saturday, and if we were both out, it would have been a lot more—my girlfriend does like a drink, and she likes her man to keep up, so she tells me.

An hour ago I almost did something stupid. Just for a moment, I considered going into town and seeing if I could find her. That's the kind of thing a paranoid, jealous boyfriend would do, and I don't want Denise to think I'm like that. Really, I just want her to be happy, and if that means she has to get this out of her system, I suppose I've just got to be patient and supportive. It's not easy, though.

The worst thing is letting my imagination run wild. Last week I watched a movie to kill time, but it was about a couple going through a breakup after the wife had an affair. The husband found out, and one night, when the wife said she was away on business, he tracked her down to a house across town. He then watched through the lounge window as some random bloke shagged his wife on the sofa. I felt sick, and had to turn it off. I've no idea how it ended.

Denise would never cheat on me, though. Why would she? I might not be the best-looking bloke she's ever dated, but I'm definitely the most considerate, the kindest, and the most loyal. She's been cheated on herself, so she knows how painful it is. No, she isn't the type. I just wish my imagination would shut the fuck up and stop suggesting she might. I wish it wouldn't conjure up images of her in some bloke's flat, at this very moment.

I need to stop this. I'll give it another ten minutes at the window, and then I'll go to bed.

Everything will be fine. I know it will.

I mustn't worry.

Chapter 26

Not since I lived at home with my parents has another human woken me from a slumber.

The disorientation continues as I stumble towards consciousness. I realise I'm not in my bed, and a random man is standing over me.

"Douglas," he whispers. "Sorry to wake you."

Where the fuck am I?

I blink at the muted light and strange figure looking down at me. Beyond his shoulder, I can just make out a vending machine and a pair of dated curtains closed shut.

Ever so slowly, realisation dawns.

"Sorry, err ... I can't remember your name."

"Andy," he sniggers. "As names go, it's remarkably forgettable."

He seems in good spirits, which I hope is why he's decided to wake me up. Surely, he wouldn't be quite so upbeat if he was about to tell me Colin died twenty minutes ago?

"Is everything okay with Colin?"

"It's good news. If you want to take five minutes to grab a coffee, I'll pop back."

"Yeah, great. I'll do that."

Andy hurries away, and I clamber off the sofa. I instantly regret the sudden movement and try to recollect if I consumed too much alcohol last night. The reason for my pounding head then filters in. As much as I'd like to lament another dreadful date, I promised Heather I'd call if anything happens with Colin, and I need to get my act together before making that call. My first priority, though, is coffee and painkillers.

Only once I'm waiting for the hot drinks dispenser to pour a large Americano do I think to check the time.

"Ugh," I groan, with good reason. It's half five in the morning.

If there's any upside, we're supposed to text Jonny an hour before we're due to start work if we're unwell, so at least I've time to do that, and to text Ady, telling him I won't need a lift today. Notwithstanding the egg-sized lump on my head and potential concussion, I'm too knackered to be humping rubbish sacks and fridge freezers today.

I send the messages and take the first sip of coffee, along with two more painkillers. I'm still feeling groggy when Andy returns.

"Feeling better?" he asks.

"A bit, ta."

"Hopefully, what I'm about to tell you will help. Colin has responded remarkably well to treatment, and we're confident he's in a much better place than he was on Saturday."

"Does that mean he'll be okay?"

"We're hoping to bring him out of his induced coma this morning, and we'll know for sure then. However, all the signs are positive."

"That's a relief. I'll call Heather and let her know."

Andy asks if I want to sit at Colin's bed until Heather arrives. I make a half-arsed excuse about waiting until he's conscious and back on the general ward. The truth is that I'm too scared to see a man I know being kept alive by machines, even if it's only temporary.

Andy departs, and I scroll through the contact list on my phone for Heather's number. I pause before tapping the call icon. Should I let her sleep a few more hours? The curtains remind me that sleep doesn't come easy when you're waiting and worried. I tap the icon.

The call tone terminates on the sixth ring.

"Hello," the faintest of voices answers.

"Heather, it's Dougie. Sorry if I woke you ..."

"What? What is it?" she splutters.

"Don't panic; it's good news. Andy just confirmed your dad's condition has improved, and they're hoping to wake him up this morning."

"I'll be there in twenty minutes."

The line dies before I'm able to ask if she wants me to hang around.

Twenty-nine minutes later, my inability to decide whether to hang around or not becomes a moot point when Heather bustles in.

"You waited," she says coyly. "You didn't have to."

I get up from the sofa.

"I, um ... it's no problem."

"I just spoke to the doctor, and she confirmed what Andy told you. She was very positive about Dad's condition."

"That's great news. You must be so relieved."

"Yes ... relieved."

Relief is a common emotion, and most of us experience it every day. We're relieved when the working day is over, or there's more money in our bank account than we estimated, or when you find a lost set of keys.

Standing here now, in near silence, I sense Heather's relief is weightier than any she's ever experienced. Staring down at the carpeted floor, and with a hand pressed to her forehead, she pulls a series of sharp breaths. Somewhere between those breaths, a sob escapes. Another one soon follows, and then another.

Heather, it seems, is unable to contain her relief.

"Hey, don't cry," I say gently, stepping towards her. "It's all going to be just fine."

My words have little effect as the tears begin to flow. I don't know what to say, but I know what I'd want to hear if the roles were reversed.

"Would a hug help?" I venture.

Heather squeezes her eyes shut. After a brief pause, she replies with the slightest of nods. I wrap my arms around her and try to ignore the undercurrent of awkwardness. I'm probably the last person she wants a hug from right now. Sadly, for Heather, I'm the only person available.

"It's okay," I gently whisper, as she buries her head against my chest.

Slowly but surely, the tears stop cascading, and her breathing settles. Strange as it is, neither of us seems in a hurry to let go. On my part, it's because I'm too content just being needed by another human. It's not the same kind of hug I received from Zoe or Shelley or even Leanne. There is a closeness, untainted by sexual chemistry or desire; the kind of reassuring hug I savoured as a child when I fell off my bike or woke up from a nightmare. It is the physical equivalent of being told that everything will be fine.

Too soon, it ends.

"I'm so sorry," Heather mumbles, as she wipes her eyes with a hanky.

"There's no need to apologise. We all need a hug now and again."

She looks up at me; her soft brown eyes still wet with tears. I can't help but wonder if the sudden lowering of her defences is because of the gift or because she just needed a shoulder to cry on.

"It means a lot, Douglas. Thank you."

Unable to maintain eye contact, she steps back and fidgets with her hanky.

"Do you, err, need anything?" I ask. "I mean, is there anything else I can do?"

"I don't suppose … no, it doesn't matter."

"No, go on. I'm happy to help."

"I don't want to be a burden."

"You're not. I promised Colin I'd lend a hand if you needed one, and I don't like breaking promises."

"Well, I don't suppose you'd mind dropping by the cafe and putting a notice in the window, explaining why we're closed?"

"No problem."

Heather rummages in her handbag and hands over two brass-coloured keys on a keyring.

"If you just say we'll be closed until next week, that would be very helpful."

"Consider it done. I need to retrieve my car first, but I'll head there straight after."

I can't hold back a yawn, and it seems the perfect cue to make my excuses.

"You'll let me know when Colin is ready for visitors?"

"Yes, I will."

"Okay, um … well, I'll drop the keys back to you in the next few days, if that's okay?"

"No problem."

"Great. Um … goodbye, Heather."

"Right, yes … goodbye."

"You too. I mean, goodbye."

I scamper away, but I'm still inwardly cringing when I reach the main exit. There's something about Heather that makes me feel … awkward, I guess. I suspect the gift had a lot to do with her willingness to accept my hug, and I don't know how I feel about that.

One short taxi ride later, I arrive at the car park. Being it's still early, there's no warden around to check my expired ticket. I hop in the car and leave before one shows up. It's a small but rewarding victory.

It takes every ounce of my concentration to remain alert on the drive to The Vale. I did consider dropping by later, but I want to get it out of the way. When I get home, I intend to crash on the sofa and stay there all day. In between naps, I also need to plan where I go next in my quest to find Miss Right. In truth, I'd be happy just to avoid meeting another Miss Nightmare.

I park up outside The Vale and trudge up to the front door. It takes a few minutes to deal with the stiff locks and finally force the door open. Only then does it dawn on me that to write a note, I need paper and a pen. I've no clue where to find either.

I begin the search behind the counter and find the pen. The pad used for jotting orders is too small so I have no option but to extend my search beyond the counter. The Vale isn't big, so there are limited spaces to explore. There's a small lobby off the main dining area giving access to the kitchen, the solitary toilet, and the fire escape. I push open the door to the kitchen and turn the light on.

I spend a few minutes opening cupboards, but all I find are cooking ingredients and utensils. Then, in a tall cupboard in the corner, I discover a metal filing cabinet. The top drawer offers a tape dispenser, which I'll need, and other stationery items such as a hole punch, stapler, and highlighter pens. I find what I'm looking for in the next drawer.

"A-ha!"

I grab the pad of A4 paper and remove it from the drawer. Unintentionally, my eyes are drawn to the letter underneath and the bold words at the top: FINAL DEMAND. The logo in the corner happens to be one I'm familiar with, in that it belongs to Ashbridge Borough Council. I shouldn't look, but curiosity gets the better of me, and I lean in to get a closer look.

I quickly wish I hadn't.

The letter states that Colin has only seven days to settle his outstanding business rates, a sum of £3,755. I pluck the letter from the dark drawer and re-read it. That's when I unearth another one below, with similar wording but a different logo—a final demand from their energy supplier. I pick it up, and there's another and another. I stop snooping at the fifth demand; from a waste contractor.

I'm no accountant, but if these handful of unpaid bills are any indicator, The Vale Cafe really is in financial trouble. No wonder Heather couldn't afford thirty quid for a new toaster.

Returning the letters to the drawer, I feel guilty for looking at them but also concerned that the building in which I-'m presently standing might not be a cafe much longer. Their plight must have been hard enough before this enforced closure, but an entire week without trade could be the death knell unless Colin and Heather have a plan to raise thousands of pounds in the coming days.

Troubling as it is, it's none of my business. Even if I wanted to help, I'd have to confess to snooping.

I write the sign and fix it to the door. I'm about to turn off the lights, but I feel compelled to take what might be my final look at the interior of The Vale Cafe. It really would be the end of an era if it closed. But, beyond my selfish reasons for feeling sad, what are Colin and Heather going to do? Alas, I have a few problems of my own, and they're currently hogging what's left of my mental bandwidth.

I lock the door and return to my car.

I've never been quite so pleased to see my sofa. After changing out of last night's clothes, I settle down for a shortish nap. If I sleep too long, I won't sleep tonight, and the cycle will continue right through to the weekend. I set an alarm and close my eyes.

The three hours pass by in a flash, but I wake up still feeling jaded. A decent lunch helps, and then I return to the sofa for an afternoon of watching television and doing next to nothing.

A text message arrives, and when I spot Shelley's name on the screen, I'm inclined to delete it, unread. However, curiosity wins the argument, and I open the message. *I'm so sorry for everything, Dougie. I've now split up with Paul so if you're willing to give me a second chance, I swear I'll make it worth your while. XX*

I delete it, and block Shelley's number.

In my haste to list all the attributes I'd like in my ideal woman, I overlooked the basics, like honesty and loyalty. Sadly, I know from bitter experience that a second chance is rarely the last chance where lying partners are concerned. I won't make that mistake again.

I turn my thoughts back to the list and what other revisions I need to make. It proves so mentally taxing that I fall asleep halfway through an episode of *Escape To The Country*.

Chapter 27

I awake, bleary-eyed, to the sound of the doorbell. Still semi-comatose, I climb off the sofa and stagger to the hallway, checking the time on the way: 5.17 pm.

"Shit."

I can't believe I slept for another three hours. Whoever is at my front door, I'm glad they called round when they did, as I might have slept through to bedtime.

The second I open the door, I'm not so glad.

"Hey, Leanne."

"Thank God," she gasps. "You're okay."

"Err, yes. I'm fine."

"Ady said you called in sick today, and you're never off sick."

"It's nothing. I bumped my head yesterday, and the doctor said I should rest for twenty-four hours, that's all."

"How are you feeling?"

"Honestly, I feel a little groggy, but I've just woken up."

"You haven't had dinner yet, then?"

"No."

She holds up her right arm and presents a Tesco's carrier bag.

"I thought you might not feel like cooking, so I picked up a few bits. I hope it's okay?"

She adopts the look of a Dickensian orphan begging for coppers. I can't say no.

"You honestly didn't have to, Leanne, but thank you."

I reach out to take the bag.

"No," she firmly responds. "I'll do the cooking. You sit down and relax."

Too late, I realise I've misinterpreted Leanne's act of kindness. I presumed she'd bought a multipack of pork pies and a tube of Pringles.

"I wouldn't want to inconvenience you," I protest. "Besides, won't Ady be expecting you home from work?"

"No, he won't," she huffs. "He texted me an hour ago to say he was meeting a mate in the pub at five."

"Oh."

"And I think we both know who his mate is, don't we?"

"Um ..."

"It makes no odds to me, Dougie. I'm past caring."

"Right."

Not wishing to fall into the rabbit's hole of Ady's alleged infidelity or appear ungrateful, I'm left with no option but to find a half-smile and invite Leanne in. Standing in the hallway, she kicks off her shoes and opens the carrier bag for me to see inside.

"It's nothing special," she says. "Pork medallions with mustard mash and garden peas."

"Sounds lovely."

"If you show me the kitchen, I'll have it knocked up in twenty minutes or so."

I escort her through to the kitchen.

"Wow! I'm impressed, Dougie."

"Are you? Why?"

"Your kitchen is spotless. As soon as I clean ours, Ady is in there making a mess which he never clears up, the lazy git."

"Sadly, there's no one to clean up after me, so I've no choice but to keep it tidy."

"And that's a crying shame," she says dolefully, placing a hand on my arm. "You deserve someone."

Her statement lingers in the silence, just as her hand lingers on my arm. I don't much care for either.

"Um, you know, Leanne, there's no need for you to cook dinner. You've already been more than kind, and I wouldn't want to take advantage."

"You're not," she replies, finally removing her hand so she can wave away my objection. "You go and put your feet up."

Part of me wants to dig in or feign a sudden headache, but I'd be lying if I said a teeny part of me isn't warmed by the situation. I guess it's just part of the routine for most couples, but as a long-term single man, no one has ever insisted they cook dinner for me or fretted over my wellbeing. I know it's not right because Leanne is Ady's girlfriend, but that doesn't mean it's not nice.

"You're a star. Thank you."

She smiles and then playfully shoos me away.

I return to the lounge and flop back on the sofa. I'm about to switch the television on when my phone rings.

"Hello."

"Um, Douglas ... it's Heather."

"Hi, Heather. Are you okay?"

"Yes, I'm fine. I was just calling to let you know Dad is now back on the general ward. They moved him this afternoon."

"That's great news. I'll pop in on Saturday if that's okay?"

"Yes. He would like that."

"Good. And, how are you?"

"I'm fine. I've just got back home, and ... well, I was just ... oh, forget it."

"Is something the matter?"

"No, just me being ridiculous as usual. I was going to ask if you ... would you like to come over for a bite to eat?"

"Um ..."

"Forget it. As I said, it was just a thought and ... my way of saying thank you for what you did."

"That's incredibly kind of you, but I was just ..."

"I must go. Goodbye, Douglas."

The line falls silent.

Perturbed, I place my phone on the coffee table. How has this happened? I now have two women who want to cook dinner for me, but neither are viable candidates for the position of my partner. Leanne is dating my closest work colleague, and Heather is just ... well, Heather.

"Everything okay, Dougie?"

I look over to the doorway where Leanne is standing, tea towel in hand.

"Err, yeah."

"Are you sure? I wasn't eavesdropping, but I heard you mention good news. You don't look like a man who's just received good news."

"It's nothing. A friend asked if I wanted a bite to eat tonight, but obviously, my dinner is already in hand."

"Your friend is called Heather?"

I nod.

"I hope she wasn't too upset."

"I'm sure she's fine. I'll likely see her on Saturday, and I'll buy her a coffee."

"Right."

Leanne disappears back to the kitchen. I switch on the television and distract myself with the news. As is usual these days, there's very little actual news but a lot of opinions and sensationalised conjecture. After a few minutes, I switch over to a quiz show where I'm more likely to encounter reliable facts.

Leanne reappears, carrying a tray.

"Dinner is served," she says cheerfully.

"Thank you."

She carefully places the tray on my lap and hands me a knife and fork.

"Give me a shout once you've finished, and I'll fetch your plate."

"Err, right. Where are you going?"

"To wash up."

"Absolutely not. You've done more than enough, and besides, I've got a dishwasher."

"I'll load the dishwasher, then."

"Please, Leanne. I insist on clearing up, okay?"

"Okay."

This is the point I expect her to leave. She's completed her good deed, and now I've told her there's nothing else to do, what reason does she have to stay?

Leanne sits down on the sofa next to me.

"Do you mind if I keep you company a while longer?" she asks. "I don't think I can face going home just yet?"

What am I supposed to say, particularly with a mouthful of mustard mash? I adopt a grimace-like smile and nod. Satisfied with my response, Leanne sits back and makes herself comfortable.

I tuck into my dinner while my guest answers the TV quiz questions. Her general knowledge is impressive, which is surprising when you consider Ady's knowledge doesn't extend beyond football, cars, and beer. They're a strange pairing, but they patently have enough in common to have stayed together for so long. Alternatively, perhaps they prove the point that opposites do sometimes attract.

I finish the meal. It reinforces my view that food always tastes so much better when someone else prepares it.

"Thanks, Leanne," I say, getting to my feet. "That was delicious."

"I'm glad you enjoyed it. Have you had enough?"

"I'm stuffed, but I could murder a cup of tea. Would you like one?"

"I'll make it."

"No, I'll make it. It's the least I can do."

"Are you sure?"

"You carry on watching your quiz."

I return five minutes later with two mugs of tea.

"Do you like quizzes, Dougie?"

I pass Leanne one of the mugs.

"I do, actually. I'm part of a quiz team at my local."

"That sounds like fun. I don't suppose you've got room for another member?"

"I'll, um, ask our captain."

"Thanks."

I retake my position on the sofa, careful not to sit too close to Leanne. As I sip from my mug and the quiz shows draws to a close, I try to formulate a polite way of bringing this surreal experience to an end. I can't deny the experience hasn't been enjoyable, but more to the point, I *shouldn't* be enjoying it. Leanne derails my train of thought.

"Can I ask you a question?"

"Sure."

"Do you like being a bachelor?"

"It is what it is. I try to make the best of it."

"Don't you get lonely?"

"Sometimes."

"I feel terrible. I've known you for so long, and it never crossed my mind to pop over and see if you're okay."

"You make me sound like an elderly relative."

"Sorry. What I meant is that it never occurred to me how much I might enjoy spending time with you."

"Oh, right."

"I mean, this is nice, isn't it? Just relaxing with a cup of tea and watching the TV."

"It is, yeah."

"I could get used to it," she chuckles. "It's so different from my evenings with Ady and his mum."

I'm not sure how different it could be, and I'm not inclined to ask. I take another sip from my mug and return my attention to a way out of this. Finally, a plausible excuse floats in.

"Um, I hope you don't think I'm being rude, but I need to go run a bath in a minute. I fell asleep on the sofa earlier, and now I ache all over."

"Of course, I don't think you're being rude," Leanne says softly. "But you really do need someone to pamper you. Dougie."

I nod and leave it at that.

"Would you like me to scrub your back?"

Leanne's question is followed by a slight snigger and a grin, leaving it open to interpretation. She might be joking, but I wouldn't swear on it.

"Tempting as your offer is, I don't think Ady would approve, do you?"

"No," she huffs. "Probably not."

We finish our tea with little in the way of conversation. To reinforce my reason for asking my guest to leave, I get up, stretch, and groan.

"I'm getting old," I remark.

"You know what they say?" Leanne says, standing up. "You're only as old as the woman you feel."

I've already debunked that adage when I left Zoe's flat feeling anything but young. I feign another back spasm.

"You poor thing. Are you sure you don't want a back rub?"

"Err, no ... thanks."

I manage to corral Leanne towards the hallway and thank her again. She insists it was her pleasure and plants a kiss on my cheek, keeping her lips pressed to my skin a touch too long.

Finally, she leaves. I shut the front door and lean against it, puffing a long sigh of relief.

That is definitely the last time I let Leanne into my home. If the circumstances were different, maybe I might now be upstairs enjoying a massage. They're not, though, and I've had enough women-related problems over the last week. Encouraging Leanne in any way—even innocently—could so easily come back to bite me on the arse.

I climb up the stairs and turn on the bath taps. It's not that I need to ease my aching bones, but I do need to sit and take stock of where I am. My previously simple life is now anything but, and the gift is proving to be the sharpest of double-edged swords. I don't want any more humiliating one night stands, no more cheaters or their psychopathic boyfriends, and I definitely don't want any more attention from my colleague's partner.

I just want Miss Right. Is that too much to ask?

Chapter 28

If Ady had any issues with his girlfriend's absence yesterday evening, he didn't share them with me on the journey to work. If anything, he seemed in good spirits.

That was until we arrived at the depot where Big Fal had parked in Ady's regular bay. A heated discussion ensued, and it only ended when Ady acknowledged there was no way he'd win a fight with his eighteen-stone colleague. It was a brief but welcome distraction from my problems—some of which are, admittedly, of my own making.

Whilst stewing in the bath last night, I had a good long think about what's happened since I took that sip of herbal tonic eleven days ago. Those thoughts coincided with a memory, a quote from one of my favourite films, *Spider Man,* when Peter Parker utters the immortal line: with great power comes great responsibility.

Without a doubt, the gift is a form of power, but have I managed it responsibly? I concluded I had not.

In many ways, I've done with it what most men do after they've purchased a new piece of tech, like one of those super-expensive coffee machines—mess around with it without any real understanding of how it works. Obviously, the gift didn't come with instructions, but even if it did, I doubt I'd have read them.

I subsequently paid the price for being impetuous through the medium of sexual humiliation and a trip to A&E. And, the less said about the unwanted attention from Leanne, the better.

After much further thought, I reformulated my list of rules last night. It evolved into a strategy of sorts, with the key aims to be patient, to limit my exposure to unsuitable partners, and to be more constrained generally. Jumping in feet first with every woman I fancy has not proven an effective use of the gift. From this moment on, I will treat my search for Miss Right like a first-time buyer treats their search for a new home. I'll take my time, search carefully and diligently, and conduct copious amounts of research before committing.

"I should have decked the gobby bastard," Ady mumbles, as we enter the meeting room.

"You'd need a sledgehammer to deck Big Fal, and you know it."

"Bigger they are, harder they fall."

"Hmm ... bigger they are, harder they tend to punch, too."

Ady scowls and digs his hands into his pockets—a sure sign he knows he's wrong but isn't willing to admit it.

Jonny ambles in and tells everyone to pipe down.

"I have to start with some bad news," he barks, arms folded across his flabby chest. "And someone in this room is responsible."

Immediately, there's a shift in the atmosphere as heads turn and shoulders shrug. Without knowing the details of this supposed bad news, it's impossible to say who's responsible for it.

"Keira has resigned," Jonny continues. "And although she never mentioned a specific name, she did say it's because she no longer feels comfortable working with one of you lot."

Ohh, shit!

As everyone around me mumbles their denial, I think back to when I declined Keira's invitation to dinner and our subsequent interactions. Could that be the reason she feels uncomfortable? What have I done?

"You didn't say anything to her?" Ady asks, noticing my frown.

"What? No, of course not."

He turns to Steve.

"What about you? You were the one who made those comments about her tits."

"Yeah, when she first started, but I ain't said nothing since. We've all been on our best behaviour after she laid into us that time."

Steve is right. I haven't heard a single sexist remark since Keira called out some of my colleagues on their behaviour. That only leaves one contender for the man who made Keira's position untenable, and that's me. However, it's not for the reasons Jonny or anyone might suspect.

"Anyone gonna own up?" my boss yells above the murmuring.

No one does. Should I?

In the silence, I consider how my confession might play out. I quickly determine it would not play out well at all. No one would believe Keira asked me out, and they'd laugh their arses off if I said I then turned her down. Within seconds they'd give me a new nickname—Delusional Dougie.

"Anyone?"

The silence continues.

"When I find out who did it, they're in deep shit. For now, though, I need a volunteer to help check the vans in and out. Anyone?"

Slowly, six hands are raised, including mine. It's the least I can do, under the circumstances.

"Put your hand down if you can't use a computer."

Five hands are lowered, leaving just mine.

"Looks like you're the man," Jonny says. "Come see me after the meeting, and I'll show you the ropes."

"Um, how long will it be before you find Keira's replacement?"

"No idea, but it'll be a good few weeks at least."

Wonderful.

I catch the look in Ady's eye. This new role means we can't leave the depot until every van has returned and the admin is complete. I don't think my colleague is best pleased.

"Knob," he mumbles under his breath.

No, he's not pleased.

It takes fifteen minutes for Jonny to show me what I need to do. It's fairly straightforward, and as long as there are no issues when the vans return, it shouldn't take long to sign them all back in. If it means an extra ten minutes on my working day, I suppose that's just penance for my part in Keira's decision to quit. I wish there were something I could do to change that, but with bins to empty and Ady to placate, it's a problem for later.

We're last to depart the depot, unsurprisingly.

If I needed reminding what a sulker Ady can be, it arrives within minutes as he shrugs his shoulders when I ask a question. He barely says a word for the rest of the morning. Ordinarily, I'd just ignore him and revel in the quiet, but today I can't help but think of Leanne. If Ady is like this at home, no wonder she's got the hump with him. I've already decided I'm not getting involved with their relationship but if he is cheating on his girlfriend, he's an even bigger fool than I thought. Leanne deserves better.

"We gonna go to The Vale for lunch?" he mumbles, as we empty the last bin on the round.

"Oh, you're talking to me now?"

"Yeah, but I dunno why. You should have checked with me before volunteering to deal with the vans."

"Yes, I should. I'm sorry, but someone had to stand in for Keira, and it's not my fault everyone else is computer-illiterate."

"Suppose not."

"Am I forgiven?"

"Whatever."

"I'll take that as a yes. Unfortunately, though, we can't go to The Vale for lunch."

"Why not?"

"It's a long story, but Colin had a scare in hospital. Heather will be at his bedside for the next few days."

"Bloody hell," he whines. "I fancied a full English today, too."

I'm about to rip into Ady for being a selfish, inconsiderate twat, but I can't stomach another three hours of sulking.

"Even if it was open, we don't have time. We're running behind schedule."

"Yeah, 'cos you had to be teacher's pet."

"Give it a rest, Ady."

My weariness sets a tone for the remainder of the afternoon. We get the work done, but there's not a lot of chat.

When we return to the depot, we're one of the last to arrive. Consequently, I don't have to wait for all the crews to return, and I'm able to complete my new duty within minutes. We leave a bit later than we usually would but not dramatically. Even so, Ady makes a suggestion on the way home—that I drive myself to and from the depot until they find a replacement for Keira. I agree, just to keep the peace. Ady drops me outside my house and drives away in a better mood than he deserves.

As soon as I pass through the front door, I check the weather forecast and hurry upstairs. I haven't visited Tinkerton Meadow since Monday, and I'm beginning to suffer withdrawal symptoms. Knowing I'm in a race against darkness and the threat of torrential rain, I dispense with a shower and quickly get changed. Then, I drive across town a little faster than I usually would.

A certain Scotsman is in the process of packing up his gear on the top of Falbert's Mount when I arrive.

"I thought you'd forgotten the way here," Kenny jokes, as I hustle over to his side.

"I've had one of those weeks."

"Anything you want to talk about?"

"Honestly, I came here in the hope of forgetting it."

"Aye, I hear you."

He then nods off to the horizon, where a dark cloud looms ominously above the treeline.

"But I'd make the most of it because that beast is coming our way."

"I saw the weather forecast, but if I can get an hour in, that'll do me."

He puts his rucksack back on the ground.

"Seeing as you're here now, I'll hang around a wee while longer ... if you fancy the company?"

"Sure."

With my private life off the agenda, we chat idly about nothing in particular as the light slowly fades. Kenny had already warned me not to expect much, and his warning proved sound. After half an hour, all I've got to show in my bird diary are a dozen Lapwing, five Meadow Pipit, and a pair of Little Grebe. On the upside, the angry cloud remains tethered to the horizon, delivering the promised rain to another part of Ashbridge.

Eventually, though, there's too little light to spot anything other than the family of swans gliding across the lake. Just as he's about to return his binoculars to their case, Kenny's mobile phone emits a pinging sound. He places the binoculars in his rucksack and checks his phone. I turn back to the lake and take another sweep of the shoreline, more in hope than expectation, and then retire my binoculars for the day.

Kenny is still frowning at the screen of his phone.

"Everything okay?" I ask while zipping up the pockets of my jacket.

"For me, aye," he replies, still eyeing the screen. "But I'm not so sure they're okay for you, pal."

"Eh?"

"Look at this," he says, holding the phone up for me to see.

I take a step closer and squint. I'm not sure what I expected to see, but it wasn't a photo of my face. It takes a few seconds to comprehend the context.

"That's you with Zoe, isn't it?" Kenny says. "The lassie from The Fox & Hounds."

It is indeed the photo Zoe took of us both in that swanky wine bar where we met on our date. She looks stunning, whereas I look like a man who didn't want his picture taken. The existence of the photo itself isn't my immediate concern.

"Why is that photo on your phone, Kenny?"

"Sara sent it to me—it's a post on Facebook that one of her friends shared with her."

"What? Why is one of Sara's friends sharing that photo?"

Kenny's chin drops a touch.

"It's not the photo they're sharing, pal—it's the message written underneath it."

"A message from who?"

"Zoe, and judging by the tone in her post, she's not happy with you."

"Why? What does it say?"

"Here, read it yourself, but I'd warn you, it's not pleasant."

My stomach churns as I take the phone and catch sight of the opening line of the post: *Sexual Predator Warning—Be Alert!*

As inflammatory as the post is likely to be, I can't ignore it. I've no choice but to read on.

This is a message to every woman in Ashbridge and the surrounding towns. The man in the photo above is called Dougie, and last Friday evening, he somehow coerced me into performing a sexual act on him. As you can see from the photo, he's middle-aged, bald, and utterly repugnant. There is no way I would have agreed to go on a date with such a gross individual unless I was drugged or tricked.

Unfortunately, the police are unwilling to question him, so I've had to take this measure to protect other women.

If this man approaches you, do not engage with him. Whatever despicable methods he uses, they are so subtle I didn't even realise I was a victim until it was too late.

You have been warned—stay away from this pervert.

Chapter 29

It's been twenty-odd years since I last stayed awake all night. The circumstances are different today, but the sense of dread is eerily similar.

From my bed, I watch on as the first shards of daylight creep over the curtain rail. Externally, the silence is absolute, but internally, the noise in my head shows no sign of abating. In a way, it reminds me of gulls—the one species of bird I have no time for. They don't sing like a Nightingale or whistle like a Robin; they squawk and heckle as tunefully as a rusty garage door being prised open.

An entire flock of gulls have continued squawking in my ear since I returned from Tinkerton Meadow early yesterday evening. When I opened my laptop and logged in to Facebook, the squawking intensified. If the original post from Zoe wasn't bad enough, it had been shared hundreds of times and attracted scores of comments. Like a fool, I read them.

Several things shocked me as I trawled through the first few dozen comments. Firstly, just how quick people are to take a position when armed with only half the facts. I was shocked but not surprised because that's how social media works. People believe what they want to believe, and why let something as insignificant as facts get in the way? Secondly, I was dismayed by the unimaginative language used in almost every comment. They contained the same limited variety of adjectives: filthy, dirty, disgusting, sick and warped. An equally limited list of nouns followed each adjective: scumbag, tosser, wanker, creep, and pervert.

I did learn something new, though. After the speed dating event, it did cross my mind that I might try online dating again, but I now know I wouldn't have fared any better than I did before. The scores of women who viewed my photo on Facebook weren't influenced by the gift—they could only see the ugly reality, and they didn't hold back in sharing their opinions.

I can only imagine Zoe's reaction when she opened the image gallery on her phone. She must have felt sick, repulsed. Considering she was already feeling humiliated after my disappearing act, it's no wonder she vented her rage on Facebook.

I got what I deserved. I might not have slept with Zoe, but I let that young woman do something I knew full well she'd never consider doing if she wasn't under the influence of the gift.

As nasty as the comments on Facebook were, nothing is as bad as my current state of self-loathing.

I grab the laptop from the bedside table and check the post hasn't reappeared. Kenny called mid-evening to see if I was okay, and he suggested I report the post as libellous so Facebook would take it down. I was in such a state of self-flagellation I almost didn't heed his advice, but then it occurred to me there was far more at stake than just my reputation. I reported the post, and it disappeared in the early hours of the morning.

Although the original post is no more, the damage has already been done. I dread to think how many people viewed and shared it before the Facebook administrators stepped in. For all I know, half the population of Ashbridge will wake up this morning with the firm belief that I'm a sexual deviant. They won't notice or likely care that the offending post was subsequently deleted.

Reluctantly, I crawl out of bed and prepare to face a day I'm dreading.

"Just get through today, Dougie, and it'll all have blown over by next week."

Not entirely convinced, I get ready for work.

I'm so distracted by my concerns for what lies ahead, I almost forget Ady isn't picking me up this morning. After wasting five minutes waiting for him, I finally remember and hurry to my car, cussing all the way. It's not the best start to a day that already promises to be a shitty one.

Despite my later than anticipated departure, I arrive at the depot before Ady and park up. I don't know if my colleagues are avid Facebook users, so there's a slight chance I might not face a grilling when I wander into the meeting room, but there's only one way to know for sure.

I turn the engine off and sit for a moment, watching the minutes tick by on the dashboard clock. Out of time, I get out of the car and slope across the tarmac to the main building. On the way, I double-check the parking bays for Ady's car, but it's nowhere to be seen. Unless he arrives in the next thirty seconds, there's a chance he'll receive his final strike. If the circumstances were different, I might be concerned for Ady, but as I push open the door to the meeting room, my thoughts are elsewhere.

In hindsight, walking in at the very last second wasn't a great idea. Every one of my colleagues is standing together in a tight group, staring at me.

"Oi, oi!" Steve yells. "Here he is!"

Shit. They know.

I keep to the back of the room, standing a few metres from the door, and prepare myself.

"You're late, Dougie," Big Fal grins. "Did you have a problem getting rid of another dolly bird this morning?"

It says a lot about my colleagues that one of them still uses the term dolly bird, and the others find it amusing.

"Grow up," I mumble.

"Ooh," they all jeer in unison.

"How'd you do it, then?" Steve asks. "We're all wondering why a stunner like that would hop into bed with you?"

"None of your business."

"Did you drug her?"

The accusation prompts a chorus of laughter. I don't know why Jonny isn't here yet, but I need to nip their taunting in the bud before it gets out of hand.

"Listen," I snap. "Whatever you read online, it's bull-shit—that's why the post was removed. But seeing as you're so interested in my love life, I will confirm I had one date with a girl called Zoe, and no, there were no drugs involved. *She* asked me out, and then *she* invited me back to her flat, where *she* initiated a sexual act. And that's all I'm going to say on the matter. Clear?"

I've worked with these men long enough to know how to defuse their childish hectoring, but there's too much ammunition to expect an easy ride. Big Fal opens his mouth to say something, but before he can get his insult out, a door slams behind them.

"Listen up," Jonny barks.

They all turn around to face our boss. I can relax for the next five minutes, and at least the worst of it is over. Like kids on the school playground, they're far worse in a large group where they can show off. Once the meeting is over, I'll only have to put up with their individual jibes.

I've never been happier to listen to one of Jonny's dull brief-ings. Halfway through it, Ady creeps in and edges up to stand next to me.

"Where have you been?" I whisper.

He shoots me a look that says he's in no mood to answer my question. If his recent form is anything to go by, he probably woke up on a mate's sofa twenty minutes ago. Quite remarkably, he looks more sleep-deprived than I do.

Once the morning brief is over, Ady heads off for a smoke while I deal with the van admin. As I suspected, the inquisition is limited to a few snarky comments and one or two questions about my strategy for attracting women like Zoe. I respond to each and every remark with a withering glare. It proves enough to quell the playground high jinks.

One by one, my colleagues all filter away as the vans depart for their daily duties. Ady, still smoking, joins me as I unlock the last remaining van.

"Any wisecracks," I say, as we put on our seatbelts. "Get them out of the way now."

"What?" he mumbles.

"You know, about that post on Facebook."

"Dunno what you're talking about."

It hadn't crossed my mind Ady might not have seen the post.

"Forget it. It doesn't matter."

I start the engine, and we set off in silence.

Despite a few idle remarks on my part, Ady keeps up the silence for almost an hour. After emptying the tenth bin of the day, we return to the cab, and I decide I've had enough of his sulky attitude.

"What's the matter with you today? Have you still got the hump about me doing the van admin?"

"No."

"What is it then? You've had a face like a slapped arse all morning."

"It's nothing," he sniffs, turning his head towards the side window.

"Ady?"

"Just leave it, will you. I'm ..."

His voice breaks into a semi-croak like he's trying to swallow back a lump in his throat.

"You're not fine if that's what you were about to say. What's up, mate?"

Slowly, he turns to face the dashboard, but he can't bring himself to look at me.

"It's Leanne," he says in not much more than a whisper. "She's left me."

"Oh shit. Really?"

"No," he snorts. "I'm just having a fucking laugh about it."

"Sorry, I didn't mean to ... I'm just shocked, that's all. I thought you were set for life together."

"So did I."

"What happened?"

Ady stares at the dashboard without answering.

"You know you can talk to me, right?"

"Nothing to talk about. She's gone, and she ain't coming back."

I wonder if Leanne finally confronted Ady with her suspicions about him seeing someone else, and the argument got out of hand. If that is the case, maybe I can help him rectify the situation, or at least get to the bottom of what he's been up to of late.

"I'm not trying to pry, mate, but you've not been yourself for a while now. Is there something going on in your life you want to talk about?"

"Like what?"

"You know, something that you might not be able to talk to your girlfriend about. Perhaps something like a meaningless fling."

He turns and fixes me with a hard stare.

"What the fuck are you talking about?"

"Nothing. I just ... you can't deny you've not been on your best behaviour for the last few weeks, staying out late, not coming home, that kind of thing. Maybe if you were in Leanne's shoes, you might fear the worst too."

"Funny that, 'cos she accused me of the same thing."

"Err, did she?" I reply, my cheeks warming. "And what did you say?"

"I told the truth, that I'd never cheat on her."

"And I'm guessing she didn't believe you?"

"Made no odds if she did or didn't, 'cos she'd have left anyway."

"Why?"

Ady's Adam's apple bobs up and down as he turns his hard stare back to the dashboard.

"Leanne has met someone else," he mumbles. "That's why she's left me."

I'm about to respond with a token platitude, but a sudden and dreadful thought steals my attention. Was Leanne using me to get information on Ady—information she could use to offset her guilt? I've no idea why she'd want to play such a game, but I guess it doesn't make much difference now.

"Mate, I'm so sorry. I don't know what else to say."

"I don't want your pity. I brought this on myself."

"There's no excuse for cheating. If Leanne was unhappy, she should have talked to you."

"She did, or she tried to. I just lied to her, though."

"I'm not with you."

"I need to tell you something," Ady says with a heavy sigh. "But, you've gotta swear not to tell another living soul, alright?"

"You can trust me. I swear."

"I've got a problem ... I'm up to my eyeballs in debt, and every day I manage to make it worse."

"How much debt?"

"I dunno, maybe four or five grand ... I lose track."

"Shit, Ady. How the hell have you managed to rack up that much debt?"

He draws a deep breath.

"Gambling."

"Oh, no."

Even armed with the truth, I can understand how Leanne reached a different conclusion. Infidelity and gambling both require an unhealthy amount of deceit, and I can only imagine a similar amount of guilt for the perpetrator. In my limited experience, I know both are usually terminal when it comes to a relationship.

"How long have you been hooked?" I ask.

"I dunno, it just creeps up on you. One day you're chucking loose change into a fruit machine, the next, you're walking away from a poker table having lost five-hundred quid. I then tried winning the money back using online casinos, but I just dug a deeper hole."

That would explain why he's been so fixated with his mobile phone of late.

"Would I be right in guessing Leanne doesn't know about your problem?"

He nods.

Any semblance of self-pity fades away as a solitary tear rolls down Ady's cheek. For all my woes, I don't think I'd want to swap places with him right now. He appears utterly broken.

Then, in a heartbeat, his demeanour changes.

"When I find out who he is, I'm gonna fuckin' kill him," he spits before wiping his eyes with the palm of his right hand.

"Who?"

"The bastard she's been seeing."

I can see what he's doing. Anger is a handy life-raft when you're drowning in a pit of despair.

"Mate, I don't think an assault charge, or worse, is going to make you feel any better, and it won't fix any of your problems, either."

"Says who?"

"Says me. I've got a vague idea how you're feeling right now, and I can tell you that there's no easy way out, but there are plenty of easy ways to make it worse ... much worse."

"How can it possibly get any worse? My life is fucked."

He won't thank me for saying it, but his life is far from fucked. I know what absolute rock bottom looks like, and despite his current plight, Ady is nowhere near it.

2nd August 2001

How did I get here? More to the point, how do I get out of it?

Denise still doesn't have a job and I'm starting to think she doesn't want one. She tells me she's applied for jobs and even had a couple of interviews, but I've only got her word to go on. Even if she is trying, it doesn't change the fact I'm struggling to keep up with the bills and support my girlfriend.

She tells me this is a test. All of it. If I'm worthy of her love and respect, I have to prove myself. That was easy at the start, but her demands are now too much, and I'm struggling.

Is it worth it?

If I'm being honest, I was so scared of losing her that I'd have agreed to just about anything. Now, I'm just scared of her—her temper gets way out of hand sometimes. I think she needs proper help but every time I mention speaking to a professional, she gets angry. Denise said she'd spoken to a shrink before, and it hadn't done her any good. Anyway, I'm the one with the problem, apparently. Whatever I do, it's wrong. If I let her have her way, I'm weak. If I stand up to her, I'm too controlling. When she gets angry there's no way to calm her down.

I can live with the mood swings, the lack of job, the laziness around the house, and even her spending my money quicker than I can earn it—I can live it because I love her, and I know one day she'll get better. What I can't live with is the jealousy.

I tried so hard in the bedroom, but the pressure got too much. The last two times we tried, I couldn't even get a hard-on. She got angry the first time, but the second, she just laughed and said I was pathetic.

She was right. I am pathetic. What kind of man can't even get hard when he's lying next to a beautiful, naked woman?

That's why I deserve to be punished, why I need to be educated. It's killing me, though.

The first time it happened was two weeks ago. Denise went out on a Saturday evening and said she'd come home when she felt like it. I didn't argue, but just after midnight, I took up my usual position at the lounge window and waited. Then, just before half-twelve, a taxi pulled up outside the house. Denise got out but she wasn't alone.

I can't even remember his name: Jamie, or Jimmy, or something. I remember the way he looked at me though, like I was something he'd trodden in, even when I gave him my last beer from the fridge. He downed it in one and then went off to use the toilet. That's when Denise told me what was going to happen.

She said that I had to prove how much I loved her, and in doing so, I might learn something. She was going upstairs with Jamie, or Jimmy, or something, and I was to wait in the lounge. She had needs, she said, and as I couldn't fulfil them, someone else had to. It was my fault, and if I didn't like it, I could leave. Tempting as it was, she made it clear I wouldn't be welcome back.

I stared at the wall for forty-nine minutes and listened to the soundtrack of some stranger fucking my girlfriend's brains out. What kind of man does that make me?

It happened again last Saturday, and Denise came home with her 'friend' again two hours ago. I'm writing this in the lounge in the early hours of the morning because it's the only way I can distract my mind from what's going on upstairs.

As punishing as it is to sit here and listen to Denise's screams and the headboard banging against the wall, at least she'll be in a good mood tomorrow, I hope. Last Sunday we went shopping together and then had lunch in a nice pub out in the sticks. It was such a lovely day, and a reminder why I put up with so much. Deep down, I know that Denise is a good person. I can't give up on her. She loves me—I know she does.

I read in a magazine that you can now buy a drug called Viagra, which helps when you can't get a hard-on. I need to book an appointment with the doctor next week to see if he can prescribe some. If I can get my act together, these Saturday night trysts will be a thing of the past as I'll be the one upstairs, satisfying Denise's needs.

It's a plan, and I'm a man in need of a plan!

The headboard has stopped banging against the wall, but I can still hear them going at it. Maybe they're on the floor, or he's fucking her up against the wall. Whatever he's doing to her, he's doing a better job than I ever have.

Why am I such a failure?

Chapter 30

I once watched a documentary about a couple who decided to sell their comfy home in suburbia and relocate to the wilds of the Pembrokeshire coast. They purchased a ten-acre plot of land and set up home in a disused hay barn with no mains electric, gas, or water. Living off-grid, they called it.

This morning, as I look out over Tinkerton Meadow, I can almost see the appeal of such a lifestyle. With most of the Ashbridge residents still in bed and my mobile phone safely locked in my car, I'm completely disconnected from the rest of society. All is quiet, and all is calm.

I'd love to think I could live off-grid, but I reckon I'd miss too many of my creature comforts. Standing here in the light drizzle, chilled to the bone, I'm only ten minutes away from a steaming hot bath. Afterwards, I can put my muddy trousers in the washing machine and then cook a hearty breakfast in a kitchen with all the mod cons.

What I don't think I'd miss is people. Well, most of them.

I popped to the pub with Ady after work yesterday, and we talked about his problems. I told him I couldn't help with his relationship, but if he had any hopes of luring Leanne back, he had to confront the reason she left in the first place—his addiction and the accompanying trail of lies. After a quick Google search, I found a charity that provides free support to gambling addicts, and I helped Ady complete the form to request a chat with a counsellor. I've got enough shit of my own to deal with, but I felt compelled to do something, even if it's just pointing my workmate in the right direction. After two pints, he said he wanted to be left alone to think, and to drown his sorrows in all likelihood.

I spent most of the evening staring at my laptop, constantly refreshing the search for my name, just in case Zoe decided to submit another toxic post. I fell asleep on the sofa and woke up at four in the morning. I checked Facebook again, just to be sure, and went to bed. I couldn't sleep.

Too cold to continue bird spotting, I return to the car and retrieve my phone from the glove box. Dreading any messages or notifications, I unlock the screen with some trepidation. There's one message from Heather, and it simply says: *3.00 pm?*

It takes a moment or two to understand why she's sent such a vague message, and then I remember.

"Ahh, bollocks."

The last time we spoke, I said I'd pop in to see Colin today, but I had planned an afternoon in front of the television, disconnected from the real world. I really don't want to go, but neither do I want to let Heather down. Still, it's safe to assume she knows nothing of *that* post on Facebook, otherwise, I doubt she'd be inviting me to her dad's bedside. It's probably safe to say Colin hasn't seen it either—he's very much of the opinion that life was better before the internet came along, and it's not for him. Sometimes, I think he has a point.

I reply to the message, confirming I'll be there at three.

The moment I walk through the front door, I head straight to the lounge and check my laptop again. Another search of my name on Facebook bears no results other than my profile. I hope to God Zoe feels sufficiently vented now, and that she considers I've been suitably humiliated.

Feeling a fraction less anxious, I grab a shower and then prepare a late breakfast. I've barely had time to put my plate in the dishwasher when the doorbell rings. I freeze.

"Please," I whisper. "Don't be Leanne."

I take a moment to prepare a bullet-proof excuse if it is. It's a slight white lie, but I'll say I'm heading off to visit someone in hospital. That should help me avoid any awkward questions regarding Ady.

On the way to the front door, my position changes somewhat. If my mystery caller is Leanne, I don't owe her anything after the way she suddenly dumped my workmate. I know he's not been entirely honest with her, but two wrongs don't make a right, and an addiction is the lesser of the two wrongs in their relationship.

I open the door. It's not Leanne.

"Oh, Dad."

"You okay, Son?"

"Err, yeah. What brings you over?"

"Aren't you going to invite me in?"

"Sorry, sure."

I stand aside, and he steps onto the doormat.

"There's nothing wrong, is there?" I ask, concerned at my Dad's impromptu visit.

"Yes, and no. Put the kettle on, and we'll talk."

He follows me through to the kitchen. I flick the switch on the kettle and invite Dad to sit at the table.

"I'll stand if it's all the same with you."

There's a slight frostiness to his tone, and the fact he doesn't want to sit down implies he's not here to pass the time of day.

"What's up then? You don't look happy."

"I'm not."

"Right."

I wait for him to elaborate. He doesn't.

"Dad, do you want me to guess what's wrong?"

"It concerns tonight."

"Nope, you've lost me. What's going on tonight?"

"You've forgotten, haven't you?"

"For crying out loud, Dad," I groan. "I've not had the best of weeks, and I was hoping for a stress-free weekend. Can you get to the point, please?"

"Unbelievable," he snaps, shaking his head. "Tonight is my presidential inauguration at the golf club ... the event my family are supposed to be attending. Remember?"

I stare back at my dad, slack-jawed and gormless.

"You know how important this is for me, but patently not important enough for you to bother writing it down on a calendar."

"Shit, I'm so sorry, Dad. As I said, I've had one of those weeks, and—"

"Save it," he barks, holding his hand out like a traffic cop. "I know what kind of week you've had, and that's why I'm here."

"Err, now I'm lost again."

He puts his hands on his hips, just as he used to do whenever he was about to deliver a bollocking to my teenage self.

"I had a call from Royston Garwood this morning, regarding your invitation tonight."

"Should I know who Royston Garwood is?"

"He's the Chair of the management committee and the one man you don't want sniffing around your business. He's a busybody and prone to making mountains out of molehills."

"And why was he interested in my invitation?"

"Because, Douglas, someone informed Royston about a message on Facebook. Fortunately, Royston himself never got to see it, but he got the gist, and that was enough for him to start asking some very awkward questions."

"What kind of questions?"

"Ones I couldn't answer. For example, is there any truth my son was involved in some kind of indiscretion with a young woman?"

My shoulders slump.

"I don't know what to say, Dad, other than I had a ... I went on one date with a woman, and it didn't work out. She then posted a wholly inaccurate account about that date on Facebook, but their administrators removed it."

"You never mentioned going on a date."

"I didn't realise I had to notify you."

"Don't be a smart arse, Douglas. I'm just wondering why you never mentioned it."

"I just didn't, okay. And, considering it never progressed beyond that first date, it validates my point—it wasn't worth telling you about."

"So, why did this woman kick up such a fuss?"

"No idea, but you know what they say about Hell having no fury."

"Hmm," he responds, his eyes narrow. "That's as maybe, but this woman's scorn has put me in a terrible position."

"I don't see how. You said this Royston didn't see the post, so what's the big deal?"

"People talk, and Royston is the worst of them."

"Do you want me to have a word with him, set the record straight?"

"I don't think that would be sensible. Better to keep a low profile."

"Fine. I'll stay in the shadows this evening, then."

Dad shuffles on the spot, scratching his chin.

"Actually, Son, I'm not sure it's a good idea you being there."

"What?"

"It'll only flame Royston's gossiping if you turn up."

Granted, I had forgotten all about Dad's do at the golf club, and even if I hadn't, I wouldn't be looking forward to spending an evening with a load of pretentious snobs, but that's not the point.

"Is that why you're here ... to rescind my invitation?"

"No, I'm here to ask if you wouldn't mind staying away. You hate the place, anyway. You've told me often enough."

"Yes, I do hate it, but that's hardly the point. I thought you wanted your family there."

"What would you have me do, Douglas? If you come along and Royston starts a whispering campaign, it'll do no good for either of us, will it?"

"If he's going to spread malicious rumours about me, it'll do him no good either. Mark my words."

"And that's another reason why I think it'd be sensible if you stay away. I can't afford any ... incidents this evening. It's too important."

I'm about to launch another counter-argument, but the futility steals my words, and I puff out a long sigh instead. What is the point in arguing for something I really don't want?

"For your sake, I'll give it a miss."

"I appreciate that, Son," he replies, patting a hand on my shoulder. "I know it's a lot to ask, but I hope you understand my motives. It's not because I don't want you there."

"You don't want me there enough to risk the evening being ruined."

"I think you'd do the same if the roles were reversed."

"I fucking hate golf, so that's unlikely."

We share a half-smile, and with Dad getting what he came for, his demeanour softens.

"How about that cup of tea, then?" he says brightly. "And if you've time, maybe a catch-up?"

He stays for almost an hour, most of which he spends talking about the holiday to the Maldives they've just booked. I sometimes wonder if I was switched with another baby in the hospital because I have so little in common with my parents, unlike Kathryn.

I see him off and return to the kitchen. Alone, the questions I resisted asking Dad then return. Was that Facebook post really the reason he didn't want me there tonight? To a degree, maybe, but I think there was another reason. Folks tend to mingle at these events, and inevitably they ask the same set of dull questions to one another. What do you do for a living? Is your wife with you? Where do your children go to school? What's your handicap?

I can imagine Dad squirming as I chat with one of his fellow members, answering those questions honestly. *Yes, mate, I empty bins and clear waste for a living. I'm forty-one, single, with no kids. I think golf is a game for wankers. Oh, and did I mention I was recently outed as a sex pest on social media?*

Maybe Dad has every right to feel disappointed with his son. What have I done with my life?

Christ, things could have been so different.

One mistake in my youth, albeit a catastrophic one, and that was that—my life veered off on an entirely different trajectory to the one I had planned. Even now, bestowed with a miraculous gift, I'm still making stupid mistakes. Perhaps I'm destined to be an embarrassment, no matter what.

Chapter 31

There are two ways to look at it. When you're not in the most positive of minds, the last place you want to be is in a hospital. Conversely, perhaps being in a hospital is a reminder that things could always be worse.

As I pass through the main doors of Ashbridge General Hospital, I'm still not sure which frame of mind I'm leaning towards. Time will tell, I suppose.

Heather texted me an hour ago to confirm which ward Colin is currently holed-up in, and I checked the route with a woman at the main reception desk. Her smile and flirtatious body language served as a reminder that the gift is still giving—her wedding ring a warning not to engage.

I arrive on the Gloucester Ward a few minutes after three, and a nurse directs me to the patient I'm here to visit. Colin is in one of four beds, grouped at the end of a short corridor. Heather is seated next to him on a plastic chair. She's the first to notice my arrival.

"Dad," she says, nudging Colin's arm. "You have a visitor."

He turns and looks up at me, grey-faced and gaunt.

"Hello, mate," he rasps. "Thanks for coming."

It occurs that Colin has become such a long-term fixture in my life that I don't think I've ever gone more than a week without seeing him. After two weeks, it is good to see his cheery smile again.

"It's no trouble. How are you doing?"

"Not bad, all things considered."

"You gave us all a scare with your little trip to intensive care. I hope it was a one-off."

"So do I, mate."

Pleasantries out of the way, I drag a chair over and sit down. The second my backside touches the plastic, Heather gets to her feet.

"I'm just going to get a cup of tea from the vending machine," she announces. "Would you like one, Douglas?"

"Yes, please."

I'm about to confirm how I take it, but I think Heather probably knows by now. She departs, and Colin turns to me.

"Heather told me how you helped her out last weekend," he says.

"It was nothing."

"Oh, it was. She had no one else to turn to, and I'm grateful you stepped up. You're a good man, Dougie, and I can't thank you enough."

"Oh, you can," I chuckle. "I'll take a free full-English when The Vale re-opens."

My mirth reaches Colin's face, but it doesn't linger long.

"I'm sorry to say it, mate, but I don't think The Vale will be reopening."

"Eh? Why not?"

"The truth is that it just doesn't make enough money. Everyone wants vegan-friendly food and fancy coffees these days, and they want it delivered. There's no room for the traditional cafe anymore."

Like the man in the bed before me, The Vale had been an integral part of my life for so long I can't imagine it closing for good.

"Isn't there something you can do to drum up more trade?" I ask.

"I don't know, but it's probably too late anyway. We've been haemorrhaging money for months, and if I don't do something now, we risk losing everything."

Thoughts of my brief visit to The Vale on Monday return, and the cache of unpaid bills I found in the kitchen.

"Are things that bad?"

"They are, and I don't have the stomach to keep fighting against the tide. I'll be sixty-eight next birthday, and my best days are behind me ... as you can tell."

"And what about Heather?"

"What about her?"

"How does she feel about closing down The Vale?"

"This decision is *for* Heather. It could be months before I'm fit to work again, and it's not fair to lumber her with the headache of keeping the place afloat. No, it's better all-round if we cut our losses and move on."

"And what are you moving on to?"

"Retirement."

"And Heather?"

"She's still considering her options, but once we sell up, she'll have a while to work things out."

I don't have the first clue what those options might be, and that's pretty poor form considering how long I've known Heather. Poor, but no different to most.

We all tend to drift through life, picking up superficial connections along the way. I know my postman's first name, and that he's been shoving mail through my letterbox for almost a decade, but I don't know anything about him. The same could be said for most of my neighbours. I know their names and that they've lived near me for years, but little else. I'm ashamed to admit I don't know that much about Heather, even though she's been cooking my lunch for the last five or six years.

"What did Heather do before she started at The Vale?"

"She held the same job she'd had since leaving school—working as a seamstress for a sweet old woman who ran a small tailoring business near us. She retired six years ago due to ill health, and that's when Heather decided to come and work at The Vale."

"Do you think she'd want to find another job as a seamstress?"

"Possibly, but … I think you know Heather well enough to understand she's a shy girl—always has been, and that makes it hard for her to meet new people. The thought of starting a new job and working with strangers is her idea of hell."

I hadn't considered Heather to be shy up until recently. I'd always considered her withdrawn, even a little frosty. I guess it bears out my theory that you never really know someone until you know them.

Our conversation meets an abrupt end as the topic returns, carrying two plastic cups.

"I should apologise in advance," Heather says, as she hands one of the cups to me. "The tea is appalling here, but it's a long walk down to the visitor's cafe."

"I'm sure it's fine. Thank you."

I take a sip. It's the opposite of fine, but I flash a smile at Heather, not wishing to appear ungrateful.

"I was just telling Dougie about our decision," Colin says.

"Your decision, you mean?"

Colin frowns at his daughter.

"If you've got a better idea, young lady, I'm all ears."

Heather glances at me and then at her cup.

"You know I haven't," she mumbles.

"It'll all work out in the end," Colin then adds in a brighter tone. "We'll sort something out."

This is the first time I've seen Colin and Heather interact beyond the walls of The Vale Cafe. There's an odd dynamic between them, like Heather is still a young girl and Colin the protective father. Maybe he thought his daughter would be married and living with a family of her own by now, but clearly life hasn't panned out that way for Heather.

A nurse approaches.

"Sorry to interrupt," she says to Colin. "I know you asked for a bath hours ago, but we're so short-staffed we're running behind. We can fit you in shortly if you like? I know it's not ideal during visiting hours."

"I smell like a baboon's armpit," Colin chuckles, turning to me. "Would you think me rude if I cut short your visit?"

"No, not at all. I can always pop back again another time."

"I'll wait around," Heather says.

The nurse confirms she'll return in ten minutes, and deep down, I'm secretly pleased. It's not that I don't want to spend time in Colin's company, but I'm just not in the mood for small talk.

"She liked you," Colin says under his breath as the nurse wanders off. "You should ask for her number."

"Um, I'm not really looking for anyone at the moment."

"Seriously? Even a lovely looking girl with a nurse's uniform?"

"Dad!" Heather groans. "Don't be so ... just don't."

"Sorry, Dougie," Colin says, rolling his eyes. "I didn't mean to embarrass you."

"It's fine."

We spend the available ten minutes talking about hospital food and how much Colin despises it. He claims he tried convincing Heather to sneak in a mixed grill, but she's too much of a stickler for hospital rules. She launches a counterclaim, stating that it's more a case of the practicalities and that she doesn't own a coat with enough pockets to house the various items in a mixed grill. She adds that the baked beans and fried egg would be problematic, no matter how many pockets are available. It's a fair point.

The nurses arrive, and I say my goodbye. With Heather not wanting to watch her dad taking a bed bath, she leaves the ward with me.

"I'm sorry about that," she says, as we wander back down the corridor.

"About what?"

"My father encouraging you to ask that nurse for her number. He's well-meaning, but I speak from personal experience when I say it's embarrassing."

"He's tried setting you up with a nurse too?"

"Not quite," she replies, the slightest hint of a smile creeping across her face. "But he did ask the porter if he was dating anyone at the moment."

"Ahh."

We walk on in silence for a dozen steps.

"Oh, before I forget," I say, delving my hand into a pocket. "The keys for The Vale."

I pass them to Heather. She thanks me with a nod.

"I didn't realise it when I put that sign up, but I guess I'll never see inside the old place again."

Heather ponders my words.

"Would you like your toaster back?"

"Um, no, you keep it. What's going to happen with everything else in there?"

"I don't know, but I suspect Dad is hoping to sell it all to settle some of the unpaid bills. Then, we hand the keys back to the landlord."

"The end of an era," I sigh. "I'm not going to lie, Heather, I'm gutted."

"If it's any consolation, so am I."

"You like working there?"

"I do. Very much."

Her confession isn't what I expected. I always thought she hated the place.

"Is there really no other option?" I ask. "If you want to continue working there."

She doesn't answer and we come to a stop by a set of double doors.

"I'm going this way," Heather then declares, nodding towards the doors. "The exit is straight on."

"Are you going in search of a decent cup of tea?" I joke, trying to lighten the sombre mood.

"I'm heading to the chapel."

"Oh, right. Sorry, I didn't mean to make light of, um ..."

"It's okay. I'm not exactly a devout Christian, but I spent an hour in the chapel last weekend, praying Dad would pull through. It seems only right I say thank you, now he's on the mend."

"We all need to keep the faith, eh?"

"Faith," she echoes in a hushed voice, "is the bird that feels the light and sings when the dawn is still dark."

She bows her head while I scramble for a worthy response to Heather's words. I open my mouth and go with the first word that crossed my mind.

"That's ... beautiful."

Seconds pass until she risks raising her chin again.

"I read it in a card when I was twelve, and it struck a chord. Sadly though, I'm still waiting for dawn's light."

I think back to the countless times I've stood on Falbert's Mount, waiting for the sun to creep above the horizon and light up Tinkerton Meadow. My faith is always rewarded, and I can't imagine that pre-dawn darkness going on for a lifetime.

Or can I?

"You didn't answer my question," I say.

"Question?"

"About The Vale. I asked if there really was no option other than shutting the door for good?"

"If there is, it's beyond Dad and me, I'm afraid."

"Maybe another mind might help. I can't make any promises, but I know my way around a financial spreadsheet, and who better to brainstorm ways to help The Vale than one of its oldest customers?"

"You'd do that?"

"Absolutely."

"Um, okay. When?"

I hadn't thought that far ahead and flounder for a reply.

"Um, err ... whenever."

"Are you busy tomorrow lunchtime?" Heather suggests.

"Not especially."

"Does one o'clock work, at our place?"

"Sure."

She finds a smile. I'd never suggest it, but Heather should smile more often because it suits her face.

"I'll text you the address."

"Okay, great. I'll see you tomorrow."

I hold the door open for her.

"Goodbye, Douglas."

She wanders up the corridor and turns left at the end without looking back. I'm left to consider if I've just added another layer of unwanted complexity to my life.

In hindsight, maybe I should have kept my mouth shut. Too late now.

Chapter 32

"That's a Jack Snipe," Kenny asserts. "Got to be."

"I'm not sure."

"Look at its ... ahh, bollocks!"

The focus of our attention flies off before we can confirm if it was a Common Snipe or its rarer cousin, the Jack Snipe. We've been standing on Falbert's Mount for almost an hour, and it's been the only spot of note, even if we couldn't agree on the exact species.

"What were we talking about?" Kenny asks, lowering his binoculars.

"You were talking about my humiliation on Facebook, and I was trying to change the subject."

"Aye, so you were," he laughs. "Good effort."

"Anyway, I've learned the lesson: stay in my own lane."

"Nothing wrong with a bit of ambition, pal. How were you to know she had a vengeful streak?"

"I wasn't, but I'd like to forget I ever met Zoe if you don't mind."

"Fair enough, but for what it's worth, Sara didn't believe a word of it, and neither does anyone who knows you."

"That's good to hear. Thank you."

"In fact, she suggested you come round one evening, and she'd cook us all a meal. I said you'd suffered enough."

Having sampled Sara's cooking before, I can't help but laugh at my friend's remark. In fairness, he's often said that his wife is perfect in every other way, so I think she forgives the occasional jibe at her culinary skills.

The laughter subsides, but my thoughts remain fixed on Kenny's marriage.

"Can I ask you a question?"

"Aye, course."

"How did you know Sara was the right woman for you?"

My friend stares out towards the horizon as if taking a moment to contemplate my question.

"I didn't know," he shrugs. "No one ever does, no more than you know if you've met the wrong person."

There's a slight change in intonation at the end of his sentence. Kenny is the only person, besides my parents, who knows the painful truth about my relationship with Denise.

"Sorry," he then adds by way of an afterthought. "I didn't mean to drag that up."

"No, you're probably right. It was a stupid question."

"There's no such thing as a stupid question, but I'm curious why you asked it."

As much as I respect Kenny's advice, I know he doesn't believe my tale of the woman in the glade and her miraculous tonic, so there's no point in answering his question.

"Oh, I don't know," I say dismissively. "I'm just feeling a bit bruised after what happened with Zoe. I don't get many chances to date so when it goes wrong, it feels like such a let down. I hoped there might be some strategy or technique to avoid setting myself up for another fall."

"Alas not, but there's one tip I'll willingly give you."

"I'm listening."

"Don't go searching for the right woman, Dougie—go searching for a friend. Find her, and there's a chance your feelings for one another might evolve into something special. But, if they don't, you've still got a friend. It's a win-win."

I ponder Kenny's advice for a few seconds, but I'm no more convinced of its merit than I'm convinced he saw a Jack Snipe ten minutes ago. I don't want a friend, and now I have the gift I can avoid wasting time with women who want nothing more than friendship from me. No one starts a family with a friend.

"Thanks, mate. I'll definitely keep that in mind."

Kenny nods, and then a sudden movement in the sky steals his attention. There's an unwritten rule between us: conversation is always secondary to spotting birds.

We remain on Falbert's Mount for a couple of hours until a drizzly mist blankets the entire meadow. As always, we curse the weather and reminisce about the summer with its never-ending evenings and crisp, clear mornings. At some point in January, we'll stop reminiscing about the old and start dreaming about the new.

On my way back to the car, I receive a text message from Heather: would I like a bite to eat when I pop over? As I've only pecked at a slice of toast this morning, there's no way I'm going to turn down the chance of a hearty lunch. As attractive a proposition as it is, it's also bittersweet in that it'll probably be the last time I get to sample Heather's cooking. There will always be another summer, but there won't be another meal at The Vale Cafe, sadly.

That thought journeys all the way back to Cargate Road as I consider and then quickly dismiss all the alternative eateries in our work patch. As with traditional pubs, cafes like The Vale are fast fading out. I think there's only one remaining in Ashbridge now, and that's in the town centre. How long it'll keep going is anyone's guess, but with pretentious coffee shops opening every five minutes, not long, I fear.

I turn into Cargate Road and park up, some sixty yards from my front door. Parking isn't usually a problem, but for some reason, there are more cars parked along the kerb than usual, and several outside my house. With the drizzle now a steady downpour, I get out of the car and hurry along the pavement. I'm just in the process of inserting the key in the lock when a car door shuts behind me. As I turn the door handle, a female voice calls out my name. I step into the hallway and turn around to see Leanne approaching.

I need a visit from Ady's estranged girlfriend like I need a third testicle.

"Oh, hi," I say apathetically.

Leanne steps up to the door and stands on the mat. She looks different from her last visit; hair styled and makeup applied.

"I've been waiting in the car for almost an hour," she says. "I probably should have called ahead."

"Probably. I've got a lot on today ... what can I do for you, Leanne?"

"Can you spare ten minutes for a chat?"

I glance at my watch. I'm due at Heather's place in an hour, and I hoped to grab a shower before I set off. Ten minutes is literally all I can spare.

"Just about. Come in."

I don't want to encourage Leanne to stay longer than the promised ten minutes, but I'm gagging for a cup of tea. I invite her through to the kitchen and, against my better judgement, ask if she'd like one. She accepts. Whilst the kettle boils, she poses a series of benign questions about my morning and what I've been up to. The small talk ends when I hand her a mug of tea and invite her to sit at the table.

"You're probably wondering why I'm here," she then says.

"I've got a vague idea."

"Did Ady tell you what happened between us?"

"He did. We went for a drink after work on Friday, and I left him drowning his sorrows."

"Sounds about right," Leanne snipes. "He probably got wasted and then went off to see his floozy."

Her bitterness is evident and, based upon Ady's version of events, a tad hypocritical.

"It's none of my business, Leanne, but I'm certain Ady wasn't seeing anyone."

"He might have told you that, but if you'd lived with him, you wouldn't be so certain … the shifty behaviour, the lies about money, the staying out all night. He was cheating on me; I know that."

It's obvious that Ady still hasn't confessed his gambling addiction to Leanne, and I now find myself stuck between the two of them, unsure which confidence I should break, if any.

"Have you spoken to him since Friday?"

"No."

"Maybe you should."

"I don't care anymore. Ady is ancient history … we're over, so fuck him."

There's a coldness to her tone, and I can't help but feel a tad sorry for Ady. I shouldn't because he hasn't helped himself, but there's no reason for Leanne to be cruel.

"I'm not taking sides here, but I'd strongly suggest you speak to Ady. Maybe he hasn't been entirely honest with you, but that doesn't mean he's been cheating."

"As I said, I don't care."

"Well, that's your prerogative, but it just seems a bit harsh dumping Ady for someone else when you might not know the full picture."

"Is that what he told you?"

"That you'd met someone else? Pretty much."

"That's not what I said. As usual, Ady only hears what Ady wants to hear."

I take a sip from my mug, glancing at my watch again. Leanne still hasn't said why she's here, and the clock is ticking. Time to nudge her along with a firm hand.

"Whatever's gone on between you, I think there's a chance to sort it out if you have a frank conversation. However—and don't take this the wrong way—I'm not comfortable talking to you behind Ady's back. This has nothing to do with me."

"That's the thing, though, Dougie—it has everything to do with you."

"Eh?"

She leans forward and rests her arms on the table.

"I never told Ady I was seeing someone else. I told him I'd met someone … and I was falling in love with him."

"Right," I sigh. "As I said, it's really none of my business."

"You don't get it, do you?"

"Err, apparently not."

"It's *you*, Dougie. I think I'm falling in love with *you*."

Stunned into silence, I stare back across the table at a woman I had only ever considered a casual acquaintance. And yet, here she is, claiming that she's falling in love with me.

This is not good. It's not good on so many levels I can't even begin to unpick them.

"I … err. Sorry?"

"This isn't how I planned to tell you, but I couldn't keep it in. You can't deny that you don't feel it too?"

"Leanne, I can't say I feel anything. I mean, you're … you're lovely, but up until forty-eight hours ago, you were in a long-term relationship with my workmate."

"And why do you think I ended it? I knew you'd never do anything behind Ady's back, and I respect that, but I couldn't ignore the chemistry between us."

"The chemistry?"

"When I came round the other evening and cooked dinner for you—it felt so right, don't you think?"

"I can't deny it was nice, sitting down to dinner with—"

"See!" she cries. "You *did* feel it. I knew I didn't imagine it."

I sit back in my chair, primarily to put a bit more distance between us. Leanne continues to stare across the table with pleading eyes, her hands now upturned as if she's waiting for me to grab them and confess my mutual feelings. This is a fucking nightmare.

I puff a deep breath and carefully consider what I say next. I don't want to hurt Leanne's feelings, but I know they're not real. The gift has confused her, and coupled with Ady's neglect, I understand why she's seeking comfort. She's searching in the worst possible place, though, and I need to set her straight.

"I like you, Leanne, and yes, I did enjoy your company the other evening, but ... I'm just a sad, middle-aged man who's become so accustomed to cooking for one, he'd have welcomed almost anyone to dinner. What you felt was my gratitude and maybe a tiny fragment of jealousy because you and Ady have what I've always wanted. That's it, though."

"You said I was attractive."

"Because you are, but I also think next door's Cockapoo is cute, but that doesn't mean I want a relationship with her."

Ignoring my point, Leanne continues her plea.

"I don't understand. I'm single, you're single, you've just said you think I'm attractive, and you enjoy my company. Why wouldn't you want to be more than friends?"

There's no arguing with any of her points, so what's stopping me from leaping across the table and scooping her up in my arms? Most blokes would.

"Because, Leanne, you still love Ady."

"Rubbish," she sneers. "Why would I waste my love on a cheat when I could be with a man who makes me feel the way you do?"

"It's not real," I reply, keeping my tone level. "And Ady isn't cheating on you. He loves you just as much as you love him."

"If he loved me, he wouldn't act the way he does. That tells me all I need to know."

With my time and patience almost exhausted, I weigh up the pros and cons of telling Leanne the truth. Ady probably won't thank me, but it's for his own good.

"The reason Ady has been acting like an arsehole is because he's not himself. He's ... he's been wrestling with a problem."

"What problem?"

"He asked me to keep this to myself, but you need to know. Ady has developed a gambling addiction."

A deep line creases her forehead. I hope she's now comparing Ady's behaviour to that of a gambling addict, and seeing the parallels. The creases deepen.

"Why didn't he tell me?" she asks.

"I don't know. Guilt, shame, or maybe he just thought it was a phase. People with addictions don't tend to realise they're addicts until it's too late."

Leanne sits back in her chair. She closes her eyes and silently pinches the bridge of her nose.

"I'm sorry I had to be the one to tell you," I say. "But do you now understand why ... why Ady needs you?"

She keeps her eyes shut but slowly nods.

"I'm such a fool," she murmurs.

I don't know if her self-confessed foolishness is because she didn't spot the signs of her boyfriend's addiction or because she's just confessed that she's falling in love with me. Either way, it's enough to bring down the curtain on our cosy chat. She pushes the chair back and stands up.

"I ... I need to go," she splutters, her eyes moist and shoulders sagging.

"Sure. I understand."

I don't, but I'm not about to offer any encouragement for her to stay. I guide her to the hallway, where she puts her coat back on. She's about to grab the door handle when she pauses and turns around.

"I need to ask you something, Dougie."

"Okay."

"In another life, one where there never was a Leanne and Ady, do you think we might have ... you know, hooked up?"

"Who knows," I reply with a tepid smile. "But if we get another go beyond this life, I'll be sure to look you up."

She rests her hand on my chest, close to my heart.

"Thank you," she replies.

She then slowly turns away, opens the door, and leaves. In the ensuing silence, I pause for a moment to give her question a little more breathing space. I reach three quick conclusions. Firstly, I do actually like Leanne. Secondly, it's a shame the circumstances are what they are because in many ways, she's close to my idea of Miss Right. And. thirdly, Ady really is a monumental tit for messing her around.

Chapter 33

Halfway down Cargate Road, I push the power button to activate the stereo. Some days I prefer to drive in silence, but on others, I like to listen to a conversational radio station where the issues of the day are hotly contested. Then, there are days like today when I'm feeling melancholy and prefer listening to music.

I jab the button for Magic FM, and an inadvertent snort of laughter escapes once I recognise the track currently playing: *The Great Pretender* by Freddie Mercury. No tune could be more apt. Here I am, pretending to be an attractive, desirable man and summarily failing. Quite remarkably, however, I've caused havoc in the lives of four different women with barely any effort on my part. Keira has left her well-paid council job because she can't bear working with me; I tempted Shelley into cheating on her boyfriend; Zoe is likely scarred for life after our brief dalliance at her flat; and my mate's girlfriend thinks she's in love with me.

"Nice work," I mumble under my breath.

Freddie finishes his lament, and another track begins. I don't recognise the song, but the voice is familiar: Celeste. If I'd heard her a week or so ago, I wouldn't have given it a second thought but now I'm destined to recall that night at Zoe's flat every time I hear Celeste's voice. Her doleful tones only deepen my self-pitying malaise, and barely a mile into my journey, I consider turning around and heading back home. There's only one reason I don't. If there's any way of saving The Vale Cafe, I need to find it. Helping Heather and Colin might just prove to be my salvation.

The address Heather gave me is on the very edge of the town boundary, in an area that was once open farmland. Over the years, the fields have been sold to developers and new homes erected. Some time ago, I recall seeing an advert in the local paper for one of the new developments, called Green Meadows. I thought the developers were taking the piss, considering the land was an *actual* green meadow before the construction machinery arrived. I'm sure the shareholders chuckled all the way to the bank with that one.

Fortunately, the sat nav guides me away from the housing developments to a narrow lane barely wide enough for a family hatchback. I trundle slowly along the lane, passing a pair of old cottages that look like they might have once housed farm workers. The lane then curves to the left and appears to end fifty yards ahead with a five-bar gate protecting the entrance to a muddy field where a horse is lazily chewing at the remaining tufts of grass.

The sat nav confirms I've reached my destination, but there's no obvious house. Then I spot a weathered sign with the number three on it, half-buried in a holly bush on my left. Just beyond the sign, and almost out of sight is a dirt track. I put the car in gear and edge forward.

I don't know what I expected Colin and Heather's home to look like, but it probably wasn't a ramshackle bungalow surrounded by wild hedgerows and waist-high meadow grass. It's what an estate agent might describe as needing work but offering enormous potential.

I reach the end of the track and pull up on a patch of weed-strewn tarmac that was once a driveway, I suspect. As I get out of the car, I stop for a second as the reason why Heather and Colin chose to live in a dilapidated bungalow with no neighbours becomes apparent. All I can hear is birdsong and the slight whisper of the wind as it rustles through the meadow grass. That is until the less-than-tranquil squeal of rusty door hinges breaks the peace.

I turn around. Heather is standing in the doorway of the bungalow.

"You found us okay, then?" she asks.

"Just about."

I step across the cracked tarmac towards a covered porch. On closer inspection, my host's attire could be a cause for concern. I've never seen Heather in anything but utilitarian clothing, which is understandable as she's always been working in the kitchen at The Vale Cafe, bar the time we met at the hospi- tal. Now, though, she's wearing a bluish dress patterned with sunflowers. It reminds me of the dresses my gran used to wear on a Sunday: pretty, but modest and old-fashioned. Even so, it's a worrying development because Heather is the last person I would want to upset if the gift leads her down the wrong path. Then again, maybe she always wears vintage dresses on a Sunday.

"Come on in," she says, as I approach the front door.

As my right foot lands on the doormat, the most mouth-wa- tering of aromas hits me.

"Is that—"

"Roast beef," Heather confirms. "I wasn't sure what you usually eat for Sunday lunch, but we always have a roast. I hope you don't mind?"

"Not in the least. I can't recall the last time I had a good roast dinner."

"I never said it would be good," she replies.

"Sorry?"

"Oh, err … I'm just joking. I can cook an adequate roast dinner."

What was clearly meant as a humorous remark missed its target because I wasn't expecting it.

With Heather's joke lying flat on the floor, I try to fill the awkward silence.

"If your cooking in The Vale is anything to go by, I'm sure it'll be great."

I offer a reassuring smile. Heather's cheeks redden, and she turns away.

"Come this way," she beckons.

I follow her along a wide hallway, across wooden parquet flooring in a warm-honey colour. From what little I've seen, the inside of the bungalow is at odds with the exterior. Like Heather's dress, it's old-fashioned and homely, but there's a certain charm to it.

We pass through a door at the end of the hallway into a surprisingly large kitchen, best described as rustic.

"Sorry," Heather says, turning to face me. "I forgot to ask if you'd like me to take your coat."

"Right. Thanks."

I slip my coat off and hand it to her.

"Please, take a seat," she says, waving her hand towards a dining table forged from oak planks. "I'll just hang this up for you."

Heather disappears back through the door while I sit down and appraise my surroundings. Besides the aroma of roasting meat, the air is tinged with a slight woody scent, probably because the kitchen cabinets are hewn from raw timber. At least a dozen potted plants of varying species and sizes soften the scene, and a vase bursting with orange and yellow flowers sits in the centre of the table, adding a splash of bright colour.

"Lunch will be about twenty minutes," Heather announces, as she bustles back in. "Would you like a glass of wine?"

On the side behind her, I notice a half-empty glass of white wine next to an open bottle. It seems my host has already indulged, and it would be rude not to join her in a glass, I suppose.

"A glass of wine would be lovely, thanks."

Heather half nods, half smiles, and turns to pour the wine. There's something a little peculiar about her demeanour that I can't quite put my finger on. It's as if she's following a rule book on social etiquette and trying just a little too hard.

"Here we are."

She places two full glasses on the table and sits down, leaving one chair between us. Strange.

"Thank you."

"I'm not a big wine drinker, so I had to ask the man in the off licence for a recommendation. I hope you like it."

I take a sip as Heather looks on, waiting for a reaction.

"Yeah, it's ... nice."

"Oh."

"Sorry, but I'm a philistine when it comes to wine. I know it's available in red, white, and rosé, but that's the full extent of my knowledge, I'm afraid."

"Thank heavens for that," Heather replies, releasing a deep breath. "I don't know why, but I presumed everyone but me knew about wine."

"You might be right, but I'm clueless."

She flashes a strained smile and then takes a long gulp from her glass. I recognise the signs of someone drinking alcohol to ease nerves rather than to savour the subtleties of its flavour.

"So, where shall we start?" I ask brightly.

"Start?"

"Brainstorming ideas to help The Vale."

"Oh, yes. Of course. Um ..."

I only spent two years working in an office, but brainstorming sessions were a regular feature in our weekly schedule, the aim being to generate ideas that might make everyone a bit richer, except those in the meeting. I'm sure they're a regular feature in every office, but I'd overlooked the fact Heather has never worked in one. She doesn't know what she's missing.

"Shall we start with the basics? Colin said you were struggling to make ends meet, so maybe we can look at the financial side of the business and see where the money is coming and going?"

"Ah, the books you mean?"

"That'd be a great start."

"Give me one minute."

Once again, Heather leaves the kitchen. When she returns, she's not carrying a laptop, as I expected, but a leather-bound ledger. She places it on the table in front of me.

"That's this year's income and expenditure," she confirms. "I have to apologise in advance—we're not blessed with mathematical minds."

"Not to worry. It's been a long time since I crunched numbers, but there might still be something useful lurking up here," I reply, tapping my temple.

I open the ledger to the first page, representing week one in the financial calendar. It's split into two main columns, one for income and one for expenses, with a section at the bottom used to note the weekly profit or loss and a running total for the year. The left-hand column is broken down by day, running from Monday through to Saturday with the daily income listed next to each day. I'm taken aback by some of the numbers.

"Is that right? On this particular Tuesday, you only took £62.15?"

"Yes. January is always a difficult month, and Tuesdays are our quietest day."

"Oh, okay."

I had no preconceived idea how much the average cafe might take on any given day, but I never envisaged it might be less than I earn.

The total income for the week isn't much more impressive: £714.80. I switch my attention to the right-hand column, which lists the weekly expenses. There's rent, rates, gas, electric, water, refuse collection, and a final entry marked as 'stock', which I presume is the produce they cook and serve. The total at the bottom of the column comes to £942.50, representing a first week loss of £227.70.

I turn the page. The numbers aren't much better, so I skip forward to February. There's a slight improvement, and some weeks they make a small profit. March continues in a similar vein, and although there are more days where they make a profit than a loss, the running total for the year has a minus sign before it. As I skip through another dozen pages, I notice there's an obvious expense missing on every page.

"I don't see any costing for staff," I remark.

"No, there isn't any."

"Eh? I know you don't have staff as such, but what about the wages you and Colin take?"

"We don't take anything."

"I'm sorry. How can you live if you're not paying yourself a wage?"

Heather glances at the ledger and then at the flowers in the vase as if their brightness might offer inspiration.

"Can I trust you, Douglas?" she asks.

"Of course."

"I know it's improper, but we live on the customers' tips."

I scratch my head and try to determine if Heather's revelation is a cunning way to avoid income tax or just a desperately sad way to scratch a living. Looking across the table at her, it doesn't take long to determine which.

"Surely, that doesn't amount to much?" I ask.

"Sometimes it can be as much as a hundred pounds in a week."

"And on a bad week?"

"Fifty or sixty."

"How can two adults survive on a few hundred quid a month?"

"We manage."

"But how? I mean, I own my own house, so I know how much it costs to run every month, what with mortgage payments, council tax, utility bills, and so on."

Heather takes another gulp of wine before answering.

"We don't have a mortgage, and there's no gas bill as we've got a wood-burning stove for cooking, heating, and hot water. We only have to pay for council tax, water, and electricity, and we usually earn enough tips to cover those bills."

"What about food and clothing?"

"We run a cafe, Douglas—how do you think we feed ourselves?"

"Valid point. And clothing?"

"I was a seamstress for a number of years. You'd be amazed what I can fashion with a few scraps of material or an unwanted garment from a charity shop."

My mind wanders off towards the question of underwear. I'm reasonably adept with a needle and thread, but I can't imagine ever trying to produce my own underpants. As for a bra, the mind boggles.

"I do alterations for a few locals too," Heather adds. "That helps contribute to our coffers. And before his hip gave out, Dad used to do odd jobs. He's a pretty good handyman ... he made this table and all the kitchen cupboards."

"But Colin won't be working again for months, and if there's no cafe, how will you earn tips or feed yourselves?"

"I don't know."

Heather then gets to her feet.

"The meat should be ready to carve. Now you know the extent of our financial woes perhaps you can put your thinking cap on while I serve lunch?"

I try to reply with a confident smile, but my mind is too busy processing a growing sense of guilt. I shouldn't have even hinted I might be able to help. Their situation is grave, at best.

As Heather hums to herself while dealing with pots and pans and baking trays, I churn over what I know, hoping inspiration might strike. It doesn't take long to conclude inspiration won't be joining us for lunch because I'm still missing some vital nuggets of information. As remote as the chance might be, if I can offer any help at all, I'll need to conduct some basic online research.

I pull out my mobile phone, but there's barely any signal, certainly not one strong enough to connect to the internet.

"Do you have Wi-Fi?" I call across to Heather.

"I'm afraid not. We don't use the internet."

"At all, or just at home?"

"It's never appealed, and Dad doesn't trust computers."

That much I do know.

"What about your mobile phone? Doesn't that have internet access?"

"I don't think so. It's on the dresser behind you if you'd care to check."

I twist around in my chair. The Nokia handset is almost as antiquated and chunky as the oak dresser itself.

"No, I don't think it does."

"Oh, well," Heather chirps as if it's of no great consequence. "Was it important?"

"Err, no. It'll wait."

I'm still puzzling how anyone can live without the internet when two plates arrive on the table. My saliva glands activate at the same time my stomach reminds me it's long overdue a fill.

"This looks lovely," I remark. "And I'm famished."

"You tuck in," Heather replies, handing me a knife and fork wrapped in a cloth napkin. "Maybe we'll think better on full bellies."

She takes another gulp of white wine. I take a sip from my glass, just out of politeness. The situation is entirely civilised, with Heather playing the model host. Alas, I can't enjoy it because I can still hear Freddie Mercury's words echoing in my head. Maybe Heather's willingness to impress is because the gift is creating the illusion of desire, or perhaps it's because she thinks I can help rescue her failing business. Either way, I'm still the greatest of pretenders.

My wine has an almost bitter edge to it. Worse than any wine I've sampled before.

Chapter 34

If there's anything worse than feeling like a fraud, it's acting like a fraud. For the first five minutes of our meal, I barely said a word. Heather kept asking if the food was okay or if I needed anything. This only added to my sense of guilt. She'd gone to so much trouble, and I was acting like a sulky schoolboy. I apologised and blamed my sullen mood on a lack of sleep.

Shaking off the self-pity, I focus on a positive.

"That was fantastic," I remark, sitting back in my chair. "Easily the best roast I've had in ... actually, I can't remember the last time I had one that good."

"I'm glad you enjoyed it," Heather replies, folding her napkin. "All the vegetables came from the garden."

"Your garden?"

"Yes, we have a large vegetable patch and a greenhouse where we grow peppers, tomatoes, cucumbers, and sometimes broccoli, although I'm not a big fan myself. It's Dad's favourite."

"You must save a few quid, growing your own veg."

"We grow fruit, too, and I bake bread and cakes ... oh, and pies, and quiches, and when I'm feeling brave, I'll take a crack at a lemon meringue pie. My mum was a wonderful cook but I'll never be as good as her. I do enjoy trying, though."

I know little of Colin's wife, but I do know he's been a widower for a long time—certainly all the time I've known him.

"Do you use your fresh fruit and veg at The Vale?" I ask.

"Not very often. Virtually all our produce comes from the Cash & Carry. It's cheaper and more convenient."

"But, it doesn't taste as good."

"I'm not sure our customers care. They want quick and cheap meals, Dad says."

Heather empties her glass and then gets to her feet.

"Shall I take your plate?" she asks.

"Yes, thanks."

"Would you like some dessert? I've made an apple crumble ... if you have time."

I look up at her with a wide grin.

"If the world were about to end, I couldn't think of any better way to spend my final minutes than tucking into a bowl of apple crumble—it's my all-time favourite pudding."

"That's a yes, then?"

"Definitely."

Heather takes our plates over to the sink and then opens the oven door. The comforting aroma of cinnamon and baked apple wafts across the room. Before serving her crumble, my host pours herself another glass of wine and calls over, asking if I'd like a refill.

"I'd better not, thanks. I'm driving."

There's no further conversation as I sit back in my chair and observe my host. I've eaten her meals countless times, but I've never watched her in action as she's always hidden away in the kitchen at the back of The Vale. She moves with an effortless grace while humming a tune I'm sure I've heard before but can't quite remember when or where.

Without warning an unexpected feeling engulfs me. It's the same feeling I get when putting on a new pair of cotton socks or climbing into bed after I've just changed the linen.

Pleasant as it might be, it has no place in this kitchen. I need to snap out of it.

"Can I, um ... help with anything?" I call across.

Heather turns around, a bowl in each hand.

"It's ready now, thank you."

She steps over to the table and places one of the bowls in front of me.

"I hope you like it."

My host places a spoon next to the bowl and retakes her seat. Forgetting my manners, I dig into the apple crumble and savour the first mouthful.

"This crumble is to die for," I remark. "The flavours ... it's delicious!"

Heather nods an acknowledgement and then opens her mouth to say something but fumbles for the right words.

"Sorry," she splutters. "I'm ... I think I've had a bit too much wine."

"Don't apologise. If it weren't for the fact I'm driving, I'd be on my fourth glass by now."

"I don't drink alcohol very often," she explains. "Or entertain guests, for that matter."

"Well, you're very good at it ... I mean entertaining, not drinking alcohol."

"Thank you, I think."

We share a smile and then return to our respective crumbles. There's a silence, but it isn't uncomfortable, and I don't feel compelled to fill it. I do, however, want to ask Heather a question. I open my mouth and say the first word of a sentence at the exact same moment Heather chooses to speak.

"Sorry," I chuckle. "After you."

"No, after you."

"I was just going to say that I'm amazed you never offered this crumble at The Vale—I'd have popped in every day if it had been on the menu."

"Would you?"

"Of course. It's amazing."

"I guess I was worried the customers wouldn't enjoy it. Besides, I don't think I could make it as cheaply as we buy frozen puddings from the Cash & Carry."

"Yes, but I'm sure customers would be willing to pay more for better quality food, especially when it tastes this good. I certainly would."

"I don't suppose it matters now," she sighs. "Unless you've had any brainwaves in the last half-hour?"

I take another mouthful of crumble and consider Heather's question. I wouldn't call it an epiphany exactly, but the dull glow of a forty-watt bulb illuminates a possible idea.

"You know, Heather, I might have something, but I need to think it through. If you can give me a day or two, I'll conduct a little research and come back to you."

"Really?"

"It's just a vague notion at the moment, but I think it's worth considering."

"I should probably ask what it is, but I don't want to know just in case it comes to nothing. There's nothing worse than getting your hopes up, only to see them dashed."

"I couldn't agree more. You're sitting with the master of dashed hopes."

"And yet, you always seem so happy, so positive."

"Do I?"

"I don't think I've ever seen you with a glum face."

I'm tempted to ask Heather how long she's been monitoring my emotions, but I wouldn't want to embarrass her. I change the subject.

"What is it you use in your crumble recipe? It's subtle, but it really makes a difference."

"Do you swear never to tell another living soul?"

"Cross my heart."

I draw a cross on my chest with my forefinger for added authenticity.

"Nutmeg."

"Ohh, of course, that's what it is."

"It's Mum's secret recipe."

"Your mum is a genius," I reply without thinking.

"Was," Heather says, gulping hard.

I drop my spoon in the bowl and bash my palms into my forehead.

"I'm so sorry, Heather. I just ... I'm terrible in female company ... always putting my foot in it."

"It's okay. It's been a long time, and I should be over it by now."

"I don't think you ever get over losing a loved one, do you?"

She shakes her head. I don't know what to say. Is it insensitive to talk about her mother or rude to abruptly change the subject? I say the first thing that comes to mind.

"Tell me to mind my own business, but how long ago did she pass?"

"It still seems like yesterday, but it was three weeks after my eleventh birthday."

"God, I'm so sorry, Heather. Losing a parent must be terrible at any age, but when you're only a child ... that doesn't bear thinking about."

"I can't deny it was the worst period of my life."

"Forgive me for raking it up. Me and my big mouth."

"Don't be sorry. I don't ... it's not something I ever talk about, and that's probably not healthy."

"Why don't you talk about it?"

She takes a long sip of wine before answering.

"The truth is, Douglas, there isn't anyone to talk about it with, apart from Dad."

My mind drifts back to an earlier conversation we had, in which Heather admitted she and Colin had no other family.

"You don't have friends willing to listen?"

The shake of her head is barely perceptible, but it's enough to tug hard at my heartstrings. I think carefully about how I should respond, but Heather clears her throat and speaks first.

"My lack of friends stems from school and what happened to Mum."

"Do you ... would you like to talk about it?"

"I don't want to bore you with my woes. You only popped by as a favour."

She's right. I did only pop by as a favour, but what kind of man would I be if I didn't sit and listen to someone who sounds like they could really do with a chat?

"You did me a favour, Heather. If you hadn't invited me over, I'd be sitting at home staring at the TV with a microwave meal on my lap. If you feel like talking, folks tell me I'm a good listener, so go for it."

"I will, on one condition."

"Name it."

"I'll talk if you finish the last of your crumble. There's nothing worse than cold custard."

"There is. Cold custard with a skin."

She makes a face that implies I'm right, but it quickly fades away as she straightens her back and leans her elbows on the table.

"Ready for the sad tale of the world's saddest girl?"

I reply with a positive nod.

"I had the happiest childhood. We lived in a nice house, and everything was perfect until Mum became sick. Dad had to give up his job to care for her, and then one day, I came home from primary school, and Mum wasn't there. She'd died that morning, and that was that. We had a funeral and then ... Dad couldn't go back to work because someone had to look after me, so we had to move from the nice house, and this place is all we could afford. It's a long way from where we used to live, and an even longer way from the life we used to live."

Heather pauses and picks up her glass. It doesn't reach her lips this time, and she returns it to the table.

"I had to start a new school, and the timing couldn't have been worse."

"How so?"

"I left a cosy primary school where I was surrounded by familiar, friendly faces and landed in a huge secondary school where no one knew me or cared to know me. A few of the teachers were okay, but the other children were ... let's just say they weren't kind to me. And, to make matters worse, I had to transition from a child to a young woman without my mum there to guide me. Dad tried his best but ... it was a difficult time."

It becomes apparent I'm not listening to a carefully considered speech but a pent-up pressure release. It's as if the words have festered in Heather's mind for years, and she simply has to air them while someone is willing to listen.

"Those five years in secondary school were just awful, and I couldn't wait to leave," she continues. "When I did, I thought life would get better, but I underestimated how much that place had affected me ... actually, no, that's not quite the right way to say it. It wasn't how it affected me—it was what it stole from me. Before Mum died, I was a bright, sociable child, and full of confidence. Secondary school stripped all of that away. Not a day goes by when I don't think back to that place and shudder."

She stops for a second and eyes my spoon, laden with crumble but hovering in the dead air between my mouth and the bowl.

"And that, Douglas, is why I'm now thirty-seven years of age, still living with my dad and working my way towards becoming a full-blown spinster."

Belatedly, she empties her glass and places it back on the table with a satisfied sigh.

"There. The end."

I lay my spoon back in the bowl.

My host has just bared her soul, shared pain she's probably never shared with anyone. What can I say in response that won't come across as trite or patronising?

"Um ... fuck, I don't know what to say."

Heather responds with a snort of laughter.

"Thank you," she adds.

"For?"

"For being honest. I didn't tell you because I was looking for sympathy. I'm not a victim, just a casualty of circumstances."

I'm aware there's a clock in the room somewhere, ticking away. Although I can't see it, I'd bet it's old but sturdy and dependable. It might have a pendulum too. I visualise it swinging back and forth, back and forth. On the fifth swing, I open my mouth again.

"Can I ask you a question?"

"Sure."

"Why tell me?"

"Two reasons, I think," she replies, nudging her bowl away. "I've drunk way too much wine."

"And the second?"

"Because, I ... no, you'll think I'm silly."

"Please, go on."

"Okay, I told you because ... I think you're different."

"Am I? Different to who?"

"Everyone."

"How?"

"I've no idea, but we're sitting here enjoying lunch and talking, and that makes you different, if not unique. I mean, I wouldn't dream of telling just anyone this, but because of what happened to me when I was young, I suffer from anxiety in social settings. Talking to people is so hard for me but, for reasons I don't understand, I feel comfortable in your company."

I have a vague idea why.

"I'm glad you felt you could talk to me, Heather."

"I'm not sure I will once the wine wears off. You must think I'm a total saddo."

"God, no," I protest. "I can empathise with much of what you've told me. My experiences at school weren't exactly a barrel of laughs, and then a few years later, I ended up in a relationship which ..."

There's a reason why only three people know the truth about my relationship with Denise. Relaying it means reliving it, and no part of me wants to.

"Go on," Heather says gently.

I look across at the woman I've known for a number of years but never really met. Granted, she's probably sunk a few glasses of wine, but she still found the strength to confide in me. There's no reason for me to tell her anything apart from trust. She trusted me, so I owe her the same.

"Can I have another glass of wine, please?"

"It's that bad, eh?" she smiles warmly before reaching for the bottle.

"Yep. it's that bad."

She fills my glass almost to the brim. I take a breath, then neck a couple of large gulps.

"Ready?"

"As I'll ever be."

I sit back in my chair. "So, this relationship ..."

9th September 2001

I thought about Christmas today. Not the one I had planned this year—that's not going to happen now—but Christmas when I was a kid. It always amazed me how quickly the world changed from the 24th of December to the 2nd of January. Just nine bloody days.

Early evening on Christmas Eve was the best because of the anticipation, and I wish I'd started writing a diary back then because I'd love to remember more about it. I do remember saying to Mum that it was like being in a tin of Quality Street because everything was shiny and colourful. That made her laugh, and she told everyone. I think Christmas as a kid is as magical as life gets, but no one tells you at the time.

Then, you get to January.

Dad didn't like the decorations up beyond New Year's Day so on the second everything was taken down and returned to the loft. The house looked bare, but there was worse to come because a day or two later, it was time to return to school. God, how grey and miserable the world felt as I trudged up the path to the school gates.

Was it any greyer than the walls of the cell I spent last night in, though? I don't think so.

Just like those nine days between Christmas Eve and the misery of early January, everything in my life has changed in a heart-beat. I didn't see it coming ... or did I?

If anyone ever reads this, I want them to know I did nothing wrong. I tried so hard to make it work with Denise, but the more

I gave, the more she took. I worked so hard. I cooked, I cleaned, I let her spend my money. Shit, I even let her screw other men in our home so she could have the one thing I couldn't give her.

It wasn't enough.

When two police officers turned up at the office and approached my desk, for one dreadful moment, I thought they were going to tell me something terrible had happened to Mum or Dad, like a road accident. What they said was almost as dreadful—I was under arrest on suspicion of actual bodily harm.

What happened next was humiliating and terrifying in equal measure. Marched out of the office, I was put in a police car and then taken to Ashbridge Police Station. I kept telling them I hadn't done anything wrong, but they wouldn't listen. They took my fingerprints, a DNA swab, and then locked me in a cell. I didn't even know who I was supposed to have assaulted.

I found out eventually when I was sitting in a windowless room opposite a detective in a shirt and grease-stained tie. According to him, I assaulted Denise this morning before I left for work. That would have been hard as she was still fast asleep in her bedroom, with the door locked. The detective asked how Denise had sustained a black eye and a cut lip. I said I didn't know, but maybe she'd got one of her male friends to hit her, to set me up. The look on the detective's face suggested he didn't believe me.

In the end, they had to let me go because I denied hitting anyone, but I had to report back in two weeks. They also said I wasn't to go anywhere near the house or Denise.

I went back to the police station yesterday, and they said they weren't going to press charges. It doesn't matter now because my life is ruined anyway. Denise called on Thursday and told me to collect my things. I hurried over there and found one bin bag with some clothes, including my diary, which I'd hidden in a jacket pocket. She said I was lucky to walk away with that as I'd left her without any money so she'd sold everything else of mine.

She also said she wasn't leaving the house, and I'd have to continue paying the rent and all the bills, or she'd tell the police I'd raped her. If that wasn't enough, she ranted on about what a useless excuse for a man I was, and she'd only ever wanted my money. I will never forget the sneer on her face, the look of utter disgust like I was nothing.

She finished by saying that if I went near her again, she'd call the police, and then the door slammed shut. Angry, I tried to get in, but my key wouldn't work—she must have changed the locks.

I returned to my car and just sat there for ages, dazed.

I am a fool.

I've just read back my earlier diary entries, and perhaps I should have had an inkling. It's easy now, in hindsight, to say I should have never let things get to where they ended, but what is it they say? Love is blind?

I don't think love is blind, at least not the kind I had with Denise. That love is vicious and cruel and … it's fucking unfair.

Dad made me go back to the police station and tell them about what Denise said, just in case she ever tried making her sick claim against me. I really didn't want to, but I went along and gave them my side of the story. It didn't make any odds. They think Denise is the victim and I'm the bad guy. How is that fair?

I haven't been able to work for weeks, and they've put me on unpaid leave. I don't know how I'm supposed to pay Denise's bills with no money. My boss said I could come back once I've got my life sorted out, but I'm not sure I can ever go back. Too many bad memories.

It's nearly 2.00 am, and I can't sleep. I just skipped back to see when I last wrote a diary entry here, in my old bedroom at Mum and Dad's house. I've got used to calling it that, rather than home, because I thought I had a new home with Denise. Now I feel homeless—homeless and hopeless.

There is a way out of this, though. I can stop the pain with the bottle of sleeping pills on the bedside table. I've been looking at that *bottle for two hours now, trying to pluck up the courage to do the right thing.*

I think I'm ready now.

I'm sorry I wasn't stronger. I'm sorry I made such a mess of things.

Maybe Denise is right—I am a worthless piece of shit, and the world would be a better place without me in it.

Chapter 35

Monday morning, and I'm scraping frost from my windscreen. It's so much quieter than usual, and I can barely make out the houses opposite due to the dense fog that descended on the street overnight. The scene is verging on eerie.

I get in the car and rub my hands together in front of the heating vent. Slowly, the interior warms to the point I can feel my fingers again. Seatbelt on, I pull away.

Knowing I'd have to defrost the car, I left the house a bit earlier than usual this morning. I'm still ahead of schedule, but it's slow going due to the poor visibility. The ponderous pace allows my mind to wander, and it doesn't take long for my thoughts to turn to yesterday and my afternoon with Heather.

It would be fair to say it didn't pan out the way I expected, but in a good way. After Heather became only the fourth person to hear the pitiful tale of my one and only relationship, she couldn't have been more understanding, more supportive. We talked for over an hour at the kitchen table and in a strange kind of way, sharing our experiences proved a cathartic exercise. As Heather put it, one reason her scars are still raw is that they've never received treatment. I told her I'd spent several hours talking to a counsellor, which helped, but those sessions only served to dull the pain. It never went away, not really.

Our woes aired, and a tenuous bond formed, Heather suggested I might like to help her refill the bird feeders in the garden.

As we stepped through the French doors, she explained that the land at the front is kept wild for the benefit of insects, but she and Colin love tending the garden at the rear. Even in autumn, it was stunning.

If hadn't been told to the contrary, I'd have guessed that the garden evolved organically, with Mother Nature herself carefully selecting the type and position of every plant, every shrub, and every tree. Heather said that it actually evolved through painstaking planning and cultivation over many years. She told me that besides passing on her talent for cooking, her mum was a keen horticulturist and they spent many an hour tending their previous garden together. My host's extensive knowledge of flora would have put even Kenny to shame.

We wandered lazily around the garden, filling each of the eight bird feeders and topping up the water in the two birdbaths. Then, we returned to the kitchen and waited for our feathered guests to dine.

It wasn't quite the same as standing on Falbert's Mount, but there were some advantages. Heather makes a smashing cup of tea, and it was nice to drink it out of a bone china cup rather than a plastic mug. What I enjoyed most, however, was being able to share my passion with someone who seemed genuinely interested; fascinated even. I can't say I spotted anything out of the ordinary until a bright-green Ring-Necked Parakeet landed on one of the feeders. They're a relatively rare sight at Tinkerton Meadow, so seeing one at close quarters was a highlight.

The fading light brought an end to the afternoon and, keen not to outstay my welcome, I made my excuses. At the front door, we both floundered when it came to the simple act of saying goodbye. After the afternoon we'd shared, just saying goodbye and merrily strolling away didn't seem right, but neither did a peck on the cheek. We settled on a brief hug that wasn't as awkward as I was expecting, considering my host had sobered up a bit by then.

The only blot proved to be the drive home. Throughout my visit, I'd managed to ignore the voice in my head, berating me for taking advantage of Heather's vulnerability. I now understand why she's always appeared so distant, and it felt like I'd cheated my way past her defences. If not for the gift, there would be no fledgling friendship.

However, over the course of the evening, I concluded that there might be a way to counter my deceit and the associated guilt. The seed of an idea that first sprouted in Heather's kitchen grew into a possible solution. I promised to call her on Tuesday with an update, so I've got some work to do, besides the eight hours of paid work ahead of me.

I pull into the depot and park up. I'm not expected in the meeting room for another five minutes, so I open the notes app on my phone and tap the folder I created last night: Project Vale. The information within is nothing more than a list of random thoughts, but I sense the awakening of a sound idea. It might have started as a passing comment, a polite gesture, but the more I think about helping Heather and Colin, the more the idea appeals. Perhaps I have inherited some of Dad's entrepreneurial spirit after all.

I'm about to add another note when the sound of squealing tyres snares my attention. I look up just as Ady's car zips past and instinctively check the dashboard clock. He's two minutes away from our official start time, so there's no need for aggressive, boy-racer driving. I've warned him about it a thousand times, but he never listens.

Ady pulls into a parking bay at the end of a row, and I watch on as he clambers out of the car, slams the door, and storms towards the office doors. His demeanour doesn't suggest a reconciliation with Leanne. After her visit on Saturday, I'm staying well out of it.

I put the phone away with a minute to spare and mentally prepare myself for another day, another week. I don't know why but I can't seem to summon my usual self-motivation today. Perhaps I need a holiday, although that in itself presents another problem—where do I go and who with? As is usually the case, it'll be nowhere and no one.

I get out of the car and trek across the tarmac.

After tugging open the door to the main building, I'm met by the buzz of conversation from the meeting room beyond a pair of doors. There's also the familiar low-key hum that's likely baked into the brickwork; a result of sweaty, filthy men leaning up against the walls over many years.

I push through the double doors into the meeting room.

As I enter, heads turn in my direction. One of them belongs to Ady, standing fifteen feet away. The second he clocks me, a scowl breaks across his face. It deepens with every stride as he storms straight towards me.

"You're a dead man," he snarls.

I turn and glance over both shoulders, curious who he's yelling at. There's no one there, and by the time I turn back to face Ady, he's almost upon me.

Ady is a man who likes to think he's much tougher than he is. I've seen him in the pub many times, acting the hard man right up until the threat of physical violence becomes a distinct possibility. At that point, he usually makes an excuse and backs down.

This time, however, he seems intent on walking the walk. More by luck than judgement, I'm able to evade a wild haymaker of a punch by ducking down at the last moment. The momentum, however, spins my workmate around until he stumbles sideways and trips over his own feet. There's no evading a thirteen stone lump of uncontrolled Ady as he crashes into me.

We bounce off the wall and land in a heap on the floor. It's then a mad scurry to gain the upper hand—I want to put some distance between us whilst Ady wants to pin me down and begin a pummelling. Much shoving, grabbing, and twisting ensues, in which Ady is unable to land a punch, and I'm unable to escape his improvised wrestling moves. We soon tire, and just when I think I might be able to escape, a referee intervenes.

"Enough!" Jonny barks, grabbing the collar of Ady's jacket.

I complete the move, rolling away and scrambling to my feet. Ady manages to stand upright but can't move as Jonny positions himself between us. Still, my attacker looks primed to continue the fight, his chest out and face redder than a baboon's arse.

"What the fuck's wrong with you?" I pant. "You're crazy."

"I'll tell you what's wrong with me, shall I?" Ady spits, jabbing his finger in my direction. "You've been having an affair with my missus, behind my back."

By their very nature, surely all affairs are behind someone's back? Perhaps now is not the time for semantics.

"Don't be ridiculous," I scoff. "You couldn't be more wrong."

"You're a fucking liar. You told Leanne about my ... you told her stuff you had no right telling her, so that you could get in her knickers."

He's right on one count.

"I told her the truth, just like I'm telling you the truth when I say nothing happened between us."

"Bullshit! I know she was round at your place three times in the last week or so ... and don't tell me you were just chatting 'cos I know you'd knob anything with a pulse given half a chance. I bet you filled her head with poison and made out to be all caring—"

"Shut it!" Jonny snaps. "Both of you."

He turns to Ady and instructs him to go outside and cool down. To be sure he complies, Jonny guides Ady towards the double doors and watches him walk away. Then, he turns to me.

"My office. Now."

Keeping a safe distance behind, I follow my boss across the meeting room to a door adjacent to the fire escape. I enter the office, and he orders me to close the door.

"Sit down," he grumbles, while flicking through a pile of papers on an untidy desk.

Long seconds pass while I wait for the anticipated lecture. I'm supposed to be the level-headed, sensible employee, so it stands to reason Jonny will expect me to explain what happened with Ady.

He finishes reading whatever needed reading and sits back in his chair. With his mop of unkempt hair, three days of stubble, and sizeable bulk, Jonny is no one's idea of a manager.

"What was all that about?" he asks.

"Ady got the wrong end of the stick, that's all."

"I overheard some of it. You've been meeting up with his missus behind his back. That true?"

"Her name is Leanne, and she came to see me because she was worried about Ady. You know yourself he's been all over the place of late."

"And what happened when she came to see you?"

"Nothing happened."

"Ady clearly thinks otherwise."

"Ady also thinks they feed bananas to cows to make banana-flavoured milk. What's your point?"

Jonny glances at the computer monitor before replying.

"We'll put Ady to one side for the moment. I was going to call you in this morning, anyhow."

"Why?"

"I heard some of the lads talking about a post on Facebook last week. Some woman claimed you sexually assaulted her."

"That claim was a lie, and Facebook removed it within a few hours."

"Why'd she say it, then?"

"Because she was angry with me."

"I'd be angry if you'd sexually assaulted me."

"Jesus wept. I didn't sexually assault her—we had a date, and I decided not to take it any further. She got angry and posted that bullshit on Facebook. There's nothing else to it, and to be frank, Jonny, I don't understand why we're discussing it. It happened out of work, so it's none of your business."

After another glance at the monitor, he adjusts his position in the chair, resting his chubby forearms on the desk.

"The reason why it's relevant is because I received some information on Friday relevant to Keira's resignation."

The mention of Keira's name is enough to make my skin prickle, but I don't respond to Jonny's statement.

"One of your colleagues claims you asked Keira out for dinner, and she was upset by it."

It's my turn to sit forward.

"What?"

"Did you ask Keira out for dinner?"

"No."

"So, the person who overheard you is lying? You never had a conversation with Keira in which you asked her out for dinner?"

My discomfort becomes indignation.

"Assuming your grass is Big Fal, he got the wrong end of the stick."

"I'm not naming names, but they were pretty sure about what they heard."

"I don't give a shit what Big Fal think's he heard. It was Keira who asked *me* out to dinner, alright?"

The moment Jonny snorts in response to my claim, I know I've made a terrible mistake.

"Yeah, course she did," he sneers. "You're really her type, ain't you."

"I'm telling you what happened."

"And I don't believe you."

"Ask Keira then."

"That's not my place, but I'm afraid I had to report this to HR, and they'll certainly be speaking with Keira."

"You reported me to HR? Why the fuck did you do that?"

"I didn't have a choice. You forget, Dougie, we work for Ashbridge Borough Council, and that means we all abide by their rules, their policies. Don't matter if you sweep the streets or work in the planning office—any impropriety must be reported to HR. Them's the rules, and I'm just following them."

"You could have talked to me first."

"Why should I put my balls on the chopping block? You can't tell me that all this stuff that's gone on—the Facebook post, Ady's missus, and Keira—is all just a coincidence?"

"That's *exactly* what it is."

"So you say, but if it turns out you're a wrong'un, and I ignored the evidence, I'll be the one getting canned. I ain't losing my job just because of your ... behaviour."

Jonny then opens the drawers in his desk and pulls out a white envelope.

"I have to give you this," he says, placing the envelope in front of me.

"What is it?"

"It's a formal notice of investigation. You're to attend a disciplinary meeting tomorrow morning."

Dumbfounded, I stare at Jonny and then at the envelope.

"This is a wind-up, right?"

"Dougie, do I look like I'm laughing?"

"I can't believe you've done this. I've worked my guts out for years ... always on time and never off sick, and this is how you treat me? You're an arsehole, Jonny. A total arsehole."

"Just doing my job," he replies, the slightest hint of a smile creeping across his face. "And part of that job is to inform you that you're now suspended until the investigation is complete."

This is ridiculous. Ridiculous and completely unfair.

"Thanks for nothing," I spit, snatching the envelope off the desk. "I'll be sure to let HR know how much porn you watch on your office computer."

"Tell 'em what you like," he replies dismissively. "Unlike your sketchy behaviour, there's no evidence and no witnesses."

I've already lost the moral high ground, but that doesn't mean I can't leave without a parting salvo.

"You do realise that IT can still determine which websites you've visited, no matter how many times you delete those porn sites from your browser history?"

Jonny's smirk evaporates, but I don't hang around long enough to savour it. Kicking the chair away, I storm out of the office and don't stop till I'm back behind the wheel of my car. I'm too angry to drive; too wound up to trust my concentration levels. Instead, I sit and seethe, gripping the steering wheel as tightly as I'd like to grip Jonny's neck. And Ady's for the matter. And Big Fal's.

I watch the digits on the dashboard clock tick over until my heart rate settles. The anger remains, but I have to admit my own culpability in all of this. That conclusion leads my anger down a different path entirely, towards the gift.

"Gift?" I hiss. "Curse, more like."

What's the point of being attractive when all you seem to attract is trouble?

I pull away, and although I think long and hard about that question, no answer is forthcoming by the time I arrive home.

There are, however, an increasing number of reasons why I preferred my old life. In many ways, I'm worse off now than I was when I was plain old Ugly Dougie. Life was a bit shit, but it was uncomplicated.

What I can do about regaining my old life, though, is a different problem entirely.

Chapter 36

The crumpled letter sits on the kitchen table. After reading it a third time, I lost my temper, screwed it up, and then tossed it in the direction of the bin. The only reason I salvaged it is because I couldn't remember the name of the woman in the human resources department I'm due to meet tomorrow: Rhona Carmichael.

Perhaps if I hadn't lost my temper, I'd have realised sooner that the fact I'm meeting a woman might be grounds for optimism. Deploying the gift against Ms Carmichael might be considered a shade unethical, but I could argue that fairness is just as important as ethics—I've done nothing wrong.

I take a photo of the letter and place the physical copy in the bin. Out of sight, out of mind.

One problem kicked down the road—if not solved—I should decide how I'm going to spend the day off I wasn't anticipating. My thoughts immediately turn to Tinkerton Meadow and enjoying six or seven hours on Falbert's Mount. However, the early morning fog is hanging around like the egg and cress sandwiches at a buffet. Besides, even if the sky were blue, how can I enjoy anything whilst I'm still as wound up as a tightly coiled spring?

I think back to Saturday, sitting at this very table with Leanne. Lesser-principled men would have taken advantage of the situation, irrespective of any friendship. I could so easily have been one of those men, but I resisted the temptation for the sake of my friendship with Ady. I might as well have committed the sin, seeing as he didn't seem to care about the truth. Arsehole.

And then there's Jonny. We've worked together for years, and although I wouldn't exactly say we're the best of mates, I always thought he'd have my back. How wrong I was. Big Fal can piss off, too, the snake. He could have spoken to me before running off to Jonny and telling tales, but no.

I guess it proves you don't know who your friends are until you need them. How am I supposed to continue working with my so-called workmates now those bonds of trust have been broken?

"Tossers."

Hard as I try, I can't quell the resentment simmering away in the pit of my stomach. It doesn't matter if I'm here or stood on Falbert's Mount; it's not likely to ease any time soon.

In need of a distraction, I get up and wander through to the lounge. I don't want to sit on my arse and watch television all day, but as short-term anger-management solutions go, it's my best hope.

From my armchair, I jab a button on the remote control and flick through the channels. The news? No thanks. A Hollywood romcom? Christ, no. A documentary about The Shetland Isles? Seen it. *Ramsay's Kitchen Nightmares*? No idea what it is.

I'm about to press the button on the remote again, but then the narrator says two words that snag my attention: failing restaurant. As I listen a little more intently, he goes on to explain how the owners of a once-thriving restaurant in Brighton are now on the verge of bankruptcy. A question is posed: Can Gordon Ramsay save the owners from financial ruin?

I don't know, but I'm intrigued enough to sit back and find out.

That intrigue continues beyond the end of the show. So much so, I search online to see if there are additional episodes available to stream. There are—five series, in fact.

I settle down to watch another episode, and it follows the same pattern as the first one. Ramsay arrives, samples a few items from the menu, and declares the food to be 'fucking dreadful'. He then sets about identifying why the food is so dreadful and what he can do to fix it, along with any other issues contributing to the restaurant's woes. The process seems to involve a lot of tears and tantrums and much swearing. In the end, all the issues are fixed, the restaurant is packed out, and the owners live happily ever after.

I watch two more episodes and then stop for lunch.

As I sit and chew on an uninspiring cheese sandwich, I think back to yesterday's lunch with Heather. I then remember something she said about never using the internet. The cogs continue to whirl, and then from nowhere, I imagine punching Ady in the face. Appealing as it is, I push the image to the back of my mind and refocus on the matter at hand. In Gordon Ramsay's show, the unifying problem across all the failing restaurants was the food. Heather's food is exceptional, at least the food I ate yesterday was. That's not to say what they serve in The Vale is poor; it's just not as good as what I know Heather is capable of creating, given free rein.

Those facts lead me to a question: what would Gordon Ramsay make of The Vale? I've only watched four episodes of his show, but I reckon he'd blame Colin for the cafe's problems. Heather's job is to cook, but Colin decides what she has to cook and where they source their produce. I think he's missing an obvious trick.

After finishing my sandwich, I gather my thoughts and return to the lounge. Whilst watching another episode of *Ramsay's Kitchen Nightmares*, I tap at my mobile phone screen, adding more and more ideas—a feat of solo brainstorming. By the end of the episode, I'm so wired I could almost forget why I'm sitting at home in the middle of the day, watching television.

I call Heather.

"Hello ... Douglas?"

Hardly anyone uses the name on my birth certificate, but it sounds right coming from Heather.

"Hi. Have I caught you at a good moment?"

"Kind of. I'm just getting ready to go and visit Dad."

I had hoped she was at home and at a loose end, but discussing my ideas with both of them together makes sense.

"Would you mind if I joined you at the hospital? I've got a few ideas for The Vale."

"You have?" she responds, her voice an octave or two higher. "That's such good news. And, yes, of course, you can drop by the hospital. I dare say Dad would welcome a bit of male company."

"Great. I'll be there in an hour or so."

I end the call and then begin to panic. What the hell do I know about the catering industry, besides my own limited experiences as a customer and a few hours watching a television show? I'm the last person Heather should be pinning her hopes on.

Then again, what other hope does she have?

I spend ten minutes swinging on an emotional pendulum; quietly confident one moment and racked with crippling self-doubt the next. It only ends once I conclude there's nothing at stake here. The Vale is as good as gone, so where's the harm in throwing a few ideas at Colin and Heather? I doubt Colin will hold it against me, but I'm not sure how I feel about seeing the look of disappointment on Heather's face. Not good, I decide.

Still, whatever the rights or wrongs of my half-arsed advice, I'd rather focus on a positive, so I continue refining my ideas during a long shower. It's preferable to dwelling on what happened at work this morning or what lies in store for me tomorrow.

I set off for Ashbridge General Hospital and arrive twelve minutes later. Knowing where I'm going this time, I manage not to get lost en route to Colin's ward. When I arrive, he's propped up in bed with Heather on a chair next to him.

"Hello, Dougie," he beams the second he notices my approach. "Good to see you again."

"You too."

I smile at Heather. She smiles back.

"You're looking in much better shape than when I saw you last," I comment, taking a seat.

"I'm not doing too badly, all things considered. How's tricks with you?"

For one fleeting moment, I imagine telling Colin exactly how I've fared since his last day at The Vale. I picture his face as I regale the story of falling down an embankment, then meeting a strange woman who offered me a potion that not only fixed my injuries but made me irresistible to women. And how I've used that new-found superpower to screw my life up.

"Same old, same old, mate," I reply. "Nothing much to report."

"Heather tells me you popped over to the house for lunch yesterday."

I glance at Heather, but her expression remains unreadable.

"Yeah, I ... err, we talked about The Vale."

"So she tells me. I hear you might have a few ideas about saving the old place."

"Possibly. I mean, not for one minute am I pretending to be an expert on the catering industry, but—"

Colin raises his hand, palm out.

"Let me stop you there. I really appreciate you wanting to help, but I think I've solved our problem."

Judging by the look on her face, this is news to Heather.

"Have you?" she says. "How?"

"I was chatting to one of the nurses, and she told me about her son and how he sold his flat in Ashbridge and used the money to buy an old farmhouse in Carmarthenshire."

"Carmarthenshire, in Wales?" I ask.

"That's the one. Apparently, property prices are almost half what they are around here. Anyhow, that got me thinking."

He turns to Heather.

"We can sell the bungalow, pay off all our debts, and there should still be plenty of money left to buy a similar property in Wales ... maybe even a place with more land than we've got now. You've always fancied having a few pigs and chickens, haven't you?"

"Well, yes ... but Wales?"

"I know it's a long way away, but what have we got keeping us here now?"

"We have a business, in case you'd forgotten."

"We *had* a business, but it's over, sweetheart—we both know it."

Heather's eyes shift from her dad to me, and she doesn't have to say a word. I understand her plea.

"What if there's a chance of rescuing the business?" I ask. "Wouldn't you prefer to stay where you are and give a few of my ideas a shot? Nothing ventured, eh?"

"Trouble is, lad, we've nothing left to venture. Heather said you took a look at the books, right?"

"Yes."

"Then you'll know we're losing money quicker than we can make it."

"I understand that, and that's why I've spent the last twenty-four hours thinking about ways you can increase turnover."

"It's too big a risk. We've already sunk all our savings into that place. There's nothing left."

"You're just going to give up without even listening to Douglas's ideas?" Heather interjects.

"Being a pragmatist is not giving up. What if none of these ideas work, and we fall deeper into debt? We could lose our home, sweetheart, and then where will we be?"

Colin places his hand on Heather's. It would be easy to label him defeatist, but he's just doing what he's always done—protecting his daughter. Judging by her sagging shoulders and resigned sigh, I suspect she knows it too.

"It'll all turn out for the best," he adds, somewhat unconvincingly. "You'll see."

A squeeze of her hand and a question about the weather puts an end to the subject. It's not my place to question Colin, so I don't.

For the next hour, the conversation feels stilted and one-sided. Colin seems keen to talk about Wales and what type of property they might find. Despite his best efforts, Heather still appears unconvinced.

At four o'clock, I decide it's time to leave.

"Thanks for dropping by," Colin says. "And I do appreciate you taking the trouble to help. If circumstances were different, maybe we might have tried a few of your ideas, but I hope you understand why we can't risk it?"

"I do."

I get to my feet and say goodbye. As I'm about to depart, Heather suggests she walks with me to the exit.

"I'll fetch us a proper cup of tea from the cafe," she says to Colin. "I can't stand that muck from the vending machine."

"Good girl. I could murder a decent brew."

We leave Colin to complete a crossword and walk in silence until we reach the main corridor.

"I'm so sorry," Heather says.

"Sorry for what?"

"Wasting your time. If I'd known what Dad had in mind, I wouldn't have asked for your help."

"You didn't waste my time, Heather. I thoroughly enjoyed our afternoon yesterday, and to be honest, thinking of ideas to help save The Vale has been a welcome distraction. I've had a few problems at work."

"Oh, no. Anything you'd like to talk about?"

"That's very kind, but ... I'm sure they'll blow over soon enough."

We reach a set of doors. Without thinking about it, I open the door on the right and invite Heather through.

"Thank you," she says, as I follow. "Men don't tend to open doors so much these days."

"I don't usually. I'm not sure why I did."

"Why don't you? Perhaps I'm old-fashioned, but I think it's courteous."

"Do you really want to know?"

"Of course."

"I went on a date, must be eight or nine years ago and, when the woman arrived, I could tell by the look on her face that she was disappointed. I wanted to counter that disappointment, so I opened the door to the restaurant and remarked how lovely she looked. She grabbed the opportunity to end our date there and then."

"Really?

"Yep, she just exploded, yelling that my comment about her dress and opening the door were hallmarks of a misogynist. She then stormed off, and that was that. It still holds the record as my shortest ever date."

Heather shakes her head.

"Why do some people have to be so mean?"

"Beats me."

We reach the end of the corridor and turn right, continuing towards the main stairwell.

"Did your luck change?" Heather asks.

"With dating? No, not at all. It's been one disastrous date after another."

It occurs that my admission is just as true now as it was a few weeks back, before the gift.

"I've never had a disastrous date," Heather replies.

"Believe me; you're lucky. I've had some so horrific that I still have nightmares about them."

"It depends on your definition of lucky, Douglas. I've never had a disastrous date because ... because I've never had a date."

My legs seize, and I come to an abrupt halt.

"Never?"

"I know," Heather huffs. "It's pathetic, isn't it?"

"Eh? No, I think you've misinterpreted my surprise. I mean ... why not?"

"As you now know," she replies with a faint smile. "I don't get out much."

There are scores of ways I could react to Heather's confession, but I don't know which would be most appropriate. I know from experience that sympathy, well-intentioned as it might be, doesn't make you feel any better. Quite the opposite, I've found. It's a reminder of what a failure you are.

Heather takes my lack of a response as a reason to continue walking towards the stairwell and for a change of subject.

"Can I ask, Douglas, do you think any of your ideas might have saved The Vale?"

I catch up.

"I'm not sure, but I hadn't factored in the precarious nature of your finances. If my home was on the line, I think I'd be pretty risk-averse, too."

"I understand Dad's motives, and I suppose his plan does make sense, but I wish he'd asked for my opinion."

"The idea of moving to Wales doesn't appeal?"

"I don't know. It's not like I've built any kind of life here, so there's not much to leave behind. I don't like the idea of leaving our bungalow, though. It's my home."

We reach the stairs and descend in silence. There are so many thoughts and unresolved emotions swilling around inside me that I can't think what to say as we approach the cafe.

"Well," Heather says with an air of finality. "I'd better get those cups of tea. Thanks again, Douglas ... for everything."

One of the unresolved emotions bubbles to the surface. I like this version of Heather, which is why I don't like the idea of saying goodbye. Not yet, anyhow.

"Um, I was just thinking ... err, seeing as you went to so much trouble cooking lunch yesterday, would you ... um, would you like to go out to dinner one evening? My treat, obviously."

Heather doesn't initially respond, and her facial features suggest a heated inner debate is in progress. Several seconds pass before she replies.

"For you to understand my answer, I need to tell you about Max."

"Who's Max?"

"A dog. A scruffy black mongrel to be precise."

"Oh."

"Not long after Mum passed away, maybe a month or so after we moved into the bungalow, Dad brought Max home. His elderly owner had gone into a care home, and Dad intervened when the chap's son said there was no choice but to send Max to a refuge. Dad being Dad, he offered to take him in. I think he realised I needed a friend as much as Max needed somewhere to live."

I nod.

"I can't tell you how much that soppy dog meant to me and how much he helped me through the grieving process. What we didn't know was that Max was already thirteen years of age when he came to us. Barely a year after he bounded into our lives, we had to take him on a one-way trip to the vets."

"Oh, God. That's awful."

"I remember Dad saying that we were blessed to have Max in our lives, even if it was only for a year. I didn't feel that way at all. I'd lost my mum, and then my best friend. Losing Max broke my heart all over again."

Even if I knew what to say, the lump in my throat would likely block any words.

"I don't wish to compare you to a dog, Douglas, but I think we might have been the best of friends if fate ... if I'd been brave enough to befriend you sooner. Even now, it'll be hard enough saying goodbye ... which is why I must politely decline your invitation."

Heather steps forward, stands on her tiptoes, and kisses me gently on the cheek.

"Goodbye, Douglas."

Unable to speak, I stand and watch Heather stride towards the door to the hospital cafe. She pushes it open and disappears inside. I then watch it swing shut, my feet frozen to the tiled floor. My stomach clenches with the familiar grip of disappointment. Yet again, the gift has dragged me into a situation that was never going to end well. I completely understand Heather's reasons for declining my dinner invite, but I now wish we'd never got to the point where I wanted to ask her.

I'm left with only one possible conclusion—the gift *is* a curse.

I want rid of it.

Chapter 37

Sitting in my car at a red traffic light, I consider a question almost worthy of its own card in the Scruples board game we played as a family. It's perhaps a macabre dilemma in that it relates to a period in English history when public executions were commonplace. On the journey from the jail to the town square, did the condemned favour good weather over bad?

Knowing you're only minutes away from meeting your maker, would you want to savour the warm sun on your skin and a bright-blue sky one final time, or would you prefer dark skies and winds so biting that death seems an attractive proposition?

I suspect I'd spend that final journey reflecting on my poor life choices rather than the weather, much like I am this morning. In a way, I'm heading to meet my executioner, although whatever happens during my meeting with Rhonda Carmichael, I'll live to tell the tale, I presume.

The meeting is set for ten o'clock, and I left home well in advance because the venue is not at the offices of Ashbridge Borough Council but the main offices of the county council, some fifteen miles away. There's a reason why I have to endure a thirty-mile round trip. A few years ago, the county council decided that operating eleven separate human resources departments in eleven separate borough councils might not be the most efficient use of taxpayer's money. It's rumoured that other local council departments might meet the same fate, but as yet,

no one has fathomed out how to keep the streets clea.
fewer people.

I checked the best place to park beforehand as the council office car park is for staff only. The nearest and cheapest alternative is a ten-minute walk, but I arrive in plenty of time. I couldn't face breakfast this morning, and as I pass a bakery even the aroma of freshly baked bread isn't enough to tempt me in.

Plodding along with my head down, I look up when the pavement ends. The county council offices are directly ahead, some hundred yards away. I'm no architect, but the building's design is as austere and joyless as Scottish pornography, I'd imagine.

I cross the road and approach the main entrance.

As I enter the main reception area, I remind myself that I have an unfair advantage over the woman I'm about to meet. It's that thought which has kept my sombre mood from slipping towards abject despair. I suppose it's not the meeting itself that's behind my lack of positivity, but the men who caused it and their betrayal. I half expected a call or visit from Ady last night, apologising for his behaviour, but that never happened.

I approach the enquiry desk, and a youngish guy with unnaturally white teeth points me in the direction of the human resources department. A few minutes ahead of schedule, the lift carries me up to the third floor of the building.

Another desk and another receptionist.

"I've got a ten o'clock appointment with Rhonda Carmichael."

"Your name, please?"

"Douglas Neil."

"She's ready for you now. Please, go on through."

The receptionist points towards a door to my right and flashes a smile. I wonder if that smile would be so wide if she knew the reason why I'm here.

I cross the carpet and rap a knuckle on a door that's slightly ajar.

"Come in."

One deep breath, and I enter.

The office is larger than I expected and tidy to the point of clinical. Directly ahead of me, a woman behind a desk stands up.

"Rhonda?" I query in my warmest tone. "I'm Douglas Neil. Dougie."

"It's Ms Carmichael, Mr Neil. Take a seat."

She sits back down without offering a handshake. It's not the chilly reception that troubles me, though—it's the stern expression on Ms Carmichael's face. In a way, it perfectly matches her business-like appearance: dark hair cut short, no detectable makeup, and a simple black jacket over a white blouse.

Sitting upright, she clasps her hands together and places them on the desk.

"Can you confirm you received my letter stating that this is a disciplinary hearing?"

"Yes."

"And, that you've waived your right to have a colleague or trade union representative present?"

"Um, I guess so."

"Yes or no, Mr Neil. Have you waived your right for a colleague or trade union representative to be present?"

"Yes."

"That confirmed, we shall begin the hearing."

There's not a flicker of emotion in her face, no sign whatsoever that Ms Carmichael is under the influence of the gift. Something isn't right, and unless her defences wane over the next twenty minutes, I could be in serious trouble.

"We are currently investigating an allegation of improper behaviour towards an employee of Ashbridge Borough Council: Miss Keira Payne. In her resignation statement, Miss Payne confirmed that her position had become untenable because she felt uncomfortable working with an unnamed male colleague."

Ms Carmichael looks directly at me, unblinking. Her gaze is so intense it feels like she's staring at the doorway behind me. For a moment, I consider turning around to check the door is closed.

"In a statement from another employee," Ms Carmichael continues. "It is alleged that you asked Miss Payne out for dinner. How do you respond to that allegation?"

With my throat suddenly bone dry, I have to cough a couple of times before replying.

"I ... I never asked Keira out for dinner."

"You're denying it, then?"

"Yes."

"Can you explain why we have a witness who claims otherwise?"

"You'd have to ask him, but he got his wires crossed. This is a simple misunderstanding."

Her expression still unreadable, Ms Carmichael then slowly turns her head towards a computer monitor. I can't see what she's looking at, but whatever it is, it only holds her attention for a few seconds.

"And what about the altercation that occurred in the workplace on Friday morning? Was that another misunderstanding?"

"It was ... something and nothing."

"Your line manager confirms an allegation of improper behaviour towards a colleague's partner. I'd hardly call that something and nothing."

"Ady got the wrong end of the stick. That's all."

"Let me get this straight. There are two recent incidents in which allegations of improper behaviour have been alleged, and you claim there's no substance to either allegation. Is that correct?"

If it's any consolation, either she's unaware of Zoe's Facebook post or, as I suggested to Jonny, it's beyond the council's disciplinary boundaries.

"There is no substance, no."

"Would you care to elaborate on that statement?"

"Elaborate how?"

"With facts, Mr Neil—facts and specific details. It's not enough just to say someone got their wires crossed or the wrong end of the stick."

"Do I have—"

My reply is cut short by a dry tickle in the back of my throat. I cough and then swallow twice in an attempt to lubricate my vocal cords.

"Sorry," I rasp. "Slight frog in my throat."

"Would you like a glass of water?"

It seems the ice queen is not completely heartless.

"Please. It must be the air conditioning."

"One moment."

I'm sure I catch a sigh as my interrogator strides across the office and out the door. I can't relax, but at least I have a brief moment to consider what I say next. Maybe I should say nothing, go with no comment responses so I don't implicate myself. But wouldn't that make me appear guilty, like I've something to hide?

Unsure which way to go, I begin fidgeting. I reach across the desk for a coaster in preparation for the arrival of a glass of water. As I adjust my position in the chair, I notice a set of keys positioned behind the keyboard. There's nothing remarkable about the keys, but they're attached to a fob with a photograph encased in transparent plastic—a bride and groom walking through a shower of confetti. The bride, dressed in a traditional white wedding dress, looks nothing like Ms Carmichael. That begs the question: why is she carrying around a photograph of a random couple?

On closer inspection, I realise why.

Dressed in a full morning suit, the groom in the photo is none other than Rhonda Carmichael.

"Oh, crap," I whisper.

As potent as the gift has proven to be, it certainly can't alter someone's sexual persuasion, which would explain why Ms Carmichael is impervious to my superpower.

I sit back in my chair, thoughts scattered. Notwithstanding my innocence, my plan to escape this hearing unscathed relied on one thing: the gift coercing Ms Carmichael's view of me. With that one defence mechanism now defunct, what do I say when she returns and repeats her questions?

Behind me, the door clicks shut. I don't need to turn around to acknowledge I'm already out of time.

Ms Carmichael places a glass of water on the desk in front of me and then retakes her seat.

"Thank you," I say, my voice barely a horsey whisper.

"Once you've found your voice again, Mr Neil, perhaps we can continue."

I gulp thirstily and then nod.

"You were about to elaborate on your statement."

"Err, which part, specifically?"

"Let me be clear. Whatever you do outside of work is none of the council's business. However, we cannot have colleagues fighting one another on our premises. As for the incident regarding Keira Payne, I'm duty-bound to investigate why she decided to leave. If it turns out the alleged advance did occur, and Miss Payne felt uncomfortable, that could constitute sexual harassment."

"Are you serious? Asking a colleague out to dinner constitutes sexual harassment?"

"No, but if that invitation forms part of wider campaign of inappropriate behaviours, that most definitely would."

"Hold on a sec. One minute I'm accused of asking Keira out for dinner, then next you're suggesting I've been harassing her. You're out of order."

"As I said, Mr Neil, I'm just trying to get to the bottom of why Miss Payne resigned. All we have at the moment is her resignation statement in which she says she felt uncomfortable working with one of her colleagues, and a witness who claims you asked Miss Payne out to dinner. You must understand why I need to ask these questions, surely?"

"I've told you I didn't ask Keira out to dinner."

"Fair enough. Do you have any idea who this colleague might be—the one Miss Payne referred to in her resignation statement?"

Ms Carmichael's question carries with it an accusatory undercurrent. Without the gift to warp her perception, it's no surprise she wants to explore the obvious narrative. She sees me how every woman has ever seen me: undesirable, unlovable, a man no one would ever want to claim as hers. In short, the kind of desperate man who bothers women.

I don't blame her for thinking it, but it doesn't irk any less.

"What's the point of this?" I ask, making no attempt to hide my bitterness.

"I'm not with you."

"I mean, what do you want from me?"

"The point of any disciplinary hearing is to establish the truth. I asked you here today to hear your version of events. It's only right and fair."

"And what if I tell you the truth and it doesn't correspond with what your witnesses have told you?"

"I can't say at this point because there are other witnesses I need to speak to."

"And who are these supposed witnesses?"

"Miss Payne, obviously. And, I'm still waiting on a report from your line manager relating to the incident yesterday morning but it's likely I'll be speaking to Mr Turner as well."

Her confirmation has implications I hadn't really considered before now. Rhonda Carmichael wants the truth because she believes it's fair, but what if the truth and fairness don't tally?

I can imagine Keira sitting in this very chair, confessing that she asked ugly Dougie out for dinner and how he spurned her advances. It's the truth, but is it fair on Keira? If she were to admit it, her work life would become a misery with a never-ending stream of stupid comments from the likes of Big Fal and Steve. She went to great lengths to keep her work relationships on a professional footing, and admitting she asked me out to dinner would undermine all that effort. Is it any wonder she resigned?

Then, there's Ady. Would he feel comfortable admitting to the head of Human Resources that he has a gambling addiction? He's already on a final warning. Harder still, could he admit to himself that his denial and dishonesty drove his girlfriend to seek help from a workmate?

"How long have you worked for the council, Ms Carmichael?"

"Is that relevant to the hearing?"

"Possibly."

"Eighteen months. Why do you ask?"

"I've worked for Ashbridge Borough Council for twenty-odd years."

"Your point being?"

"I assume you looked at my personnel file before this meeting?"

"Naturally."

"And what does it say?"

"I can't tell you unless you formally request a copy of the file."

"No need, because I've already got a fair idea what it says. I've only ever had a handful of sick days, I'm punctual, hard-working, and to the best of my knowledge, there's never been a complaint lodged against me from either colleagues or management. Would you say that's a reasonable assessment?"

"I would concur, broadly speaking."

"So, considering my long-standing service and impeccable employment history, would you be willing to accept my word that nothing untoward occurred?"

"Why would I do that?"

"Because I don't want you to interview Keira or Ady. Corroborating my version of events could make their lives difficult, and that's not fair."

"You're asking me to close this hearing without interviewing witnesses whose evidence could potentially prove you're guilty of gross misconduct?"

"Their evidence won't prove anything other than my innocence."

"So you say."

"It's the truth."

Ms Carmichael straightens her shoulders.

"I'm afraid that's not an option, Mr Neil. I have a duty to thoroughly and methodically investigate all possible breaches of our employment policies. Based upon your record with the council, I might be inclined to believe you, but it doesn't matter what I think—it matters what the evidence states."

"Fair enough."

In the time it takes to stand up and push my chair back towards the desk, I reach the most impetuous of decisions.

"You've left me with no other option, Rhonda—I quit."

"I'm sorry?"

"I resign. You'll have it in writing this afternoon."

"But ... what about the investigation? Aren't you being a little hasty?"

"If I resign, there's no need for you to interview Keira or Ady. In fact, you can tell Keira that I'm leaving and maybe she'll reconsider withdrawing her resignation. She's incredibly good at her job, you know."

With the head of Human Resources sitting open-mouthed, I turn to walk away. I cover five feet of carpet before turning around.

"Sorry, one last question: how long have you been married?"

"Is that any of your business?"

"No, but seeing as the hearing is now officially over, humour me."

After a brief pause, she replies.

"Two years last month."

"Belated congratulations on your anniversary, and I hope you enjoy many more. Some people are destined never to find love, so you should be eternally thankful you found it."

The thinnest of smiles cracks across her tundra-like face.

I turn around and walk on, not stopping or considering what I've just done until I reach the lift. Thirty seconds and scores of thoughts later, I pass through the reception area and out the door.

Putting one foot in front of the other, I plod back in the direction of the car park, waiting for a wave of regret to land. What the hell was I thinking? Fifty yards becomes a hundred and then two hundred, but the anticipated regret fails to materialise. Instead, I feel surprisingly serene.

Slowly, my thoughts clear, and a new perspective takes hold. Maybe the anxiety I suffered before the meeting wasn't down to the risk of losing my job, but the fear of change. I've tried so hard to find love that I've ignored the possibility that there might be other ways to live a fulfilling life. In that sense, I've forsaken my career and spent two entire decades treading water whilst waiting for the right woman to come along. No wonder I don't feel regret.

I turn a corner, but my thoughts continue heading in the same direction.

Since the moment I fell down that bank, fate has conspired with the gift to monumentally change the course of my life. Without either, I wouldn't currently be walking away from a disciplinary hearing and a job I thought I'd never leave. The gift never delivered Miss Right, but it has forced me to consider how I might spend the rest of my working life. Do I want to look back when I'm in my sixties and rue wasting another couple of decades?

I pass a coffee shop and pause for a moment. Has my need for an injection of caffeine ever been greater? I think not.

I'm no fan of overpriced coffee shops, but with time on my hands and fresh thoughts to process, I push open the door and step inside. The aroma of freshly roasted beans instantly justifies whatever price I'm about to pay for a cup of tepid brown liquid.

I approach the counter and order a coffee and a much-needed bacon roll. When the barista asks, I confirm I'll be eating in.

I choose a table near the window and sit down. Now the anxiety has settled, my hunger has returned. Alas, it only takes one bite of the bacon roll to determine it's not a patch on those served at The Vale—the bacon limp and the roll dry. It's such a pity Colin has made up his mind about closing the cafe, but on one level, at least, I admire his bravery. He had a decision to make, and he made it, and even when I tried to influence that decision, he held firm. Not many people would be so quick to give up on their business, sell their home, and relocate halfway across the country, but Colin considered his plight and acted accordingly.

Admiration isn't the only emotion at the table, though. A tiny part of me envies Colin's clean slate. However, as much as I'll miss my frequent chats with Colin in The Vale, I'm disappointed that I won't have the opportunity of getting to know Heather a little better. It would have been lovely if I'd had the chance to invite her for an afternoon at Tinkerton Meadow.

I might have even offered to cook her a meal, or asked her to accompany me to the cinema.

The disappointment sits heavy. I sweep it away by thinking of my next move. I won't be heading to Wales, but there's no reason I can't consider an equally radical plan. People do change careers late in life, although working for Ashbridge Borough Council was only ever a job—no one could call keeping the streets clean a career. Nevertheless, what's stopping me now? Why can't I have my own clean slate?

Whether my snap decision turns out to be the right decision for Dougie Neil remains to be seen, but I'm certain it was the right decision for Keira and Ady.

I finish my late breakfast and ask the barista where I can find the toilets. Coffee goes through me like water through a sieve, and I'd rather avoid crossing my legs on the fifteen-mile journey home. He points to a door on the far side of the coffee shop.

Once I've emptied my bladder, I wash my hands, keeping my eyes fixed on the tap to avoid the large mirror behind the sink. As I'm about to leave the toilets, an elderly chap enters. I stand aside and let him pass.

"Thank you, young man."

"No worries."

I step into the corridor that leads back to the coffee shop. As I reach the midway point, the door ahead swings open. A woman hurries towards me, eyes on the mobile phone in her hand. A few steps later, she looks up.

We both freeze and stare at one another.

"Dougie?" she gasps. "Is that ... is that you?"

In a physical sense, she's vaguely familiar. Her voice, however, is unforgettable.

My mouth bobs open, but it takes a monumental effort to cough a name out.

"Denise?"

Chapter 38

•

Time appears to stand still. We both remain motionless in the silent corridor; her eyes fixed on mine and mine on hers. Not quite trusting that this isn't a surreal out of body experience, I study her features and compare them to the woman I once lived with. Her hair is shorter and a darker shade of honey-blonde. The lips I've kissed countless times are as plump as I remember, but they're now edged with fine lines; the price of her nicotine addiction. What doesn't appear to have changed much is her body. Denise could eat or drink anything she liked, but it never seemed to alter her slender frame.

"Oh. My. God," she blurts, taking a step forward. "It *really* is you."

I can feel my heart pounding away at twice its usual rate. The dry mouth which temporarily suspended my meeting with Rhonda Carmichael returns. Dehydration might explain why my mind is currently shrouded in an impenetrable fog.

Denise takes another step towards me—no more than five feet away now.

"Dougie?" she chuckles, waving a hand in the space between us. "Anyone in there?"

She drops her hand, but her eyes remain firmly fixed on my face. I've seen this expression before, but never whilst looking at me. The last time I saw it, Denise was standing in our kitchen looking up at Jimmy, or Jamie, or whatever his name was. Minutes later, all giggly and playful, she dragged him up the stairs to our bedroom.

Barely three heartbeats pass before a powerful wind blasts the fog from my mind. The remaining scene is as crisp and clear as a spring morning on Falbert's Mount. My senses alive, I can see everything I need to see.

"Your hair," I remark flatly. "It's shorter. It's darker too, isn't it?"

"A bit," she smiles. "I need to keep the grey at bay, so it's out of a bottle. You look … different."

"Do I? How?"

She takes yet another step towards me, tilting her head slightly.

"Hmm. I'm not sure, but the years have been kind to you, Dougie. Really kind."

They haven't. Denise isn't seeing the real me—she's seeing what the gift wants her to see.

"That's certainly nicer than the last words you said to me … if you can remember?"

Her smile instantly dissolves.

"You probably hate me, but I'm no longer the woman you once knew—that crazy cow is long gone."

She draws a sharp breath before continuing.

"There are no excuses for what I did to you—none. But, you need to understand how messed up I was back then, mentally and emotionally. I was just a stupid kid … we both were."

She delivers her words with the rapidity of a machine gun. It's how she used to get her own way, by talking at me without drawing breath, pushing home her argument, and never pausing to let me speak.

"Is that it?" I ask impassively.

"For what it's worth, I am sorry. And, if it makes you feel any better, life has been pretty shit for me over the last twenty years."

"And you think it's been great for me?"

"I don't know. Has it?"

"Not particularly."

"In which case, I'm doubly sorry."

"It's a bit late for apologies."

"You're probably right," she sighs. "And I'd understand if you spat in my face and walked away, but can I ask you a question?"

"You can ask."

"Do you ever think about how life might be now if things had worked out differently for us?"

"You mean if you hadn't had sex with random blokes in our bed or threatened to tell the police I raped you?"

"As I said, Dougie, I wasn't in a good place back then, but don't make out it was all awful. We had some good times too. Great times."

"Maybe, but my memory can't see past the psychological abuse, strangely enough."

"You don't remember the first time we made love?"

Before I know it, we're standing almost toe-to-toe. She's so close I can smell the same cocktail of cigarettes and perfume I so vividly recall from our first night out together.

"That wasn't so horrific," she purrs. "Was it?"

As I consider Denise's question, a Venn diagram forms in my mind's eye. There are two circles side-by-side—one labelled hate and one love—overlapping at the edge. I've resided in that overlap for so many years it feels like home. If I hadn't loved Denise so much, I couldn't possibly have carried all this hate for so long.

The question I then ask myself is, which is the stronger emotion?

"Whatever good times we had, Denise, I'll only ever be able to remember the bad because there were far more of them, for me anyway."

"That's a shame," she replies matter-of-factly. "Up until I went off the rails, I genuinely thought we had a future together."

"Jesus wept," I snort. "Went off the rails? Is that how you remember it?"

"What do you want me to say? I behaved like an utter bitch, and treated you worse than a dog? Does hearing that make you feel any better or change what we went through?"

Remarkably, the dynamic has shifted to such an extent I'm now the one scrabbling around for an appropriate retort.

The mental fog drifts back in.

"I ... what do ... fuck this. Get out of my way, Denise. I'm going, and if I don't see you again for another twenty years, it'll be too soon."

I take a step to the right with one eye on the door behind my psychotic ex-girlfriend.

"Wait, Dougie. Please."

"For what? Is your boyfriend with you? Maybe you'd like to call him in, and I can hide in the toilets and listen to you fuck, just for old time's sake. Is that what you want?"

Panting hard, I realise my hands are so tightly balled that my fingers are on the edge of cramping up. In truth, my hands are not the only body part racked with tension.

Denise dips her chin and swallows.

"I deserved that," she says in a quieter voice. "And if you want to go, I understand, but please let me say one thing before you do."

Still simmering, I can barely bring myself to look at her, let alone reply.

"I did love you. I genuinely did. Seeing you now has made me realise that."

I close my eyes and drag my mind two decades back into the past. I'm in a therapist's office, listening to his calming voice telling me that I'm stronger than I know, and words alone cannot harm me.

A hand gently touches my upper arm.

"Dougie?"

Dragged back to reality, I open my eyes.

"What?" I reply through gritted teeth.

"Do you think this could be fate? Us meeting here like this?"

And then it hits me—a sudden, intense heat. I've almost become used to the slight warmth that seems to accompany the gift, but this is on a whole different level. The only time I've ever felt anything like it was one summer when Ashbridge recorded record temperatures, and I was humping waste into the back of the van on my own. Decked in protective clothing and with the midday sun bearing down, I almost passed out with heatstroke.

A raging thirst arrives.

"Are you okay, Dougie? You look a bit flushed."

"I ... I need water."

"Come with me."

Panicked, I let Denise guide me through the door to the coffee shop. She then sits me in the nearest chair and hurries over to the counter, returning seconds later with a bottle of chilled water.

"Here," she says, handing me the bottle and pulling up a chair. "Take a drink."

If I wasn't so perturbed by the prospect of bursting into flames, I might have been taken aback by Denise's sudden, and out-of-character, concern. I open the bottle and gulp back the cooling water.

"Any better?"

"A bit."

She then places her hand on my forehead like a mother might do when checking a child's temperature. Ironic, as the Denise I knew didn't have a maternal bone in her body.

"You're still a bit clammy."

Delving into her handbag, she pulls out a packet of ibuprofen.

"Take a couple of these. If you're coming down with a fever, they'll help."

Acting on autopilot, I press two pills from the blister pack and swallow them with another gulp of water.

"Listen," Denise then says. "I was heading to the loo when I bumped into you. I'm desperate, but I don't want to come back and find you're gone. Will you wait for me ... please?"

I'm more concerned with regulating my body temperature but respond with a half-nod.

"I'll be two ticks, okay."

She hurries away to the toilets, leaving me alone to gather up my scattered thoughts. There are many, and they're all over the place.

I raise a hand and press it to my forehead, much like Denise did. I'm warm but not burning up as I was back in the corridor. What the hell happened? It was like stepping from an air-conditioned aircraft that's just landed in some sub-tropical clime. Now, though, I'm back in my seat with the cabin door closed.

What could have triggered it?

I think back to the moment it hit me. I didn't do anything, and neither did Denise. One moment she was talking about fate and the next ...

"No," I gasp. "No way."

Two men seated at the adjoining table glance over at me, both sporting a quizzical stare. I flash an embarrassed smile and turn my attention to the tiled floor, where three of my most prominent thoughts are now gathered together.

The gift.

Denise.

Fate.

Was this chance meeting really chance? On my walk here, I questioned whether the gift had sent me on a path towards a new career; an opportunity to start a meaningful new chapter of my life.

And then, I stopped for a coffee.

I could have kept walking or chosen a different coffee shop. I could have left Rhonda Carmichael's office a minute earlier or a minute later. Jesus, if I hadn't stopped to let that old bloke in the toilet pass, I'd have left before Denise entered the corridor. Our paths would never have crossed.

But they did.

In twenty-odd years, I've never considered how I might feel if I ever saw Denise again. I might have occasionally wondered how her life panned out, but such pondering never ended well. I tried to imagine her living a shitty, unhappy life as penance, but it made no odds. By that point, the damage was done.

So, why is she here?

I let that question stew for a moment until my stomach suddenly knots in a tight spasm. The cause could be gratification or existential dread—I'm not sure which.

If there's one way to silence your demons, it's to confront them as the devil. Denise was right when she suggested we're not the same people. I am now in possession of a miraculous gift, and she's a benign, middle-aged nobody.

Is this the point of everything?

"How are you feeling?"

I look up just as Denise retakes her seat.

"What are you doing here?" I ask.

"Err, I just went to the loo. Remember?"

"I mean, what made you walk into *this* coffee shop?"

"It's the same coffee shop I use whenever I happen to be in town."

"And why are you in town?"

"Tuesdays are my day off. I broke a nail this morning, so I had to pop into the salon."

"You weren't planning on coming into town today?"

"No, and I wasn't planning on spending thirty quid on a set of acrylics either. Thankfully, they had a cancellation, so Georgie was able to squeeze me in."

It seems Denise's being here is the result of another set of fluke events.

"Why do you ask?"

"No reason. Forget it."

Silence pulls up a chair.

"I'm, um, just going to grab a coffee," Denise says. "Will you wait one minute for me?"

"Why? I think we've both said all we needed to say, haven't we?"

"I don't think so, no. One minute, please."

To avoid a negative answer, she gets up and returns to the counter. I watch her go and try to detach the woman I'm looking at from the evil creature I once lived with. Watching her interact with the barista, I could almost trick myself into believing it's not the same person. I can still see the physical similarities, but I suppose it's like leaving your home town and returning twenty years later. You instinctively focus on what's different rather than what's the same.

She leans forward to tap her bank card against the payment terminal. As she does, I can't help but notice her denim-clad backside is as pert now as it was the last time I saw it. I hate myself for thinking it, but I can't deny that I'm still attracted to her. Is that normal?

Against a backdrop of all-consuming hatred, I'd almost forgotten I once loved this woman. It might have been a long time ago, but no one ever forgets their first love or the one who stole their virginity. In my case, it's the same person and, in the early days of our relationship, before we moved to Norton Rise, I couldn't have loved any human more than I loved Denise. That was, I suppose, the fundamental problem with our relationship—I loved her far, far more than she ever loved me, if indeed she ever did. Evidence suggests she didn't.

Denise thanks the barista and returns to the table.

"Sorry about that. Where were we?"

"You asked me to wait one minute for you. That minute is up."

"Do you have to be somewhere?"

"That's none of your business."

"No, it's not, but it could be."

"What's that supposed to mean?"

She sips from her coffee cup and then casually crosses her legs. For someone who was just told they're out of time, she appears unhurried.

"Cards on the table. I don't believe in random coincidences. I think we were meant to bump into one another this morning. Don't ask me why but seeing you again has just … I don't know. I can't stop looking at you, and in the interest of transparency, I'm sitting here thinking of all the unspeakable things I'd love to do to you right this moment."

Once again, she fixes me with the same look she kept for Jimmy, or Jamie, or whatever his name was. Lustful would be a good approximation.

"Are you single?" she asks, almost as an afterthought.

I nod.

"Me too. I was married, but we split up four years ago."

"Why?"

"He cheated on me. I came home from work early one day as I wasn't feeling too clever and found him shagging my best friend on the sofa."

At least her ex-husband had the decency to keep his infidelities secret. Still, if there's such a thing as karma, I bet Denise felt it that day.

"Not nice, is it?"

"No, it's not. I'd like to say I learned my lesson that day, but I wasn't lying when I said life hasn't been kind to me. Before I met my cheating shit of a husband, I'd already suffered more setbacks than I care to recall and enough regrets I could fill a book."

"And where would our relationship feature in that book of regrets."

"If you'd asked me yesterday, I'm not sure I could have answered you. Then, fate threw us together this morning, and now I've got a whole new list of regrets ... with your name at the top."

If I'd just met her, I'd have zero doubts about her sincerity. It comes across in her voice, and it's there in her eyes for anyone to see. The trouble is those same eyes were once dark and foreboding, and I can't forget that.

Denise pulls her chair a few inches closer to mine—close enough I can feel her thigh touching mine under the table.

"Would you let me cook you lunch?" she asks.

"Lunch?"

"Yeah, you know—the meal between breakfast and dinner."

"Spare me the sarcasm."

"Sorry. I just thought you might like to come back to my place, and we can ... talk."

"I don't think we've anything to talk about."

"If you're referring to our past, I'd agree with you. There's nothing I can say to change it, or to undo the pain I caused. However, I'd like to talk as two strangers who bumped into one another in a coffee shop. Two strangers who are attracted to one another and like the idea of seeing where that attraction takes them. Maybe it'll lead nowhere, but there's only one way to find out."

What Denise is suggesting is tantamount to a clean slate.

"Who said I was still attracted to you?"

"A woman knows, Dougie. She just knows."

Denise suddenly gets to her feet.

"It's up to you," she says. "Come with me now and see if I can't prove to you that I'm not that stupid girl, or you can stay here and spend the rest of your days wondering. Either way, I'm glad we bumped into each other—I truly am."

She waits for a reply. I empty the last few mouthfuls of water from my bottle and stand up.

Denise's smile returns, broader than I've ever seen it, and she offers me her hand.

"I'm afraid my cooking skills still aren't great, but I'm a dab hand at beans on toast."

I look down at her hand. Is this really what fate intended?

Chapter 39

Staring into the fridge, I can't decide if I'm hungry or not. It's gone six o'clock, so I should be hungry, but my stomach is still too knotted to receive food.

I close the fridge door but not before snatching a can of beer from the shelf. I might not have an appetite for a chicken risotto, but my need for the calming influence of alcohol has never been greater.

Before I can even snap the ring pull, the doorbell chimes.

Putting the can on the side, I stomp through to the hallway. I'm not in the mood for guests, and there have been far too many of the uninvited variety of late.

I open the door.

"Oh. It's you."

Ady stands with his hands tucked into the pockets of his jeans.

"You got a minute?" he asks.

"I was about to start dinner."

"It'll only take a minute, I swear."

"If you've come to have another pop at me, you can forget it."

"Nah, it's nothing like that. It's ... look, I'm sorry, mate. That's what I came to say."

If his forlorn expression is anything to go by, he at least looks sorry.

"Alright," I sigh. "Come in."

I don't stand on ceremony and head straight back to the kitchen. Ady follows me through and, despite not being asked, I notice he's kicked off his shoes.

"Beer?"

"If you've got one spare, ta."

I open the fridge again and hand Ady my second-to-last can.

"Cheers," he says with a nod. "I did pop round earlier, but you weren't in."

"No, I've had a hectic afternoon, what with one thing and another."

"Job hunting?"

"Not yet, no. I've been ... actually, it doesn't matter where I've been. Why are you here, Ady?"

He runs a hand across his stubbly chin.

"First things first, I need to say sorry for what happened at work yesterday. I was bang out of order."

"Yeah, you were."

"What can I say, mate? I don't always think about what I'm doing until it's done. It was a stupid thing to accuse you of and ... I wish I could take it back."

"Alas, you can't. But, I accept your apology."

"Dunno how I got it into my head you were seeing Leanne. I mean, no disrespect, but if she were gonna cheat on me, I'd expect it to be with someone better looking than me."

"No offence taken."

"Or intended."

"Hmm. Anyway, are you two still not on speaking terms?"

"She moved back in last night after we had a proper talk."

"Oh. I thought she'd confessed her love for another man."

"She only said that to make me realise I'd been taking her for granted. It bloody worked, too."

"So, there is no mystery man?"

"Nah, thank God, but she did tell me you two had been chatting about my problem."

"I didn't mean to go behind your back but—"

"It's alright," he interjects. "I know you were only trying to help, and it was my fault for not fessin' up sooner."

"Are you back on track now?"

"Yes, and no. I've gotta get my act together otherwise I will lose her, and for good. She made that clear."

"And, are you going to get your act together?"

"I've booked a session with a counsellor for the end of the month, and I've given all my bank and credit cards to Leanne. She's now in charge of my spending."

"That's a good start."

"Yeah, and if I can clear my debts within a year, we're gonna start saving up for a deposit so we can buy our own place. It might take a couple of years, but it's about time I started thinking about the future."

"Christ, you really have turned over a new leaf."

"Yeah, I'm trying," he says, shuffling his feet. "But I didn't pop over just to apologise. Is it true you've handed in your notice?"

"I didn't think it'd take long for the news to get out. Yes, I resigned this morning, and I'm using my outstanding holiday to cover my notice period. I'm afraid that it's for me at Ashbridge Borough Council."

"Is it 'cos of what I did?"

"Not really. Yes, I was pissed off with you yesterday, and Big Fal and Jonny, but I've been coasting through life for far too long. Quitting just seemed like the right thing to do."

"I thought you liked the job."

"So did I, but things change—people change. In the same way Leanne shocked you into changing your ways perhaps I needed a jolt to realise I need to change mine."

"What are you gonna do?"

"That's a good question. Honestly, I'm not sure yet, but I spent most of the afternoon formulating a few ideas. Let's just say I'm excited by what lies ahead, but I'm also shitting myself."

"No chance I can change your mind then?"

"Afraid not, mate. You're not the only one who needs to get their act together."

"Fair enough, but work won't be the same without you."

"I'm sure you'll cope."

"I'll try," he replies with a rueful smile.

Ady stays for another twenty minutes, but just before he leaves, he tells me he heard a rumour while waiting to sign the van back in earlier. Apparently, Keira is returning to work next week after withdrawing her resignation.

We say goodbye with a manly hug, and I promise I'll attend a leaving do that Ady seems keen on organising.

Just as he steps through the front door, an unanswered question pops into my mind. I hesitate before asking as it's not really of any relevance, but if I don't ask now, I might never know the answer.

"Ady, I've got a confession to make."

"Yeah?"

"I might have seen a text message on your phone from someone called SCK. And, I might have mentioned it to Leanne."

"I know," he says with a knowing grin. "She told me."

"Ah. Sorry, mate."

"It's alright. I know you were only looking out for her."

"You're not angry?"

"I'm a bit pissed off that you couldn't just ask me, but nah. Water under the bridge, mate."

"Dare I ask who SCK is?"

"Not an ex-girlfriend, that's for sure. SCK is Sean the Card King—that's what he calls himself. He's the bloke who taught me how to play poker, and got me hooked."

"So, that evening he referred to?"

"That was one of the only nights I've ever won a few quid. Turns out Sean the Card King wasn't much cop at playing poker ... or teaching it."

"Clearly not," I chuckle. "Seeya, Ady."

I return to the kitchen, and I'm about to grab another beer from the fridge when a thought strikes—Keira wasn't the only woman who suffered at the hands of the gift. Thankfully, it sounds like my former colleague will be okay, but while I'm trying to get my life back on track, there's someone else who deserves an apology and some kind of explanation.

I close the fridge and put my shoes on.

After a brief detour to Tesco to buy the biggest bunch of flowers available, I drive to a street I last visited in a state of mild intoxication. I've no idea if Zoe is at home, but if not, I'll leave the flowers at her door and a brief note asking her to contact me.

I park up and somehow manage to navigate my way to the block where Zoe's flat is situated. With mounting nerves, I climb the stairs and ring the doorbell. I can hear Celeste's voice crooning away inside—confirmation I'm literally about to face the music.

The door opens.

Dressed in jogging pants and a hoodie, Zoe stands in the doorway with her mouth agape.

"You," she finally splutters.

"Hi, Zoe."

She continues staring at me, perplexed. Even when I hand her the flowers, she seems unsure of her own eyes.

"Could I talk to you for a moment?" I ask.

"Err, I suppose. Come in."

"No, I'll stand here if it's all the same. I wouldn't want to in-trude, or ... I only dropped by because I owe you an explanation and an apology."

Much like Ady did earlier, Zoe shuffles awkwardly on the spot.

"I think it's me who owes you an apology," she then says in a low voice.

"The Facebook post?"

She nods, avoiding eye contact.

"I'm not going to pretend that didn't sting, but I understand why you did it. I'd have been just as angry if someone walked out on me like I walked out on you."

Zoe turns and places the flowers on the floor just inside the hallway. I'm not sure I'd like to know what's going on in her head as she still seems confused.

"I don't understand," she then admits.

"What don't you understand?"

"Why I felt so disgusted by your photo. Now you're here, I want to rip your clothes off."

"I get that a lot," I smile. "I suppose you might call it the strange appeal of Dougie Neil. I can't explain it, but I can explain why I walked out on you."

"Go on."

"While you were in the shower, I noticed a framed photo on the chest of drawers."

"What photo?"

"I think it was you, your sister, and your parents."

"Oh, that one."

"I guessed I'm probably closer to your dad's age than I am to yours. It made me realise that what we were about to do was wrong on so many levels—I just couldn't go through with it."

"I told you I didn't have a problem with the age gap."

"No, but it wasn't just the age gap that bothered me."

"What then?"

"You're young and beautiful, and I'm ... not. We were never meant to be together, Zoe, and I shouldn't have taken advantage."

"You pissed off without even saying goodbye. Do you have any idea how cheap that made me feel?"

"I've got a fair idea, and I can't apologise enough. I'm not that experienced with women, and I suppose I just panicked. That's not an excuse, but please understand that I just wanted to avoid making a difficult situation worse for both of us."

"Okay," she sighs. "I accept your apology."

"Thank you. And, if it's any consolation, the sex would have been dreadful. I did you a favour."

"Story of my life, Dougie," she snorts. "I seem to veer from one dreadful relationship to the next."

"Maybe take a change of course then. You don't need a man in your life, Zoe, and you certainly shouldn't settle for anything but the best. You've got a lot going for you."

"Do I?" she huffs. "I work as a barmaid in a shitty pub, and I live in a shitty flat."

"Yeah, but you can change your situation with a bit of effort. As it is, you're young, fit and healthy, and you've got a sharp mind if you choose to use it. I think you undersell yourself."

"You sound like my dad."

"I'm sure he only wants the best for you. Most dads do—even though we don't always realise it."

Apology delivered and accepted, Zoe asks if I'd like to come in for a glass of wine and a chat. I decline but tell her I'm always on the end of a phone if she wants to talk. What I lack in looks I make up in my ability to listen.

It's just a shame I've spent so long listening to a nasty little voice in my head.

Chapter 40

I've only ever had two job interviews in my entire life. Two.

It's funny, but I prepared so hard for the interview with Temple-Dane Auditing that I can still remember every question they posed and every answer I gave. One of those questions came to mind this morning as I stared out of the kitchen window: where do you want to be in five years?

The last time I answered it, I replied with a canned answer. The chap interviewing me probably didn't care about my plans, only that I was ambitious and willing to commit to Temple-Dane for the foreseeable future.

Now, I can answer that question with absolute honesty. It won't be easy but seeing as I've nothing better to do this morning, unless I want to risk standing on Falbert's Mount in a thunderstorm, I can at least give it my undivided attention.

I quickly realise that five years is a stupid timescale to consider. So much can happen that it's impossible to plan that far in advance. Twelve months is a more realistic target.

Where do I want to be twelve months from now?

As I watch fat droplets of rain chase down the windowpane, I begin unpicking that question. Only then do I realise the question itself is flawed. What I *want* is irrelevant.

I've spent my whole life wanting. I wanted a girlfriend, and when I finally got one, I wanted her to treat me the way I wanted to be treated. I also wanted to be better in bed and earn more money at work. Neither happened.

Even when my life collapsed, post-Denise, I kept on wanting. I wanted to hide away from the world. Then, when I stumbled upon the gift, I only considered what I wanted. Shit, I even committed my wants to a wish list.

Not once have I asked myself what I need or questioned if any of those needs are within my control.

Always wanting, never getting.

Every time I visit Tinkerton Meadow, I want to spot the rarest of birds. However, I know with absolute certainty that wanting to see them is a futile pursuit. Birds will do whatever they want, and no man can control them. And yet, that's how I've lived my life—waiting and wanting, wanting and waiting.

Madness.

I make a cup of tea and sit down at the kitchen table. There, I reframe the question: where *will* I be twelve months from now?

It's strange how shifting a few words in a question completely changes the context. If I am going to be somewhere in twelve months, I must plan accordingly. Sod fate, and screw waiting for other people to make it happen for me. It's about time I decided where Dougie Neil is heading, and how I get there. And, if those I choose to join me aren't willing, so be it. I'll carry on without them. I might need to deviate or adjust my plan as I go, but the destination is far more important than the route I take.

Twelve months from now, I will be where I need to be. No question.

I sit back in the chair and smile. It's incredible what a difference twenty-four hours and a new-found sense of belief can make.

I owe much of it to a conversation yesterday afternoon. It's taken a long, long time to realise it, but if you take control of a situation, people tend to follow your lead. They see the fire in your eyes, and they know you intend to make good on your promises. They know you've turned a page. They understand you're not the person they thought you were.

Buoyed, I grab my laptop from the lounge and boot it up.

The forecast suggests the thunderstorms will peter out by lunchtime, so that gives me three solid hours to thoroughly plan my strategy for the next twelve months. Once I've committed that strategy to digital ink, I might treat myself to a few hours at Tinkerton Meadow. Maybe if Kenny is there, I'll share a few details and see what he's got to say. I suspect he'll think I'm insane, but my mind is made up—sometimes you've got to go with your gut instincts.

The hours roll by, and I'm so entrenched in my planning that I almost miss lunchtime. Only a grumbling stomach saves me from an afternoon of hunger. I make a sandwich and nibble it whilst continuing my work. By two o'clock, I think I'm done. My eyes and back certainly are—it's been a long time since I spent so many hours on a chair, staring at a screen.

I finish by making a note on my calendar twelve months from now. Briefly, I consider naming my project after the woman I hope will join me on the ride, but I don't want to be premature.

The final task complete, I close the laptop and sit back in the chair. A quick stretch and a check of the sky beyond the kitchen window, and I'm good to go.

When I arrive at the Tinkerton Meadow car park, it's empty. It's rare I ever get to visit at this time on a weekday, so I can't say if this is the norm, or not. One thing is for sure—Kenny isn't here. I toy with the idea of calling him, but he's probably hard at work, making up the hours lost to rain this morning. Maybe he'll drop by later to snatch an hour of spotting before the light fades.

After zigzagging my way along the path to avoid the many puddles, I reach Falbert's Mount and carefully ascend the grassy slope. When I reach the top, I take a second to catch my breath and take in the view. Recently, the views have ranged from uninspiring to drab, but today the scene before me is nothing short of spectacular. I look up to the soft grey clouds slowly drifting across a blue canvas; the sun's rays breaking through like searchlights and catching the ripples on the lake. If I believed in such things, I'd say that such a fine view can only be a good omen.

That thought gains traction over my first hour on Falbert's Mount. Besides the usual visitors, I spot a Lesser Redpoll, five Siskin, and a Goshawk. Wherever Kenny is, he'll regret being there once I share this afternoon's spots, and I've still got at least an hour of daylight remaining.

Barely thirty minutes later, I look up and rue my earlier prediction. The clouds have coalesced, and the sky now resembles a sodden grey blanket. Still, it's been a decent couple of hours, and until the rain arrives, I'm happy to stay just where I am.

Despite my optimism, the sky continues to darken at a worrying rate. The weather app warned there might be showers late afternoon, but it didn't mention the end of days. Out on the lake, my avian friends are departing in number, as if they can sense what the sky is about to unleash. I should seriously consider following their lead.

Resigned to my fate, I remove the binocular strap from around my neck and begin popping the lens covers back in place. As I fumble with the last one, a violent gust of wind blasts across the Mount, whipping the lens cover from my fingers and depositing it in the long grass on the top of the bank.

"Bugger."

I take half a dozen steps forward, squat down, and firmly grasp the lens cover between my thumb and forefinger. It's just as well the grass is long, or the cap would have continued down the bank and landed in the marshy ground at the bottom. Thanking my lucky stars, I pop the cover back on the lens and tuck the binoculars into my pocket. With one final glance across the lake, I turn to leave.

Keeping my head down to avoid being blasted in the face by another gust of wind, I suddenly catch sight of movement in the corner of my eye. It seems odd that a twitcher would turn up this late in the day, in this weather. I look up and glance to my left.

"What the ..."

Shocked by the vision before me, my heart almost falls out of my arse.

"Hello, Douglas."

I squeeze my eyes shut and open them again. She's still there.

"You?"

With her cloak flapping against the wind and the string of raw opals around her neck, there's no mistaking the woman before me. The last time I saw her, I was lying up against the trunk of a silver birch on the far side of Tinkerton Meadow.

"How are you?" she asks as if we were just casual acquaintances bumping into one another in a supermarket.

"Me?" I scoff. "I've had the most wonderful couple of weeks, cheers."

"I'm pleased to hear that."

"I was being sarcastic. What the fuck did you do to me?"

"I gave you what you needed, Douglas. Nothing more, nothing less."

"No, you ... you, poisoned me."

"It couldn't have been a particularly effective poison, could it? You look very much alive and well."

Touché. I'm not the only one willing to deploy sarcasm it seems.

"Do you have any idea what I've been through because of that damn tonic?"

"Yes."

"Oh, I bet you ... what?"

"I said, yes. I do have an idea what you've been through."

"Jesus," I gasp. "Have you been stalking me? What kind of nutter are you exactly?"

"You should calm down, Douglas. Think of your blood pressure."

I stare back at the woman, open-mouthed.

"I am calm," I eventually growl. "And, I would like some answers. Please."

"Of course," she replies.

Her expression remains completely impassive, just as it was that day in the glade. Even with the wind pulling at the hood of her cloak and whipping up the ends of her hair, there's nothing in her features to suggest she's in the slightest bit bothered.

"What was in that tonic?" I ask.

"Does it matter?"

"Of course, it matters. I could have ..."

She slowly raises her right arm and shows me the palm of her hand. Instinctively, I stop talking.

"If you're going to ask questions, Douglas, make them worthwhile. We have limited time."

Looking past my frustration, I can see the common sense behind her statement. Knowing what was in the tonic is irrelevant—knowing what it's doing to me isn't.

"Why didn't you warn me about the effects?"

"Would you have listened if I'd told you? I think you might have found it difficult to believe me."

Again, she's probably right.

"I don't wish to press you, Douglas, but we are running out of time."

"Fine, I ... err."

Why can't I think of a single question?

Noting my temporary paralysis, the woman steps forward until she's only feet away. I say step, but with her long cloak hiding her legs, she could be on wheels for all I know.

"Um, who are you?" I eventually splutter.

"A friend."

"Call me old-fashioned, but I prefer my friends to be a little less ... odd. And it helps if I know their name, too."

"Not in this case," she says, the merest of smiles breaking her pristine face. "But I think you'll find out in the fullness of time. For now, though, you still haven't asked the question you really want to ask."

"What question?"

"The one relating to your gift. In your shoes, I might want to know if the effects are permanent."

"Right ... yes, good question. Are they?"

In almost an exact reproduction of the first time, she dips a hand into her pocket and pulls out a small bottle containing a brownish liquid.

"This is the antidote, for want of a better word."

She holds the bottle out, intimating I should take it. Cautiously, I raise my hand.

"Assuming you no longer *want* what I gave you," she adds.

Unless her weirdness extends to time travel and mind-reading, there's no way she could possibly know I spent most of the morning examining my wants and needs. And yet, she definitely emphasised the word.

My hand remains static, hovering in the air inches from the bottle. Taking it won't change anything, but even its existence is enough to throw my mind into a spin. I've made plans, and those plans assumed the continued existence of the gift.

"If I drink that, women will no longer find me appealing?"

"Some women. As was the case before you took the original remedy."

"No, that was *all* women."

"Now, now, Douglas," she scolds. "We both know that wasn't the case."

"It wasn't? I must have imagined all those years of rejection and enforced celibacy. Silly me."

Too late, I wish I could take back the reference to enforced celibacy. My cheeks burn.

"You're referring to your search for a partner, I presume."

"You presume correctly."

"And yet, you'd already met her, long before that day I found you."

"Eh? I had?"

The woman's eyes narrow a fraction. She nods just once.

"Who is she?"

"You already know. And, you also know that life has not been kind to her. That is why you need one another."

"Eh? You're not making any sense. I don't ..."

"Take the bottle."

"It's just as well I'm struggling to ask coherent questions. You're not very good at delivering straight answers, are you?"

"Our time is nearly up, Douglas. Please, take the bottle."

"I'll take the bottle, but ... but what about this woman you claim is my ideal partner?"

"What about her?"

"If I no longer have the gift, will she be interested in me?"

"There's only one way to find out."

"But, by then it'll be too late. I don't want to go back to the life I had."

"And yet, you consider your gift a curse, do you not?"

Not for the first time in the last five minutes, my mouth bobs open. No words follow. How in God's name does she know my inner thoughts? Is this a trick of some sort, like the stage hypnotist Ady told me about?

"It is not a curse, Douglas. It just gave you what you needed, nothing more."

"And what did I need?"

"Take the bottle. Now."

I force my hand towards hers. Holding a small glass bottle should be of no consequence, but by implication alone, it means I'm at least willing to consider giving up the gift.

The bottle passed to my shaking hand, the woman smiles the broadest of smiles.

"The rest is up to you," she says.

"Yeah, but what—"

Behind me, the sudden snap of wood snares my attention. I spin around, and there, barely twenty feet away, stands a female roe deer. I've seen hundreds over the years but never this close. If she's fazed by the close presence of a human, she doesn't show it. A few seconds pass, and then deer casually saunters back down the bank, out of sight.

I turn around.

"Did you ..."

There's no one there to hear my question.

How long did the deer capture my attention? It was probably no more than five or six seconds but long enough for the woman to leave unnoticed.

As the first spots of rain arrive, I scan the immediate area. There's no cover or hiding place for several hundred yards. Not even Usain Bolt could cover that distance so quickly. Confused, I scuttle over to the far edge of the Mount and survey the southern bank. No sight of anyone; no sound other than the wind and the patter of raindrops hitting my coat. With confusion edging towards disbelief, I circle the entire perimeter of the Mount, looking near and far for the woman. It doesn't take long to establish she's long gone. How? I have no idea. Where? Not a clue.

The fruitless search over, my attention turns to the small bottle I'm clutching in my hand. It would be so simple to cock my arm and then hurl the bottle far over the edge of the Mount. It might not reach the lake, but it'd certainly be lost in the boggy reed-beds.

I study the bottle and innocuous-looking liquid within.

"Gift ... or curse?" I whisper.

The question is carried away on the wind, unanswered, as I continue staring at the bottle. My trance is then suddenly broken by a rumble of thunder overhead.

Time to leave.

I carefully stow the bottle in my coat pocket and hurry back to the car park. By the time I click the seatbelt into place, it's near-impossible to determine the scene on the other side of the windscreen, such is the torrent of rain pounding the car.

So much for the weather forecast.

I arrive in Cargate Road with barely any memory of the journey home; my mind unwilling to shift its attention from what occurred on Falbert's Mount and the small glass bottle in my pocket.

Soaked to the skin, I step through the front door with a completely different mindset to the one I had when I left a few hours ago. Then, I felt sure of what I needed to do, the steps I had to take. Those plans are now subject to one monumental decision. I can't move forward until I make it, but I'm so scared of making the wrong decision I could easily spend the rest of my life dithering back and forth.

However, as I strip out of my rain-soaked clothes in the hallway, one overarching thought dominates my mind—this situation is almost too insane to comprehend. From the moment Keira first batted her eyelashes at me to randomly bumping into Denise yesterday, my entire world has been turned upside down. Those two events, and everything in between, are all connected to one person—the woman in the cloak.

Who is she, and why has she singled me out? More to the point, what am I supposed to make of those statements she made on the Mount barely half an hour ago?

If I hadn't experienced the potency of her tonic first hand, I'd have already dismissed her as a crazed loon. For that reason alone, I don't doubt that the small glass bottle will deliver exactly what she promised—an end to the gift.

What she failed to disclose, however, is the identity of the woman who could supposedly be Miss Right. All I know is that I've already met her. If that is the case, what was the point of the gift?

Now, that is a question worth considering.

I remove the bottle from my pocket and place it on the coffee table in the lounge. Then I dump my clothes in the washing machine and head upstairs for a bath. A long soak might help me unpick the knotted ball of questions currently rolling around my head.

An hour later, I'm back in the lounge, seated on the edge of the sofa. The bottle is where I left it, in the centre of the coffee table.

I know that there's nothing to be gained by prolonging the moment. I pick the bottle up and walk through to the kitchen.

Standing at the sink with a view out to my rainswept garden, I carefully remove the cork bung.

"Last chance to change your mind, Dougie."

I don't change my mind.

Task complete, I grab my mobile phone and scroll through the contacts list until I find a recent addition. I then compose a text message: *I'd like to talk to you about the future. Can you come over to my place if you're free?*

I add my address and tap the send button.

Now, all I can do is wait.

TWELVE WEEKS LATER...

Chapter 41

Wrapped in a windproof coat, I hurry along the High Street. I pass a fish & chip shop and smile. It's a takeaway I've avoided for the last twenty years because it reminded me of my first night with Denise and our first kiss. Seeing it now is like seeing it for the first time; untainted by memories I've spent so long trying to forget. Now, those memories are an irrelevance.

I return to the car and check the app on my phone. It confirms my deliveries are complete, but my working day is far from over. I'm about to tuck the phone back into my pocket when it beeps to signify an incoming text message. It's from Kenny, asking if I'm still alive and, if so, if I fancy meeting him for a few pints tonight. I've barely seen him of late, what with everything that's been going on. And, being a cold, dark January, opportunities to visit Tinkerton Meadow have been limited.

I send a reply, saying I'd love to meet up. We've got a lot to chat about.

Maybe it's because I'm getting older, but I seem to feel the cold a lot more these days. It doesn't help that the outside temperature has barely crept above zero all week. I turn the ignition key and set the car's heater to maximum. I'll give it a minute before setting off.

There's a sudden tap on the side window.

I turn and look straight into the face of a female parking warden. She gestures for me to open the window. I oblige.

"Are you coming or going, sir?" she asks.

"Sorry, I was just going. I'm trying to get some heat back into my hands. They're like blocks of ice."

"Tell me about it," she chuckles. "I'm wearing two pairs of gloves."

"Well, you know what they say: cold hands, warm heart."

"Shush," she replies, putting a finger to her lips. "Us wardens have a reputation to protect. We can't have people going around saying we're warm-hearted."

"No, I suppose not," I smile. "But thank you for not ticketing my car."

"No problem. I'll give you a couple of minutes to defrost, okay."

"Thank you."

She replies with a smile and then continues down the street, checking the windscreens of each vehicle she passes. I don't want to stretch my luck or her goodwill and slip the gearstick into first.

Ten minutes later, I pull into the car park. It's gone two o'clock, but there are still more parked cars than available spaces. I grab the delivery bag from the boot and make my way to the front door. Inside, there's a gentle hum of conversation across the ten occupied tables. Behind the counter, Colin is in the process of taking payment from a middle-aged couple.

"That's two lunchtime specials and two wheatgrass smoothies, right?"

The man confirms their order.

"That'll be £24.00 exactly, please."

"Worth every penny," the woman says enthusiastically. "We'll definitely be coming back."

I pull open the door to the kitchen and enter just as Heather is plating up an order.

"Excellent timing," she declares. "Can you take this to table eight, please?"

"For you, madam, anything."

Heather then wipes her hands on a cloth before carefully placing the two plates on a tray.

"That's the last one," she says. "It's been non-stop since you left."

"How many covers, roughly?"

"I lost count after forty."

I do a few quick sums in my head. If we haven't passed the thousand-pound mark today, I'll be amazed. It's a remarkable improvement over the business that once occupied this building.

Within a week of resigning from Ashbridge Borough Council, I visited Colin in hospital and proposed my grand plan. I offered him virtually all my savings in return for a fifty per cent share in The Vale Cafe, but with certain conditions attached. The first of those conditions related to a pile of unpaid bills, and that Colin used the money to clear them. He agreed without hesitation. The second condition related to his daughter. I would only conclude the deal if Heather agreed to stay on. Having spent many hours talking through my ideas with Heather, I already knew she was on board. Colin couldn't say no, and reading between the lines, I think he was beginning to have doubts about the move to Wales, anyway.

Deal struck, it was time to put my plans into motion.

Having never operated a business before, I needed advice from someone who had. When I first mentioned taking over The Vale Cafe, I half-expected Dad to pour scorn on the idea. To my surprise, he couldn't have been more encouraging. He helped me put a business plan together, and we worked through most of the challenges I'd potentially face. Even with my lack of experience in the catering industry, he never once wavered in his support. To my utter amazement, he even suggested he'd like to invest in the business. In return for a measly one per cent share, he offered me twenty thousand pounds. We both knew it wasn't an investment in the true sense—he just wanted to give my fledgling business the best possible chance of success. That support meant a lot.

On the day he transferred the funds to my account, we toasted the new venture with one of Dad's best malt whiskies. What he then said brought a tear to my eye. Dad explained that he was never disappointed *in* me—he was disappointed *for* me. He said that every parent wants their child to have the best life possible, but he and Mum felt I'd become stuck in a rut of my own making. They were right.

With funding in place and my confidence stoked, I set about refurbishing The Vale. We redecorated top to bottom, purchased new furniture, and invested heavily in up-to-date equipment for the kitchen. Then came the moment we had to order new signs.

One key part of my plan to move the business forward involved the menu. I'd sampled what Heather could create when using the right ingredients, and I knew customers would be willing to pay good money for top-quality, freshly cooked, organic food. Most of the recipes that Heather chose for the menu came from her late mother, so it seemed only right to acknowledge Elizabeth Emsley's contribution. I ordered the new signs, and Lizzie's Kitchen was born.

On the same day the contractor put up those signs, Colin was discharged from hospital. I'd already agreed to pick him up, and as a surprise, we took a detour to the cafe where Heather had organised a little unveiling ceremony. Colin is rarely lost for words, but he was so choked with emotion we couldn't get a word out of him for five whole minutes. When he finally swallowed the lump in his throat, he wholeheartedly agreed we couldn't have chosen a more fitting name.

Besides updating the building and the menu, I also commissioned a website where customers can order a range of quality sandwiches and other homemade snacks. Part of my new role is to deliver the orders to various shops, offices, factories, and warehouses across Ashbridge. The service is still in its infancy, but we're already processing scores of orders and generating more profit than The Vale ever did. It seems I'm not the only one who's sick of bland supermarket sandwiches.

Besides being able to order their lunch, the website also allows customers to book a table. We're open five days a week from 8.00 am till 4.00 pm, serving breakfast, lunch, and afternoon tea. Within a few weeks of launching Lizzie's Kitchen, we'd already amassed dozens of five-star reviews on Facebook. I credit that feedback to Heather's talent in the kitchen and Colin's cheery manner with the customers. I wasn't sure Colin would want to be involved, but now we've removed the financial millstone from around his neck, he's in his element. The three of us make a great team, and some days I need to pinch myself because we've achieved so much in such a short space of time. My only regret is that I didn't spot the opportunity years ago. Mind you, it's taken this long to realise that there's more to life than waiting around for Miss Right to appear.

Ironically, though, she did turn up in the end. And, lo and behold, I already knew her.

A few days after I politely declined her offer of lunch that day at the coffee shop, Denise and I arranged to meet for dinner. The look on her face when I waltzed into the restaurant was priceless. Without the gift to sway her judgement, I wasn't the attractive proposition she'd so willingly agreed to meet. I was just plain old Dougie Neil—the man she ditched when we were kids. I could have tortured her by insisting we sit through three entire courses, but I only ever intended to stay long enough to say what I needed to say.

The conversation didn't go exactly as I intended.

As much as I wanted to vent, the only emotion I could muster was pity. Denise clearly isn't the same screwed-up psycho who messed with my head all those years ago, but she's still searching for something I doubt she'll ever find. I've finally managed to forgive her, but in all honesty, the forgiveness was more for my benefit than hers. By letting go of the anger and the resentment, I could finally see our relationship for what it was—a toxic infatuation, much like Ady's gambling addiction.

Unlike Ady, I let my infatuation fester for far too long. That evening at the restaurant, I finally confronted it.

"I'd better get this to table eight before it gets cold."

I hustle back through the door and deliver the tray to the two women waiting at table eight.

"Two cottage pies," I say, transferring the plates to the table.

"Thank you," they coo in unison.

"Is there anything else I can get you?"

"No, thank you," the older woman replies. "I just hope we have room for a pudding. We both love the sound of the apple crumble."

"Well, speaking as a crumble connoisseur, I can promise it'll be the best you've ever tasted."

I leave the two women to their lunch and, just as I'm about to return to the kitchen, the front door opens. A chap in a Royal Mail uniform enters, carrying a large, flat parcel.

"Parcel for Colin Emsley," he announces to no one in particular.

"That'll be me," Colin replies from the counter.

The delivery driver hands over the parcel in return for a signature and then departs. I've got a good idea of what he's just delivered and step over to the counter.

"Is that what I think it is?" I ask Colin in a low voice.

"It's almost two weeks late, but yes," he replies, matching my hushed tone. "I can't wait for her to see it."

"When are you going to put it up?"

"I'll wait till the last customer has left, but it'll only take a minute to hang. If you can keep Heather in the kitchen, I'll give you the nod once it's up."

"Righto."

The package contains a large framed picture of Heather's mum, and there's a space on the wall behind the counter where Colin intends to hang it. When I first suggested the idea, I wasn't sure how Colin would react, but he seemed just as keen that we prominently display a picture of 'Lizzie'. He took over the task, sourcing a suitable photograph from his collection and placing an order with a local portrait studio. We decided to keep it a secret from Heather, so it'll be a nice surprise, hopefully. As the only photo of Lizzie I've seen is a sepia-tinted Polaroid from their wedding day, almost forty years ago, I'm also looking forward to seeing it unveiled.

I return to the kitchen. There's a steaming mug of tea waiting for me.

"You're a lifesaver. I need this."

"Only another hour to go, and then you can put your feet up."

"True, but I won't be able to keep them up all evening. Kenny wants to meet up for a few pints."

"You could sound a bit more enthusiastic. You haven't seen him in weeks."

"I know, and I am, but ..."

"But?"

"I was kind of hoping we could spend the evening, um ... snuggling."

"Ohh. I see."

The word 'snuggling' would not be my euphemism of choice, but it kind of stuck after Heather first used it two weeks ago. Full of nervous excitement, we checked into a posh hotel, and although we planned to enjoy the restaurant and spa facilities, we never left the bedroom. I'll never forget our first snuggle together or the five subsequent snuggling events that followed. What made it particularly special, besides the four-poster bed and Jacuzzi in the en-suite, was the fact it was Heather's first time. To all intents and purposes, it was my first time, too—the first time I'd physically connected with someone who wanted me for who I am.

And yet, twelve weeks ago, I had no idea if Heather would even want to be my friend.

As I stood at my kitchen sink weighing up the pros and cons of the gift, I considered how many problems it had caused. I also considered Kenny's advice: the strongest relationships typically begin with friendship. How could I build a friendship, or a solid working relationship with Heather on a foundation of deceit? She had to know the real me, which is why I sipped that strange herbal tonic.

To this day I still don't know for sure if the gift really affected Heather. When she popped over to see me that evening, she didn't act any differently from the last time we were together. In fact, she seemed genuinely enthusiastic about the prospect of becoming my business partner. So much so, we talked until midnight. However, as we said goodnight on the doorstep, she did pass comment about the night I found her alone on a bench outside the hospital. Heather couldn't put it into words exactly, but she admitted she felt safe in my company; an inexplicable sixth sense strong enough to offset her shyness.

It's strange to think it, but if wasn't for my disastrous date with Shelley and the subsequent trip to A&E, that moment with Heather outside the hospital would never have happened. In a way, I suppose you could argue that the gift threw us together that night, but it played no part in what happened in the days and weeks after I sipped the antidote.

As we spent more and more time together planning our new venture, it became evident that we were slowly drifting past the point of friendship. It was only then that Heather admitted she'd liked me since those early months when she first started working at The Vale. I, like an idiot, took her shyness as a sign she didn't like me. Maybe in one respect, the gift helped me overcome my self-doubt and that's why we eventually connected. For that, I'll be forever grateful.

The night we shared our first kiss, I returned home on a cloud. I couldn't sleep, so I did something I should have done years ago—I gathered up all the old diaries from my time with Denise and consigned them to the recycling bin. I then logged into Amazon and ordered a new diary, intent on recording new memories ... better memories.

"It's Saturday tomorrow," Heather says. "Unless you've got any other plans, we can spend the whole day snuggling."

I place my mug on the counter and pull her into my arms.

"That sounds like my idea of heaven."

"But you're cooking," she sniggers. "I've done enough this week, don't you think?"

"Yes, you have, and you deserve spoiling."

We enjoy a long, lingering kiss until reality bites. We've still got work to do.

I help Heather tidy the kitchen while clearing the tables as the final customers drift away. Just after 4.00 pm I bolt the front door and turn the sign.

"Five minutes long enough?" I ask Colin as he unpacks the framed picture.

"Perfect."

With Lizzie's Kitchen closed for the day, I empty the cash from the till and transfer it to the safe in the kitchen. Our new till is connected to an app on my phone so I can tally the day's takings on the sofa at home, rather than standing at the counter for half an hour at the end of a long day.

"All done in here," Heather says. "And I'm knackered."

"You know, if business continues on the same trajectory, we should consider hiring another pair of hands."

"Do you think we can afford it?"

"I think so, and as much as I'm proud of what we've achieved, I don't want us to become slaves to the business. Money isn't the be-all and end-all—I just want us to be happy."

"Well, you're doing a very good job so far. I've never been happier."

"Good, because there's plenty more where that came from. I've got big plans for you, Miss Emsley."

Heather moves towards me and puts her hands around my waist.

"Do you? What might those plans involve?"

"You'll have to wait and see."

She looks into my eyes, and in some way, it's almost as if she knows what I'm thinking. Dad once told me that if something seems too good to be true, it generally is. When it comes to Heather, that cliché couldn't be more wrong. She seems too good to be true because she is, and so is what we have. Neither of us has broached the subject yet, but I can see a future where we're husband and wife, and maybe there are one or two additions to the Neil clan. I'm almost certain that's what Heather hopes for too.

The kitchen door opens, and Colin pokes his head in.

"Not disturbing you two lovebirds, am I?"

Heather's face flushes pink.

"No, um ... we were just discussing business."

"Course you were," Colin responds with a wry smile. "Can I borrow you for a minute?"

"Sure."

He then beckons his daughter through the door. I follow closely, keen to see the look on Heather's face when she sees her mother's picture on the wall.

"Close your eyes," Colin says.

"Why?"

"Just trust me."

Heather duly obliges, and Colin slowly guides her towards the counter, where he places his hands on her shoulders.

"Keep those eyes shut," he says. "I'm going to count down from five, and then you can open them."

Keen to save a special moment, I open the video app on my phone and begin recording. I can't see the portrait from my position near the kitchen door, but I've got a great view of Heather's face. It's her reaction I want to capture.

"Five, four, three, two, one. Open your eyes and look up at the wall."

Heather blinks three times and then gasps.

"Oh, my Lord. It's ... it's beautiful!"

Because Colin is standing behind his daughter, I'm able to capture both their faces in one shot. Heather clamps her hands across her mouth, her eyes wide and full of love. Colin is staring up at the picture of his late wife as the camera catches him biting his bottom lip.

I continue recording and slowly step towards Heather and Colin, keeping their faces in the centre of the screen. All I need to complete the video is a final shot of the portrait itself. I join my girlfriend and her father, then slowly turn around while tilting the phone towards the wall behind the counter. The framed picture then appears in the centre of the screen.

I stare hard at the digital image, unwilling to believe the evidence of my own eyes. A glitch in the phone's software, surely. I slowly lower my arm and look up at the woman in the portrait. There is no longer any doubt in my mind who she is. I recognise her mane of straw-coloured hair and glacier-blue eyes. I recognise the string of raw opals around her neck.

"Douglas," Heather then brightly announces. "This is my lovely mum, Lizzie."

I continue staring up at the picture. Nothing makes sense, and yet, somehow, everything now makes perfect sense.

"That's ... that's your mum?" I gulp.

"I know," Heather chuckles. "Alas, I didn't inherit her looks but I hope I inherited her kind heart."

Still shell-shocked, I turn to the woman I was always destined to be with.

"I ... I get it now."

"Get what?"

I look back at the portrait.

"Thank you, Lizzie. You have given me the greatest gift any man could ever want. A real gift."

Heather squeezes my arm.

"That's such a lovely thing to say, Douglas. Wherever she is, I'd bet Mum is very happy that we found one another."

"I'm sure you're right," I reply, unable to take my eyes off the portrait. "More right than you'll ever know."

THE END

Before you go ...

I genuinely hope you enjoyed *The Strange Appeal of Dougie Neil*. If you did, and have a few minutes spare, I would be eternally grateful if you could leave a (hopefully positive) review on Amazon. If you're feeling particularly generous, a mention on Facebook or a Tweet would be equally appreciated. I know it's a pain, but it's the only way us indie authors can compete with the big publishing houses.

Stay in touch ...

For more information about me and to receive updates on my new releases, please visit my website: www.keithapearson.co.uk

If you have any questions or general feedback, you can also reach me or follow me on social media ...
Facebook: facebook.com/pearson.author
Twitter: twitter.com/keithapearson

Acknowledgements ...

This novel is dedicated to the memory of Ron Tuohy—erstwhile member of The Broadhall Social Club and all-round decent bloke.

I'd like to offer a massive thank you to all my diligent beta readers who helped clean up the draft manuscript: Caron McKinlay, Kay Dadson, Adam Eccles, Tracy Fisher, and Roy Taylor. I can't emphasise enough how much your keen eyes and feedback helped.

A huge thank you must also go to my brother, Mike, who helped with research.

Last but not least, sincere thanks to my editor, Sian Phillips. I've run out of superlatives for her contribution over the last seven novels (or it could be eight ... I lose count).